Flight of the Hawk

OTHER TITLES BY G R GROVE:

Available from all booksellers:

Storyteller

Available from Lulu.com:

**Guernen Sang It: King Arthur's Raid On Hell And Other
Poems**

Guernen Sang Again: Pryderi's Pigs And Other Poems

* * * * *

For further information about the **Storyteller** *series, see*

http://tregwernin.blogspot.com
or
http://aldertreebooks.com

Flight of the Hawk

The Second Book
in the Storyteller Series

G R Grove

Lulu.com

Published by Lulu.com
Lulu Press, Inc.
Morrisville, NC, USA

Copyright ©2007 by G R Grove. All rights reserved.
First Edition: November 2007

ISBN: 978-1-4303-2851-3

Set in 12 and 18 point Garamond and 10 point Arial by Aldertree Books, Denver, Colorado, USA.

Front cover image based on a design by Urweg jewelers (http://www.urweg.com), Salida, Colorado, USA.

For further information about the Storyteller series, see
http://tregwernin.blogspot.com or **http://aldertreebooks.com**

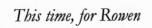

This time, for Rowen

— CONTENTS —

1 Londinium
2 Llys-tyn-wynnan
3 Pengwern
4 Viroconium
5 Deva
6 Aquae Arnemetea
7 Manucium
8 Bremetanacum
9 Olenacum
10 Eboricum
11 Virosidum
12 Cataractonium
13 Luguvallum
14 Corstopitum
15 Hencastell
16 Bramburgh
17 Trimontium
18 Dun Eidyn
19 Alt Clut
20 Caer Iddeu
21 Dun Moreu
22 Dundurn
23 Dun Nottar
24 Cromar

Picts

Manau

Strathclyde

Antonine Wall

Gododdin

Aeron

Bernicia

Goddeu

Hadrian's Wall

Rheged

Deira

Elmet

Gwenydd

Powys

SAXON LANDS

Dyfed

Deuheubarth

Dumnonia

····· Roman roads
• Towns

G R GROVE 2007

Map of Britain in the mid-6th century.

Prologue: The Storyteller

Blood and fire, gold and steel and poetry, a river's voice in the silence of the night, and the shining strings of a harp—all these and more I have known in my time. Steep mountains, dark forests, and the endless song of the rain; music and laughter and feasting in the fire-bright halls of kings; a dusty road, and a fast horse, and a good friend beside me; and the sweet taste of the mead of Dun Eidyn, with its bitter aftermath: a dragon's hoard of memories I have gathered, bright-colored as a long summer's day. Now they are all gone, the men and women I knew when I was young, gone like words on the wind, and I alone am left here in the twilight to tell you their tale. Sit, then, and listen if you will to the words of Gwernin Kyuarwyd, called Storyteller...

Another Samhain night, another audience. I have never been one to promise what I cannot perform. It was with the words above that I started this tale of my adventures on Samhain night a year ago, and those of you who were with me then got full measure, as I think, and a little over, in my first telling—tales of how in my youth I left my home to be a traveling storyteller, and how I met the great bard Taliesin himself, who had sung for King Arthur, and was sent by him to his own old master Talhaearn to learn the essentials of the bard's craft. So it was that I came to winter among strangers that year at the Prince Cyndrwyn's court of Llys-tyn-wynnan in the hills of western Powys, instead of going home to my own people in Pengwern as I had planned. But by the time the wild geese flighting up from the south brought the spring north with them again, many of Cyndrwyn's folk were no longer strangers to me, nor I to them. Indeed, I was feeling very much at home there, and beginning to put down roots—not something that a bard should ever do!—when fate, in the form of Taliesin, took a hand in my affairs once more, and sent me off a-wandering again. And that is the story I will be telling you tonight.

The Hawk

It began on a bright spring evening two days before Beltane. The birds were singing passionately in the new-leafed trees; the cattle were lowing in the green fields outside the court; and I and my girl Rhiannedd were seated on a rough wooden bench close by Cyndrwyn's mead-hall, passing some moments pleasantly enough until it was time to go inside for dinner. I had my arm around her slender waist, and was just about to kiss her, when we were interrupted by the sound of approaching horses.

Into the muddy courtyard there rode three men, and two of them, to my astonishment, were familiar to me. The slight, dark man in the lead, Taliesin Ben Beirdd himself, I would know, I think, at the world's end—always supposing that he himself wished it!—and his apprentice Neirin mab Dwywei's dark red hair and lean build were hard to disguise by any light. The third man, a fair-haired youth who rode behind them and led their packhorses, was a stranger to me.

With a startled word to Rhiannedd, I leapt up and ran to meet them. "Taliesin! Neirin! By all the gods, what brings you here?" Then there was confusion and shouting in the courtyard as others ran to greet them or to hold their horses, to carry word to the Prince and make ready his hospitality, or merely to participate in the excitement. In the midst of it all, I found myself face to face with Taliesin himself. "Gwernin!" he said smiling, and reaching out he took me by the shoulders and looked me up and down, his blue eyes sparkling in his dark-bearded face. "Yes, I was right. Being with Talhaearn suits you, I think. And you have grown."

It was true: I had grown a finger's breadth over the winter, and was now as tall as he. It seemed very strange, but I had no time to ponder it, for Taliesin had released me to Neirin, who stood beside me grinning, and had turned to greet the Prince and my master

Talhaearn. I did not see what passed between them, for Neirin had flung an arm around my shoulders, and was introducing his companion. "Gwernin, this is Pedr mab Rhys, from Dyfed. He is wanting to learn the harp, and Taliesin has brought him along to take your place while you are gone."

"Gone?" I cried. "Where am I going?"

Neirin laughed. "To the North with me, I hope! But only for the summer! Na, na, but I should have let him tell you the story himself—no doubt but that I have spoiled it."

"Now that you have begun, go on!" I said. "But first let us take your horses to the stables, and you can tell me as we go. Besides, there will be less of a crowd there while they are all gathered around our masters, and we shall have more chance to speak!"

"How was your winter?" Neirin asked as we walked. He too had grown over the winter, I thought, though not as much as I; but then he had been the taller already.

"Good," I said, and thinking back I smiled. "Most of it, at any rate! And yours?"

"Good indeed. Your town of Pengwern where we wintered is a most fair place, and her Prince very generous. He loaded Taliesin with treasures, and could hardly be persuaded to spare him for a few days to make this trip. Indeed, I thought at one point I would have to come alone to make my request, and glad I am that I did not—Talhaearn would have made short work of me! How do you get on with him now?"

"Very well, nowadays," I said with a laugh. "He is no easy master, I can tell you, but he has taught me much—if only to know how little I really knew!"

"That is the first lesson," said Neirin seriously, "and the hardest. I mind me well when I first came to Taliesin: *hai mai*, I was full of myself! But he soon showed me the error of my thinking." And he chuckled reminiscently.

Cyndrwyn's chief groom was waiting at the stables with boys to take the horses, so Neirin and I loaded ourselves with harps and saddlebags and went out again, leaving Pedr behind to deal with the gear on the pack-ponies. "I do not know where they will be putting you," I said, "but come to our hut first and leave your gear. Then we can talk properly, and I can introduce you to Rhiannedd."

"Oho!" said Neirin, his amber eyes shining. "This has the sound of news! Should I remember her?" He and Taliesin had spent some days at Llys-tyn-wynnan the previous autumn when I was new there; that was how we first became friends.

"I do not know," I said, shouldering aside the leather door-curtain and beginning to set down my load on the stone-flagged floor. "You will have seen her, I know, but there are others more memorable at first glance. I will let you decide."

Neirin grinned. "A good winter indeed, I think you must have had! Though I was not lonely in Pengwern myself. Where now?"

"The hall: I want to see what is passing between our masters. And you still have not told me about this trip we may be making, or about Pedr. He had little enough to say for himself."

"I doubt we gave him a proper chance," said Neirin, falling into step beside me. "He is here because Taliesin wants to borrow you from Talhaearn to be my companion on a mission, and feels that he should provide the old man with a substitute while you are gone. Their discussion, I think, should be well worth the hearing!"

"I hope we are in time," I said, and laughed.

We found Taliesin still talking to the Prince, while Talhaearn stood by with an expression on his craggy face that spoke to me of gathering storm. "Ah, Gwernin!" said Cyndrwyn as we came up. "I have been offering Taliesin the guest lodgings across the courtyard from yours for himself and his party. Would you take them there?"

"Gladly," I said, keeping a weather eye on Talhaearn. "Neirin and I have just been stowing some of their baggage in our own hut, so…"

"Let us all go and get it, then," said Taliesin, "and you can be our guide, Gwernin. Prince, we will talk more at meat, if it please you. Talhaearn, give me your company now, please." And he swept us off with a hand on blind Talhaearn's arm, gesturing to myself and Neirin to go ahead as he did so. "So here you are again, and unexpectedly as ever," I heard Talhaearn say behind us. "What are you playing at this time, Gwion?"

"A diplomatic mission, as I said: can you doubt it?" I could hear the laughter in Taliesin's voice, and Talhaearn's snort in response. "Na, na, Father of Awen, we will talk of it soon enough, and I hope you will not be displeased. Wait you only until we are indoors and private."

"As you please, as you please," said Talhaearn, and was silent until we reached our lodging. As Neirin and I were leaving with the baggage, I heard him say, "What news from Rheged?" But the curtain closed and I lost Taliesin's answer.

"Phew!" said Neirin as we crossed the court again. "We are well out of that, I am thinking! Ho! Pedr! This way!"—waving to his companion, who was standing irresolute and burdened at the entrance to the stable-yard. As he came up I saw that he was Neirin's age or a little older, a well-grown handsome young man, with the golden hair and blue eyes you often see on the Saxons, and sometimes on the Irish as well. His voice when he spoke sounded pleasantly of the southwest. "I thought I would never find you," he said. "This place is like a maze!"

Neirin chuckled. "You would not say that when you had seen Deva, or any of the old Roman towns."

"I have seen Caerwent," said Pedr, "but that is mostly straight lines. This is different."

"Did you pass through Caerllion on your way?" I asked. I had been that way myself a year before, at the start of my adventures.

"Let me think: no, we went by Severn-mouth, and up through Glevum: another Roman town, and bigger than Caerwent, but fewer people in it. A place of the dead; I did not like it."

"Well, well," said Neirin peaceably, as we entered the guest lodging. "That is as it may be. Put the packs down over there, and let us sort things out."

At this point a kitchen boy arrived with a flask of wine and three cups on a tray, saying, "Cyndrwyn sends it for the bards."

"I will take it to them," I said, and the boy grinned and left. Pedr made to reach for one of the cups, but I pulled the tray back in surprise. "Pedr, I meant what I said."

Pedr frowned briefly. "My apologies," he said. I looked at him for a moment longer, my brows raised, and he continued unwillingly, "I thought you meant for us to share it ourselves; we are bards, too."

"Speak for yourself," I said reprovingly. "I am Gwernin Story-teller, and I serve Talhaearn." And turning, I went out of the room with the tray. Behind me I heard Neirin's voice speaking to Pedr; the words were muffled, but the tone was not kind.

At the door of my own lodging I paused, hearing the rumble of Talhaearn's voice within. But I had been in this position before; balancing the tray one-handed, I tapped on the door-post and went in. "Wine from the Prince, masters," I said; and setting the tray down on a low table, I filled a cup with the strong red wine and took it to Talhaearn. His color was high, and he was frowning, his bushy white brows almost meeting in the middle, but he took the cup readily from my hand and drank. I turned back to do as much for Taliesin, but he was already helping himself. Before drinking he poured a few drops, neatly and deliberately, onto the floor in libation. Looking up he caught my eye and smiled. "No, Gwernin, not about you this time," he said. "Though that will come soon enough, no doubt. Has Neirin told you my plan?"

"Part of it, Lord," I said, and looked at Talhaearn. "Master? Do you know?"

"Not yet," said Talhaearn. "He has only told me that the North is a tinderbox, about to burst into flame, and the Saxons are stirring again in the east, and Cynan Garwyn is doing his best to foment war in the south and west: nothing of great moment, you perceive. Why, what is it that he has yet reserved? Something to do with you, Gwernin, I feel." He did not add, "as usual," but I felt it in the air.

I turned back to Taliesin. "Will you tell him, Lord? It will come more completely from you."

"Gwernin," said Taliesin lightly, "are you trying to force my hand? Well, then," and he turned to Talhaearn, "it is true I have come to ask you a favor, Iron Brow, though I would have preferred to choose my own time for the asking. The North being, as I have said, a tinderbox, I am sending Neirin up there this summer to gauge the accuracy of my news and do what he can to soothe things down in his own home country, while I do my best to restrain Cynan. And as he is still young, and only one man, I thought to give him company on this trip by borrowing Gwernin from you for a few months. I have brought a young man with me to serve you while he is gone, Pedr mab Rhys by name, who says he wishes to learn the harp and the other arts of the bard. I think"—and here he grinned unexpectedly—"that you will soon get his measure. Treat him as you will, Father of Awen: perhaps he will last out the summer!"

At that Talhaearn smiled grimly in his gray beard. "Well, we will see," he said, and then to me: "Gwernin? What do you think of this? Are you ready so soon to leave me?"

At that I went down on my knees beside his chair. "Master," I said, "you know I am not. I admit that the adventure tempts me, but it is for you to decide, yea or nay. I will do as you desire."

Talhaearn's expression softened a little. "Well, well," he said, "you are very docile. Is it only my company you would be missing, I wonder? Never mind; but do you come back to me in the autumn, and strive not to forget all my teaching in the meantime." And he laid his hand for a moment on my head as if in blessing. "Now go along with you; Gwion will see me to the hall when it is time."

The next two days were busy ones. Taliesin and Neirin were staying to keep the Beltane feast with Cyndrwyn before they left, the one for Pengwern again and the other with me for the North. Talhaearn was continually thinking of last-minute instructions or bits of advice for me, some of which I managed to remember. And for myself, I had an urgent desire to spend as much time as I could with my dear dark-haired Rhiannedd before I left.

She had taken the news philosophically, though whether she believed my promises to return I am not sure. "It will be as the gods allow," she said once when she saw I was troubled, and she smiled up at me so sweetly, her blue eyes so full of understanding, that I could not but kiss her. I had introduced her to Neirin, not without qualms, but he took the measure of our relationship at once, and although he teased me, he treated her like a sister. For her part she soon lost her awe of him, and dealt with him much the same, for all of his high birth—his mother, as I had heard, was own sister to Gwallawg King of Elmet—and the fierce, shining look that came on him sometimes when he played or sang in hall, which led some folk to call him "Taliesin's Hawk." Pedr, on the other hand, she took in dislike at once, and I cannot say that I was sorry, for there was no denying he was a very handsome man.

Now Beltane, as you know, is *Calan Yr Haf*, the beginning of summer, when the plowing is over, and the first crops in, and the increase of the land begins to be felt. When the bonfires that would be lit that evening were sinking, we would drive the cattle between them for protection and increase in the coming year. It was the custom, too, for men and women, those who desired this sort of blessing, to leap or run between the fires themselves; it was also a form of unofficial hand-fasting.

Rhiannedd and I would not be leaping the fires this year. We had talked long and long about it, for during the past winter I had come to know that I loved her, and she loved me. But I had no way to support a wife: no land, no livelihood, no way to raise a bride-price. By my own actions in choosing the bard's path against the wishes of my family, I had cut myself off from my kindred and my possible inheritance in Powys Cynan. I was free-born, yes, and had some status in Cyndrwyn's *llys* as my master's apprentice, and lately also from my own talents: but that was all. Some day, perhaps, when Talhaearn was satisfied with my training, I might become *bardd teulu*, the bard of the retinue: so I was becoming unofficially already. Some day, perhaps, I might be a *pencerdd*, a Master Bard, myself. But these possibilities were long years in the future: not enough to build a life on now. All this Rhiannedd and I knew and had discussed; but knowing in the head is not knowing in the blood. And we were very young.

On Beltane Eve the two of us stood near the fires hand in hand, as we had stood at Midwinter; but this was a calm, mild night, not one of icy cold. We watched as the black and brown cattle were driven bawling between the fires, the cows with their new calves at their heels and the sparks flying wild about them; and after the cattle, the sheep, with the sheepdogs barking behind. Then, as the flames were dying down, the men and women went through: the young ones running and laughing, some of them holding hands; the older ones more deliberately. At last, when it was very late, and few folk were left, I looked at Rhiannedd, and she looked back at me, and something passed between us. Then we, too, ran between the sinking fires, holding hands; and that night we did not go back to the court at all, but spent the time together on the green hillside, with one cloak beneath us, and another above, and the pale stars of summer overhead. And when we went home in the dawn, still hand in hand, we knew that we were bound as sure as any, though no priest had blessed our union—no mortal priest—and no bride price had changed hands. And the next day I took horse with Neirin and we rode north.

But that, O my children, is a story for another day.

The Road North

I mind me well that summer morning when Neirin and I rode out of Llys-tyn-wynnan on our way north. The sky was a high clear blue, the early sunlight glittered on a million dewdrops, and all the earth was clothed in tender green of a thousand different shades. Around us the birds sang loudly—a little too loudly for my taste, for last night's feasting and beer-drinking had gone late, and I was not feeling my best in consequence. With the other two pack-ponies on a lead behind me, I jogged lazily along at the rear of our party on the black one I had borrowed once before, watching Taliesin and Neirin deep in conversation ahead of me, and remembering my parting from Talhaearn. "So," he had said musingly, looking toward the two of them where they stood in the dawn-pale courtyard—for he was not wholly blind, and in the half-light he could see shapes and colors—"Taliesin flies his hawk at last. Well, well, it is full time. But I wonder, will that one ever come to the glove again, once he has felt the wind in his wings?" And he had smiled a little, and gone on to give me a list of instructions which I could not now remember. I hoped Pedr would take good care of the old Bard while I was gone, but I admit I had my doubts; Pedr the Fair did not seem like the sort to take good care of anyone but himself.

A pleasanter memory was Rhiannedd, and the night we had spent together after leaping the Beltane fires. These thoughts kept me entertained for some time, while we made our way down out of the hills and into a wider and wider valley, and the bright morning changed to a warm midday. A mile short of Caer Einion we turned northeast, following the trace of the old road which runs up Dyffryn Meifod. It was at this point I realized that Taliesin was not going straight back to Pengwern, but was coming with us as far as Deva.

"Yes," he said when I asked, "I want to visit with Prince Cyndeyrn there, for he too is Cynan's cousin, and may have some influence on him. And besides"—and here he grinned like a boy—"I have been too long indoors this winter, talking endlessly to old men in the smoky torchlight; I need a while in the clean air and sunlight to remember who I am!"

"Gods protect us," said Neirin, mock-gloomy. "It will rain the rest of the way!" And we all laughed.

So it came about that three of us, and not two only, rode into Deva the following evening over the Romans' stone-built bridge, having spent the previous night in a village on the edge of the hill country. And true to Neirin's prediction, it was raining, a small mizzle rain that had been falling steadily all day, seeming like nothing when it started but gradually soaking through the thickest cloak. By now I was wet to the skin, my hair plastered to my face and rain dripping from my chin and trickling down my neck, but this was the least of my misery. I had never ridden so far or so long before in my life, and every part of my body from my neck to my knees was telling me so. I was almost ready to get down and walk, despite the mud and filth of the road, and I hoped desperately that we would be spending more than one night in Deva.

Nevertheless, I looked around me with interest as we left the bridge, for although Deva, like all the Roman towns, had lost a considerable amount of its past grandeur and population, it had been a great seaport in its day, and was still the largest city I had yet encountered. Indeed, as we made our way through the fortress gate and along the stone-paved street to the Prince's compound, I almost forgot my misery in wonder. When we reached the courtyard, however, I slid to the ground with a groan, and had to stand for a moment clutching the black pony's mane before I could trust my legs to bear me.

"Sorry I am, Gwernin," said Taliesin, dismounting beside me. He sighed and stretched, then pushed back the hood of the leather rain cape which had kept him fairly dry. "I forgot you were not used to riding so far. But this ill, at least, practice will cure. Come into the

hall with me now, while Neirin leads our horses on to the stable."
And taking his saddlebags, he turned to the doorway where folk
were waiting to greet us. I looked up at Neirin, still mounted, who
gave me a rueful grin from the shelter of his own hood. "*Sa*, do you
go with him," he said. "I will be seeing you in a little while." So
handing him the pack-ponies' lead-ropes and taking down my
saddle-roll, I followed Taliesin into the hall.

Inside the door I stopped, for after the darkening twilight outside, the long room seemed ablaze with light and fire, and sweet
with the scent of the resin-rich torches. Beside the central hearth
Taliesin stood talking to three tall, richly dressed men, one of them
grey-bearded and the other two young. As I watched, a fair young
woman in a red gown of fine-spun wool came down the hall toward
them, bearing in her two hands a great silver cup. Smiling, she
stopped and offered it to Taliesin with some soft words I did not
catch. He took it with an answering smile and drank, and gave it
back to her. Then turning, he saw me and motioned me forward. I
came, trying not to limp, and stopped beside them.

"Be welcome in our hall, stranger," said the young woman, offering me the guest cup. I took it, and looked into her face, and was
caught. Her eyes were as green as forest shadows, and her hair as
golden as the broom, and her clear skin like pale heather honey: and
she smiled faintly at me in perfect consciousness of her beauty. I
stood there like a fool with the cup in my hands, until at last
Taliesin's voice recalled me to my senses. "You had better drink,
Gwernin," he was saying, and I could hear the ripple of amusement
in his voice. "You are keeping the Lady Denw waiting." Blushing, I
muttered something disjointed, and drank, and returned the cup,
and could not have said afterwards whether it contained water or
wine.

An hour later I was happier than I had ever expected to be that
night—a state due, not to the Lady Denw's beauty, but to one of
the old surviving Roman features of Deva which I had never before
encountered: hot baths. Our travel-stained clothes stripped off and
taken away by servants to be dried and brushed, the three of us

were sitting shoulder deep in a sunken pool of steaming water in the Prince's bath house, warm to the core and almost too relaxed to move. All my clenched muscles had untied themselves, and even the raw spots where I had been too long in contact with a saddle were losing their sting. Neirin seemed to have fallen asleep where he sat, and Taliesin's eyes were half-closed, though as I watched he opened them and sighed, and sat up straighter. "We will have to get out soon, I suppose," he said, pushing the damp hair back out of his face. "I could wish more kings still kept to the Roman ways." And he reached over and jogged Neirin. "Wake up, Little Hawk."

Neirin opened his amber eyes and smiled. "A very fair dream I was having, and now you have spoiled it." He yawned. "*Hai mai!* And now I am hungry! Do you suppose we can still get supper?"

"We can try," said Taliesin, and stood up, scattering water everywhere.

Warm, dry, and in clean clothes, I felt a different man. The evening was not so far advanced as the rainy twilight had made it appear, and we found that feasting was still going on in the hall, where we were made welcome. Taliesin was seated at the Prince's own table, while Neirin and I found places lower in the hall and were rapidly provided with wooden cups and bowls by the well-trained servants. The food was abundant and good—spit-roasted beef came into it, as I remember, and fish of some kind, and little brown barley loaves—and the drink was clear golden mead. The latter I sipped with care, remembering its potency from one or two previous occasions.

Neirin was watching the high table, where Taliesin sat talking with the grey-beard I had seen earlier, who must be the Prince Cyndeyrn. Some sort of question must have been asked, for Taliesin was shaking his head and smiling; then he glanced in our direction, gestured at us, and shook his head again. "Na, na," said Neirin under his breath. "That was not well done—tomorrow will be soon enough."

"For what?" I asked, puzzled.

"Performance. There was no need to press him, and he straight from the road. And it is not as if the Prince had no Bard himself." And this was true: I had previously noted a tall, dark man near the end of the high table dressed in what looked like a singing-robe, who seemed vaguely familiar to me from the previous summer. "Bluchbardd," said Neirin, following my gaze. "And he is good enough of his kind, though not of our masters' standard. You should be thinking what you might perform tomorrow, if they ask you."

"Me?" I said, startled. Over the winter Talhaearn had impressed on me strongly that as his student I was not to perform without his permission.

"Yes, you." And Neirin grinned. "I am not going to do all the work this summer, and I know you are a good storyteller. So do you think of it, and be prepared."

"I might," I said slowly. "But my master—"

"Talhaearn has loaned you to Taliesin, and he has loaned you to me," said Neirin, still grinning. "For this while, *I* am your master, and I say you are to perform. Is it not good?"

"It is," I said, and grinned back at him. "But mind that you treat me well!"

"That," said Neirin, making his mouth prim, "goes without saying." Then he laughed. "*Hai mai!* But we will have fun!" And I laughed with him.

By and by Bluchbardd got up from his seat at the high table and took a performer's stance, and a young boy brought him his harp. I listened critically to the song that followed. It was, as Neirin said, good enough of its kind—better, indeed, than I could do myself in those days—but predictable. Apparently much of the audience thought so too, for there soon began to be a background hum of conversation, and the applause that followed was half-hearted. A second song fared no better; then the singer sat down, and the babble of voices in the hall rose to its previous volume. "Not hard for you to better that," I said to Neirin.

"*Sa,* we will see. An odd place, this." I nodded; I had felt it too: there was something strange about this court and its people, something hard to put my finger on, and I thought it centered around the Lady Denw. She was seated now at the high table between her younger brother and Taliesin, and all the light of the hall seemed to shine on her fair head. It was she who drew the gaze, not the dark singer Bluchbardd and his unheard praise. He was watching her now as she talked to Taliesin, with something like hunger in his face. The sight stirred a memory in me which I could not quite recall, a memory of ill-omen. I carried the thought to bed with me that night, but found no answer in my dreams.

When I awoke the next morning in the guest-house, Taliesin was already up and gone, and Neirin was dressing. "We are at liberty to explore," he said grinning. "And the rain has stopped, no doubt because Taliesin is indoors talking again: come and see!" Flinging on my second-best tunic—I had only the two—I followed him to the feast-hall in search of breakfast. It was not so late as I had at first feared, and many of the folk of the court were seated there still, breaking their fast with fresh wheaten bread and cheese, and cold roast meat from the night before.

Taliesin was at the high table again with the Prince and his sons, and I noticed with interest that the Lady Denw was with them once more as well. This morning her gown was of a pure dark green, like oak leaves in midsummer, and her hair seemed to have brought some of the morning sunlight indoors. For the most part she sat quietly at her father's side, now and then adding a word to the conversation, but her eyes were on Taliesin, though I could not see that he paid her much heed in return. I watched them as I ate, but got nothing by it, and by and by Neirin and I arose and went out to explore the town.

Much of Deva, I found, was in origin a Roman fortress, and a large one at that, built to house many hundreds or thousands of soldiers, while the civilian settlement which grew up outside its brown sandstone walls was much smaller. After the Eagles left, however—whether with Maxen Wledig when he marched on Rome itself, or in some later campaign—the settlement outside had gradually moved within the walls, so that now most of the people lived there. The Prince's compound enclosed the old Commander's house and the headquarters building, and was itself a defensible space, but between it and the river-gate through which we had come the evening before was an extensive range of red-tiled, half-timbered buildings. Under the Eagles they had been barracks and storehouses, kitchens and mess halls, but now they were workshops and homes for all the trades and people that make up a town. In the streets the smells of wood-smoke and horse-droppings mingled with those of fish and seaweed from the broad brown tidal river outside, and the warm morning was loud with the crying of gulls and of children. It seemed a busy, bustling place to me, though no doubt it would have looked a pale shadow of itself to the people who built it so many lifetimes ago. Neirin and I wandered through it at our leisure, inspecting the goods in the workshops and the fishing boats at the wharf, and watching the people in the streets. There were some very pretty girls among them, as we pointed out to each other.

"Yes," I said, after Neirin had managed to get a smile from one passing beauty, "she is very well indeed, but nothing compared to the Lady Denw. What do you think of *her*?"

"Fine indeed," said Neirin, grinning, "but no meat for us, I am thinking."

"Na, she will be looking higher for a match—or her father will be. It did seem to me," I said, picking my way carefully, "that she was much taken with Taliesin, though I could not see that he was interested."

"Na, na," said Neirin easily, "he will have other things on his mind. He is not much of a one for the women in any case, though he does not dislike them; likely it will be the same for us when we reach his age, for he is not young."

"Maybe," I said, frowning a little dubiously, "but in the meantime—look at that one! Can you get her to stop and talk to us, do you think? You are better at this than I am!"

"I can try," said Neirin; and he did it, too.

In the late afternoon we came back to the guest-house and found Taliesin sitting cross-legged on a bench in the sun, with his harp in his hands and an inward-looking expression on his face. He greeted us absent-mindedly, then roused himself to give us our instructions for the evening. And when it was time for meat, we went again to the hall.

This time Neirin and I were seated closer to the high table as part of Taliesin's entourage. He himself was dressed more formally tonight, and wore the silver circlet I had seen on him once or twice before, and the great enamel-set golden brooch which Neirin said had been of a gift from Arthur the High King, in the far-off days when Taliesin served him and first got his title "Chief of Bards." Whether because of this, or because of something in his bearing, he seemed taller tonight, a larger, more shining presence, so that all eyes went to him again and again, and when he stood up presently from the high table to sing, the silence in the hall was immediate and total. Neirin, who had brought his own harp with him to the hall, had gone up earlier by pre-arrangement, and now stood ready to accompany his master.

The song which Taliesin sang that night began with praise of Arthur as the great warrior who had defeated the Saxon armies:

"I sing a great King, Arthur Chief Dragon—
I saw him destroy men, I saw his delight!
Great Bull of Battle, strong Pillar of Britain,
Bright-blood-stained Wolf he was, red-shafted Spear!
Once here beside this same City of Legions
Dead of all England he spread on the field.
Charging upon them he led in the front line—
Ravens grew red as he splintered their shields.

You broke them wholly, Arthur War-Leader,
Many a man you trampled in mire,
Marshes ran red beneath your rich vengeance,
Five kings you slew in a single charge!
Forcing surrender on Sussex's raiders,
Back to the beaches you hurled them in woe—

> Nor let them leave without their sore wounding—
> Reaper of corpses, most fierce to your foes!"

So far, so good; but Taliesin did not stop there. Best in war Arthur was, but also best in peace:

> "Greatest of Britons, generous gold-giver,
> None could surpass you in peace as in war.
> Kindest of kings, best gift you gave us—
> Peace in our fields, peace in our homes!
> Gifts from our God garnered in safety—
> From your iron hand no raider could reave!
> Strongest you stood, standing above us,
> Steadfast and stern, great Lord of all.
> Like the high God, none could defy you,
> None could defeat you, thrice-honored king!"

For this, said Taliesin, Arthur would be remembered:

> "Though at cruel Camlann you won your last battle
> And into the West then you sailed from our sight,
> Down through all ages your legend will burn still—
> Brightest of Britons, our great beacon-light!
> Until this world, darkness-enveloped,
> Winds to its end, your name will be known—
> All bards that be praises will sing you,
> And in high heaven build your new throne."

At the end the hall was full of breath-held silence. Then the applause began, a pounding, shouting tumult that seem to shake the roof-tree itself. When it died down at last Taliesin sang again, a shorter, simpler song but no less potent, praising the Prince Cyndeyrn, his strength in war and in peace, his strong sons and beautiful daughter. Then he sat down again, and the Lady Denw with her green eyes and faint smile came to bear him the mead-cup from her father the Prince, and in a little while the hall returned to its customary conversation.

By and by Bluchbardd sang in his turn, with no better results than on the previous night. But before that I had seen him watching Taliesin, his dark face darker than ever with anger, and a look in his eyes which I would not have wanted turned on me; and a small finger of cold stroked down my neck and was gone, lost in the mead-bright warmth of the hall. Then Neirin asked me if I had decided which story I might perform if asked, and in the ensuing discussion I forgot Bluchbardd and his troubles, if that was what they were.

We stayed one more day and night in Deva, but Taliesin did not sing again for our hosts. Instead he set Neirin to harp for them, and me to tell one of my stock of tales; and both of us were well received, and well rewarded. And if our rewards stopped short of the Lady Denw's admiration, neither did we collect any enmity from others, which was just as well.

But that, O my children, is a story for another day.

The King in the Ground

A day's ride east of Deva the traveler on the old Roman roads has a choice: to turn left for Mamucium and the north, or right to rejoin the great south road to Londinium. If you want to go due east, you can take one choice or the other and then work back towards your goal, or you can head straight for the Peaks, cutting across the marshy land between as best you may. Like all choices, each of these three has its consequences: Neirin wanted to go first to Elmet, and so we chose the middle way.

We had parted from Taliesin the day before outside Deva, on a cool grey morning that promised neither sun nor rain. The previous afternoon he had gone out into the town and returned with a present for me: a hooded leather rain-cape like his own. It was tied behind my saddle now, and from time to time I touched it, and remembered how he and Neirin had embraced at parting, briefly but hard, all their good-byes already said the night before. After that Neirin had been silent for nearly half a day, a most unusual state of affairs with him, and then had recovered his voice and spirits with a bound. Since then he had barely stopped talking.

Now we sat our tail-switching ponies beside a stream, contemplating the way forward. The game trail we had been following had died out in a dozen smaller branches, and nothing much larger than a hare could have penetrated the tangled briars and brambles before us. The stream banks were muddy where they were not choked with reeds, and the peat-brown water of the stream itself hinted at worse ahead. Altogether the prospects were not inviting.

Neirin slapped irritably at the cloud of insects buzzing around his face. "I am not knowing which way next," he said, "but I think if we sit here much longer we will be eaten alive, and the horses with us."

"Back, then," I said, turning my pony, "and follow that bit of ridge to the right. Trees are more likely to be dry-footed than reeds."

"We can but try," said Neirin, and "Hup! Come on, you!" to our packhorse, who had decided to graze. We splashed back across the muddy ford we had crossed earlier and scrambled up the bank. The afternoon was overcast and warm, and sweat was trickling down my back under my tunic. Maybe, I thought, it would be cooler under the trees.

Certainly it was darker. After a little casting about we found a deer trail, and followed it as best we could—deer think nothing of jumping an obstacle that a horse cannot pass!—hoping that it was taking us in the right direction. It was hard on the level ground to tell up-slope from down, and harder under the oaks to tell east from west. I began to suspect we were riding in circles, and soon I knew it, when we came for the second time to a fallen tree from which our horses had brushed the moss in passing. "Now what?"

"Am I a Druid, or a seer, to give you the answer?" asked Neirin glumly, running his fingers through his sweat-dark hair. "I thought this would be easier; we could see the hills so clearly this morning. Where have they gone?"

"Maybe it is 'where have we come?' instead?" I said, thoughtfully scratching the back of my neck where an insect had been dining. "I do not have the feel of the land here at all. It is like riding through fog."

"Yes, you are right. Well…" Neirin closed his eyes for a moment and seemed to be listening. Then he pointed to the right. "That way." As if in answer there was a distant rumble of thunder, and a little breeze touched our sweating faces for a moment and died away. We looked at each other, then shrugged and turned the horses to the right, into another deer-trod that looked the same as all the rest. But slowly as we went along the ground began to rise, although the forest—and the sense of riding through fog—was as thick as ever. The light was fading fast; now and again we heard the thunder again, and it was coming closer. Neirin looked about him as he rode and shook his head from time to time. "Na, na, na, I cannot," he said, half to himself. "But … somewhere … Gwernin, stop a moment. I need—to get down."

I pulled up my pony, concerned, and took the packhorse's lead rope and his own reins from him. "Are you ill?" I asked. He certainly looked pale enough.

"Na, but—I have to—be *still*." As he spoke Neirin was sliding down from his horse to stand, swaying slightly, in a listening pose, feet well apart, head up, but with his eyes still closed. As I watched him the thunder spoke again, very close now, and from nowhere a wind began to rise, a cold wind with the smell of rain in it. I shivered, and my hand went again to my new rain-cloak, as much in reassurance as in immediate need.

Then three things happened at once: Neirin cried out a word I did not know, in a voice between triumph and pain; there was a flash of light and an enormous rending crash as lightening split a nearby oak; and the threatened rain began to fall in torrents. For a moment, still half-blind from the lightning, I had my hands full with the horses, who wanted to bolt. When I could see again, Neirin had disappeared.

A cold tide of panic flooded through me. "Neirin!" I called. "Where are you? Are you hurt?" I got no answer; in the noise of the storm I could scarcely hear myself. If Neirin was on the ground, the horses, still barely under control, might tread on him. Keeping a tight grip on the reins, I dismounted, meaning to tie them to a tree. Then the earth slid out from under my feet, and I was falling.

Only my grip on the reins and the lead rope saved me. As I clung to them, my feet over empty air, my body battered against stone, the frightened horses backed away, and backing, hauled me out of the pit that had opened beneath me. I lay on the muddy ground gasping, half-drowned by the rain pouring down on my face; then with a convulsive heave I rolled over and got to my feet. Somehow I got the horses picketed, then searched on hands and knees the place where Neirin had been standing, as well as I could guess, when he disappeared. The pit into which I had almost fallen was close by; its earthy breath rose fog-like into the rain and wreathed about the trees. I called Neirin's name again and again into its mouth, but got no reply. Then, as clearly as if he spoke into my ear, I heard Taliesin's voice, giving me the rain-cape. "This should give you shelter when you need it most," he had said.

I stood up and went to the black pony, and took the rolled cape from the back of the saddle where it was tied. It went on easily; almost at once I felt warmer, and with the rain no longer beating on my head, less confused. I turned back to search again for Neirin, and as I did so I saw with the corner of my eye a light coming through the trees. I blinked and it was gone, but when I turned my head I saw it again. It was a lantern.

The room was pleasantly warm, sweet-scented with smoke from the brazier. "Do not you be looking at the edges," said Neirin's voice behind me. "That is the hard part. Once we are in we will be safe, until we go out again... Ah, that is good!" And he stepped past me and set his lantern down next to another one on a table which stood against one wall. Turning, he smiled faintly. "Do you sit down," he said. "He is with the horses now, but he will be back soon."

"Are you not hurt?" I asked. It seemed as reasonable a question as any. "I was afraid you fell."

"Na, I am not hurt, or at least, not from falling," said Neirin, seating himself on a bench by the brazier and holding out his hands to the fire. He was almost as wet as I was, and there was blood on his cheek and forehead. "It will be well with me. Only do not ask questions; I doubt me I have answers. Even Taliesin cannot explain it, not in words. Do you sit down; it is better that way."

I pushed back the hood of my rain-cloak and sat down by the brazier. The fire felt good on my cold hands. I was dimly aware that my body was strained and bruised, and would be very sore tomorrow, but it did not seem to matter. Everything was a little out of focus, and that was best.

The door opened, and a man came in, a tall black-bearded man in a white robe. "Be welcome, friends," he said. "Will you have drink?"

"Gladly," said Neirin. I looked sideways at him, wondering, but he was still smiling. The black-bearded man poured something from a blue-glazed pitcher into two wooden cups, and handed them to us; then he went and sat himself down in a high-backed oak chair on the other side of the brazier. "Drink, friends, and be welcome," he said in a pleasantly husky voice. "No harm there is in it." Neirin drank, and after a moment I followed suit. It seemed at first to be water, with a faint, herbal aftertaste, but it spread a warmth in me like the finest mead, and the pains of which I had been dimly aware receded.

Watching us, the stranger nodded approvingly. "That is well," he said. "If you have hunger, there are nuts and cheese beside you. Will you eat?"

"Gladly," said Neirin again, and helped himself, and passed the bowls to me. The cheese was soft and fresh, ewe-milk cheese, and the nuts were hazelnuts. I ate, and hunger I had not noticed faded.

The room was quiet except for the fire; there was no sound of storm, no rattle of rain on the house, no voice of wind without. We might be in a cave, but if so, a very comfortable one. There was apple-wood in the brazier, and the table was polished oak; the walls were lime-washed stone, and the floor of glazed tiles. When the stranger entered, there had been no sound of storm outside, and no light. But perhaps it was night, and the storm had passed.

"Gwernin," said Neirin's voice beside me, "do not you be thinking so much. Look only at what is before you: it is better thus. Lord," he said to the white-robed man, "we thank you for your hospitality. Will you tell us your name, and such of your story as we may know?"

The stranger smiled, showing good teeth. "I have no name now, Noble One," he said. "It is gone: it was taken: I gave it away. Call me Claddedig, if you will: the Buried One: for such is the name of the King in the Ground."

"Ah," said Neirin. "I knew it. We are privileged, Lord, to meet you here. Is there any of your story you can tell? I would not press you."

"No," said Claddedig. "No… It is well. A long time now it is, since I have had visitors. Will you tell me *your* names?"

"Neirin," said Neirin, "son of Dwywei, daughter of Lleenawg Elmet. My father was Cynfelyn Eidyn, Mynyddog Mwynfawr of Dun Eidyn. And—Gwernin?"

"Gwernin Storyteller," I said, "son of Gwenfrewy, daughter of Cadell Coch, of Pengwern. I do not know my blood father, Lord; my name-father was Ynyr son of Huwel."

"It is well," said Claddedig. "So—a story then." And he smiled. "In the years after the Romans came to Britain—you know it, do you not, my children?"

"We do," said Neirin. "Go on."

"Yes… In those days, there was much—disruption—in the land. Mona was burnt, and many good men killed. Boudicca raised her rebellion, and died of it. Caradawg was betrayed to the Romans, and taken away in chains, to what fate we did not know. And many worse things"—and Claddedig showed his teeth here in a snarl—"were done. Some of them, I grant you, by the Britons. But still…"

"I have heard that tale," said Neirin. "Go on."

"Well… In the years after Boudicca died, the Romans reaved much treasure from this land. Gold and silver, my children, were the least of it. They pillaged also our language, our customs, all the forms that made us who we were. For who are you, my children?" asked Claddedig.

"Those who would presently be Bards," said Neirin. "You know of what I speak: go on."

"Yes." And Claddedig smiled again. "The keepers of the Word: the keepers of the Name: in effect, all who came after me. For I was the Chief of my Order: and for that, to save that, to *guard* that, I was put into the ground."

"I knew it," said Neirin. "For so my master taught me: go on."

"Ah," said Claddedig, and was a while silent. "The Romans broke our language: the Romans broke our customs. So I have said. They did more than that: they did worse than that. They would have made this Island a land without a people: a people without a land. Do you know, O my children, who I was?"

"A Druid: a Priest: a Prince," said Neirin. "And more than that, and less than that, and wholly that. A maker, a shaper, a remembrancer: one tied to the earth, and the heavens, and the seasons. Is there more?"

"Yes," said Claddedig, "and no: all of these, and none of these I was. Will you hear a questioning?"

"Yes," said Neirin, "go on."

"*Sa, sa,*" said Claddedig, "here it is then:

> "Who is the King within the Ground,
> Why is the Stone within the Ring,
> What is the Bell that makes no sound,
> When will the New Lord come in spring?

"Can you answer?"

Neirin sat for a while, and then covered his eyes with his hands, and leaned forward as if very tired. "You are the King within the Ground, that is clear," he said after a moment, "and I think, if I must, that I could give a name to you, Lord; but the rest I cannot answer now: I am too young, and I am too old, and I am too weary. The New Lord, I think, should come at Beltane: and yet I am not sure. Will you go on?"

"I will," said Claddedig, and he smiled. "Well, then, as I said, the Romans broke that which they did not understand, and profaned that which they did; and from one end to the other of Britain they made a desolation, and called it a peace. It was right, then, that something ... someone ... should be set to counter them, that our land should not wholly die. In the year in which this was decided, there were few of us left: and I was most senior. And so it fell to me, after due deliberation, to make and to be the Sacrifice: to make and to be the Chosen One: to make and to be the Guardian at the Gate."

"Yes," said Neirin, "I understand you well: go on."

"Ah," said Claddedig. "Will you come and see the treasure I guard?"

"Gladly," said Neirin, and stood up. "Gwernin?"

"Gladly," I said, and followed them.

It was a long way, it was a short way; it was very deep, and very shallow, in the earth. It was a great hall beneath the ground, piled with every sort of treasure that could excite a man's desire. It was a place empty and dark and forsaken. We stood at the doorway, and looked out, and saw—and did not see—both of these. With every heartbeat in my breast the vista changed: treasure and emptiness, gold and darkness, life and death. "Gwernin?" said Neirin again beside me.

"Yes," I said, "I see it, and Not-It. What is the answer, Lord?" This was the first time I spoke to Claddedig myself, and I felt his smile beside me in the darkness.

"O my children, I am glad," he said, "that those who will be Bards have eyes yet to see. Noble One, will you tell me the answer?"

"Yes," said Neirin, and he sighed. "You guard the spirit of Britain: the truth within the language, the language within the mind, the mind within the soul: you guard the past, and the present, and the future of our people. While you are here, the tongue of our people will endure, and with it the knot, the soul, the spirit of our land. Do I speak truth?"

"You do, Little Hawk," said Claddedig. "Let us go back to the room."

When we were seated again in the warmth, he poured a drink for each of us from the blue-glazed pitcher. "Yes," he said then, raising his cup, "I know now who is your master. A blessing on him, and on you, and on those who come after you: it is for this, O my children, that I went into the ground. Now, the testing is over, but I am times and times a-lonely here: do you stay with me this night, and entertain me, and my blessing will go with you hereafter. Is it fair?"

"It is very fair," said Neirin, and he smiled. "Will you hear a tale? For I know that my friend Gwernin has one ready…"

Somehow, somewhen, somewhere, we found ourselves in the forest again, with our horses; and it was dawn. But the last conversation that passed between Claddedig and Neirin—I do not remember it all, though now I understand it—concerned the way of his dying. For the Consenting, as he said, is the all…

But that, O my children, is a story for another day.

In the High Hills

Elmet is a land of contrasts. It stretches from the Low Peaks in the south to the Pennine Gap in the north, from the Western Wall above Aquae Arnemetiae to the eastern hills that fall by slow stages to the Saxon plain. Much of it is moorland and mountain, little peopled or visited, broken here and there by deep and fertile valleys. Once it was a big kingdom, but bit by bit it has been nibbled away by the Saxons in the east and northeast and by Rheged in the northwest, until only the rocky core is left. But rock can be very strong, and falcons are no less fierce for nesting high. On the high tops the old ways still linger, and stone circles are more common there than churches.

After our experiences in the marshy country to the west, and our steep climb up the Western Wall, Neirin and I were glad to stop for the night at a shepherds' camp, where we were made welcome by the tough brown herders and their women and children. All summer they spend up there, from Beltane to Samhain, and care little for the goings-on below, but bards and storytellers they value above gold. Indeed, so warm was our welcome that we stayed three nights, and might have stayed much longer if we had so wished it. Night-times we sang and told stories by the fire, and daytimes we spent walking or lazing on the dry sheep-cropped turf; and bit by bit the silence of the high places soaked into us, and made us whole. Also the shepherd girls were very friendly, and the beer was good, so that all and all, we were almost sorry to move on.

We were going first to Aquae Arnemetiae, where we hoped to find Gwallawg Elmet, Neirin's uncle. "Not," as Neirin had said to me the day before, lying stretched out like a cat in the sunshine while one of the shepherd girls rubbed his back, "because I love him or he loves me over-much. He has never forgiven my mother for preferring the North to Elmet, or the man of her own choice to the one he would have chosen for her."

"Did you not grow up here, then?" I asked lazily, half-asleep myself with my head in another girl's lap. She bent over me and smiled, and her dark hair tickled my face.

"Na, na," said Neirin, "I got my birth and my raising in Manau, with my Gododdin cousins, and only came south to this country when I was of an age to bear arms. And then I compounded my offense: for it was here Taliesin found me, not long after, and took me for his prentice, so I have never really lived in Elmet at all. But the general lay of the land here I know—well enough, at any rate, to find Aquae, where Gwallawg has one of his chief courts. Then we will be seeing—what there is to see." And he rolled over and pulled his little dark girl down for a kiss, and we spoke no more for a while.

I was thinking back to that conversation as we came down the last hill to Aquae Arnemetiae, which in our tongue means "the Waters of the Goddess of the Sacred Grove." This was a holy place time out of mind, as hot springs often are, and although the Romans had taken it over and made it largely theirs, some of its ancient aura still clung. Nowadays the town was the usual mixture of British wood and thatch over Roman stone which was beginning to be familiar to me. Aquae differed only in having relatively more stone than wood, and also in lacking a defensive palisade: an indication in itself of how secure—and how distant from its enemies—this falcon's nest was.

Neirin had guessed right: Gwallawg was in residence. A big burly red-headed man with only a little grey starting in his abundant beard, he greeted us friendly-wise, though the embrace he gave his nephew was somewhat perfunctory. Aside from their general coloring there was no resemblance; Neirin, I thought, must take after his father. Gwallawg accepted our stated reason for the visit— that Neirin was set free by his master for a summer's journeying, and was on his way north to compete in a bardic competition in Manau at the Lughnasadh Fair—readily enough, and went straight on to his own concerns. He swept us into his fire-hall, talking non-stop, ordering one servant to take our gear to the guest-house, another to bring food and wine, a third to build up the fire and bring lamps. As he began to tell us of his last-year's raiding successes against the Saxons of Deira and Bernicia, I perceived that uncle and nephew were not so unlike after all. It might be one reason for their lack of friendship.

"Iffi will think twice," he was saying, "before he comes raiding in my domains again, I can tell you. We met them near Verbeia, and caught them in an ambush where the valley narrows; many a corpse they left behind them when they fled. If only Rheged had joined with me, we could have wiped them out; but so it is ever with Urien: he is more likely to attack his neighbors than combine with them against our mutual enemies. If you are going to his court on your way north, boy, you should go with care, for he does not love my bloodline, and he has reason." And he smiled grimly.

"I will remember," said Neirin soberly. "What news of the Saxons this spring?"

"Very little so far, but their raiding parties will be abroad before long. Do you carry weapons? I saw none about you."

"Only a knife. Bards are generally safe."

"Ha! Not from the Saxons!" Gwallawg grinned. "Is that all your master has taught you? I will find you a sword before you leave, if you can use one."

"I can," said Neirin tautly, his eyes sparkling and a flush rising into his thin cheeks. "And my friend Gwernin can as well." He compressed his lips, as if holding back angry words. For myself, I tried to keep the surprise out of my face; swords and I were not well acquainted.

"Good," said Gwallawg. "Then I will see you two here this evening. Perhaps you will show me then what you *have* learned." And he turned away and went out without pause, shouting for his chamberlain, and leaving us to find our way to the guest-house by ourselves.

"Have you been back, since Taliesin took you?" I asked as we unpacked our saddlebags.

"Once," said Neirin. His color was still high. "But I had him with me then. I should not be letting Gwallawg bait me so, I am too easy a target. I knew this would be hard. I should not have brought you here."

"Why not?" I said lightly. "It is only for a few nights, and my heart tells me we will see worse in our wanderings." And that was a true word.

Neirin sighed. "Yes, you are right. Let us walk outside; the need is on me for fresh air. And I can show you something— interesting."

From the court he led me to a little hill. Halfway up it were stone-built ruins of a circular building. "This is part of it," said Neirin, pushing aside the willow-herb and ivy that half blocked the entrance. "They do not use it now; the Christian priests have their way here instead. The Romans—improved—this place, but the core is older."

Within the ruined walls was an open space, partly overgrown, and in the center a carved block of stone. I looked with interest at its front, but the figures were too worn to recognize. "Here," said Neirin, going up to it, and placing both hands on the top. "Just— here."

I put my square brown hands beside his freckled ones. At first there was only the chill of the stone, there in the shade of the ivy-grown walls, and the distant call of a bird in the trees outside; then I began to feel something more. The world around us grew paler, out of focus, in a way I was coming to know. There was a sound that was not a sound, and the faint echo of a presence recently familiar to me. I took a deep steadying breath, and looked up to meet Neirin's eyes. He nodded. "Yes. He was here."

It cost me an effort to lift my hands from the stone. Slowly the world came back into focus, and the air warmed toward summer, which had been winter-cold. My mouth was dry; I spoke with difficulty: "Claddedig?" Neirin nodded again; his eyes were wide and dark. I wondered what he was seeing. Then he too lifted his hands deliberately from the altar block and stood back, and sighed.

"Yes," he said. "Taliesin showed it to me, when we were here before, but I did not know…" He shook his head as if to clear it. "Come, there is more."

"I am not sure I am for *more*, just now," I said, striving for lightness as I followed him out of the ruin. "What else do you have to show me here?"

Neirin looked back and smiled. "Nothing so … heavy. I swear it. Is it that you are afraid?"

"More and more, with you," I said, smiling back at him. "I think it is a Druid that you are."

"Na, I am not. But—come you, and see. It is not far." He went on up the hill, and I followed. Around the crest were young oaks, their leaves still golden-green with spring, and mixed with them two or three dark hollies. They spread a shadow over the hilltop all out of proportion to their size, like a memory of things past. I shivered as I went under them, but I followed Neirin.

At the crest he stopped and turned round, his gaze going up into the small trees that were not small from below. "Do you see it?" he asked. His eyes were bright. I shivered again; I had felt the Old Powers before. What he was seeing I did not want to see, but I had no choice. The light was fading even as I stood there, fading to dark green dusk, and again there were the sounds that were not sounds, that were memories of sounds: the echo of a brazen horn, faint and far-off, like the horn of Gwyn mab Nudd, and the sound of voices chanting. I closed my eyes and felt myself falling.

Then warm hands had mine in a hard clasp. "Gwernin," said Neirin's voice close beside me, "it is well with you: open your eyes." I did so: we were in the grove, and sunlight was pouring through the young oaks to dapple the grass around me. Neirin was on his knees beside me, looking down at me anxiously, his dark red head cocked a little to one side and his amber eyes narrowed in concern. When he saw I was back in my body, his face relaxed. "It is sorry I am, not to have warned you," he said. "I had forgotten… It took me like that the first time, too. Can you sit up?"

"Yes," I said hoarsely, and did so. I looked around at the trees and the sunlight, and felt the peace that lay on the place now, and a deep calmness entered into every part of me.

"Arnemetia," said Neirin softly. There was birdsong in the branches, a small sweet piping, and a little wind rustled the leaves. We sat for a long time listening to it. Only with the approach of evening did we rise and go back down the hill to Gwallawg's court.

The torches were lit in the mead-hall that night, and fire burned on the central hearth, for though the day had been mild, Aquae lay high in the hills. Gwallawg kept no *pencerdd* in his hall just then, but he had a harper—a dark young man not so many years older than myself—who played for us during the first part of the meal. When hunger and thirst were satisfied, Gwallawg turned to Neirin, sitting beside him at the high table. "Well, Sister's-Son, have you a song for me?"

"Na, na, Mother's-Brother," said Neirin lightly, "let me wait until tomorrow, that the song may be worthy of this hall. My friend Gwernin, I know, has a tale ready for you and would gladly tell it."

"So I do, Lord," I said, as Gwallawg turned to me. "Would you hear the tale of Maxen Wledig, and how he won a wife, and the High Kingship of Britain as well?"

"Gladly," said Gwallawg. "Speak your tale."

This was one of the stories I had learned from Talhaearn the past winter, though it is not a winter-tale as such, and I enjoyed the telling of it, and the gradually increasing look of interest and engagement on Gwallawg's bearded face. "Well," he said at the end, when the applause of the hall had died, "you at least have been well-taught, young man. Who is your master?"

"Talhaearn Tad Awen," I said, not without pride, "and if I have a little lived up to his reputation I am glad, though I am the least of his students."

Gwallawg smiled, and took a silver bracelet from his arm, and gave it to me. "Well have you done so," he said. "I hope my sister's son can do half so well tomorrow." And with that he rose up and left the hall.

The next morning I woke in the green dawn to see Neirin by the door. "It is out I am going, Gwernin," he said, when he saw I was awake. "I will be back with evening; bide you here in the court this day." And before I could answer he was gone, leaving me wondering. I spent the day as I was bidden, and talked some time to Gwallawg's young harper, Padarn, who came from the lands of the southwest near that other Aquae which is dedicated to Sulis, and had in his blood-line and his face much of the Roman. And with evening Neirin returned, though saying no word of where he had been that day.

When the feasting was over that night, Gwallawg turned to his nephew as before. "Well, Sister's-Son," he said, "are you ready now to show me what you have learned, or do you need yet more time to prepare?"

Neirin smiled faintly. "Since you offer it, Mother's-Brother, I will take a little longer: tomorrow night I will be more ready. And I know that my friend Gwernin has yet another tale prepared that you will enjoy…"

"Indeed I have, Lord," I said. "Would you hear a tale from Ireland, of the warrior Cuchulainn and how he took up arms?"

Gwallawg laughed shortly. "It seems I have no choice, since my sister's child is yet unready for his work. You I know to be well taught. *Sa,* I will hear that tale gladly."

So I told the tale that I had told once before to Cyndrwyn's young men while we stood the wolf-guard that past winter, and it was as well received by Gwallawg and his war-band, for it is a tale that appeals to all of the warrior-kind, whatever their nation. And at the end Gwallawg took another silver bracelet from his arm, and gave it to me. "I hope," he said then, "that my sister's boy-child is ready with his art tomorrow night, for the day after that I ride north, and would see you both a little way on your road."

"I will be ready, Mother's-Brother," said Neirin calmly enough, though the tell-tale flush was mounting in his cheeks.

"Do you see, then, that you are," said Gwallawg shortly, and he rose up as before and left the hall.

Again I woke in the green dawn to see Neirin by the door. "I am going out now, Gwernin," he said, "but I will be back tonight."

I yawned. "I suppose you know what you are doing," I said sleepily, "but are you sure you would not like company? I can be ready in a moment."

"Na, na," said Neirin, and he laughed softly. "Do not you be worrying: I know what I am about. I will see you tonight," and he was gone before I could protest more. And that day passed as had the day before; and at evening he came back to the court.

When the feasting was over that night, Gwallawg turned to his nephew as before. "Well, Sister's-Son," he said, "tomorrow I take the war-trail. Have you anything to show me before I go, that I may see the worth of your teaching, and your teacher?"

"*Sa, sa,* I do that," said Neirin. "I have a song for you, Mother's-Brother: weigh it as you will." And he stood up, and took the singer's stance, and he began.

"A golden song for a golden one,
a bright song for a bright fallen star:
she is gone down into deep darkness;
my heart within me is heavy as stone.

A golden song for a gold sister,
a bright song for one bright as day:
she is gone out forever from Elmet;
my heart within me is winter-dark.

A golden song for a gold lady,
a bright song for one briefly loved:
she is gone out now from Manau;
my heart within me is empty and cold.

A golden song for a golden one,
a bright song to warm my cold heart:
heavy green turf grows now over Dwywei:
who will not weep with me here for her loss?"

Gwallawg looked a long time in silence at his nephew when the song was done. "*Sa, sa,*" he said at last, and I could hear the tears in his voice. "I will weigh it and reward it." And he called to a servant, and had a heavy chest brought into the hall and opened. From it he took a sword in a jewel-set scabbard, a weapon for a king, and held it out to Neirin. "Take you this, Sister's-Son, as a small part of the value of your song: I repent me that ever I spoke against your master or his teaching. Hereafter you will both be welcome in my hall."

Neirin looked long at his uncle and the offered gift, and I saw there were tears on his own cheeks as well. Then he nodded. "*Sa, sa,* I take it as it is offered," he said, "provided only"—and here he smiled with that special warmth that lit up his face—"that you find some weapon as well for my friend Gwernin, who has defended me nobly while I prepared."

"I might," said Gwallawg, "do even that." And with a smile the equal of Neirin's own, he reached into the chest again, and from it drew a second, only slightly lesser, weapon, which he gave to me. And the next day when we rode out with his war-band, we both rode armed; and well it was for us that we did so.

But that, O my children, is a story for another day.

Blood and Fire

The price of glory is blood. So do the men of the war-band pay for their mead-feast, and for the golden gifts given them: with their blood, and if need be, their lives. But glory—and treasure—is bought also with the blood of others, and thus does the raider live, like a wolf, by his weapons. And in order for the wolf to eat, something—or someone—must die.

On the bright morning after Neirin had made his singing in the fire-hall of Elmet, we rode out with that Prince and his retinue on the Romans' old road north. Gwallawg was going roundabout to his target in order to set us on our way, and also to spy out the southern marches of Rheged while avoiding Saxon scouts from the east: for with summer all war-bands were stirring. The first day's ride took us to Mamucium, where we camped in the grass-grown remains of the old brown Roman fort. A second and longer day by a good straight road would take us over the hills to Bremetenacum, on the edge of Rheged's territory. From there Gwallawg meant to cut back east on the cross-Pennine road that leads toward Eboricum, passing through Olenacum and Verbeia and harrying the western flanks of Deira, while Neirin and I rode on north alone.

Such, at least, was the plan; but on the second evening as we were approaching Bremetenacum a messenger met us in haste, a blood-spattered man on a hard-ridden horse. "Lord," he said, hardly waiting to draw rein, "the Saxons are out—they have passed Verbeia and will be closing in on Olenacum by now. We knew you would be on the road, and I came this way in hopes of finding you. Come you now, and we can catch them while they sleep!"

"Na, na," said Gwallawg, "let me think. We have come a long ride already today, and Olenacum is half as far again." And he sat his big bay stallion in silence for a moment, running his fingers absently through his curly red hair and frowning. "Na," he said then, "we will stop here to eat, and tend the horses, and rest for a while. Then we will ride on with you, friend, at moon-rise, and take them just before dawn, when their sleep will be heaviest and their sentries tired. Rhys, Cadfan, take the men on into camp and see to it. Sister's-Son, do you ride this war-trail with me?"

"Gladly," said Neirin, his face alight. "It is long and long since I carried a spear in battle!"

"*Sa, sa,* I will find you one then, and one for your friend as well," said Gwallawg, grinning. "Let us ride on. And you, friend"— this to the messenger—"let you ride with me and tell me all that you know. What is their strength?"

"Two or three score, Lord," said the man, turning his horse to ride with us, "about the same as yours, so far as I could judge. They are burning as they come, Lord, and driving off the cattle."

"They will pay *sarhaed* for that tomorrow," said Gwallawg. "Come you now, and rest and eat with us, and we will find you a fresh horse: then tonight you can show us the way."

So it was that very late that night, as the old moon was westering and the pre-dawn light beginning to show along the eastern horizon, I found myself sitting my pony with half of the war-band on the road just west of Olenacum, while Gwallawg and the other half circled round to strike the Saxon's camp from the east. The night was very quiet where we were, so quiet I could hear the distant voice of the river we had forded earlier, and the call of a hunting owl in the copse near us sounded loud. Now and then there was the faint jink of metal as one of the horses moved restlessly, or the creak of leather when one of the riders shifted his weight. The spear shaft in my hand felt heavy and unfamiliar, but at least I knew what to do with it; I had ridden on one or two cattle-raids as a boy, before I left Pengwern. I felt the old excitement rising up in me now, the anticipation which stirs the blood and sets the heart beating faster, and tightened my grip unconsciously on the light cavalry bucker I carried in my left hand. I looked at Neirin beside me and saw his teeth flash white in the moonlight as he grinned. Every moment now the light was growing. When would Gwallawg strike?

Even as the thought formed in my mind, I heard the distant smother of sound, pierced by shouts and screams of pain, and the high bright notes of a hunting horn. "Now!" said Rhys, the troop-leader, and we broke from a stand into a trot, and then a canter, a ragged body of horsemen roughly centered on the Roman road and heading for the Saxon watch-fires just outside the old walls. Then we were in amongst them, and the world was a swirling red confusion which I cannot now well remember or describe. Only brief glimpses of it stay with me: the snarling face of the Saxon who took my spear in his throat, and the dark gush of his blood as I tore the point free again—the first man I ever killed; the blow from a Saxon sword that cleft my light shield of wicker-work and leather, and would have taken off my arm if I had not had that shield; the other sword-blow that might have killed me in its turn had not Neirin beside me cut off the man's head with his new blade before it could land, and the fountain of blood from the severed neck that splattered us both; the second man I speared—in the belly, that time—and the way the spear was torn from my hand, half pulling me from the saddle as my pony carried me onward; the screams of wounded men and horses, and the hot bright pain in my leg where someone's steel went home; and my clumsy efforts with my new sword to be more of a danger to the enemy than to myself or my friends.

Then the Saxons—those who survived—were gone, streaming away to the east with Gwallawg and half his men in pursuit, and I was sitting on a broken wall blinking in the early sunlight while Neirin slit open my blood-soaked trouser leg and bound a linen rag around the oozing gash in my left thigh. He himself was bleeding from several minor wounds, but seemed not to notice it; he looked up from his work and grinned in sheer high spirits, and I grinned back, the excitement of battle still fizzing in my blood. "*Sa, sa,*" he said, "that was a night to remember! But we must get you some sword practice, brother: have you ever so much as held one before?"

"Not above once or twice," I admitted, laughing. "My uncle was a free man, but no warrior. It was only spears for me: I never thought to have a sword of my own."

"No great matter, that," said Neirin, straightening up and wiping his bloody hands on the skirts of his filthy tunic. "*Hai mai!* I could do with breakfast! Let us go and see what the Saxons have left."

What they had left was not good seeing. The little town beside the remains of the old marching camp had been half-ruined already, but the Saxons had finished the work. Whatever could burn had done so; acrid smoke still rose from the charred timbers and caught in the throat, and it was not like the clean smoke of a hearth-fire. Here and there in the street there was a body, human or animal. One of them had been a girl, much the same age and coloring as the shepherd girls on the high tops above Aquae. This one might have been pretty, too; I could not tell. I stood and stared; I could not help myself. Neirin, seeing I had stopped, looked back. He frowned, his dark brows almost meeting, and his nose wrinkled in disgust; then he took my arm and walked me along. "Come you on, Gwernin," he said. "There is nothing to be done here. Come you on." And I came. But that was the day I really began to hate the Saxons. Now that I am old, I know that all armies do this on occasion, for there is evil, as there is good, in every race of men upon the green earth; but until that morning I had not seen the face of war.

At the end of the village we caught up with some of our own men, who had killed a cow and were spitting the meat to cook. They had found a store of heather-beer, too, and shared some of it with us. I drank it off as if it had been water, but it took the sick taste out of my mouth, and presently that and the smell of the sizzling cow-meat reminded me that I was hungry. The surviving townspeople had begun to trickle back from the wooded hills where they had spent the night with such of their possessions as they had been able to save when the raiders came. Someone gave me a barley-bannock, and I sat chewing it and waiting for the meat to be done, resting my leg and wondering if I could get a woman to sew up my trews where Neirin had slit them; I had only the one other pair in my baggage-roll, and those were my good ones.

Toward mid-morning Gwallawg came back with part of his men; the rest, I gathered, were still harrying the fleeing Saxons. After he had seen to the horse-lines and dismissed his troop to eat and rest, he joined us for breakfast. He was in a good humor, his hazel eyes twinkling above his bushy red beard, for we had killed twelve or thirteen of the raiders at little cost to ourselves, and looked likely to recover most of the stolen cattle. It was while he was sitting by our fire, a hunk of dripping meat in one hand and a horn of beer in the other, that we became aware of a disturbance coming our way. Then the soldiers around us fell back to allow two of their number through, who were half-carrying and half-dragging a third man between them. They threw him down in front of Gwallawg, where he got slowly to his knees: a fair-haired youth not much older than I, with his golden beard just starting, and his face covered in blood from a gash on his forehead. It did not need his long-sleeved tunic or his sullen expression to tell me what he was: a Saxon prisoner.

Gwallawg's eyebrows shot up, but otherwise he did not move. "*Sa, sa,*" he said, "and where did you find this beauty?"

The soldiers grinned, standing behind their prize with their hands suggestively on their sword-hilts. "Near the outer defenses," said one. "We were clearing the bodies and saw this one move. He looks to have been trampled in the first rush."

"That is his misfortune," said Gwallawg, looking the boy over. "I see you have not robbed him." For the prisoner still wore a fine belt with an elaborate bronze buckle, and broad silver bracelets on his wrists.

"Na, na," said the other soldier, "we brought him in all his finery so that you might admire him. Like enough we will get the remains when you are through." And there was general laughter. I saw the prisoner's eyes flick around the circle before going back to Gwallawg, but he kept his head well up. Whether he understood our speech I could not tell, but he could not much mistake its meaning.

Gwallawg spoke suddenly to him: "Who are you? What is your name?" And getting no response, he repeated it in the Saxon tongue: "*Hwæt is ðin nama? Hwa aert ðu? Saga hwaet ðu hattst?*"

"*Ic hatte Wulfstan*," said the boy in surprise, and then he shut his mouth. To Gwallawg's further questions he returned no answer, only glaring in sullen defiance, until the Prince shook his head.

"I have no more time for this, and I doubt he knows anything useful." And he nodded to the two soldiers. "Take him away and cut his throat."

The prisoner understood *that*; his eyes grew wide, but still he maintained his silence. The soldiers behind him laughed and took him by the shoulders to drag him away. And I surprised myself by lurching to my feet, saying, "Wait, Lord."

Gwallawg turned to me, surprise in his face. "Gwernin? Have you a claim here?"

"No, Lord," I said, "but surely it is a waste to kill him out of hand? There must be some better use for him." I would not admit, even to myself, that the prisoner's courage had moved me.

Gwallawg sighed with barely contained impatience. "What would you suggest? Here we are on the war-trail, ready to ride on in a few hours, you to the North and I in pursuit of my enemies. Would you drag this Saxon trash along with you, to cut your throat while you sleep? I would not."

I looked at the Saxon, still on his knees, dumb-sullen. "Na, na," I said, "Nor would I. But he must have some value. He and his kind have caused much damage here—give him to the townspeople, to work as a slave in the rebuilding."

Gwallawg laughed harshly. "An apt punishment! Will he thank you, I wonder?" And to the soldiers: "Brân, Rhun, let it be with him as the Storyteller says; but the two of you can have the trinkets. Take him first to the smithy, to put chains on him, lest he run." And cramming the rest of his breakfast into his mouth, he stood up and headed off to inspect the town.

I stood for a moment watching the soldiers drag their prisoner away; then I sat down again, for my leg was hurting, and looked around at Neirin beside me. "Did I do wrong?" I asked, remembering the little dark girl, dead in the street—and dead in such a way! But killing this boy would not bring her back to life.

Neirin smiled a little and shook his head at me. "Na, I would not be knowing. But I think you have more forgiveness in you than I have, for all that you are no Christian." He stood up and stretched down his hand to me. "I am going down to the baggage train to check on our gear, before our pack-pony disappears, harps and all. Do you come with me, or would you rather rest?"

"I will come," I said, and took his hand, and he hauled me to my feet again. "I am for leaving this place as soon as we well may." And we went away to look for our ponies, and I thought no more of the young Saxon and his fate—or at least, not that day.

In early afternoon Gwallawg bade us farewell, embracing us both cheerfully, and rode off with his war-band to follow up the pursuit, advising us to spend the night in Olenacum before setting off cross-country to cut the Roman road again south of Calacum. But we had seen enough of Olenacum, and we took ourselves and our tired ponies back across the ford and up the long slopes to the moors; and that night we camped in the silence of the high places, and washed ourselves and our bloody clothes in a little peaty stream that chuckled through the heather there; and when we slept, we slept sound. And the next day we set our faces towards the North, and rode on toward the court of Urien Rheged.

But that, O my children, is a story for another day.

Tristfardd

It took us many more days than it should have to reach Luguval-ium, that fine city on the old Roman Wall where Urien Rheged had his chief court, and I was the cause of the delay. The wound I got in the fighting at Olenacum festered and would not heal, and we had to stop more than once on the way to rest it, and to renew the herbal dressings that Neirin and I contrived between us: for I had learned a little herb-lore on my travels, and Neirin knew rather more than I. Still, I had some anxious days and uncomfortable nights before our efforts began to have effect, and the ugly red streaks above the wound cleared at last, and the jagged cut itself ceased to drain and closed cleanly. I carry the scar of that first battle to this day, but it was a good lesson: since then I have always remembered that prevention is easier than cure, and have been more careful in the cleansing of wounds.

Had it not been for that mishap, our ride north would have been pure joy. The weather was mostly fine and warm, and made camping a pleasure rather than a hardship; Neirin found time to give me some lessons in swordsmanship, though perforce mostly on horseback until my leg healed; and we talked all through the sunny days and half the pale nights, sharing songs and stories as well as our own personal tales. But the moon which had been waning when we waited for the fight at Olenacum was new before we reached Luguvalium, and too much of our summer had already slipped away.

Into every summer journey, however, some rain must fall. It was while we were still some way south of Brocavum, following the climbing road that leads up the Lune valley toward the pass through the hills, that our golden weather left us. The clouds which had been thin and pale when we awoke that morning grew lower and darker as the day wore on, dropping to brush the high hills to our east with their dangling fringes, and then to veil the whole country-side with a blue-gray mist of rain. We put on our rain-cloaks, checked the coverings of our gear on the pack-pony, and rode on, but we were glad to see a steading ahead of us in the valley that evening, and smell the hint of blue wood-smoke that mingled with the rich scents of the rain-wet earth.

The farm-folk were glad of company, for many of their people were up on the high fells with the sheep and cattle. They welcomed us into the big thatched house-place and brought us to the fire, which was grateful after the chill of the rain. When they found we were bards, their pleasure knew no bounds, and that night after we had eaten we entertained them, I with my tale of Arthur and the Three Truths and Neirin with some of his harping.

"That was good playing indeed," said the gray-haired farmer afterwards. "It is long and long since we had a harper in this hall, and longer since we heard such a good one, for men who wake their music for kings stop seldom at such a place as this."

"There was once one who did," said his old wife beside him. "Though his music was not so bright and fair as yours, lad."

"Aye, that is true," said the farmer. "Sad was his music, and sad his fate, the poor man, though some say he deserved it. The Sad Bard, they called him—*Tristfardd*." And looking at me, he asked, "Do you know his tale, lad?"

"I have heard of him," I said slowly. "But you who have met him should know his tale better than I, who only heard it told once by my master Talhaearn."

"Na, but we are not storytellers," said the wife smiling. "Do you tell it to us as you have heard it, far away in the South."

I looked at Neirin, and he nodded. "*Sa*, let you tell it, Gwernin. I should like to hear it again as well."

"Very well," I said. "This is the tale of Tristfardd, *Pencerdd* to Urien Rheged, as I heard it once from my master." I paused a moment thinking, to gather the stands of the story as I remembered it, and then I began.

"Urien King of Rheged you will know well by repute, living so close to his lands as you do. He has not now a Chief Bard in his court, nor has he had one for many years, only lesser bards who come and go with the seasons. But once he had such a man in his service, and that one was called Tristfardd.

"Three sorts of music there are that a harper-bard must command: the music of joy, and the music of sleep, and the music of sorrow. All of these Tristfardd could play, but it was in the last, the *cerdd drist*, that he excelled, and so he got his name.

"In those days Urien was a young king, recently come into his lordship in Rheged. And young also was Urien's wife, Modron ferch Afallach, and she was of surpassing beauty. As he played one night in Urien's *llys*, Tristfardd gazed upon her, and as he looked, he fell under the spell of that beauty, so that every part of him was filled with love and desire for Urien's wife. And she looked upon him, and though he was not comely, the enchantment of his music entered into her heart, and she loved him in return. And when Urien was next away from his court, they found opportunity to be together, and to fulfill their love; and they were happy. But when Urien came back, they were apart again, and miserable. And this went on for some time.

"At last Tristfardd could no longer bear this having-and-not-having, and he determined to go away. For three years he wandered throughout the land of Britain, without once coming near to the court of Rheged. And in all that time he had no peace, and his heart was eaten up with longing for Urien's wife. And he knew that it was the same for her.

"Finally he decided to try and see her again. It was then autumn, with the winter closing in, and threatening soon to shut all the ways with snow, and the thought of spending another half-year away from Modron was more than Tristfardd could bear. So he set out toward the court of Rheged. It was cold, wet weather, and as he drew near to Urien's *llys* it grew worse, so that by late afternoon he was so chilled and weary that he was forced to stop for a while in the shelter of some woods and build a fire to warm himself. And while he was trying to light the fire, with the wet wood hissing and spitting and refusing to burn, he heard a horseman coming; and peering through the cloud of smoke around him, he saw a tall man on a bay mare. As the man came closer, Tristfardd saw that he was all muffled up in a heavy hooded cloak against the rain, so that nothing could be seen of him but his beard, which was gray-streaked like the pelt of a badger. Tristfardd called out to him, and asked him if he had been recently at Urien's *llys*.

" '*Sa*, I have that,' said the stranger.

" 'And was Urien then at home?' asked Tristfardd.

" 'He was there when I was there,' replied the stranger.

"Then Tristfardd asked the stranger to carry a message to Urien's wife, and beg her to meet him tomorrow at a place near the court which they both knew well. And the stranger agreed, and rode on his way. But what Tristfardd did not know was that the stranger with whom he had been speaking was Urien himself; for in the three years since they had last met, Urien's beard had turned gray.

"When Urien arrived home, he told his wife what had happened, and he ordered her to meet Tristfardd the next day and send him away. And she went; but as soon as she and the Bard saw each other, they knew they could not bear to be parted again. Even though she warned Tristfardd that Urien knew of their love, he would not leave her, and she could not bring herself to send him away.

"When Modron returned to the *llys*, Urien asked her if she had done as he ordered, and she admitted that she had not. Then Urien was angry, and he took his sword and went out to slay the Bard. But when Tristfardd saw him coming he knew him, and begged Urien to spare his life, and to let him stay at the court where he might at least see the Queen, for without the sight of her his life was not worth the living. And Urien agreed, on two conditions: that Tristfardd should no longer entice Modron to love him, and that he should never again speak to Urien himself of his desire for her. Tristfardd swore that he would keep to these terms, and he returned with Urien to the *llys*. And that night Tristfardd sang again in the hall of Urien Rheged, and he had the sight of the Queen in his eyes to comfort him, and she had him in hers."

I paused, thinking back to the stormy evening last autumn when I had first heard Talhaearn tell that tale. It had been told then as a caution to our Prince's young wife and one of his lords. Now it was told to entertain, and yet I could hear in memory the very pitch and cadence of my master's voice. Trying to match it, I went on.

"So things continued for half a year or more. But at last neither the Queen nor the Bard could bear to be always seeing each other, and never touching, and so they found a chance when Urien was away to come together in secret, and they once more became lovers.

"One day when Urien went out hunting, he took Tristfardd with him on a whim as one of his party. After they had killed their deer, they shared around a skin of strong wine, and Tristfardd, who was weary, drank more of it than he ought. Presently his horse went lame, and as they were then approaching a river, Urien took the Bard up behind him on his own mare to ford it.

"As they were crossing the river, Urien said, 'A fine little mare this is indeed, who bears the both of us on her four slender legs.'

" 'Fine also,' said Tristfardd, the wine speaking through him, 'are the *two* slender legs that bear us both.'

" 'Ha!' cried Urien, 'I see that you have broken your vow, and taunt me again with your lust for my wife!' And on reaching the bank, he pulled out his sword and slew Tristfardd, so that the river ran red with his blood; and that place has ever after been called *Rhyd Tristfardd*. And from that day to this, there has not been a Chief Bard in the court of Urien Rheged."

"Ah, now that was well told," said the farmer when his folk had finished their applause. "And I do think you have the kernel of truth in it, though maybe the tale has grown somewhat in its travels."

"That may be so," I said, smiling. "But this is how I heard it. What would you reckon, then, is the truth that I have not heard?"

"Hmm," said the farmer, and he rubbed his blunt brown nose. "I am no storyteller, and it would come somewhat bald and plain from me."

"Na, husband, you are none so bad," said his wife comfortably. "Do you tell the tale to the lads as we know it here."

"Oh, very well," said the farmer, and he paused a moment, pulling at his gray beard and frowning. "Some of this," he said slowly, "we heard from a traveler, not long after the thing happened, and some of it I know for myself, by my own eyes and ears." He stared for a moment longer into the fire, and shook his head, and began.

"I saw the man called Tristfardd three times in my life, though only once to speak to, and I cannot claim to know his mind, or why he did what he did, or even what that was. True word it is, that men will do strange things for want of women." And here he met his wife's eyes, and they smiled briefly at each other; then he went on.

"The first time I saw the Bard was eighteen or twenty years ago, around about the time of Camlann fight. I was a young man myself then, and not long wed to my lass here, and I had still a young man's eye for the girls, though I say it as ought not. My cousins and I had driven some of our sheep up to Brocavum over the pass for the autumn market there—the prices are sometimes better than at Calc to the south of us—and we were there when Urien and his party came by, bringing home his bride. And a great company he had with him, and a strong war-band as escort, for the times were unsettled. But I saw his lady wife in her horse-litter, pulling back the curtains to look at the people and smiling like the sunrise; and I saw the Bard riding near her, with his harp-case on his shoulder. And she was shining fair as a bright spring morning, when the early sun touches the mist and sets it afire; but he had a face on him dark and bitter as a cold winter's day, and he was not young. They came, and they passed, and I took my attention back to the sheep-pens, which was as it should be, and thought no more of them then.

"The second time I saw the Bard was two years later, or it might have been three. I remember my lass here had been brought to bed a while before that with our first-born, and we had been holding the naming-feast that day, and were making merry afterwards. It was autumn again, not long before Samhain, with the cold weather coming on—winter comes hard in these hills. Raining it was that day, with the burns running full, and going on for dark when he came to our door for shelter. Truth to tell, I would not have known him again, but for the harp case, for he was all alone, and wet as a trout as well, having come away from the court, as it seemed, with only his horse, and his harp, and the clothes he stood up in, and little enough besides."

"Ah, I remember," said his wife nodding. "We brought him to the fire, and warmed him with ale, and loaned him one of your old tunics, love. And by and by he began to look like a living man, and toasted my boy, and even played us some music. But times and times, when no one was speaking to him, he would go quiet again; and then he looked like a man who has seen the Wild Hunt, and had them on his heels." And she shook her head at the memory.

"Well, well, that is as may be," said the farmer. "I remember he stayed with us a day or two, until the rain let up, and then he was away to the South. Not so long afterwards we heard he had cut a man in a fight, in the King's own hall, and Urien was wanting to lay hands on him. But I reckon the man survived, for we heard no more of the tale."

"Na, and I never believed it myself," said his wife. "He was no man to be fighting, was the Bard. He was too gentle. I wish I could remember all of the song he sang for me, the night before he left us; so sad it was, and yet so sweet!"

"Hmm," said the farmer. "I would not be knowing about that. Myself, I would say he looked a good man of his hands, but women see these things differently." And he fell silent, staring into the fire.

"What was the third time, then, that you saw him?" Neirin asked after a while, and the farmer looked up at us again.

"The third time—yes, the third time," he said. "Another two years, was it, wife, or was it three?"

"Three," said his wife, and sighed. "It was the year our second boy was born, who died in the Black Winter."

"Mmm, yes," said the farmer, and his mouth was wry. Neirin and I made sympathetic noises. "Well," he said, "to finish the tale… I had been up to Brocavum again to the autumn market, and was coming back on my own, when I heard away off in the hills the sounds of a hunting horn, and dogs barking, and men hallooing and shouting. Somewhere ahead of me they crossed the road, and their noise was louder then. I heard a horse neighing in fear or pain, and a scream that might have been an animal, and might have been a man. Presently I met them all coming back along the road—more like a war-band than a hunt, they were, laughing and shouting as men will when their blood is up, and Urien in the midst of them, the loudest of them all. There was a led horse at the back, but no sign of any game, nor any plunder, either; and I thought that was strange, but it was none of my business. It was only when I came to the ford on the River Lyvennet that I saw what they had been hunting, or rather who: it was the Bard."

"Was he dead?" I asked after a few moments, when he seemed disinclined to go on. The farmer looked up again and shook his head.

"Not quite," he said simply, "but he was beyond speech, as a man may be when he has a boar-spear through his body, and half his blood poured out on the sand around him. I got down and looked, but there was no helping him, though I did what I could. Afterwards I pulled out the spear, and piled the stones over him, and came away." He sighed. "We did hear afterwards that the Queen was main sick all that winter, and like to die, but in the end she recovered and was brought to bed around Beltane of a boy. That would be Urien's second son, would it not, wife?"

"Aye," said the woman. "His first-born was one of twins, so they say, and fair as their mother is fair, though Urien is black."

"So he is," said the farmer, and yawned. "Well, that is my tale, lads, and time it is now for bed."

"Indeed, and we thank you for it," I said. "But tell me this: did you ever hear of a reason why Urien killed the Bard?"

"Na, I never did," said the farmer, getting to his feet. "And after what I saw, I was not inclined to ask. But one part of your tale at least is true, lad: from what I hear, Urien is generous to entertainers, and welcomes them all. But he does not keep them long about him, and from that day to this, he has never had a Chief Bard at his court. So have a care, when you stand in the court of Urien Rheged."

"Indeed, and I will," I said, and Neirin echoed my words, though he looked thoughtful.

But that, O my children, is a story for another day.

The Court of Urien Rheged

Luguvalium—the place of Lugh-on-the-Wall—was as great a town as any I had so far seen in my journeying. More: it was still a living town, with undamaged buildings and running fountains. It lay at the west end of the great Wall of Hadrian, where that eighty-mile-long barrier comes down from the hills to the sea—the Sea of Rheged, some call it, though the north side of that wide bay is a different land, with a different Lord.

It was just before sunset when we rode in through the town gate, and the warm western light seemed to burn in the red tile roofs and mellow brick-work. We were tired and hungry, for the south end of Rheged is little peopled, being mostly marsh and rough moor-land; and once we had reached the Eden valley and found Urien was not at Brocavum, we had pressed on up the good Roman road without pause. Still, the abundance of this court was legendary, and we looked forward to a good dinner that night.

I noticed as we rode in that the people of the town looked well-fed and well-pleased with themselves, the shops and markets busy and profitable. Luguvalium had been the headquarters of the Roman army in the North, and thereby weathered disturbances which had damaged other towns, and clearly its good fortune had not entirely departed. As we came to Urien's court in the center of the place, I wondered about our welcome, but Neirin had been right: we were both of us wearing our harp-cases, slung baldric-wise on their shoulder-straps, and it seemed that this was all the identification needed here: soldiers at the gates of the *llys* waved us through, boys came running to hold our horses, and other servants led us to a guest-room along the east wall. Wine and water appeared like magic, and we were bidden make ourselves comfortable, and come to the fire-hall at our leisure, where we would be welcome. It was so easy we could hardly keep from grinning at each other.

On inquiry Neirin found that the bathhouse here still functioned, so we went there first to wash off the dust of the road. It was twilight by then, and we did not linger, but the cold plunge was refreshing. After that, clean and in fresh clothes—my best and Neirin's next-to-best—we made our way to the hall. It was easy to find, and not only for its size: music and voices and firelight poured out from its doors like a river. We found seats at one of the trestle tables near the lower end, and at once servants brought us bowls and cups, and platters were passed our way, full to overflowing with meat and bread and other good things. I hardly noticed what I ate for looking at the high table and the people there: and they were well worth the seeing.

At the center of the table sat a big man in healthy middle age, richly dressed in robes of black and scarlet and gold. His beard was streaked with grey, but his long hair, held back by a band of gold, was still dark, and his broad face was deeply tanned. Beside him sat a woman, and it was she who caught and held my attention. Almost as tall as the man, she was as different from him as she well could be: pale clear skin she had, and hair that was almost silver, and strange dark eyes, and with it all great beauty. And yet I saw in her a deep sadness; so might Gueneviere have looked after Camlann fight, when all that she had lived for had died. I turned to say as much to Neirin—no on else would have heard me in the tumult of that hall!—and saw his gaze was elsewhere, on a tall young man and woman who had just entered by a door at the upper end of the hall. They were both richly dressed, as like the pale woman as they well could be, and clearly brother and sister; they came along behind the table, pausing to speak to her and the gold-crowned man, and then found themselves places and sat down. I looked at Neirin again, and this time he nodded. "Urien himself, and his wife Modron, and their twins Owain and Morfudd." His gaze went back to the high table; he drew a deep breath. "*Sa, sa,*" he said softly, "never did I think that a woman could be so beautiful."

"Yes. She burns like a still flame," I said. "So beautiful, and yet so sad."

"Sad?" Neirin looked round at me in astonishment; then he grinned, and his eyes began to dance. "*Hai mai!* I think we are not looking in the same place, at all: it was the daughter I meant, and not the mother!" And his gaze went back, as if against his will, to Morfudd where she sat beside her brother Owain, all unaware of his regard. For myself, I looked thoughtfully at Neirin for a moment, and then reapplied myself to my supper; I felt I was going to need all my strength before long. I remembered well the tale of Trist-fardd, who had once loved Modron the Queen too well and died of it, and I did not think a traveling bard would be a welcome suitor for the only daughter of Urien the King.

"Na, na, na!" said Neirin later that evening in our lodgings; he had been saying it for some time. "Of course I would not be doing such a thing; I am remembering our mission here as well as you are. It is only—it is only—" He paused, running his hands distractedly through his dark red hair and rumpling it still further. "By all the gods!" he said, half to himself. "Never did I think that such a thing as this could be happening to me!" He gave a reluctant laugh. "And she has not so much as seen me! I am well served, maybe, for some of my past adventures. But I must be speaking with her somehow, I must!" And he flung up from the bed where he had been sitting, and began to walk around the room again in a hasty, restless way, as if unable to keep still.

I yawned; I could not help myself: it had been a long day. "Well, if you must, then you must," I said. "You are the leader of this expedition, after all. But do you come to bed now, and get you some rest; you will not see her the sooner for all this pacing about."

"Na, na, I cannot; there is no sleep in me tonight. I am for the fresh air: maybe it will cool me." As he spoke Neirin took his cloak from the bench by the wall and flung it over his shoulder. At the door he looked back, grinning. "Do not you be worrying: I am not for running my head in a noose. I will see you in the morning." And before I could argue he slipped out, closing the door softly behind him, and leaving me in great uneasiness to get what rest I could.

He was as good as his word: I was roused at dawn by the sound of the latch, and in he came, light-footed as ever, dropping his cloak on his unused bed and bending down to take his harp from her case. Sitting on the bench, he began to check her tuning, his movements delicate and unhurried, and his lean fingers deft on the silver harp-key. I frowned a little, wondering if he had been walking in the rain, for his hair was wet, and plastered around his face in curling tendrils; but his clothes seemed dry enough. He caught the questioning look in my eyes and grinned ruefully. "The bathhouse was open, so I went in: cold water has its uses." And he struck a run of notes and began to play, softly and hesitantly. I lay listening for a while, and drifted off to sleep before I knew it. When I woke again it was full morning, and Neirin and his harp were gone.

It was the music that led me to him in the end. I had made my way halfway around the *llys* by then, looking and occasionally asking questions, but though I met several other entertainers on my quest, no one would admit to having seen a red-headed man with a harp. Either they were as common as sparrows here, and not worth the noticing, or Neirin had discovered how to make himself invisible: a possibility not to be discounted in Taliesin's pupil. I looked into the hall, the bathhouse, the stables, the kitchen quarters, and several empty courtyards, all to no avail; but at last a distant snatch of melody caught my ear, and a familiar voice. Harp-song is not as carrying as drums and trumpets, but a garden wall cannot contain it. The gate was closed, but the drooping limbs of an apple tree offered at once a way in and a concealment; I chinned myself on a branch, found a purchase for my feet, and looked over the wall.

The garden was small, and clearly very old; perhaps it had belonged to the Commander of the North, when the *llys* itself was part of a Roman fortress. At one end was a fountain, where water flowed from the mouth of an ancient stone lion to trickle into a mossy basin and vanish. At the other end, seated on a wooden bench, was Modron the Queen, with her daughter and two other young women beside her, their fine woolen robes bright as a bed of summer flowers again the grey stone wall. And in front of them was Neirin, sitting cross-legged on the stone-flagged garden path, and looking very much at home, with his harp in his lap and the morning sunlight glowing like fire in his red hair. Even as I watched the Queen smiled, and said something I could not catch, and he began a new piece, the piece he had been playing in our room that morning. After a while, in and around the phrases of melody, he began to sing. It was not like any song I had ever heard a bard make before, where the harp is usually there to strengthen the beat of the words. But Neirin's harping was not like any I had ever heard before, either; maybe that was the difference. The women were watching him intently, their eyes bright and their mouths a little open, as if to drink his words.

> "Silver flows now bright as moonlight;
> Cool lady's light calling my name.
> Now from their home, free they come riding,
> Bridles ringing, bridging the sky.
>
> Locked away, lost in cold darkness,
> Silver sparkles, shining in night.
> Arrow's flight, unerring archer,
> Strikes her target, shines silver-bright…"

Frowning, I was trying to make sense of this rapid steam of words and music, when abruptly I felt a grip on my ankles. The next moment my feet were jerked out from under me and I came crashing down from my perch, scraping my face and hands on the wall as I did so, to land hard on the path below. At the shock my left leg gave me a sharp stab of pain, but I rolled and came to my feet, to find myself facing a dark boy a year or so younger than myself. "Why did you do that?" I asked indignantly, trying to keep my voice down—for music was still floating over the wall, and I did not want to interrupt Neirin's performance with a brawl.

"Why were you looking into our garden?" asked the boy in his turn. "And who are you, anyway?" His face was flushed with anger, and he had a long knife in his right hand, which he held as if he knew how to use it. I took in his good clothes and boots and his air of authority, and came to an unwelcome conclusion: despite his complexion, this was another of Urien's sons. Best, I thought, to go warily; and I smiled inwardly, remembering the farmer's advice.

"I am Gwernin Storyteller," I said peaceably. "I am sorry, I am a stranger here; I heard the harp-song, and wanted to see who was playing. I thought it might be a friend of mine. Do you know who it is?"

"Na," said the boy, and frowned, listening. "I do not know— but he is very good!" He became aware of the knife in his hand, and sheathed it. "I am sorry," he said. "I thought you were a thief."

"Well, I am not." He was a tall boy, almost my height, black-haired and black-eyed, and with something of his mother in his face. I smiled at him. "I have told you my name: what is yours?"

"Cadell, son of Urien King." Tentatively he smiled back at me. "What sort of stories do you tell, Gwernin? We have not had a good storyteller here in some time."

"I tell many kinds of tales, Prince," I said. "Would you come with me now to the hall, and hear one? And perhaps there may be food: for I have not eaten today."

"That," said Cadell, grinning, "I can make sure of. Let us go to the hall now, and when you have eaten, I will gladly hear a tale."

So it came about that I spent some part of the day telling tales, and when Neirin and I went to the hall that night, I was called first to perform. He did not mind; he himself had come back to our room that afternoon with a dreamy, inward look, and seemed to be attending to no more than half of what I told him. Teased, he laughed and admitted it, but said he was tired, and stripping off his tunic lay down and slept at once. Come evening, though, he was awake and alert, with a look in his amber eyes that promised mischief.

I had given some thought before-hand as to which tale I would tell, and eventually settled upon the story of Cuchulainn's training with Scáthach in the Western Isles. This tale, though Irish, contained no bothersome romance, nor any references to British kings or kingdoms; moreover, there was enough blood in it to please most war-bands. So indeed it proved; I was well applauded, and got a rich gift of silver from Urien. It should, I thought, be enough to buy me a new pair of trews in the town, with plenty left over.

Then it was Neirin's turn. He had dressed with care that evening in his best clothes: a knee-length tunic of fine-combed wool woven in a pattern of dark red and blue checks, which should have clashed horribly with his red hair and yet somehow did not, and dark woolen trews beneath it. The black leather of his belt and boots gleamed softly with polishing, and the bronze fittings on his belt and knife sheath glittered like gold in the torchlight. His hair was pulled back and tied at the nape of his neck, and his young mustache (better than mine, alas!) was oiled to make it seem more solid than it was. And his harp was as fine as he himself. He walked up the center of the hall from where we had been seated, and took his stance beside the high table, where he could see Urien and his two eldest children with a single glance. He looked around the hall calmly—I saw his master in him that night—and then began to sing.

> "Great King of the North, your hand is heavy
> on all your enemies, on all your foes.
> They groan in anguish—Urien's their master.
> From his hard hold they cannot escape…"

I let out a sigh, but only half a sigh; so far it was a straightforward praise song, but it was not over yet.

> "Fairest of women, your wife beside you,
> and her fine daughter, equally fair…"

Well, that was safe enough…

> "As you in arms crush all before you,
> so do all fair ones before them despair…"

Careful, Neirin!

> "Blesséd of Kings with such blesséd children,
> blissful the court wherein they do dwell;
> blushes I bear; 'tis bliss to be near them;
> best of all beauty, God's great gift to you."

He stopped; there was applause; Urien said something com-
plimentary and Neirin replied. Then, after taking the silver present
he was given, he took three steps to his left, went on one knee
before the Lady Morfudd, and offered it to her. There was a sudden
dead silence in the hall. I groaned, and wondered how fast I could
saddle the horses. A frown like a thundercloud gathered on Urien's
brow. Morfudd's eyes were locked with Neirin's. She said a few
words, and his head came up, as if he replied. Then she smiled, very
sweetly, and with another word reached out and closed his hand
over his would-be gift. For just a second her fingers clung to his;
then with a word she released him and sat back in her seat.

Slowly, like a man mortally wounded, Neirin stood up. He
bowed first to the lady, and then to her father, then turned and
came back down the hall. I glanced once at his face, and then away.
Behind him Urien's thundercloud-look had changed to heavy
satisfaction, and he was beckoning to another performer. Neirin
walked on past me and out of the hall, and the darkness beyond
swallowed him up. I stayed where I was for a good long time, to
give him privacy, and by and by told another tale at Cadell's request.
But when at last I went back to our room, Neirin's bed was empty,
and his cloak was gone.

He had at least left his harp. I took heart from this, and lay
down to wait for him. Eventually I fell asleep on top of my blankets. Towards morning I woke, stiff and chilled, and found that he
had come back, but so quietly I had not heard him. He was lying
face-down on his bed with his head on his arms, but I could tell
from the tension in his shoulders and his harsh breathing that he
was not asleep.

"Neirin?" I said after a moment. Silence. I chewed my lip
thoughtfully, and tried again. "Neirin? Is it tomorrow we are
leaving?" Still silence. I rolled over and sat up on the edge of my
bed. The scar on my leg was itching, and I rubbed it absently with
my thumb. "Neirin? What did she say?"

At that he turned and looked at me. In the faint light from the
window, his face was blotchy and pale, his mouth set hard, but his

amber eyes were blazing with something like anger. He looked more like a hawk than ever, and a dangerous one at that; I would as soon have touched him as a falcon mantling over her kill. Instead I got up and went to the bench by the door for the flask of wine and the two cups I had brought away with me from the hall that night. Neirin took the cup I gave him without a word: drank, and choked, and drank again until it was empty. Then he sighed, and some of the anger seemed to go out of him. And at last he answered me.

"She thanked me," he said flatly, "very prettily, and told me she is to be wed next month. She asked me to keep the silver I had offered her as a bride's-gift, for the finest praise poem she had ever heard. She will be marrying Rhydderch Hael of Strathclyde, and hopes I will sing for her there in his hall after the wedding feast. And that is the whole of it."

"Well," I said practically, "if we are going to get to Alt Clut and away again before the wedding, we had better leave tomorrow. But first, I think you need a little sleep, or I shall have to tie you on your horse by afternoon." I filled our cups again, and raised mine. "To better luck at the next court we visit," I said. And Neirin smiled faintly, and touched his cup to mine, and echoed my toast: "To better luck!"

So ended my first visit to the court of Urien Rheged; but it was not to be my last.

But that, O my children, is a story for another day.

Goddeu

The back of a pony is a good place for thinking, especially when the pony in question is ambling slowly up a straight Roman road on a fine, warm, early-summer's day, and there is no urgency in either your traveling or your arrival. So it was with me on the day we left Luguvalium, passing out through the north gate of the town which was part of the old Roman wall itself. For the Eagles who manned that wall, in the days before they flew south again forever, this had been the end of the world, the edge of civilization itself. Now it was just a long wall: sometimes—but not always—a boundary; some-times—but not always—a defensive barrier. On the summer day when Neirin and I rode north, it was both, and neither: for it was the northern boundary of Rheged, and again it was not. North of it for a way there stretched a debatable land, presently claimed by Gwenddolau of Arferet, at whose court we would be stopping that evening if all went well. Beyond his lands to the west was yet another kingdom, and one not always friendly either to him or to Rheged: the land of Aliffr Gosgorddfawr, Aliffr of the Great War-Band, and his twin sons Gwrgi and Peredur. Farther north up the coast was Elidyr Mwynfawr of Aeron, and beyond him, Rhydderch Hael of Alt Clut. Neirin had told me that all these kings and princes were close cousins, but that did not make them better friends; on the contrary, they fought among themselves like a pack of starving hounds over one big bone, even as their fathers had done before them, and when the Saxons came at last it was to prove their undoing. But that bloody day was still far in the future, and no one then believed it would ever come, least of all Urien Rheged himself, who was to be in some sort its cause.

On this sunny afternoon, though, as I jogged along on the black pony's back, I was feeling distinctly pleased with myself. Before Neirin dragged me away from Urien's *llys* that morning, I had received a valuable present, and the way of it was this. After the previous day's adventures, I had been first to wake for a change, and had slipped out of our shared room to see to the ponies, leaving Neirin still deeply asleep. Crossing the courtyard in the cool of early morning, I met Urien's son Cadell, bent on some business of his own, and greeted him. "Gwernin!" he said, his dark face brightening. "I liked your stories last night. Do you know more of the Irish ones? I have not heard those before."

"Indeed I do, Prince," I said, "but alas, I cannot stay to tell them for you. My friend Neirin is on his way to a bardic competition in the Gododdin lands, and we have lost too much time on our way already, because I was injured." And I touched my left leg in explanation, where the faint bloodstains and the crudely mended rent in my trews—I was wearing my old ones that morning— showed clearly enough what had happened.

"Was it a fight?" asked Cadell with interest, his eyes following my gesture.

"It was, with Saxon raiders."

"Oh! I wish I could have been there!" and his dark eyes sparkled. "But you cannot leave already! You are the best two entertainers we have had here in a long time!"

"Thank you, Prince," I said, smiling. "That is good hearing. Maybe, when we come south again in a few moons, we can stop here again. But now we must be going, this morning if possible. And I must go and see to the horses first."

Cadell sighed. "Well, if you must, then you must. But do you come back again when you can, Gwernin. Maybe, when I am a man grown, I will have my own court, and you will join me there?"

"For a while, I will, if my travels allow it," I said, and went on to the stables.

It was some little while latter, when we were on the very point of departure—Neirin, indeed, was already in the saddle, anxious to be gone, and I was checking the black pony's girth one more time before mounting—that I heard Cadell's voice calling me. "Gwernin! I am just in time," he said, coming up beside me, a little out of breath, and with a bundle of cloth in his arms. "This is for you."

"Why, thank you, Prince," I said, taking the bundle. It looked like a cloak or blanket, and a well-worn one at that.

"Don't unwrap it until later," said Cadell, and grinned. "I know you need some new ones, and there was no time to get anything made; but Owain would never miss these, and anyway I will tell him when he comes back from the hunting. They may be a little long, but I expect you won't mind that."

I turned back one corner of the cloak nevertheless, and saw the bright new cloth within the old. "What—?"

"Trews," said Cadell, still grinning. "Father gave you silver, but I thought these would be more use." And he could see by my answering grin that I agreed.

"There it is," said Neirin, recalling me from my day-dreaming. "On the hill—do you see it?" He had been quiet that morning, no doubt engaged with his own thoughts, which would have been heavy enough. I looked where he pointed, at a chain of three steep, forested hills ahead of us. Our road was heading toward the tallest, which showed cleared patches on its side and crest, and what might be old fortifications. "The tower on top?" I asked.

"Na, though that is a part of it. Lower down, where the new stockade shows above the old walls. That is Gwenddolau's western court—Hêncastell, the men at the ford called it—where he should be tonight. And so should we."

"Is it another old Roman camp?" I asked, to keep him talking and pass the time.

"It is, and the last we will be seeing for a while and a while, I would think. There are not many in the land between the Walls, and those are mostly along the East Road, or so Taliesin says. I have not been that way myself, so I would not be knowing." He fell silent again for a while; then his irrepressible good humor bubbled up, and he laughed ruefully. "I am thinking he will not be too well pleased with me, after yesterday. It was my job to come and observe, not to make myself memorable before Urien and all his company! *Hai mai*, but I have made a mess of it!"

"Umm," I said, remembering a day last year when Taliesin had not been well pleased with *me*... It was not a memory I cherished. "That is not good. Will he beat you, do you think?"

"Na, na, nothing so easy." And Neirin gave a little shiver, for all that the day was warm. "I would not be minding *that*. He will just—*look*—at me..." He sighed. "Well, I have deserved it. But by all the gods, I doubt me I could have done otherwise, once I had seen her..." And he lapsed again into thoughtful silence until we reached Gwenddolau's court of Hêncastell.

This was a set of wood and thatch buildings, a long way down the scale of impressiveness from the ones we had just left, and surrounded by a new palisade, on which men were still working. The whole lay within one corner of an old Roman fort, part of whose stone was being robbed to reinforce the new walls. I gazed at them thoughtfully as we rode in; I must admit that if I had Urien for a near neighbor, I would have been looking to my defenses myself. In fact I found that this was not Gwenddolau's only reason: his neighbors to the west were restless, too. He had another court farther east at Castellum—we had passed near it that morning—but this was his current favorite. He was restoring the watch-tower on the hill above as well, and kept it manned: a prudent Prince, in fact.

Despite the make-shift nature of some of his arrangements (no bathhouse: I must admit that I mourned), his hospitality was generous enough. Even though his guest-house was wattle-and-daub and reed thatch, not stone and tile, the beds were clean and comfortable, and the welcome in his mead-hall warmer than that in Urien's, because more personal. He was younger than Urien, with a lively face and a long, curly mane of red-gold hair, and his eyes were a sort of greenish-brown, like a forest stream. Much of his land was forest as well—Goddeu, some called it, the southern end of the great Forest of Calidon—and the oaks and pines of that old woodland wrapped the hill on which his fortress lay. Winters were cold here, snows sometimes lay deep, and the wolf-packs were never far from his walls; but all the wolves in Calidon could not match his neighbors for fierceness, and he had need of a strong fortress, and a strong war-band, to hold the corn-lands and pastures we had ridden through that day. The oddest thing about him I did not learn until later: Gwenddolau was no friend to the Christus, and there were no churches in his lands.

I told that night, at his urging, the tale of Gwydion mab Dôn, and how he stole Pryderi's pigs, and brought them to Arvon. Now Gwydion, as you know, was a magician, and a warrior, and a trickster, and in some sort a god in the land of Gwynedd in north Wales. The tale of how he went to Dyfed in the south, and by trickery made off with the magical pigs belonging to Pryderi son of Pwyll, the lord of that land, is one that begins in lust, and ends in blood with the death of Pryderi, and many other good men besides. It is the center of a knot of tales about the Children of Dôn, which conclude with the miraculous birth and rearing of Llew of the Skillful Hand, he who is celebrated at summer's end in the Lughnasadh festival, which the Christians call Lammas. In some versions of that tale Gwydion is Llew's uncle, and in some versions his father, but in all of them his magic is older and darker and it may be more powerful than Llew's, and though Llew afterwards came to rule for a time in Gwynedd, Gwydion was not defeated; and although he may have been imprisoned for a time, he has not wholly withdrawn from that land, as I had cause to know.

That night I told the story of the stealing of Pryderi's pigs, and the battle which resulted, and I told it with vigor. Gwenddolau's war-band were all young men like their Lord, and very merry, but they quietened to listen as I spoke, and when I told how Gwydion fought Pryderi, man to man on the great sands of Y Traeth Mawr, with the red blood running down both of them from their wounds and coloring the sea around their feet like wine, they cheered the ending as heartily as if they had been Gwynedd men themselves.

Neirin, coming after me, gave me a wink and a grin, and bettered even my tale in blood-shed, with a story from the Pictish lands which I had never heard before. It told of a band of warriors, outnumbered and cut off by a detachment of the red-crest Romans when first they came to the lands of the North. All the other Picts had been falling back dismayed before the solid masses of the Roman army, all but the men led by this one chieftain Bridei.

" 'Brothers,' said Bridei to his warriors then, 'we are the shield-boss of the north, we are the spear of the Goddess. If we die here today, it is a little thing, and our blood and that of the Romans whom we kill will nourish the land we love. But if we flee, the Romans will conquer, and our people and our tongue will be wiped from the face of the earth. I am for battle, for a short life and long fame in the mouth of the bards. Those of you who have drunk my mead, let you pay for it now in the red wine of the spears, and make a wolf-feast and a crow-feast of all who come against us!' And taking his spear in his hand, he charged the Romans so fiercely that five-score of them fell before him, and his warriors did likewise, so that in their dying they made a great slaughter, and the Romans who survived were three days in the burning of their dead. Then seeing this the other war-bands of the Picts were shamed, and they came together and attacked the Romans, and defeated them, so that those who survived fled south out of the land of the Picts, and came never north to trouble them again. And the son of Bridei the warrior, whose name was also Bridei, came in his time to be Lord over all his people, and his line after him; and his people are still free, and there is still a son of Bridei ruling in their land today," said Neirin. And again the war-band cheered.

All in all, it was a merry evening we had there at Hêncastell, and the feasting was hearty, with deer-meat from the forest, and salmon from the river, and plenty of heather ale to wash it all down. Gwenddolau had us up to his high table afterwards, and toasted us in clear golden mead, which went down very gratefully; and if his presents were less rich than Urien's, I for one did not mind. Whatever came after, he was a very fair Prince, as fierce in warfare and generous in peace as any I have known.

Afterwards I stood at the guest-house door, letting the mead-fumes clear somewhat from my head and gazing up into the pale twilight of the northern sky. There was a black speck up there, slowly turning, which might have been a soaring eagle. It brought back memories of the summer before, and my own encounters with Gwydion mab Dôn, whose favorite form it was for travel. I wondered where, in this world or another, that restless spirit was now, and what he was doing. But the eagle—if it was an eagle—passed on, and in a while I turned and sought my bed. Neirin was already asleep, but his snores did not keep me awake for long.

In sleep, in dreaming, I saw the eagle again, and spoke to him as Gwydion; but if he answered, I cannot remember what he said. I should, of course, have remembered that naming calls…

But that, O my children, is a story for another day.

The Old Man of the Forest

The old Forest of Calidon stretches from the Wall in the south to the Great Glen in the north, and even beyond. Mountains rise out of it, islands in an ocean of trees; here and there the low ground is cleared by men for corn-lands and pasture. But the name and the nature of the North lies in its forests, and especially Gwenddolau's land of Goddeu: for *Goddeu* in the common tongue means trees.

The morning after our coming to Hêncastell, Neirin and I were in the mead-hall breakfasting on cold bread and deer-meat and small ale and discussing where to go next, when our host himself came up to us. "Good day to you, Lord," Neirin greeted him. "What is your pleasure?"

"Why, to ask the two of you to stay here for one more night at least, and entertain me and my company," said Gwenddolau, smiling. "For I have seldom heard performers who pleased me more. And also to show you, if you will ride with me today, a thing that may interest you: for I think you are both seekers on the path of wisdom."

I looked at Neirin; almost he shrugged. "Gladly, Lord," he said, turning back to Gwenddolau. "We are at your pleasure. When will you ride?"

"Not so soon that you cannot finish your meal," said Gwenddolau, still smiling. "I will see you in the courtyard, then, in a while and a while."

After that, as you may imagine, we finished our breakfast at speed and went to saddle our ponies. Gwenddolau met us as he had promised, and we soon rode out, accompanied by a half-dozen of his *teulu*, for in those days in the North even the princes—especially the princes!—did not ride alone. At the outer gate of the fortress we turned left-handed, away from the Roman road on which Neirin and I had ridden in the day before, and followed a well-beaten track that ran anti-sunwise around the hill and through a saddle to the north. Almost immediately we were under the trees, a heavy canopy of oak and pine that changed the bright morning sunlight to green twilight. The track dropped steadily for some time, then came to a cross-roads. This time Gwenddolau led us right-handed into a broader road, but one still roofed over with forest. Now and then a dusty beam of sunlight found its way through to shine briefly on his fair hair and green cloak, and the big roan horse he rode; then the twilight closed in on us again.

The path was too narrow to ride abreast, and Neirin and I followed Gwenddolau, with the men of the *teulu* behind us. The air was heavy with the scent of leaf mold, and now and again we heard a crashing of something heavy in the brush on either side of the trail, and the calling of birds from the branches above us. We splashed through a stream, climbed and dropped and climbed again, but seemed on the whole to be following a shelf on the south side of a deep valley. Presently the hillside became steeper, and I caught glimpses of a loud-running river off to the left at the bottom of its canyon. We crossed another stream, running fast through its rocky slit of a bed, then climbed a steep slope where my pony's hooves slipped in the black mud as he plunged after Neirin's speckled grey. Then we were on another level stretch, but still in deep green twilight.

In a little while we reached a fork in the track, and without slowing Gwenddolau took the right-hand, less-traveled branch. Now the path was narrower, and we were brushing through undergrowth on either side in a strong smell of bruised leaves. Suddenly we came to a clearing, and Gwenddolau pulled up his big roan. Looking past Neirin, I saw the track ended here.

Ahead of us was a circle of seven stones—big grey stones, shaggy with moss and lichen, twice the height of a man. They stood on a low, stony mound, and around them the trees fell back, as if giving them plenty of room, and let the sunlight through. Despite this, and the stillness of the air in what had earlier been a breezy morning, the place was not warm. It was quiet there; I could hear distant bird calls and the far-off chittering of an angry squirrel, but in the Place of the Stones nothing moved except ourselves and our horses, who shifted restlessly from foot to foot instead of standing still. Gwenddolau had dismounted, and beckoned us to do the same. I slid slowly down from my black pony, and one of the *teulu* took his reins, as others were doing for Neirin's and Gwenddolau's mounts; but I noticed the young men were quiet, and careful to stay near the entrance to the clearing. Then I followed Gwenddolau and Neirin into the circle.

At first it seemed that nothing had happened. The rough grass of the clearing lapped around the stones wherever the rocky soil gave it root as in any other such place, and there were small blue flowers here and there among the grass. The stones themselves had clots of harder, lighter-colored stuff in them, making zigzags of white against the gray, and the lichens on them were bright patches of orange and gold, like the bright threads in Gwenddolau's tunic, or the sunlight on his long, curly hair. In the middle of the circle was a bare patch, black with the memory of old fires, and beside this he stopped and turned back to face us. In the silence of the clearing, our footsteps sounded loud; and louder still was the silence when we stopped, with the fire-mark between us and Gwenddolau.

Slowly then the light began to change. Paler it grew; greener, and bluer, and grayer, as if a fog was rising out of the ground; and in it a faint sound, like the chiming of bells. And when I looked outside the circle, there was nothing there, only shadows, moving shadows of green and brown, like trees walking. I looked at Gwenddolau, and he was smiling, looking back at us as if nothing untoward had happened. And yet as the light faded he glowed all the brighter, in green and gold and amber-brown, like the forest trees themselves. Beside me Neirin was shining like red and amber flame in the twilight, and I myself, when I looked down, showed blue and green and silver. And outside the circle the shadows grew darker, and the chiming of bells died away into silence.

Then Neirin laughed, and spoke a word I did not know, and between one breath and the next, the morning was as it had been before. Gwenddolau's smile grew broader, and he nodded. "Yes," he said, as if continuing a discussion, "I thought that was the way of it. You have the look of him, for those who have eyes to see."

"How long have you been coming here?" asked Neirin.

"Oh, a while and a while," said Gwenddolau, and he started back toward the horses. "I was younger than you are now, the first time I came. But you would be knowing that well enough, would you not? Come along back to the *llys*, and I will tell you the rest of the tale." And all the way back to the court we rode in silence; but I noticed the men of the retinue looking sideways at us from time to time, and one or two of them, when they thought I did not see them, making the sign against evil which was old before ever the Romans came across the sea to these shores.

"It was along towards mid-winter," said Gwenddolau to us later, "and I in my seventh year, when first I found the Place of the Stones, and knew it for what it was. It was an open winter that year, and I was out on my pony, as boys will be. I followed the track that we took today, and came to the stones and the clearing. And in the middle of the circle I saw a man, piling wood for a fire—for a midwinter bonfire—in the place where you saw the burnt mark today. He was an old grey man, old as the mountains, with long white hair and a long white beard, and a grey-brown cloak around him hiding what else he wore. Being the child that I was, I came up, all fearless, to greet him and ask him what he did there. And he looked at me— his eyes, under a thorn-bush tangle of brows, were blue as the shadows that lie on the snow at twilight, and his face as full of lines and ridges as the bark of an old oak-tree—and he smiled and greeted me by name, as if he had been expecting me.

"He showed me the different kinds of wood he was gathering, and told me the names of the trees from which the wood came, and their strengths and weaknesses, where they grew and how old they were. I was all that afternoon with him, and came back the next day, and the one after that. I wanted to come and watch him light the bonfire on midwinter eve, but he said it was too far, and not safe for so young a boy to be abroad in the forest that night. 'Come back at midsummer,' he said, 'and you may find me here again.' I raged against his prohibition, but I obeyed him. When I rode back the next afternoon, hoping against hope, there was only the mark of the fire in the circle; that, and on a stone close beside it, one green oak-leaf, green in the depths of winter. I took that for a promise, and kept it; but it soon turned brown, and withered away as do all mortal leaves."

Gwenddolau paused, and drank from his wooden cup. It was afternoon of the same day, and the three of us were sitting, very friendly, on benches in the shade of his apple-orchard, helping ourselves from plates of ewe-milk cheese and barley-bannock and a jug of good brown heather-ale that sat on a rough wooden table between us. Above us a few puffy white clouds drifted slowly past, and a warm summer wind rustled the apple leaves. It was as far from mid-winter as you could well get: and yet not far enough.

"At seven years old," Gwenddolau said, "mid-winter to mid-summer seems half a lifetime. I did not quite forget the old man, but he was not at the front of my mind on the bright summer day—as fair as today!—when I next went riding by the Stones. Indeed, I almost passed by the place entirely, but as I approached it I heard a kind of piping, very soft and fitful on the breeze. And I turned my pony into the path, and came to the stones—and there he was again, seated on the trunk of a fallen oak at the clearing's edge and playing on a small wooden pipe. As I came up he ceased his playing and greeted me. 'You are late," he said, and gestured at the pile of wood in the center of the circle, and I saw it was as high and as complete as the one he had built there last winter, needing only a spark on the tinder to set it alight.

" 'But must you be leaving already?' I asked. 'Cannot you stay here for a few days, and teach me more about the trees?'

"He looked at me a long time without smiling; it was as if he weighed me with his eyes. 'Come down from your pony, Gwen-ddolau,' he said at last. 'Come down and walk with me for a while. I cannot stay, no, but I can give you some teaching before I go—if you will it so. But it will not be light or easy, for I have not much time. Will you come?'

" 'Yes,' I said, and slid down off my pony, and tied his reins to a nearby branch. The old man stood up, and tucked his pipe through his belt, and held out his hand to me. And I saw then that his cloak was like the mist that rises over the marsh at evening, and his tunic the color of the oak-leaves behind him, and his eyes as green as the forest shadows themselves. And just for a moment I was in awe of him, and afraid.

"He smiled very faintly—it barely stirred his long mouth, but still I saw it through his grey-brown beard. 'Will you come?' he asked again softly. 'You may not have another chance.' And I drew a deep breath, and took his hand, and we walked into the circle."

Gwenddolau sat staring into his cup for a while, and sadness and memory moved in his face. Then he looked up and met our eyes. "You saw it this morning," he said. "Not many do. But that was only the beginning, the outer edge. I cannot walk alone to the places he showed me that day, I have not the strength, nor the power, nor the will—the focused will—that it needs. But I saw this land, and its shaping; I saw the forest in all its ages. I *was* the land, and the trees, and the stones; I was the mid-winter, mid-summer fire—they are both the same. I was clouds, and snow, and rain, and rivers; I was the deep green sea; I was sunlight and moonlight, and always, always the trees. Root and trunk and branch and leaf, oak and alder and pine and fir, grass and bramble and reed that bends— I was all of these. I was seed and shadow, I was wind and mountain, I was wolf and stag and boar, I was eagle in the sky and salmon in the stream. I ate and was eaten, I drank and was drunk, I lived and I died, and at last—at last—" He gave a deep sigh. "I was Gwenddolau again, walking with the Old Man of the Forest, and I saw a battle, a moving army, a moving forest of trees.

"Out of the south they came, and out of the north, and they met on a high place in the center of Britain. Their champions came before them, and fought between the lines; branches were broken there, clear blood flowed. Alder and ash and thorn were there, swift in their fighting; oak and yew and fir strove slow and long. From morning to evening they fought there, while the sun went round the sky. There were men among them: priest-kings, Druids, magicians. I do not know why they battled; I do not know who won. At last the dark came down, and all was over; then I found myself back in the circle with the old man. Together we struck the sparks and lit the bonfire; together we watched it catch and burn. When I had taken my pony to water, and tied him out for the night to graze, I came back and sat beside the old man on his tree-trunk, and watched the moving pictures in the fire. 'You cannot be, Gwenddolau, what you once would have been here,' he told me towards morning. 'Men and their ways have changed, and all the Druids are gone. You can only be what you are: a bright memory in a fading place, a bonfire that dies at dawn. But this much I can give you: while you keep faith with the Old Ways, they will not fail you, and you will be King in your country for a while and a while.'

" 'Cannot you stay with me and help me, Master?' I asked him.

" 'Na, na,' he said, and for a moment he looked human, and weary. 'My time here is done. But light the fires for me at summer and winter, and tell the tale that I showed you to the bards who will come: for they are now the remembrancers, the memory of the people, and of the land." And he stood up, and embraced me, and walked away into the mist that had come with the dawning, and was gone. And at sunrise I saddled my pony, and rode home"—and here Gwenddolau grinned unexpectedly—"and got a beating from my father for staying out all night! But tell me now, what do you think of my story? For I think that you saw enough this morning to know that it is true."

Neirin and I both nodded. "Yes," said Neirin. "The shadows outside the circle … before I said the word of releasing."

Gwenddolau smiled. "You have been well taught. I do not have that power; I only know what I have seen. But it is enough, for now, to help me keep my kingdom, while I honor the Old Powers. The Oak-Priests may be gone, but not all their knowledge is lost." He sighed, and stretched, and stood up. "Be welcome and at ease, as if this court were your own," he said. "I have tasks now to accomplish, but we will meet again at evening, and then it will be your turn to entertain me." And he laughed, and went striding briskly away through the orchard, the sunlight touching his red-gold hair to flame.

Neirin sighed, and reached out absently for more bread and cheese. "Hmm—hmm," he said between bites, "Taliesin did not tell me about this, and yet I know he has been here."

"He seems to have told you quite a lot else," I said, helping myself as well. "Is it something you could share?"

"Hmm? Oh, the—magic, I suppose you would be calling it." And Neirin smiled and shook his head. "Na, na, he will have to teach you that himself, when you are ready. I have not the right as yet—I am still a prentice in this." Then, seeing my disappointment, he added, "I am sorry."

"Ah, well," I said. "If you cannot, then you cannot." I grinned. "I am for harp practice, and there I know you *can* help me—if you can stand the sound of my playing!"

"I think I can endure it," said Neirin, solemn-faced, and then grinned back at me. And stuffing the last bites in our mouths, we went away to the guest-house, leaving the crumbs behind us for the birds.

That night I played my harp in hall for the first time, and played it well; and afterwards Neirin told a tale he had learned from Taliesin, of an eastern king called Iskander and how he went to war. And the next morning before we took horse and rode west, Gwenddolau the Prince embraced us both like brothers. "I will not say good-bye," he told us then, "but only wish you the Sun and Moon on your pathway, until I see you again, for I know in my heart that I shall." And indeed he was right, and when we returned it was to be for an adventure well worth the telling.

But that, O my children, is a story for another day.

The Irishman's House

Did you ever reach a point on your journey where nothing could go right for you, where every decision you—or your traveling companion!—made was wrong, and every attempt to correct previous mistakes only made things worse? Not long after we left Hêncastell, Neirin and I reached that point. Compared with what came later, our misfortunes were nothing much, but at the time it almost drove us apart.

The trouble began when we decided to go west, meaning to spend some time at the court of Aliffr Gosgorddfawr. He was, after all, a significant player in the politics of the North, being married to Urien Rheged's sister Efryddyl, and therefore often allied with Urien. Certainly it would have been good to find out what we could about his intentions toward his neighbors, especially as we had so signally failed to acquire much information at Luguvalium. Unfortunately two things which had been helping us up to that time— good roads and good weather—now changed abruptly. There were no Roman roads leading into Aliffr's territory, which should have been a warning in itself, and almost as soon as we left Hêncastell it began to rain.

The rain was the worst part. Not a soft mountain mist, this, but a serious downpour, which went on, and on, and on. Such roads as there were turned to squelching black mud, and then to bog; fords were impassable brown torrents; landscape and our sense of direction alike vanished in a gray-green fog. Day after day, with only occasional short breaks, the rain came down. It was no weather for camping, but some of the places where we found shelter were not much better. An earth floor is all very well in dry weather, but it fast looses its charm in a flood. The huts where we stayed were damp and exceedingly smoky—wet firewood does not burn well—and generally full of other unhappy people; and our value as traveling entertainers was often offset by the need to find a relatively dry place for us to sleep, usually at someone else's expense. Our bedrolls and our clothes were all damp, except when they were dripping wet; and our harps were cranky and out of tune when they were not completely unplayable—wet horse-hair strings cannot be tuned. And to make it worse, we seemed to be following Aliffr and his sons around their domain, always two or three days behind them. His courts, when we came to them, might have been drier than the poorer farmsteads, but had not a much better welcome for us otherwise, having just been eaten empty and drunk dry by Aliffr's large retinue. Barley-bannock and stale cheese was the best we got, and glad we were to get it, never mind bacon or beer. Finally we gave it up as a bad job entirely, and decided to head north for Aeron. Neither the weather nor the lodgings, as we thought, could get much worse.

It was Neirin who was asking directions, so it must have been his fault. We took the track our informant indicated up the glen; we turned right where we thought we were supposed to turn. Then we climbed, and climbed, and climbed. Clouds were above us, and sometimes below us, and always on either side. Now and again through the rain and the dripping oaks and pine-trees we caught a glimpse of mountains: not so high as those which I had seen last summer in Eryri, but certainly high enough to block our path. At last, after a steep scramble, we reached the top of the pass, and as if to cheer us, the sun broke through the clouds. That was when we realized we were going, not north, but east.

What do you do at such times other than curse? We did that in full measure, and with poetic elaborations, but it did not mend matters. The sun was unimpressed, and soon vanished behind a craggy summit in the west. Here in the north at high summer we would have twilight for a long while yet, but it would not serve us under the clouds. We had not passed any visible dwelling on our way up; and if we went on the way we were heading we might still have to camp, and would have to back-track tomorrow as well. We ought, of course, to have stopped where we were; there was a lake not far below us, and even a little grazing by its shore for the ponies. But it was Neirin's decision, and Neirin chose to turn back. As he later admitted, he was still eager to get to Alt Clut and away again before the wedding party from Rheged arrived; and so we started back down the pass into the rain.

We were almost past the worst of the steep patch when it happened. Neirin's gray, who was leading, lost his footing and went down the rest of the pitch at a stumbling run, and fell at the bottom. Before I could get to them, they were both on their feet again; but the pony was clearly shaken, if nothing worse; and Neirin, who had fortunately gone over his shoulder and rolled free, did not look to be in much better case. He had got up and caught the reins, but was leaning against the gray with his right arm over the poor animal's back, as though the two of them were supporting each other.

"Are you hurt?" I asked, sliding off my black pony beside him.

"Na, na," he said, frowning, and trying to see the pony's left foreleg, "but the fear is on me for Brith—ah!" And he staggered, and only saved himself from falling by a grab at the saddle-horn.

"Do you sit down," I said, getting an arm around him and easing him back to the ground. "Where are you hurt?"

"Only my ankle," said Neirin, gasping and clutching it. "Do you—see to the pony, I am—well enough."

"Hmm," I said, running my hands down the gray's leg and feeling him flinch a little. When I tried to lead him forward he stepped out reluctantly, limping. "Well, you are not going any farther on Brith tonight, that is for sure. Do you get up on Du and we will see what sort of shelter we can find. Can you stand?"

"Yes, I—ah! Gods!" Neirin fell back, cursing loudly. Somewhat reassured by the volume of his complaint, I bent and helped him up again. He could barely set his left foot to the ground, but fortunately none of our ponies was tall, and with a certain amount of shoving on my part he got into the saddle. Giving him the leading-rein of the packhorse, who had been waiting patiently all this time, I took hold of the lame pony's headstall and began to lead him slowly forward.

"Gwernin," said Neirin, a long, cold, wet while later, "I am thinking there is a light ahead." I looked up, peering through the rain. At first I saw nothing, but then there was a flicker of firelight through the trees. "By Pryderi's pigs," I said, "I hope it is shelter! Even if it is a giant's cave, I am going in—I cannot remember what it feels like to be warm!" And I turned my attention back to the muddy path before me, dimly visible in the light reflected back by its puddles from the cloudy sky.

The lodging we had found was not, in fact, a cave. Set well back in the trees against the steep valley wall, it was a long, low building with a thatched roof which looked more like the houses I later saw in the Saxon lands than anything a Briton would build. Only the gleam of firelight through an unshuttered window and the smell of peat-smoke from the fire gave it away. Still leading the lame pony, I picked my way through the shadowy masses of low scrub that surrounded it and reached the yard. "Hello, the house," I called, not wanting to surprise anyone, though indeed our stumbling advance had been far from silent. Behind me I heard a "snick" as Neirin loosened my sword in its scabbard where it hung at Du's saddle bow. "Just in case," he said quietly. "I am thinking this place is—a little strange." Then with a belated barking of dogs the door to the house opened, and I wondered whether we had reached a giant's den after all.

The man who stood in the doorway was big enough in all conscience. When he held up the lantern he was carrying, the better to see us, it showed us a body massive as an oak tree, with arms and legs like the tree's limbs, and a mass of curly dark hair and beard around his face. "Who comes?" he asked, in a bass growl. "Name yourselfs or pay th' price."

"Traveling bards," Neirin called back in his trained performer's voice. "Lost on the mountain and in need of shelter. May we come in?"

"Come for'ard and show yourselfs," growled the giant suspiciously. "How many of ye are there?"

"Only the two of us," I called back. "And one of our ponies is lame."

"Well, I s'ppose ye must come in," grumbled the giant. "Follow me to th' stables." And he came out and headed for the end of the building, still holding up the lantern to show us the way. Behind him in the doorway I saw two or three other people—normal-sized people—silhouetted against the light of the room behind them, but I was too busy with Brith to pay them much heed.

The stable, which was entered from the far end of the house, proved surprisingly spacious. There was plenty of room for our three ponies, and twice as many more, besides the one elderly horse who was already in residence. At the entrance Neirin slid down cautiously and stood for a moment leaning against Du, in the listening pose I had seen him take before. A flash of metal at his side caught my eye, and I saw that he had slipped my sword-belt over his shoulder baldric-fashion on top of his rain-cape, and was wearing it with the hilt well to the fore. I met his eyes for a moment; he grimaced and shook his head, but made no move to stop me as I led the gray pony inside. Instead he followed me, limping badly but walking on his own.

"Stall yer ponies where ye will and come in," said the giant, hanging his lantern on a hook in one of the crossbeams. "There be water in th' well outside and hay in th' store-place yonder. When ye be done we will find ye some stew and a bed for th' night. I be Aitan Mor." And without waiting to hear our own names, he turned away and headed for a door at the far end of the stable. We looked at each other and shrugged, and began to care for our wet and weary ponies. By the time they were all three unsaddled, rubbed down, fed and watered, and their tack sketchily cleaned, I could have easily fallen down in the straw beside them and gone to sleep, but the thought of hot food kept me on my feet for a little longer. Neirin, who had done most of the grooming while I carried hay and water, looked as weary as I.

"How is your ankle?" I asked, taking down the lantern and turning toward the house-place door at last.

"I am thinking it is not broken, but I will not be for running any races soon," said Neirin, limping after me. "Gods send we have a dry place to sleep tonight, for I am purely tired." And he yawned hugely.

"Is it safe here, do you think? You said it felt strange."

"I—I am not knowing. But our choices are not many. Do you keep alert"—another yawn—"Gods! so far as you may!"

"I will try," I grinned, and pushed open the heavy wooden door. Firelight and a cloud of peat-smoke met us on the threshold, and set me to coughing. Mixed with the peat-smoke was the wonderful odor of hot food. I could see a stewpot hanging over the central hearth-fire in the long dark room, and it drew me irresistibly. Out of the smoke a figure loomed up—a woman, by her voice. "Drop your traps where you will," she said, "and come to the fire." I did as she said gladly. By the fire there were benches; I sat down beside Neirin, and took the wooden bowl of hot stew I was given, and fell upon it like a starving wolf. There was barley-bannock to go with the stew, and small beer in a wooden cup, and all of it was more wonderful to me than the mead-feasts of kings. It was little heed I paid to anyone or anything else in the room that night: and this was a mistake. But indeed I was moving in a haze of exhaustion; and now that I was warm, and getting food in my belly, I could hardly keep my eyes open.

At last when we could eat no more the woman showed us where to sleep: two of a series of empty box-beds along the long north wall of the room. Neirin sat down on the edge of one and began with some difficulty to take off his boots; the twisted ankle had swollen badly. "Do you need help?" I asked, pulling off my own.

"Na, na, I can—ah!—do it." Followed a series of gasps and quiet cursing.

I yawned and lay down, pulling the rough woolen blankets over me. "Well, do you tell me if you change your mind," I said drowsily, and closed my eyes, drifting on waves of sleep. If Neirin answered me, I did not hear him. In a little while, the house was quiet but for the sound of snores.

I woke to gray morning light and the aroma of oatmeal porridge cooking. For a while I lay listening to the sounds of the rain on the roof, and the soft talk of women—three or four of them of different ages—and the occasional bass growl of a man's voice. There seemed to be some sort of disagreement in progress, but it was not loud, and it stopped when I yawned and sat up.

"A good morrow to ye, boy," said the bass voice, and I saw it was the giant who had welcomed us last night—if welcome you could call it. "I ha' been looking at yer horses—that gray is dead lame. Ye will be wi' us some days, I am thinking."

"I am afraid so," I said. "I hope we can entertain you while we are here. I am Gwernin Storyteller, and my friend is Neirin the Bard."

"Be ye, then? Well, we will see." And with that cryptic remark the big man turned back to his breakfast, while I got up and went to see to the ponies, leaving Neirin still asleep. I had almost finished the feeding, grooming and mucking out when he appeared, barefoot and limping. "*Hai mai!*" he said, yawning and combing his fingers through his tangled red hair. "You have done my work as well as your own! There was no need, but I thank you."

"It does not matter," I said, combing burrs out of the brown pack-pony's tail and avoiding his restless hooves. "I had nothing else to do; we are not going anywhere today. Do you feel of Brith's leg."

"True that is," said Neirin with a grimace, straightening up and rubbing the pony's nose. "Poor fellow, you are as lame as your foolish master. Na, na, I have no treats for you this morning; be content with your dry stable." And he began to check over our tack, looking for anything that still needed cleaning. There was not much.

Finishing with the pack-pony at last, I washed off my hands in his water-bucket and dried them on the skirts of my tunic. "Let us go to breakfast; anything else here will keep, and my belly is empty, if yours is not."

"*Sa, sa,* mine as well." Frowning, Neirin put the bridle he had been polishing back with the others. "I cannot make this place out: stabling and beds for a dozen, and yet only the man and the few women."

"Yes, it is odd," I said. "Maybe they will tell us more today; to ask would be bad manners." And with that I opened the house-place door, and we said no more on that subject for a while.

As the day went on, we found there were five women in the household, and none of them related. Aside from one old gray-haired dame who seemed to be in charge, they were all fairly young, and one of them—Hunedd was her name—no older than I myself. She was naturally the one who interested me the most—a little brown thing with hair like ripe barley, but shy, shy. I could see she had caught Neirin's fancy as well. He was in a light mood that afternoon, and soon had her giggling, while I watched almost in silence. The other women went about their tasks quietly, and what they thought about it all I could not tell, but the gray-haired dame seemed pleased.

Toward evening the big man—Aitan Mor, I remembered he had called himself—came back from wherever he had been, shaking himself on the threshold like the wet dogs who were with him. There were three of these, big gray-brown brutes the size of a month-old calf who stretched themselves out yawning by the fire, their green eyes gleaming with its light. Their master flung himself down in a rough-hewn wooden chair beside them, stretching out his muddy boots and taking the horn of drink that one of the women brought him. Looking over at us, he smiled. "Ha, ye are still here, then. Can ye gi' us a tale tonight, after meat?"

"Gladly, Lord," said Neirin. "What would be your pleasure?"

Aitan Mor drank deep from his horn, and wiped the foam from his curly black beard with a hand the size of a shovel. "D'ye know aught of th' Irish tales? For an Irishman it is that I be."

"I know a few, Lord," I said. "Would you hear a tale of Cuchu-lainn?"

"That would be fine," said the giant. "Start it now, an' ye will."

"At your pleasure, Lord," I said. "This is the tale of Cuchulainn's weapon-taking, after he heard the prophecy of the Druid Cathbad..." And I told the tale that I had told several times before.

At the end the giant sighed. "That was not bad, for a Briton," he said, and for some reason he looked almost sorry. But the women were serving us the evening meal, and I thought no more of it that night.

This, then, was the pattern of my life for the next few days, while the rain came down, and Aitan Mor was sometimes there and sometimes gone, and the gray pony continued too lame to travel. If the rain had ever stopped I might have walked around the place, and seen some things which would have made me think, but as it was I stayed inside and practiced my harp by the peat fire in the long smoky room. It was on the third afternoon, going out to the stables for some reason, that I came upon Neirin kissing Hunedd in the shadows of one of the stalls. I had come quietly, and they did not hear me. After a moment I turned and left, and I do not think they heard me go. For myself, my chief emotion was jealousy: jealousy of Neirin, who seemed to me to be marked out by fate to get the one available girl, supposing there was only one available, while I—I remembered my rival Goronwy calling me "horse-boy" last winter—I got the hard work, and nothing else. But then, I was only a farmer's son, not sister's-son to a King...

I had almost talked myself out of this mood by the time Hunedd, and later Neirin, came back from the stables, but his warm good-humor that evening almost set me off again. The tale I told for the company's enjoyment was a dark one, and I lay awake afterwards listening to the snores of the sleeping household and the never-ending drip, drip, drip of the rain from the thatch. So I was still awake when someone quiet and light-footed, and later someone else walking a little lame, got up and made their way one after the other to the stables, and much, much later came back. Indeed I slept hardly at all that night, but still I was up before Neirin, and had done all the tasks in the stables and was eating my porridge before ever he arose, heavy-eyed but cheerful, from his bed. And that morning I spoke to him as little as might be.

He noticed it, of course. A great one for noticing, was Neirin: and well he should have been, after four years and more with Taliesin. And that afternoon when I was standing outside the stable, gazing up at the clouds and wondering if the rain had finally stopped, he followed me out to talk to me. Talking was not what I wanted then, and I answered at first with grunts, but there was no stopping him. "Gwernin," he said after a few abortive comments on the weather, "what is the matter with you today?"

At that I rounded on him. "What do you think is the matter, then?"

"I am not knowing. That is why I asked."

"Can you think of nothing that would be annoying me? And you so clever," I said bitingly—or so I meant it, but I probably sounded merely sullen.

Neirin was quiet for a moment, frowning and looking at me. "It might be that I can. But better it would be if you told me."

"It might be," I said, counting on my fingers, "that I am tired of sitting here and watching it rain. It might be that I am tired of doing my work and yours too. It might be that I am knowing what you were about last night in the stable. It might be—it might be—" I stopped, trying not to say in anger something I would regret afterwards.

Neirin had listened with a gradually darkening brow. "As to the rain," he said slowly, flushing up in the way he always did when angry, "I cannot be stopping it myself. As to the work, you could have woken me earlier any morning, or left my share for my waking. And as to last night, I am thinking that is none of your business. Is there more?"

"Yes," I said, "there is more. I may not be a king's daughter's son, nor Taliesin's prentice, but I do my share of the work and something over, and I do not imperil myself and my mission for the sake of a few minutes' pleasure, or a girl's bright hair. Which is more than I can say for you, Neirin son of Dwywei—!"

At that point in my oration, Neirin hit me in the face, and what came after was somewhat confused. I know I hit him back several times, and took several more blows in my turn; I know there was a good deal of pushing and shoving, and rolling on the ground and punching. And I remember, toward the end of things, lying on my back in the mud and looking up at Neirin's bloody face and blazing amber eyes, while trying and failing to pry loose his fingers which were slowly choking the life out of me. Then, as my vision darkened and swam, there was suddenly a deluge of cold water on the both of us; and as a second bucket-full followed the first we fell apart, choking and gasping.

"You fools!" said a woman's voice above me in a furious, urgent whisper. "You stupid fools, here fighting each other, and they all the time making the slave-chains ready for you. Can you not see what is before your face? Oh, you fool, you fool—!"

I was still busy coughing, but I saw Neirin look up at that. "What are you meaning?" He asked quickly. "Hunedd, what do you mean?"

"Hush! hush! Do you want them to hear? Oh, that I was ever born! What sort of place do you think this is, and you so wise?"

"That is what you must be telling me," said Neirin, wiping blood off his face. "Gwernin, are you hurt? Hunedd, what is this you are saying?"

Kneeling in the mud, I tried to speak, choked, tried again. "Na, not to mention. I—" At that point I went into a coughing spasm that bent me double. I could not see what Neirin was doing, but the urgent whispers went on behind me while I did my best to throw up everything I had eaten for the last three days. At last, when I could attend again, I found Neirin was kneeling by me and shaking my shoulder, and there was a bucket of water beside me. "Come you on, Gwernin," he was saying. "Sorry I am, but there is no time for this. Wash your face and your mouth, brother, and get up. We are in trouble."

Shaking my head to clear it, I did as he said. In the stable Hunedd was starting to saddle our ponies. "Hurry, hurry!" she said. "I overheard the Big One telling his woman—they will be here at dark, and then you are lost! Go and get your gear—I will finish this! Pray God they have not hidden your swords! Only hurry!"

"What are we going to do about Brith?" I asked Neirin as we gathered our belongings, watched by the frightened younger women and cursed by the gray-haired dame. Fortunately Aitan Mor, as usual in the afternoons, was elsewhere, or our fate might have been different.

"We will try and lead him, and hope he can keep up," said Neirin, heading back to the stable. "We can be taking turns on Du. Come on!"

"And how far will you get, running and riding?" I asked as we loaded our gear on the packhorse. "You are still as lame as Brith."

"That is my problem," said Neirin, tight-lipped. "He and I must do what we can." Then, turning to Hunedd, who now stood silent beside us, "What will they do to you? Will you come with us?"

At that she smiled sadly. "Na, na, they will not hurt me— much. My man is one of them—it is too late for me. Go you now, no more talking! They will be here soon!"

Neirin nevertheless pulled her into his arms and kissed her hard. "That, then, for memory," he said, and let her go. "Gwernin, mount up, we must leave." And handing me the pack-pony's lead rope, he took hold of the gray pony's halter and led him out of the stable into the rain.

I have known fear in my time; I have fled on foot from a Saxon war-band, and seen the Wild Hunt go by, and waited at dawn for the Opening of the Gate. But for sheer panic flight I have never known anything to equal that night. Down the path in the rain we went, slipping and sliding in the mud, fearing all the time to meet a body of oncoming horsemen or Aitan Mor and his dogs. After the first mile I stopped to try and make Neirin get up on Du in my place, while I led Brith. "Na, na," he gasped—he had just fallen for the third or fourth time. "This is my fault, and I will—do my share."

"Do not be such a fool," I said, trying to take the pony's halter away from him. "You are wasting time, brother, and hurting yourself to no profit. I do not want to spend the rest of my life as a slave in Ireland, even if you do. Must I knock you out and tie you to the saddle, or will you show sense?"

At that Neirin laughed and released his hold on the pony. "Na, na, you need not do that," he said, and gripped my shoulder briefly before mounting. "Only take care of Brith." Truth to tell, the gray pony was holding up better than his master; but four legs are more stable on a muddy trail than two.

On we went then in head-long flight, while the rain came down and the light faded toward evening. Twice I heard horsemen coming and got us off the road in time to hide, standing in the dripping trees with our hands on the ponies' noses and our hearts in our mouths. One of the second clump of horsemen was Aitan Mor, identifiable even in the twilight by his huge bulk and his great dogs running at his side. One of them looked our way—I saw the green gleam of its eyes—but fortunately the rain had washed out most of our scent, and the wind was blowing toward us. After that we waited a long time before going on.

At the place where we had turned right to go up that ill-fated pass—and I thank the gods still that we could spot it in the darkness!—we turned right again. I walked for hours with my ears at the prick, expecting every moment to be overtaken, but no one else came. Maybe Hunedd put them off our scent; maybe, knowing how far it was on this road before you reached shelter, they had expected us to double back the way we had come. Instead we went north, over the mountains towards Aeron, and sometime after dawn, when Neirin was slumped half-asleep in his saddle and I myself, still leading the gray pony, was walking in a daze, we came to a friendly farmstead where they took us in. I was so weary I had not even noticed until then that it had stopped raining.

We stayed at the farm for some days, until Neirin and the gray pony were recovered. Warm indeed was the welcome we got there, and the food and beds and beer were all good; but best was the farmer's three friendly daughters, who were all of them very sorry to wave farewell to us when we left…

But that, O my children, is a story for another day.

Mist on the Water

There is nothing like the sound of steel on steel. Not the smith's iron hammer hitting metal, nor the priest's brazen-tongued bell, and certainly not the tap-tap-tapping of the craftsman, or the thud of the forester's axe striking wood—none of these has the same urgency, the same ringing voice, the same battle-shout as the cry of steel on steel. Even when the blows are slow and careful, their note is unmistakable: they catch the listener's ear; they stir the warrior's heart; and they promise blood.

Blood-spilling, however, was what Neirin and I were trying to avoid that day, as we exchanged slow practice sword-stokes in the shade of a broad green oak which stood dreaming in the drowsy, bee-loud heat of summer. Since our narrow escape from the house of the Irishman, we both felt it was time and more that I learned to use the sword King Gwallawg had given me. Neirin had set me first to pell work, and many a young tree in Aeron now bore the scars of my assault. But trees—well for me!—do not swing back at you once you have hit them, to lop a limb in return for the one you may have lopped. Slowly and cautiously, we had gone on to the next stage. So far our injuries had been slight, but it was just as well that Neirin was fast on his feet, for my aim was still erratic, and he had had some close calls.

"Enough," he said at last, stepping back but maintaining his guard. I lowered my sword and wiped the sweat from my eyes with my free hand.

"I can go on," I protested. "I think I am getting the rhythm of it now."

"*Sa*, I am sure that you can." Neirin grinned and pushed his dark red hair back from his face. "But when you start to tire is when you make mistakes, and I am not such a master of this craft as to always be sure of catching them. Besides, it is hot, and I am hungry."

"There is truth in all of that," I said, sheathing my sword. The weight of it still felt strange at my side, strange and exciting. "But I am yet waiting for you to show me the stroke you promised, the one that finishes a man's fighting, if not his life."

"Get the staves, then," said Neirin. "I am not for letting you try that one on me with steel, not with you so unpracticed."

I went to the packhorse, who was grazing placidly at the edge of the small meadow, and fetched the two wooden swords in question. These were straight pieces of oak, roughly carved into hilts at one end and blunt at the other, heavy enough to bruise or break bones if used vigorously, but not to kill. The farmer who had housed us when we first fled the Irishman had carved them for us at Neirin's asking. I tossed one hilt-first to him, and took up my guard with the other. "It would be better," I said, "if we had shields as well."

"Sa, it would," Neirin agreed. "And so we should in battle. But these will serve our purpose today. Now, do you stand still and watch." And while I watched he cocked his sword arm, his shield arm coming up automatically to balance it. Then smoothly he brought his wooden sword around and down, stepping forward as he did so, to lay it firmly against my left shoulder near the base of my neck. "That is the blow," he said. "It does not need to go deep to disable. Strike there, and your enemy will lose his shield if he still has it, and likely his life as well. So. Stand still and let me be doing it once more. Good. Now, do you try it. Good. Na, not so hard—I am not wanting a broken collarbone today! Stand. Now, again!"

"What do you do—in a fight," I asked after a while, gasping slightly, "if you have—no shield?"

"You must be fast. Swing again—so!" And Neirin jumped back at the last moment, parrying as he did so, so that my stroke missed him. "Again. Now, your turn. Faster! Good. Good. Enough!"

I switched my wooden sword to my left hand and stood panting and rubbing my bruised shoulder. "How did you get so good at this? Is Taliesin a sword-master as well?"

Neirin laughed. "Na, if he is I have not seen it, though I would not put anything past that one! I got my training as a boy in my father's court, that is all. But I am out of practice—it is lucky I am not fighting for my life today!"

"You did well enough in battle," I said, remembering. "You took a man's head off, and saved my life in the doing!"

"Na, that was different," said Neirin, turning toward the pack-pony with our wooden swords. "I was mounted and he was not. *Hai mai*, but I am hungry! Let us eat now, and then ride on."

"Is it tomorrow we reach Alt Clut?" I asked, taking my saddle-bags from Du where he stood grazing on a lead, and dropping to the mossy ground under the oak.

"Tomorrow or the next day, I am not sure," said Neirin, sitting down beside me. "What do we have for our nooning today?"

"Bread and cheese mostly," I said, investigating the cloth-wrapped package. "But fresh and plenty of it. The old woman was generous." Making our way slowly so as not to overwork Neirin's pony, whose left foreleg was still tender from the fall he had got in the mountains, we had stayed the night before at a farmhouse not far north of the court of Elidyr Mwynfawr where we had been previously entertaining.

"Good," said Neirin, reaching for the cheese. He grinned. "Where is your share?"

I knocked his hand away. "Here, as you well know. Wait while I cut it in half. I am all your retinue, you should treat me better."

"*Sa, sa*, but I do: I am for eating it all myself, so you may stay lean and agile. You must be faster than you were today, if you are going to be a warrior."

"True, O great leader," I said, dividing the bread as well and quickly seizing my half. "But I cannot fight to defend you if I am weak from hunger: bear that in mind!"

"Na, but I think I prefer you slower," said Neirin through a mouthful of cheese. "Then I shall run quickly away, and leave you to fight the enemy. Is it not a good plan?"

"Huh," I said, "you will not win much word-fame that way. And you are eating my half of the cheese as well as your own."

"Here, then," said Neirin, handing back what remained. "But I shall have plenty of word-fame, for I shall survive to make the song."

"And will you praise only yourself, and not your brave retinue?" I asked. "That will be poor dealing!"

"There are precedents," said Neirin, yawning and lying back with his arms behind his head. "Let you bravely guard my sleeping, then, as if I were Maxen Wledig after his hunting."

"Na, I am not that brave," I said, lying down as well, "but we should be riding on soon." I got no answer, and in a little while I was asleep as well.

It was the coolness that woke me, as the sun dropped behind the trees to our west. I sat up, blinking and yawning, then nudged Neirin, still snoring beside me. "Wake up, O great leader. We have lost the better part of the day."

Neirin opened his amber eyes and stared at the sky for a moment, then sat up briskly. "*Hai mai*, so we have. Well, we had better ride on, and that soon."

"No doubt of it," I said, going to my black pony where he grazed on a tether and taking his bridle from where it hung on the saddle-horn. "But where are we going?"

"We shall know when we get there," said Neirin, tightening the strap on Brith's saddle.

"That," I said, "is a true word." And in a little while we were on our way.

It was close to sunset, and the air was thickening into a haze that promised fog before morning, when we came out of the trees and saw the lake before us. Like a polished mirror it lay, reflecting the silver-blue of the evening sky. On the far side, bordered with reeds and rushes where wading birds were calling, a dark hill rose, fleecy with oak forest, but the near side was plowed fields and pasture, with a cluster of farm buildings near the shore. Behind them, seeming to float on the water, I saw a *crannog*, a small man-made island connected to the land by a causeway. Blue wood-smoke rose from the thatched longhouse on it, and joined with that from the farmstead. Children were driving the cows into the cowshed for milking, and their voices mingled with the lowing of the beasts and the birdcalls in the still evening air. The hoof-beats of our ponies sounded loud on the dry earth of the track as we rode down the last hill, and some of the farm-folk looked up to see who came; but two riders and a pack-pony were not enough to alarm them, and most of them returned to their tasks, except for a boy who went running to the crannog, and a gray-beard who met us at the gate as we rode in. "I greet you, lords," he said courteously. "Be welcome."

"Not lords," said Neirin, swinging down from his pony, "but entertainers, asking lodging for the night."

"All the better," said the man, smiling. "This will please my lady, for our lord is gone to Alt Clut, and taken his singer with him, and there is no music in our hall." And he called to stable-lads to take our ponies, and himself led us through the farmstead and along the narrow causeway to the island.

I looked around me with curiosity as I went, for I had never seen a crannog before; they are a form of defense more common in the north of Britain than in our land of Wales. This one was not the largest of its kind by any means, nor yet the smallest, being perhaps twelve paces across, but it was large enough to hold the reed-thatched long-house and a couple of smaller huts besides. The island itself looked man-made, though it may have been built up on a shallow spot in the lake. Certainly the water around it was too deep for wading, even now in the dry summer, and would have provided a formidable defense against raiders, while the causeway was narrow enough to be held by one man against many. All of this I noticed in passing and then forgot when I saw the woman who awaited us in the house-place doorway.

Not young, she was, and yet not old. Her dark hair, streaked with silver at the temples, was uncovered and gathered in thick plaits, coiled on her head like a crown, and held with bronze pins whose ends shone with bright enameling. Her gown was long, and made of fine wool in some color between blue and green, embroidered around the neck with twining vine-like tendrils in threads of red and saffron-yellow. Tall she was, and her fine-boned face was severe, and her eyes were large and dark. In her slender hands she held the guest-cup of pale carved wood edged with silver. "Drink, strangers," she said smiling, "and be welcome in my hall." Her voice was as dark as her eyes, husky and musical. Behind her in the doorway were two or three young girls, by their looks her daughters.

"A blessing on the house, and all within it," said Neirin, taking the cup and drinking deep. "Neirin son of Dwywei is my name, and my friend is Gwernin Storyteller." And he passed the cup to me.

"A blessing on the house, Lady," I said, and drank in my turn. The drink was clear golden mead, faintly flavored with some aromatic herb I did not recognize. I smiled and gave her back the empty cup, wishing it had been larger, for the bread and cheese that Neirin and I had shared at noon was a distant memory, and I was both hungry and thirsty.

"Come you in, then," said the woman. "Our household is not large, for my lord is gone to Alt Clut for the King's wedding, and we will be glad of your company this night." And we followed her into the house.

After the luminous twilight outside, the hall seemed dark at first, warm with the heat of the day and of the fire that burned on the stone-lined central hearth, sending up its smoke to wreath the rafters. We had entered in the midst of one long side of the place, either end of which was partitioned off with wicker panels hung with bright-dyed loom-work. Over the hearth-fire a cauldron, suspended on a chain from the roof-beams, was sending up savory odors that reminded me again how long it was since I had eaten. Benches went round the walls, and trestle tables were set up, ready for dinner. We settled ourselves in the places the woman showed us, setting aside our harp-cases, and even as we did so two stable-boys came hastening after us with the rest of our gear, and deposited it along one of the end-walls. Others of the household followed them into the hall, and in a little while the evening meal was served. There was meat from the cauldron—pig-meat, I think it was— sweet barley-bannock and fresh ewe-milk cheese, and horn after horn of clear golden mead, refilled assiduously by the little dark-eyed daughters. I drank it down happily—too happily, as it developed. By the time I rose to give the company a tale, I was more than a little mazed with drink, and had hard work to command myself and tell my piece as I should. Neirin, going before me, seemed to be feeling the same; if his harping was not bad—and it never was!—some of the pieces he played were certainly not as I had usually heard them. The company, however, which by then included most of the farm-folk, seemed to find nothing amiss, and cheered us both heartily.

"That was well done," said the woman when I had finished my tale, and came to take my seat again—she had seated us at her right and left hand in compliment—"and yet I wonder," she added, turning to Neirin, "if I might beg a little more of your music in a while, when they have cleared away the tables. I have never heard its like before—it is most wonderful!"

"Surely," said Neirin, smiling, but his glance went for a moment to the full mead-horn he held in his right hand, and I could tell as clearly as if he had spoken that he was wondering whether to drink it or not, and deciding that there was no way to get rid of it without causing offence. What with the mead and the warmth of the room his color was already high, and if his head was spinning like mine he was in trouble.

"Lady," I said, "excuse me, please—I must go out for a moment."

"I too," said Neirin, taking my cue. "Then, as soon as they have cleared the tables, I will gladly harp for you, Lady." And he followed me out the door, and around the corner of the hall to a place suitably private. The horn-full of mead went into the lake along with other liquids, and we both gave a sigh of relief.

"Sorry I am to waste it," said Neirin as we were walking back, "but it would not have done—it would not have done at all. Taliesin will have enough to reproach me with already when I come home, what with my doings at—at Urien's court. Gods, but I—!" He stopped, and for a moment I saw his whole face clench in bitter unhappiness, and knew that beneath his normal merriment he had not forgotten Urien's daughter, that shining girl who was soon to wed the King of Strathclyde at Alt Clut.

"Well," I said after a pause, "however badly you might play tonight, I do not suppose Taliesin would hear of it. He is far away in the South, after all."

Neirin laughed, and laughing looked himself again. "That," he said, "shows how little you yet know him! When you have been with him as long as I have—!" And he shook his head, and would say no more.

The haze I had noticed at sunset was changing already into fog, rising in wisps from the water around us, and making globes of light around the torches by the door. The coolness was welcome on my hot face. At the far end of the causeway I saw one or two faint lights around the farm buildings, but the long northern twilight of midsummer made them almost unneeded. Morning would be gray and slow-dawning; after the amount I had drunk already, this was just as well. Following Neirin back into the hall I yawned, thinking of my bed. But that was to be a while yet in coming.

Inside there had been a transformation; the trestle tables had been taken down and stacked out of the way, and all the household had gathered at one end of the hall, ready to listen to Neirin's playing. Seeing this, his head went up a little, and he grinned at me, then went to where his harp waited. I settled myself inconspicuously beside a couple of good-looking young women, but got little profit by it: they were watching Neirin while he first checked his tuning, then went and sat on the stool which had been placed for him near the fire. "What sort of music shall I play, Lady?" he asked our hostess.

She looked at him, and her severe expression lightened as she gazed: for young though he was, Neirin was good to look upon. "Play what music moves in your heart tonight," she said at last, and smiled. "That will be good enough."

For a moment Neirin sat frowning as if in thought; then slowly, as though hearing the notes somewhere inside him, he began to play. Isolated notes grew into phrases; phrases into a stream of bright sound; and then suddenly amidst the music there were words. It was like the harping I had heard him make in the Queen's garden at Luguvalium, but matured and focused through some inward lens; it spoke not to the mind, but to the heart, words and music working as one. I cannot tease out the words to repeat them, any more than I can sound the shining notes themselves; I can only remember how it made me feel. That harping spoke of love and longing and loss; of homesickness so strong it was like a physical pain, for a home so far in the past it could never be recovered; of all the hopeless futility that a man or woman may know in a long life, condensed into one unbearable moment. I found tears on my cheeks, and I know that I was not the only one. And then the harping changed, and it spoke of hope: the hope that comes with the arrival of springtime after a bitter winter, with the birth of a longed-for child, with new love after great loss. Slowly the music died away, like mist streaming off the lake when the sun rises; the words were gone, and it was over, and there was only Neirin: a young man sitting on a stool by the fire with a harp in his arms, his head bent over it as if in exhaustion, and a dazed look on his face like one who has been possessed and used by a force almost greater than he can contain, and then been released to be himself again.

That was the first time I saw him summon the *awen* to such an extent. I am a storyteller, a master of my craft: I work with words, and with them I can move men's minds and hearts; but Neirin was a Bard, and a great one, and he stood that day on the threshold of the mastery that he would later own; and there is in me a gladness still that I was there to see it.

When the Lady of the hall came to give him a horn of mead with her own hands, he took it and drank, and smiled his thanks. But it did not seem to affect him at all; it was if the *awen* had burned out of him everything else he had drunk that night, leaving him sober, and more than sober, but also more at peace than I had seen him since Luguvalium. It was I that night, and not he, who lay awake in my blankets thinking of a girl I had left behind: thinking of Rhiannedd back in Llys-tyn-wynnan, and the time we had spent together all last winter; thinking of the night we leapt the Beltane fires, and wondering if she was well, and if she was thinking of me at all; wondering too if the seed I had sown that night had taken root. Autumn suddenly seemed very far away.

Before we slept Neirin and I spent a little while outside, looking out across the mist-blurred lake and letting the mead-fumes clear somewhat from our heads. As I stood there, I was aware of the warmth and loom of a body behind me, and turned to see the Lady of the place. "I came out to thank you again for this evening," she said, "and also to ask—"

"What would you ask, Lady?" I said after a moment.

"I had a son once," she said. "All here know the tale, or some part of it, but I would tell it to you."

"Gladly would we hear it," said Neirin. "But should we not go back inside, and sit at our ease?"

"Na, na. The night is better for this tale, and the breath of the lake—the mist that lies on the water. It will not take long in the telling." Saying which she stepped forward between us, and set her hands on the wicker-work wall that edged the crannog, and stood so looking out into the darkness. A little while she stood there silent, and then, not moving, she began slowly to speak.

"I had a son once—na, that is not true! It was two sons I had once, and two years between them. The elder boy was dark and brave and bonny, and in him was great joy; but the younger was brown as you are, Storyteller, and he was never happy. Whatever his brother had, always he wanted the same, whether it was honey-cake or petting, toys or weapons or praise; and mostly he got it. But there was one thing he could not get for begging or weeping: and that was my father's sword.

"My father was lord of this holding, and having no sons yet living when he came to die, he settled it on me, and on him who married me. And he left his sword to me also, to hold in trust for the first of my sons to kill his man in battle, and come home bearing the proof of it. A fine sword it was indeed, made by a master sword-smith, with the twisting lines of the steel running through it like blue and silver flame. I hung it on the wall of the house-place in its sheath, and often I would take it down to clean and oil it, for my father had taught me how such weapons should be kept. And my elder son looked on it when I did so with joy and admiration; but my younger looked on it with anger and greed: for being two years younger, never was he likely to outdo his brother in battle, and come home first to claim it.

"And indeed in time my elder son went first into the fight, and killed his man, and came home with the head to prove it. Then I gave him the sword with delight and with relief, for I thought that now the competition would be ended. But I reckoned without my second son's nature. Not long after that, warriors came from the north raiding our cattle, and all the men-folk of the place pursued them, and my two sons with them. And our men came back with the cattle, but they brought back with them my elder son's body slung over his pony; and none had seen the blow that killed him. And my younger son came back wearing the sword.

"The blood of the Druids is in my family, and sometimes I can see the truth, whether I would or no. I looked that day at my elder son dead, and my younger son living; and when my younger son saw my face, the blood went from his, and he would not meet my eyes. And I said to him, 'Give me your brother's sword.'

" 'Na,' he said, 'it is mine now by right of inheritance.' But I did not speak, and after a moment his face burned red with shame and with anger, and he took off the sword and gave it to me. And a few days later he sought his father's permission to go and join the retinue of our King; and he got it. And so he rode away, and I have not seen him since. But my father's sword went into the earth with my elder son, though it is not the Christian custom. And now I have no sons at all."

"Thank you, Lady," said Neirin after a little while, "for telling us this tale. But why have you told it?"

"You are bards," said the Lady, with a trace of a smile in her voice. "Tales are your business, and so I give you mine. But if you should ever meet the man who was once my son... Bleiddig was his name..."

"What should we do?" Neirin asked. "What would you have us tell him, if we meet?"

"Na, I do not know," said the Lady, and sighed. "I would have said, perhaps... Let you tell him that he has a mother still. And yet I do not know... I will leave it, Singer, to your heart, and to your *awen*." And with that she turned from us, and went indoors, and we followed her.

The next morning dawned gray and misty, and when I woke it was to find the day well advanced, and everyone but us already up and about their business. It was almost midday before Neirin and I mounted our ponies, and that day we did not stop for sword practice, but rode on to the north until we found another, humbler farmstead which took us in for the night. And the evening after that we reached Alt Clut.

But that, O my children, is a story for another day.

The Rock of Alt Clut

The Rock of Alt Clut drops sheer on three sides to the blue-gray sea at its feet. Only on the green north side, the landward side, is the slope gradual enough to have allowed the building of a road to the top, and even there it must wind back and forth as it climbs. The twin peaks of the summit are unequal, and the smaller western one supports only defensive works and a watch-tower on its top, but the eastern peak is crowned with the fortress—and the palace—of the King of Strathclyde, whose brown stone walls rise straight from the living rock, as strong as any fortress in the North. Below it on the level shore is a village of farmers and fisherman, prospering alike on the bounty of earth and sea, for Strathclyde is a rich kingdom, and well did her King Rhydderch deserve his by-name "*Hael*," which means "the generous."

On the day we arrived at Alt Clut, I had been watching the Rock from my pony's back since early morning without feeling I was getting much closer to it; for coming north from Aeron as we did, we needs must make a long eastward detour around the gradually narrowing Clyde estuary to a point where the river herself could be crossed at low tide. It was a pleasant enough ride on that midsummer day, for the land was fair and green, and the hot sunshine was tempered by a salt breeze from the waters to the west. North of the estuary I could make out a line of blue mountains, hazy with distance and summer heat. "Alba," Neirin had called them when I asked. "The land of the Picts: the one part of Britain which the Romans never conquered. We are almost up to their old northern wall: do you see it over there?" I looked where he pointed, and could make a low green earthwork snaking across the country, crowned here with the remains of a tower and there with a belt of woodland which mostly hid it. A long time now it had been going back to the wild; in a few more lifetimes of men no one would notice it. But the Rock of Alt Clut, growing closer now at last, would stand as a fortress forever—or so it seemed to me then.

We were not the only travelers heading for it that day by any means. Rhydderch Hael's impending marriage had drawn noble guests from many kingdoms, as well as merchants, entertainers, and sundry other folk, until it seemed the whole North was on the move. Not far ahead of us on the road was the royal party from Aeron, who had passed us the night before, and coming up behind us I could see another group, even more splendid. In a little while I recognized on the banners and shields of the warriors the Black Boar of Rheged upon his red field: we were being overtaken by the wedding party itself. "Do you look behind us," I said to Neirin, who was riding beside me deep in thought.

"*Hai mai!*" he said when he had looked. "My fate is upon me! *Sa, sa,* I will meet it as it comes." And he grinned, and set to work brushing the summer dust from his clothes, and tidying his red hair. "Do you make yourself fine, Gwernin."

"I am fine enough already," I said, grinning back at him. "They must take me as I am. But we had better rein aside and give them the road." And I suited my actions to my words, turning Du and the pack horse onto the grassy verge between the road and the crop-land beyond.

"True that is," said Neirin, reining in his gray pony beside me, and turning to look at the Rheged party. "Ah, but they are a brave sight!"

This, I thought, was no exaggeration. Urien Rheged, wedding his daughter Morfudd to the richest king in the north, had gone out of his way to challenge that description. The round shields of his war-band, riding before and behind his party as an escort, were all painted red and black with his device. Their spear-points and shield-bosses glittered like silver as they came, and the red cloaks they wore were pinned at the shoulder with brooches of bright bronze. At their head rode Urien himself, tall and splendid on his black stallion with its red and gold harness and saddle-cloth, and his golden circlet sparkling in the sun. Beside him rode his two eldest sons, fair-haired Owain and dark Cadell; and behind him in two horse-litters came his wife and daughter, followed by their maid-servants and various officers of the court; and men-servants leading a train of well-laden baggage-mules; and finally the rest of the *teulu* making a splendid rear-guard. They came, and they passed, and we sat in a cloud of their dust listening to their retreating hoof-beats. The only one who had seemed to notice us at all was young Cadell, who had waved to me as he rode by; for all the rest we might have been invisible. So much, I thought, for making ourselves fine; but I did not say so.

"Well," said Neirin after a moment, shaking his reins to set his pony in motion again, "that was not so bad. But I am thinking we will be lucky to find a camping-place in the fields tonight, never mind a bed on the Rock, what with all the high folk who are coming to this hand-fasting; and I will be having as much chance of coming to the Lady Morfudd's notice as a sparrow has of nesting on the sea!" And he laughed and rode on, and I laughed with him.

In the event, we fared better than we expected. This was partly due to our prosperous appearance, for we were well dressed, well-mounted, well-armed, and wearing the harp cases which proclaimed our profession. The gate-guard at the bottom of the castle ramp let us by without question, and his brother at the top saw no reason to disagree. Our ponies we bestowed with the rest in the over-crowded stables, and we were heading for the great hall, in hopes of finding a corner there in which to bed down, when one of Urien's *teulu* stopped us. "You are the two southern bards who were at Lugh a while back, are you not? Gwernin and—and—"

"Neirin," said Neirin, smiling. "You were wanting us?"

"*Sa, sa,*" said the man. "Not I but another. Come with me, please," and we did so. He led us through a maze of buildings, all of them very full of people, to the doorway of a small guest-house close by the east wall of the fortress. "I have found them, Lord," he said, and to my delight I saw young Cadell come out, fastening his belt over a red wool tunic that set off his dark hair and eyes. "Thank you, Rhys," he said to the man, and to me, "Gwernin! I saw you on the road and sent Rhys to look for you. Do you have a lodging? Ours is very full, but I think we can fit two more in if you like."

"Thank you, Prince," I said. "That would be most welcome; we feared we would be lucky to find space in the fire-hall with such a crowd here."

"That is settled, then," said Cadell, grinning. "Come you in! Oh! and you, too, Neirin, if it please you."

"Gladly, Prince," said Neirin, looking amused, and followed me in. The room was small, and as Cadell said, very full already, partly because he was sharing it with his brother Owain and at least one other person, and partly because big fair-haired Owain was kneeling in the midst of it, digging in a mule-pack like a dog who has mislaid his bone, and scattering clothing everywhere. He looked up as we entered, frowning a little at the sight of us. "Have you seen my new belt?" he asked his brother. "I thought surely it was in this pack, but I cannot find it."

"I expect it will turn up," said Cadell. "Owain, you remember Gwernin and Neirin, I spoke to you about them."

"Oh, yes," said Owain, his brow clearing, "the two southern bards. Well, and I expect we can fit them in somehow. Morfudd will be pleased to see the harper; I remember she was much taken with him. Cadell, do you look in your gear and see if Cai has packed my belt there by mistake; I need it *now*." And he returned to his digging.

"Put your things in the corner," Cadell said to us quietly. "Then I think you had better leave for a while; there will be no peace here until Owain has found his belt. I will look for you in the fire-hall later." And he turned back to his brother, saying, "Yes, Owain, I will look now," while Neirin and I did as we were told and went out, taking only our harp-cases with us.

"Phew!" I said as we tried to retrace our steps through the maze of buildings. "Our gear will no doubt be safer, but there might have been more room in the hall."

"Hmm?" said Neirin absently; he seemed hardly to notice where he was going, and a little, rueful smile kept tugging at the corners of his mouth. "I wonder—what did you say?" And he blinked as if coming out of a dream.

"Never you mind," I said, grinning. "Let us see if we can find the hall again. What a tangle this place is! I wonder how long it will be until dinner? My belly is empty!"

"*Sa, sa,* and mine as well." Neirin sighed and fell into step with me. "*Hai mai!* A tangle it is indeed, and who knows the ending?" And I do not think he was referring to the palace when he spoke.

By evening the Rock was as full of people as an egg is of meat. The benches in Rhydderch's fire-hall were crammed with kings and sub-kings, princes and single-valley lords, and we were lucky to find a seat near the door with two or three other bards. The steward was arranging performances, but few of the singers could be heard above the non-stop background clamor of voices, the clinking of cups and dishes, the shouts of running children, and the snarling of dogs who quarreled in the rushes over discards from the tables. The little group of us by the door had captured a platter of roast pig-meat and a jug of red Gaulish wine, and were busy making the most of it before someone asked us to perform, or worse, to yield our place to another batch of lordlings. Neirin seemed to have recovered from his absent-mindedness, although I saw him stealing glimpses at the high table from time to time. I did not blame him; it was a company worth seeing.

Rhydderch Hael was in the center, of course—a tall, wide-shouldered man some years younger than his prospective father-in-law, with a wealth of amber necklaces half-obscuring the embroidery on his heavy purple robe, and a gold circlet almost the twin of Urien's holding back his dark curls. Beside him was his bride-to-be, her pale hair glowing like a golden flower in the smoky light of the torches, and her flower-face aloof and still, but smiling—a quiet smile that could have covered anything from joy to despair. On her other side sat Urien, resplendent as usual in red and black and gold, with Owain and young Cadell next to him. Of his Queen there was no sign; presumably she was dining in her chamber after the long journey. The rest of the table was taken up by a number of other kings and princes, only one of whom was familiar to me: Elidyr Mwynfawr of Aeron, with whom Neirin and I had recently stayed. He was a man of much Rhydderch's years and build, though lighter complexioned and with a surly, dissatisfied expression, as if he always suspected he was getting less than his desserts of goods or gear or praise. Beside him was another king who looked vaguely familiar, though I was sure I had never met him before: a thinner, darker man than most of his peers. "Who is that?" I asked Neirin, pointing. "The man in the red and green tunic beside Elidyr?"

Neirin looked, and for a moment his eyes narrowed and his mobile mouth set hard. "That is Clydno Eidyn," he said levelly. "King of the Gododdin lands."

"You must know him, then," I said. "He looks no older than Rhydderch; he cannot have been king for long."

"Na, na," said Neirin, still in that oddly level voice. "He was crowned five years ago, when his father died: I mind it well." And then, almost as an afterthought, "He is my half-brother." And he drank off his wine, and stood up, and walked away from the table like one who goes to seek the fresh air, leaving me staring after him.

I found him by and by on the castle ramparts, looking out south and west over the sea, his hands set wide apart on the brown stone and his head well up, like a hawk about to take flight. I came up quietly and leaned my arms on the warm stone beside him. The sun was low down now in the northwest, and all the wave-tops in the estuary were brushed with gold. It reminded me of something, of somewhere long ago. Bright sun-dazzle dancing on blue water, blazing, blinding, and in it the singing of the birds... Harddlech a year ago. I smiled. "I wonder what Taliesin is doing tonight?"

Neirin looked at me quickly. "You are reading my thoughts again, brother. Na, na, I do not know... He has set me a hard task, harder than I knew. I had forgotten"—and here he turned back to the sea again—"how little love I had for my half-brother, and he for me."

"You had better tell me, then," I said peaceably. The sea-breeze was pleasant up here, my belly was full, and truth to tell I was feeling a little sleepy.

Neirin was silent for a while. "I am not knowing where to begin," he said at last.

"At the beginning. Your mother married Clydno's father?"

"She did, against my grandfather's wishes. He would have had her marry Pabo Post Prydein, an old man even then, but one whose borders march with Elmet. But some chance of war or fortune brought Cynfelyn Eidyn to her hall, and once she saw him she could not think of other men." Neirin smiled. "She told me the way of it often enough when I was a child. 'He had my heart,' she used to say, 'from that first moment, and I had his.' And as Gododdin is a rich land—they call the king there '*Mynyddog Mwynfawr*,' the Wealthy One of the Mountain—my grandfather let her have her way. I do not think she ever regretted it, though she never saw Elmet again, and sometimes she missed it. She used to tell me tales of it when I was small, of Aquae and its hot springs, and its oak-crowned hill..."

"What was she like?" I asked, feeling the homing-hunger on me as well, though I had not thought of Pengwern for so long.

"Very bright," said Neirin, "bright and warm, a warmer, redder gold than that girl in the hall tonight... Well, and so I got my rearing in Manau, with my cousins and half-brothers. I did not come much in Clydno's way, for he was a man and had taken valor while I was learning to walk. But for some reason—I never knew why—he took against my mother. And once I understood this, in the way that children do, there could be no peace between us. So when she died"—he stopped and was silent for a moment—"when she died, and my father not long after, I would not stay in Eidyn. I saw my half-brother crowned, and then I rode south." He laughed. "And that was a mad thing to do at my age, but I survived it—I will maybe tell you the tale of it one day!—to find a cold welcome at my uncle's court. Then Taliesin came, and my life changed again." He sighed.

"Maybe we should go down," I said after a while, "and see what is passing in the hall."

"*Sa, sa,* that is a good idea." Neirin smiled. "And I have a better one."

"What is that?" I asked as we started down the stairs.

"To find some more of that Gaulish wine before our friends have finished it all—and get drunk!"

If we did not put Neirin's plan entirely in effect, we did get rather merry that evening, and when we finally found our way back to Owain and Cadell's lodging and collapsed on the straw pallets someone had brought in for us, we had no trouble sleeping, and were not awakened by our co-lodgers' return. And if we felt a little fragile the next morning, we were not the only ones by any means. In the feasting for Rhydderch's wedding, mead and wine flowed like water, and many a merchant was merry; and whole herds of shaggy black cattle and acorn-fed swine were slaughtered on the plain below the Rock. Three days he feasted us before the hand-fasting, and three days after. The spits and cauldrons in the kitchen-court were never empty, so that the aroma of roasting meat outdid even the odors of many men and dogs and horses, and there was a thronging in the hall most hours of the day or night. Minstrels did well; I myself got many a silver arm-ring for my tales, and Neirin was summoned to play his harp for the ladies in their bower, and went around for hours afterwards in a blissful dreamy mood which much amused me. And on the fourth day, which was Midsummer's Eve, Rhydderch and Morfudd were joined in marriage privately in the chapel, and blessed afterwards in full public view by the chief holy man of the district, the sainted Kentigern himself. He and his monks had come over from their *clas* some little way east of the Rock, founded on good land that Rhydderch himself had given them; *Glas-cu* they called it.

In those days Kentigern was still young, a tall, wiry man with a warrior's build, and his hair thick and dark where it was not tonsured, and no gray in his beard. He preached a fiery sermon afterwards, and did a good job of it, though I was not moved by his content. And that night Rhydderch did not sit late at the feasting, but went early to his bride in Christian bliss. But the Midsummer fires burned as always in the country round about, and if the people there were not celebrating in the old ways, I would have been much surprised.

As for Neirin, he sang that night around the courtyard fires for the war-bands until he was hoarse, and came very late and very drunk to his bed, and was the worse for it the next morning. He spent the three days after that performing much as usual about the court and the campfires, but he did not talk much, and I mostly left him alone. Late on the last afternoon, however, he came into the hall while I was telling a story and sat down near the back of my audience, and I could see at once that something about him had changed. I went on with my tale to its bitter ending—it was one of my Irish ones, "The Death of Cuchulainn," which I was telling again for Prince Cadell at his request—and got my due applause. Cadell himself, sitting in the front of the small crowd, was drinking it in as always, and when at last I told how the raven came and settled on the hero's shoulder, I saw his eyes bright with unshed tears. "What it must have taken, to have had such courage," he said to me afterwards. "I will miss your tales, Gwernin, when we part tomorrow, but I will hold you to your promise to return and visit me one of these days."

"I am not sure when that will be, Prince," I said, "for I must go back to my own master this winter and continue learning my trade. But when the gods allow it, I will certainly come."

"Which way are you going next?" asked Cadell. "North into Pictland, or east to Dun Eidyn?"

"Some of both, Prince," said Neirin, coming up beside me. "We are going to the bardic competition held in Dun Eidyn at the Lughnasadh, but first we may take a swing through Bannawg and Manau."

"That would be worth seeing," said Cadell. "Perhaps some year I can go. Well, good luck to you when you get there. I will see you this evening," and he grinned, "always supposing you come to bed before dawn!" And he turned and walked away.

"Bannawg?" I said questioningly.

"Well, it may be farther north than that," said Neirin, chuckling, and I saw the mischief look was back in his eyes. "I have had speech with my brother in the courtyard just now, and he has invited us to travel with him on a circuit round his borders. And as we have yet a month to fill before the Lughnasadh Fair, it seemed good to me to accept his offer—if it please you?"

"You are the leader of this expedition, remember," I grinned. "Yours is the decision—and yours the blame if it goes wrong! But what has happened to put you in this different mood? Not just having speech with your brother, I think." Looking him over more closely, I noticed a shimmer of bright crimson silk inside the neck of his tunic. Neirin saw the direction of my gaze, and his smile went a little awry.

"A farewell present," he said. "She summoned me to play for her once more this afternoon, and gave me her scarf at the end of it. But I am knowing when I have had my dismissal." He sighed. "It was a bright dream while it lasted. Ah, well, I doubt me I am for marrying young—and at least now I can show you Manau with a whole heart!"

"That will be a thing worth the doing," I said. And indeed I was right.

But that, O my children, is a story for another day.

Tree of Thorns

It was hot that afternoon in the shelter of the hills with the sun beating down on the heather, so hot that the aromatic scent of it hung heavy on the still air. Nothing moved in the valley but the eagles, circling on the thermals above, and our little knot of horsemen ambling along the dusty white road below. Runnels of sweat ran down my face, drawing muddy lines in the dust there, and soaked my brown wool tunic so that it clung to my chest and back. In the heat of the afternoon no one wanted to talk, not even Neirin. Around us the *teulu* rode silently, with no sound but the soft thudding of the ponies' unshod hooves on the track, and the occasional creak of a leather girth, or the chime of a bridle bit as a fly-bitten pony shook his head. The little river not too far to our left looked cool and inviting amidst its alder and willows, and I gazed at it with longing from time to time, but it seemed that Clydno Eidyn was not in the mood for a swim.

We were two days out from Alt Clut by then on our circuit around Bannawg, with one more day's ride ahead of us before we reached Caer Iddeu, Clydno's strong point at the west end of Manau. So far there had been little enough talk between the brothers, and Neirin and I had been treated much like part of the retinue. The night before, in a stave-built hall beside one of the great lakes of that region, we had performed by turns, singing and telling tales and harping, while Clydno had sat on his skin-draped bench talking quietly to the lord of the place, and later had gone off to the guest-lodging while we bedded down in the hall with the rest of the household. All in all, not a promising beginning, and I rather hoped we would not be spending the next month before the Contention in the same way. In that, as it turned out, I was to get my wish, though not in the way I expected.

"Not far now, I am thinking," said Neirin beside me, and I came back out of my musings to see a ford ahead, where a second stream came leaping down from the hills to the south to join our river. On the far side of it was a settlement, little more than a cluster of thatched huts inside an old earthen bank, with a pattern of corn-fields outside it stretching along the level land by the stream, green with the growing barley. Beyond them to the south, the slopes rose steeply to a frowning ridge crowned with cliffs, while to the north-east our road led on over lower hills.

"Time enough, for all of me," I said. "I hope there is plenty of heather ale tonight—I am parched clear through with this riding in the heat. A dip in that stream before evening would not come amiss, either."

"That at least I think we can manage, once the ponies are seen to," said Neirin, and grinned. "It will surely be a while and a while before we get our dinner, though it will be welcome enough when it comes. For a company of this size, they will be some time cooking."

In this I found he was right, though Clydno had sent a rider ahead to warn the local chieftain of his coming. Once the horses were cared for, most of our troop sat down in the courtyard or the hall to stay their stomachs with beer and barley-bread, but after the first round of each, Neirin and I headed for the river. By the time we got there, we were more than ready to strip off our sweat-soaked clothes and plunge in.

In its summer bounds the stream was not large—nothing like the broad brown Severn in Powys where I grew up, or the Clyde where we had crossed it on our way to Alt Clut—and it could be waded easily enough in its shallower reaches, but we found a wide pool under the willows which was deep enough for swimming, and wonderfully cool after the heat of the day. We rolled and splashed in it until we were clean, and rinsed the dust and sweat from our clothes, then stayed some time floating in the silken embrace of the water, looking up at the summer-pale sky and listening to the bird-song in the branches above. At last we climbed out, and hanging our wet tunics over the bushes to dry, lay down on the grassy bank.

The chirring of the grasshoppers in the bracken was like a lullaby, but our empty bellies, said Neirin, should keep us awake. And he was nearly right.

It was the sound of movement in the nearby bushes that brought me back to full consciousness: not a stealthy movement as of an approaching enemy, nor yet the brief rustlings of some small creature in the summer-dry grasses, but the sound of someone walking and stopping, walking and stopping, as if searching for something. Rolling over, I sat up to see who it was, giving Neirin a poke in the ribs as I did so. "Wake up," I said grinning. "We have company." And reaching for my trews, I stood up to face the two girls who had just come out of the willow-brake upstream. Their giggles at being confronted with a naked stranger made me blush, but they did not run away. Indeed, after some conversation, they were persuaded to sit down with us and share the basketful of sweet little wild strawberries which they had been gathering for Clydno Eidyn's entertainment that night. It was a pity, as Neirin said afterwards, that there were none left for dinner when we had finished, but gathering wild fruits was always uncertain, and what Clydno had not seen he would not miss.

The younger girl, Beilo, was dark and round and jolly, and she and I soon struck it off very well, while her pale-haired sister Anghenell had eyes only for Neirin, and he for her. They were soon feeding each other the ripest strawberries, taking turns to hold one by the stem while the other nibbled the fruit away. This led in time to kissing, and then to other things. Meanwhile Beilo and I took care to get our share of the berries, and then went off with the basket to look for more. It was the happiest afternoon I had passed in a long while, and I still remember it with pleasure.

Hunger and the sinking of the sun in the west eventually sent us all back to the Dun. Here I found that due to the size of the company, and the closeness of the smoky hall on that summer evening, tables and benches had been set up for us in the courtyard instead. Neirin and I followed our new friends to the kitchen and there got our food first, so that we could entertain the rest during the feast. Hastily though we ate our portion, it was as good as any served to Clydno Eidyn that evening, and later we got other delights as well. There were, however, no strawberries left for the meal.

In the pale northern twilight, the pinewood torches around the courtyard flared smoky and golden by turns, shedding their flickering light on faces young and old, stern and happy, high-born and low. One wizened little man seated close by the Lord of that place wore a wooden cross on a thong outside his gray-brown woolen tunic, and I remembered Beilo had mentioned a visiting priest in the house. Maybe that was what led me to tell the tale I did, later in the evening—that, or the sight of the new moon caught in the twisted branches of a hawthorn-tree which grew behind the mead-hall. At any rate, this is the tale I told, as I first heard it told around the feast-fires of Alt Clut by an Irish teller, a man whom I had never seen before, and never saw again.

"Once there was a wise man, a Druid, and he lived alone in a house at the very center of an oak grove, beyond the northern hills on the Island of Môn. He was an old man, and had lived there a long time, gathering wisdom from the trees and the stars, and serving his forest gods. When he was young, there had been many of his kind in the land, but that was long ago. The Romans had come and hacked down the forests with their bright steel, and the Christians had come with their bells and their prayers and their crosses. Now there was only this one man who had still the knowledge of the past, and he had no students, no followers to come after him and serve the gods in his way when he was dead. And for this his heart was sad. But because he was a wise man, he did not go forth to seek followers; neither did he trouble his gods day and night with prayers. Instead he looked into the water, and into the smoke, and into the fire, and he waited for what was to come.

"It was on a Midsummer night, a night of storm, a night of rain and wind and thunder, that his fate came to him. All evening he had been as restless as one in fever, and yet his body was cool and his mind was clear. At last, in the hour of greatest darkness, he heard a knock on the door; and he rose up from his bed, and went and opened it. As he opened the door, the draft stirred his banked-down fire to flame, and by its light he saw a girl wrapped in a gray cloak, with long pale hair streaming around her pale face, and her eyes wide and dark. He looked at her for a moment, and she looked back at him. And then he brought her inside, and led her to a seat by the hearth, and built up the fire until it burned bright and warm. He brought her a stone cup filled with red wine, and on the rim of the cup their hands touched, and their eyes met, and they knew each of them their fate. But all he said was, 'You have come, then, Lleuad,' and she said, 'I have.' And he made up a bed for her by the fire, on the other side of the room from his own bed, and the next day he began to teach her his art.

"In the old days, or so they say, the Druid kind would spend twenty years at their studies. However that may be, these two did what must be done in a year and a night. They rose early, and they worked late. They wandered the forest before dawn, at midday and by moonlight, in warm summer days and in bitter frost. And all the while the Druid taught his knowledge and his learning and his wisdom to the maid, and she drank it in like a thirsty plant.

"At last their work was done, and she was blessed with the red earth and the black, the white crown and the green, the golden circle and the knife of stone, and heard the words that no one has spoken since. And when the thing was over and finished, the maiden called Lleuad (which in the common tongue means 'the Light One,' and is used for the name of the Moon) was herself the Druid, and he that had been the Druid was only a man. And he looked at her then with a man's eyes, and saw that she was beautiful; and she looked at him with a Druid's wisdom, and she smiled. 'Where shall it be, then, beloved?' she asked; and he said, 'Let us walk by the shore.'

"By the shore they walked, where the thorn trees grow all one way, bent by the wind. Now the Christians sometimes call their cross the Tree of Thorns, for the iron thorns by which their God hung suspended on it. But the thorn-tree of our lands is the Haw-thorn, which bears white blossoms at Beltane and red berries at

Samhain, and in the summer gives shade. And in its shade the two of them sat down, and watched the setting of the sun, and the rising of the moon; and all night long they lay in shadows dappled black and white with the moonlight. And in the dawn, or so they say, the woman stood up and walked away; and where she went no one knows. What became of the wise man I cannot tell you, for no one has seen him since that night; but on that headland the hawthorn tree under which they lay still grows, and with its blossoms and its fruit blesses the seasons."

When I finished my tale, I saw the Christian priest was frowning, and so were one or two others, including Clydno Eidyn; this is always the risk nowadays when one speaks of the Old Ways. But what I remember most clearly from that night was a boy, sitting in the front of the crowd at the feet of a man who might have been his father. His pale eyes were wide and shining in the torchlight, and his corn-colored hair was summer-bleached to silver. I looked at him as I finished, and I smiled, and his face lit up in response. Then I was taking my bow to the applause of the crowd, and making my way back to my seat among the *teulu*, passing Neirin as I went, and I did not see the boy again that evening.

What I did see—and hear—somewhat later was Clydno Eidyn having words with Neirin. "It was not seemly," I heard him say, "to affront the good Father so to his face with a tale of pagan magic."

"*Hai mai!*" said Neirin, his face flushed in response. "I was not myself knowing that this is a church, or a *clas*, where we entertained tonight. Well, well, we will both of us be more careful another time, if you are so tender to the priests! But you were not a monk when last I knew you."

"If that was meant as an insult," said Clydno coolly, "it is wide of its mark. You have been a long time away, boy; you must learn to know me again." And with that he turned on his heel, and walked away to rejoin his host. Neirin saw me watching, and raised his eyebrows and shrugged. As for Clydno, neither then nor later did he speak to me directly concerning my choice of material; it was almost as if the quarrel was between him and Neirin alone, and I only the excuse for it, though how or why it arose I could not say.

After the feasting that night Neirin and I did not sleep with the *teulu* in the smoky darkness of the hall, but spread our blankets in a patch of deep grass in the apple orchard, close by the earthen wall of the dun. A quiet, sweet-smelling place it was, there beneath the summer stars, and easy of access; and though we did not sleep early, when we slept at last we slept well, and woke with the dawn ready to be on our way.

It was while I was saddling Du in the courtyard the next morning that I saw the pale-haired boy for the second time. "Lord," he said breathlessly, coming up to me, "I wanted to tell you how much I enjoyed your tale last night, and to ask—to ask—"

"What are you for asking, then?" I said, smiling. He was perhaps ten years old, if that, but very serious, and with something in his manner that seemed familiar to me.

"To ask where one might find"—he paused and looked around, but no one was watching—"such learning as that old man had, in the story. We only have the Christian priests here, and they will not teach such things."

"Na, I am not knowing that myself," I said; and then to Neirin, as he came walking up to join me, "Here is another seeker after wisdom."

"Hmm," said Neirin when the question was explained. "Hard that is to answer. I am thinking, if that is your path, you will find a way if you look—or maybe it will find you. When you are older, go to the south, to the lands of Goddeu: the old wisdom still lives there, a little, under Gwenddolau the Prince."

"Goddeu," said the boy, repeating the name. "And the Prince Gwenddolau: I will remember."

At that moment a woman's voice called from the buildings behind him: "Llaloiken! Where are you? You have work to do now!"

"Coming!" cried the boy, and was off, his pale hair streaming behind him as he ran. I saw Neirin frown, and cock his head as if hearing something behind the words. But it was time for us to mount up and ride, on our way to Caer Iddeu, and I thought no more of it, although much later I remembered that moment, and the new moon that had shone the night before.

But that, O my children, is a story for another day.

The Green Branch

For the Celtic peoples of Britain, the carrying of a green branch is a request for a parley, a sign of a truce, or the mark of an ambassador. Seldom if ever has its sanctity been completely disregarded, even by the Saxons. But this is not to say that all who advanced under its protection came safely home afterwards, for men are not predictable, and ill deeds may come of good intentions, or even by accident: that is the lesson of Camlann. Beware, then, the adder on the battlefield.

The truce—if it was a truce—between Neirin and his half-bother Clydno Eidyn was still holding as we approached Caer Iddeu, after a long, leisurely ride through the valleys north of Bannawg. Situated in the partly rebuilt remains of a Roman fortress, Caer Iddeu occupies a steep hill above the river Forth at the lowest ford on that river before it becomes tidal, and guards the western end of Manau. This is a fine green land, mostly flat and good for corn where it is not marshy, which wraps around the west end of the Forth estuary. Caer Iddeu sits on its northwest border, staring across the valley at the strongholds of the Picts.

"Na, na, they are not painted," said Neirin in answer to my question. We were riding some way back in the party and having our own conversation. "That is an old Roman tale. I have seen a few with their clan marks tattooed on them, but that is nothing. Otherwise they are much as we are, if perhaps a little leaner and darker. Manau is a land where we mix and blend. Look at Erp over there"—he pointed to a dark young man in the retinue—"or for that matter my brother or myself; no question but we have the Old Blood in us, if not too much of it."

"Do you speak any of the language?" I asked.

"*Sa,* a little. Or I used to; I doubt me I remember much now. Around here it is no more different from British than the Irish is; it may change farther north." And he grinned, and added a few words in a tongue I could not understand.

"That is different enough for all of me," I said. "Has your brother said yet why he invited us along? You started to tell me something the other day, and we were interrupted."

"Na, he has not, not in so many words. I did not tell you the way of his asking, did I?"

"Na, you had other things on your mind," I said, and suppressed a yawn—the warm afternoon and the leisurely gait of our ponies was making me sleepy. "Tell me the way of it, then."

"He stopped me in the courtyard that afternoon," said Neirin, "and asked me where I was from. 'You should know,' I told him— *hai mai*, I was not at my most diplomatic that day!—'But if you are in any doubt, let you be asking Anhun your father's sister, or Kynan the Harper, or your own mirror.'

" 'I do not need to ask them,' he said then, and he laughed. 'You have grown taller with the years, boy, but not more civil! What are you about these days? It is a long time since you left us.'

" 'I have been learning my trade in the south,' I said, 'and am set loose for the summer to journey with a friend. We are on our way to the Lughnasadh Fair at Dun Eidyn, for the Contention of the Bards. Do you have some objection?'

" 'Na, na, I do not,' he said. 'I heard your singing last night in the hall: you have been well taught. Let you ride with me tomorrow and be my harper for some days, and we will talk more. Does that please you?'

" '*Sa,* it does,' I said in surprise. 'We will come with you some way, at least.' And it was done. But I wonder now... If there was more to it than curiosity, he has not yet told me so."

"Belike he will do so soon enough," I said, and looked thoughtfully at the lean dark shape of Clydno Eidyn, riding some way ahead of us amongst his men. An active, energetic, intelligent prince he was, so far as I could judge, past his first youth but not yet old. He had spoken courteously to me at Alt Clut, and praised my storytelling. "Do you still dislike him? He seems civil enough to me."

"I—am not knowing," said Neirin, frowning. "He has not been unkind, it is true, but—ask me in a month! For we will be with him that long, unless we go off on our own."

"Ah, well," I said, and yawned, "it will not hurt us to rest for a while, after our recent adventures. And you can give me more lessons."

"Of which sort?" asked Neirin, yawning in his turn. "Gods! You have me started now!—Harp, or sword, or poetry?"

"Any, or all. You are my master at all three."

"As for the sword, most men are, who own one!" We both laughed; it was true. "As for the rest, we shall see. Like enough we will have a plenty of time to fill at Dun Eidyn. Let you be telling me again what teaching you had from Talhaearn this past winter." And I did so, and it kept us busy for the rest of the afternoon's ride, and into Iddeu castle.

When we came into the hall that night, I was surprised to see that Clydno had guests, and guests of an unusual kind. Three tall dark men, very well dressed in jewel-bright robes of crimson and gold and green, were standing beside him at the high table. They made me feel plain and simple, clad though I was in good brown and black wool over Owain's best trews. Only Neirin shone them down, in the red and blue checkered tunic he had last worn in Urien Rheged's hall. I had looked my surprise at him that evening when he put it on, but he had only grinned, saying, "When you find yourself in Pengwern again, you too will dress in your best. I got my birth and much of my raising here; I would not be wanting them to think I had fared less well since I left them."

Truly, in that garb, and with the torch-light picking out his bronze brooch and belt-fittings and shining in his red hair, he looked as much a prince that night as his brother. His mustache, too, had come on amazingly in the last month, and his beard was beginning to grow. Noticing it afresh, I ran my thumb and forefinger absently over my own upper lip and chin, and sighed. There were more hairs there than had been there last winter, but light brown does not show well against tanned skin. Contemplating my lack of adornment, I almost missed Clydno's gesture summoning us to be introduced.

"Here is my half-brother Neirin and his friend Gwernin Story-teller," he was saying as we came up. "Neirin, these three lords are come to us from the court of Nechtan son of Drustan, King of the Southern Picts. I will let them tell you their mission to us them-selves."

"Greetings, Neirin brother to Clydno and Gwernin Story-teller," said the oldest of the three, a dark-eyed, solemn-looking man whose pointed beard showed more gray than black. He spoke our language very well, but with a lilting accent I had not met before. "We have been sent by our King Nechtan to ask a favor of Clydno King of Gododdin. Our King would send an embassy to Mailchon the King of the Northern Picts, in an attempt to make peace between our peoples, for there has been much blood feud and much needless killing amongst our tribes this past year. But his problem is this: who shall he send as an ambassador, when all of his nobles, even we ourselves who stand here"—and he gestured at himself and his two companions—"come of those same tribes, and partake in some degree of the same feuds? So in his wisdom he has sent us here, to ask his friend the King of Gododdin if one of his lords would undertake this mission for us. And behold, says the King of Gododdin! Here are you his brother, Neirin son of Cynfe-lyn, newly returned from years of study in the South, and a Bard! You have clean hands and a clean heart in this matter; you partici-pate in no blood feuds; and you are dear to the gods by your calling as well as by your birth." He paused for a moment, and spread out his two hands in a stylized gesture of appeal. "Here am I, Talorc son of Uoret, asking in the name of my King Nechtan whether you, Neirin, will do this deed, and carry the Green Branch north for us as our Ambassador."

"This is a great thing you are asking of me," said Neirin, but his amber eyes were sparkling at the challenge, and I saw the mischief-look come and go around his mouth. "I must think on it some while, and take council with my brother of Eidyn, and with my friend Gwernin."

"Of course," said Talorc, and smiled. "That is understood. Let you give us your answer tomorrow, if you will, and whatever it is, we will try and be glad of it; but I find it in me to hope that it will be 'yes'." And with that we all took our places at table, and the feasting began.

"*Sa, sa,*" said Neirin to me later that evening in our lodging, "of course I am going: how not? My brother says neither yea nor nay, but I can see that he expects it, and would think less of me if I declined. And indeed, it is less I would be thinking of myself, as well!" But he was smiling as he said it, that bright confident smile I knew so well, and which usually meant trouble.

"That is not your only reason, and you know it," I said, grinning back at him. "Ah, well, they do say the Pictish women are fierce; it is good I shall be there with you to protect you, and to keep the King's sister from your bed!"

"Well, that is the one thing I am not sure of," said Neirin, and his face became all at once more serious. "It is a fine thing for me to be risking my own head in this matter, but I have no right to risk yours as well. It is in my mind that you should stay here in Manau until I return."

"What do you mean?" I asked blankly, but with a sort of sinking in my belly. "Taliesin sent me along to help you, and our journey is not yet over. Have I done aught to offend you, that you should wish to leave me behind?"

"Na, na, of course you have not." Neirin frowned down at the belt buckle he was polishing. "But this embassy was not part of his plan, and my heart misgives me to be taking you with me on it. Gwernin, do you not argue with me; I cannot explain it, but it is so. You must stay here."

"Well," I said after a moment, "I suppose someone must remain behind to bear the news to Taliesin, after you vanish without trace in the North. Only"—I paused a moment to steady my voice—"only I could wish it were not me."

At that Neirin put down his belt, and came and took me by the shoulders. "Brother," he said, low and earnest, "believe me, I would rather have you at my back than any other. And it will not be for long; I will surely be back for the Lughnasadh Fair, and the Contention."

"I know," I said, and sighed. "Well, you have had your way: make your preparations. Only do you behave yourself this time, and leave the women alone!"

"I will," said Neirin, and grinned. But his mischief-look was back, and I was not sure I believed him.

The next day, though, he looked solemn enough, standing young and straight and shining as he was, and giving his answer to Talorc and the others in open hall. And the morning after that he was gone, riding off with the Pictish lords and their retinue without a backward glance. They were going first to speak with King Nechtan in his great fortress of Dundurn, and then on into the trackless North—for so I thought of it. For myself, I stood for a long time on the ramparts in the hot morning sunlight, watching their dust cloud slowly recede up the straight trace of the old Roman road, and thinking I could still catch, now and again, a glimpse of Neirin's dark red hair like a faint and fading ember at its center. Then I came down with a heavy heart to practice my harping. Neirin had left his own beauty in my keeping—"For," he had said, "it is not as a harper I am traveling this road"—and I tried my hand with her first; but she was sullen and uncooperative without her master, and after a while I put her away and went back to my own dear one. In times of sorrow the familiar things are best.

After that the days went by slowly. King Clydno lingered on in Manau for no reason that I could see, riding out about his lands in a desultory fashion, now east to Alloa to visit his fledgling monastery there, now south into Bannawg for a day's hunting, but always coming back at evening to Caer Iddeu. Now and again he took me with him, and asked me questions about Rhun mab Maelgwn

Gwynedd and the other lands and princes of the South. If he felt any interest or concern about his half-brother, he did not share it with me; indeed he hardly mentioned Neirin at all, and I was not in a position to inquire of his motives or intentions.

Instead I made acquaintances in the retinue, and began to learn a few words of Pictish from Erp, the dark young warrior Neirin had pointed out to me, and who I found had been one of his childhood friends. I also came to the attention of Cenau, their *penteulu*, who liked my bloodier Irish tales and honored me with a seat beside him at the feasting. He was a grim young man some few years older than I myself, but a tough, experienced fighter, related by blood to Urien Rheged though his cousin Llywarch Hên. A chance remark about swords led to him giving me lessons most evenings; he had a sure hand and a quick eye, and his teachings saved my life more than once in after years.

Six or seven days after Neirin left, I began sleeping badly. I would wake in the middle of the night from some confused dream of darkness and pain, with my heart pounding and the cold sweat running on my body, and Neirin's voice still ringing in my ears, calling my name. Then I would lie awake, trying somehow to make contact with him in my turn, but without success. After a few days the dreams came less often, and less intensely, and this worried me still more. I did not think Neirin was dead, but I did not know what to do; the truth was I could do nothing, either to learn his fate or to help him, and it fretted me unbearably. I finally admitted as much one afternoon to Erp, with whom I had grown friendly, when he asked me what was wrong. To my surprise he took it seriously, but he had no more of a solution to my problem than I did; all we could do was wait, and that we did most anxiously as the days crept by.

At last the news came, and it was bad. I knew it as soon as I saw the dust cloud approaching up the white summer road, if only by the speed of its motion; no good news would travel at that pace. I knew it still more by the look of the horsemen when they came in sight: by their grim faces, and their dirt-spattered armor and clothing, and their hard-driven horses. And I knew it most of all by the face of Talorc son of Uoret when he dropped down from his mount in Clydno's courtyard: a Talorc who seemed ten years older than the bright-clad messenger of half a moon ago, with a bitter mouth, and grief-shadowed eyes, and dark travel-stained clothing. "Lord King," he said as soon as he saw Clydno Eidyn, "I bring you ill news: the embassy has failed, and your brother is held hostage. All the rest were slain, save only one, who was sent back, grievously wounded, to bear the tale."

"That is ill news indeed," said Clydno. "How did it happen?"

"By the gravest misadventure," said Talorc. "One who rode in our party had lately lost his brother to a feud. There in King Mailchon's court he saw his brother's slayer, and recognized him by a silver chain he was wearing, which had been the dead man's badge of office in his tribe; and seeing the murderer alive and exalting, as he thought, in his triumph, this man lost his discipline and his reason, and drew his sword and attacked his brother's killer. The fight became general, and many died, including all of our party except one man of the retinue, and your brother Neirin."

"Was my half-brother injured?" asked Clydno, still with an unmoved countenance and nothing but curiosity in his voice.

"Lord King, I do not know," said Talorc, his own eyes bright with unshed tears. "The one who brought the news did not see the end of the fight; he knew only what his captors told him before they brought him to the border and set him free. They said they were holding your brother for a great head-ransom, because he was in charge of the embassy; they are demanding the honor-price of a prince. And my King will pay it," said Talorc in a voice of bitter shame, "because it was he who sent your brother into this peril, and because it was a man of his own choosing who caused this disaster! I come only to bring the news; what we have wrought for you we will attempt to mend. I will not stay to longer trouble your peace." And with that he turned to his horse, whose bridle he still held, and groped rather blindly for the saddle-horn.

"Wait, Lord!" I said into Clydno's continuing silence. "Let me come with you." And I ran up and grasped the old man's arm to keep him from mounting.

Talorc stared at me blankly, and after a moment recognition moved in his ravaged face. "You are the Storyteller," he said, "the young man's friend. Yes, get your gear, you may ride north with us."

"Wait!" said Clydno Eidyn. "Gwernin, you would do better to bide here, and let the Picts resolve what they have made. This is none of your business."

"Na, but it is!" I said, turning toward him, and my voice sounded harsh in my own ears. "I do not leave my brother in peril, whatever you may do, Lord King. I have stayed here idle long enough!"

Clydno gazed at me for a moment in astonishment, as if I had struck him; then he shrugged. "Take some of my *teulu* with you; I will not have it said I sent you out alone."

"I will take two, at least, if they will come," I said, looking around the courtyard. "Erp? Cenau? Will you ride this trail with me?"

"Of course," said Clydno's *penteulu* with his grim smile, and "*Sa, sa,* most gladly," said Erp, and went to saddle our horses without more ado. So in a little while the three of us rode north with Talorc and his company, on our way to Dundurn and King Nechtan's court, leaving Clydno Eidyn silent still behind us.

But that, O my children, is a story for another day.

Gold and Steel and Silver

The honor-price of the King of Gwynedd (or so say the judges) is one hundred white cows and a red-eared bull for every cantref that he rules, and a rod of gold as tall as the King himself and as thick as his little finger, and a plate of gold as broad as the King's face; and the price of the King's son and heir is a third that of the King himself, but without the gold. The Picts, however, though fond of cows, were even more fond of silver, and so their valuation was different—though not as different as all that, as I found to my dismay. Even three hundred cows take a lot of driving, and leave a lot of cow-dung behind them, not to mention the trouble that may be caused by the bulls. And then there was the metal…

"Three rods of gold as long as the King's arm, and as thick as his thumb; and nine times their weight of silver. Five hunting horns, mounted and stemmed with silver, and all with silver fittings on their straps. Five silver chains of office, each double-linked and as long as the King's fore-arm. And five swords with gold and silver and precious stones set on their hilts and scabbards, each as good as that carried by the King himself. Gold and steel and silver: that is what we will be taking," said Talorc to me as we drew near to Dundurn that evening. "We will need a little while to gather it all together, but not one minute longer than we must. The cattle drivers started yesterday, as soon as we heard the terms."

"That is a mighty ransom for one man," I said. "Who will go with it?"

"I myself, and no other," said Talorc, and his lean, sad face with its pointed graying beard seemed to harden as he spoke. "It is my right."

"It is my right to go also," I said firmly. "Neirin is my friend."

Talorc looked at me for a moment, and then nodded. "Yes. You may go with me, and your two followers if they wish; if four of us are not enough, an army would do no better. But I wonder, I wonder…"

"What?" I asked after a moment. "What do you wonder?"

"Whether any of us will come safe home again." And he sighed, and turned his face toward the distant fortress.

"Talorc," I said after a while, "if your people have a series of honor-payments, why do you have blood feuds? In Powys or Gwynedd, if a man is killed, the kinship must pay *galanas*. Does that not happen here?"

"It does, and it does not," said Talorc, and his mouth looked as if he had bitten into a sloe. "Within the tribes there is such justice, most of the time. Sometimes within a kingdom, if the King is very strong, as our King Nechtan is now. But between kingdoms, who shall judge, and who shall enforce payment? And Mailchon of Ce just now is old, and his grip on his people is weak, and his lords see the chance to lead raids for their own enrichment, and do not count the cost. I hoped that this embassy would perhaps be a way forward out of the bloodshed; I hoped for too much, and I fear that your friend has paid the price of my folly."

"What do you mean?" I asked. "Surely when we bring the ransom, they will let Neirin go?"

"They may," said Talorc, "if he is still alive." And with that we reached the gates of Dundurn, and spoke no more for a while.

Nechtan the King of the Southern Picts held great state. In his high hall that night, bright with mead and torches, I was honored as a prince, when all I wished for was food and bed and sleep, and to hasten north as soon as might be. He seated me at his left hand, and spoke gravely to me of Neirin, his youth and brilliance and beauty, until I felt like a fellow-mourner at a funeral feast. As soon as I could I fled to my lodging to avoid such consolation, taking Cenau and Erp—who had feasted with Nechtan's war-band, and therefore were more cheerful—with me. "Friends," I said to them then, over a cup of wine—Cenau, with his usual forethought, had brought some with him from the hall—"if you have any good counsel, give it to me now, for I need it."

Cenau looked at me and then at Erp, and they nodded. "My counsel would always be, 'Do not despair!' " he said, with a twisted smile on his square brown face. "If these folk were sure that Neirin mab Dwywei was dead, I do not think they would be gathering his ransom in such haste. Trust in the Good God, I say, and in a sharp sword—but mainly in the sword!" And he gave a short bark of laughter, then sobered. "Na, na, Storyteller, you know that you can count on both of us to the last drop of our blood, for the love that we bear him. I remember him before he left Dun Eidyn, a bright boy-child proud of his first spear, eager and open, and I new-come to his father's *teulu* as I was then."

"*Sa, sa,*" said Erp, his dark eyes smiling, "and I knew him younger than that; I was in the boy-pack with him. Never a mean thought or action in him, Neirin *bach.*" And he gave a soft laugh. "But I do not think this is the sort of counsel you wanted, Story-teller."

"Indeed, friends, it is not," I said, and felt myself close to weeping. "As for me, you know my heart—I showed it clear enough to Clydno Eidyn this morning. But I am glad you are with me. Have they lodged you well?"

"With great honor," said Cenau. "Gwernin, I know you are worried, and you are right to be so. Rest you now, so well as you may, and we will do the same: that is the best service you can give Neirin tonight, for I think tomorrow we ride north, and in some haste. Good night to you now." And he clapped me on the shoulder with his hard hand, and went out taking Erp with him. After a moment I pulled off my boots and tunic and lay down, and did my best to sleep. But all that night I dreamed I was seeking Neirin through some dark place of mists and shadows: seeking, and not finding. And glad I was when the sky beyond my window paled toward dawn, and I could arise.

Nevertheless, it was midday before we rode out, I on Taliesin's black pony and Talorc on a tall bay mare who over-topped Du by at least two hands. The gold and silver and other treasures were loaded on packhorses for faster traveling, and a dozen men from the retinue went with us to lead and guard and tend them, though their task would end at the border; beyond that point only the four of us would go on. A fine summer's day it was, warm and dry and breezy, and the corn-fields shining green-golden with approaching harvest in the sunlight, but I noticed it no more than I would have snow or rain. All my mind was bent on Neirin. Halfway up Dyffryn Mawr we made it that day; the next day would see us up with the cattle drive, and the day after that to the border. It could not be too soon for me.

By the time we reached it, I was heartily sick of cows: their sight, their sound, their smell, and above all their dung. The three hundred of our herd left a squishy trail up the great valley, roughly centered on the faint trace of the old road, a buzzing, fly-mad carpet of muck from which our ponies' hooves kicked up a continual splatter of greenish-brown filth. The bulls, of course, caused their own special problems, each wanting to fight the others for control of the herd, but the efforts of three teams of cow-herds with raw-hide ropes and tethers had so far prevented any final disaster, though I was more than once reminded of the ending of the Táin Bó Cúailnge. Still I had to admit that the moving mass of black cattle made a fine sight—from a distance!—against the summer-green landscape, but I was not sorry when we crested the final hill and the herdsmen drove their charges into their improvised enclosure on the wide flat bluff above the sea, a little way north of the old fort of Dun Nottar, where the Cowie Water comes down from the hills to form the border between North and South Pictland. Nor was I sorry to leave them all to the cow-herds, and ride down to the fort with Talorc and my two friends to spend the night with the local lord.

It was in Dun Nottar that I came face to face with the grim reality of what had befallen Neirin's party. Until then I had only been prey to my own fears and imaginings; there I saw the thing itself, in the shape of Anile, the sole survivor of Neirin's retinue, and Talorc's youngest son.

He had been near to death when the Ce men brought him to the border, and his recovery was still uncertain. Loss of blood from his many wounds had weakened him, and even if he lived he might never ride to war again. The head wound which had felled him at last had taken from him the use of his left eye, but his remaining one brightened at the sight of his father when Talorc and I came into his room, and there was nothing wrong with his tongue.

"Na," he said in answer to our questions, "I am not sure how it started; I was not watching. It was Llif, I know, who was first to strike a blow against one of the Ce men, but as to who began it, I cannot say. Only that the rest of them drew and were on us so quickly, it seemed as if planned. Then there was tumult and shouting, and our men falling. Neirin tried to stop it—you could hear *him* over the battle-noise!—but the Ce men paid no heed, and gave no quarter. He and I were the last standing, and what came to him after I fell, I do not know."

"Was he wounded then, do you know?" I asked.

"A little, I think, but I could not be watching. We took all the blows for him that we could, because we were his bodyguard, but he is a good fighter, and fast. I saw him kill at least one man who would have had me otherwise."

"There is hope, then, that he lives," said Talorc, on his knees by his son's bed. "They would not else be demanding his ransom, surely."

"Where and when was the fight?" I asked.

"In the main hall of the court at Cromar—that is the chief dun of one of their sub-kings. We had just arrived, and were waiting for their King to come and greet us. I am not sure what delayed him. I remember, at the end, there were many more people rushing into the hall—the number of them sank my hopes of getting free—and two other voices were shouting, almost as loud as Neirin, and one of them a woman's! Not screaming, you understand, but shouting for us to stop! But little good we got by it. Then the sky fell on me, and I saw and heard no more." Anile closed his remaining eye wearily and sighed.

"All that you could do, I know you performed," said Talorc, squeezing his son's hand, and at the jerk of his head I went out and left them together. It was a while and a while before he joined me in the main hall for dinner, and his long, sad face was grimmer and sadder than ever, but he said no word more that evening about what we had heard.

Nottar fort stands on a headland, with sheer drops to the sea on all sides and only one narrow neck of land tying it to the bluff above. It was old when the Romans passed by, and has changed little since. I have seen few places in my travels more perfect for defense: one of them was Tintagel in Dumnonia. With strong walls around me, and a good dinner in my belly, and the sweet conviction that tomorrow, or the day after at most, I would be seeing Neirin again, I fell asleep that night to the crying of the gulls—fell asleep to dream.

In that dream I was an eagle flying high above the country, soaring on outstretched golden wings. I saw the blue sea breaking around Dun Nottar; I saw the hills to the north, and the broad green plains of Ce beyond them; and to the west I saw the mountains, heaving up their grim gray summits toward the sky. And a voice in my mind, which might have been Taliesin's, and might have been Gwydion's—odd that I had never noticed before how alike they were!—said clearly, "You must take the Eagle's Path. You must take it: there is no other road home." Then I was lying on my bed in Dun Nottar, blinking in the faint light from the window, and knowing that soon it would be day.

The Ce men were waiting for us that morning, standing around a campfire on the far bank of the Cowie. A good number of them there were, not much different to look at than our own lot. Three of them were clearly in authority, judging by their bearing, and the bright colors of their clothing, and the way the others deferred to them. The one who caught my eye, though, was a big burly man dressed in a red and orange checker, and darker even than the run of his fellows. Talorc, seeing him, said dryly to me, "Finaet Du, son of Girom: a sub-king to Mailchon, and his chief rival. Do not trust him."

He and I rode down to the bank of the stream, and stopped there. Behind us were the retinue with the packhorses, and the cowherds getting their charges in motion. Talorc called out in a voice like a trumpet, which I would hardly have expected from so lean and old a man as he, "Behold, I am Talorc son of Uoret, come from my King and Lord, Nechtan son of Drustan of Dundurn, bringing the ransom demanded for our ambassador Neirin mab Cynfelyn. Who among you speaks for Mailchon son of Bridei?" And he repeated it in the Pictish tongue. The echoes bounced back from the hills, and for a moment all men were silent, leaving only the cries of the gulls over the saltings and the sounds of the restless cattle to break the morning quiet.

Then Finaet hailed back, first in Pictish and then in British: "Finaet son of Girom am I: I speak for Mailchon son of Bridei. Bring the ransom forth!"

"*Ie*, we will do so," called Talorc. "But come you first to meet me."

"I come," said Finaet, and mounted a tall black horse held for him by one of his followers, and rode down the short way to the stream, stopping with the horse's forefeet in the water. "Speak!"

"Good," said Talorc in a lower voice. "This is Gwernin Storyteller, blood-brother and friend to Neirin mab Cynfelyn, come from Dun Eidyn with his two followers to see that all goes fairly in this exchange—I am speaking in British now for his benefit, for he does not know our tongue. The four of us will bring the gold and steel and silver to your King Mailchon ourselves; the cattle you may drive. Are you ready for them?"

"I am," said Finaet. "Have your men drive them through the ford and we will take them. But first show me what you carry with you."

"Am I a merchant, to unload my packs for your approval?" asked Talorc haughtily. "We will show it to your King Mailchon when we arrive at his court; if he is dissatisfied he may say so then."

Finaet's bushy eyebrows rose in surprise, then he nodded. "Well enough: if you bring short weight, on your head be it." And he turned back to call out something to his men in Pictish. Then to us: "We are ready."

"It is good," said Talorc, and turning to the cow-herds waved his arm in a "forward" gesture. "Come you on, Gwernin. I think we will ride ahead of the cattle today." And with that he spurred forward splashing into the stream, and I followed him, with Cenau and Erp behind me leading the pack-strings. At least today we would not be riding knee-deep in cow-shit; I grinned a little to myself at the thought.

That day we rode a long trail, first up the Cowie Water and over the border hills, and then by various ways through thick-growing oak and alder along a broad, east-flowing river—the River Dee—while all the time the hills rose higher and higher before us and to our left, growing at last into mountains. Now and then we passed villages with their corn-lands lush around them, for this was a rich land, and packs of dogs and children came out to bark and stare. Towards the end of the day, riding now in the blue shadows of the mountains, we splashed through a pebbly ford in the river to follow a muddy track which led us northwest, alongside a frog-loud marsh, to a quiet green valley. Ahead of us, at the very foot of the mountains, I saw a *llys* of some kind: a low wooden wall enclosing a wooden hall and various out-buildings. Torches flared at its gates in the summer twilight, and the breeze was fragrant with wood-smoke and the smell of roasting meat, and the faint cool mountain scent of pines. Wearily we rode into the courtyard in Finaet's wake, and reined our tired ponies to a halt, and men ran to take our bridles. Finaet spoke a few words to Talorc, who turned to me and said, "This is Cromar valley, one of King Mailchon's courts. He says, dismount and be welcome."

Stiffly I slid down from my black pony, and nodded to Cenau and Erp. "It seems we are here—wherever 'here' is. Let them unload the ponies, but keep close. And Erp"—gesturing the dark man closer—"do not you be letting them know that you understand them, if they do not know already."

Erp gave me a quick, tight smile. "Na, the same thought was in my own mind, and I have been very stupid today whenever they spoke to me; they do not know." And he and Cenau took our gear from behind our saddles, and came over to stand beside me while the local men unpacked the led ponies and carried the heavy bundles into the hall ahead of us, with Talorc and the rest of us following.

At the far end of King Mailchon's hall was a sort of raised platform, and on it a heavy chair and several stools and benches. In the chair sat a gray-bearded man, very richly dressed in checkered clothes of red and blue and purple, who could only be the King himself. He looked up curiously at us as we came, and then his eyes slid sideways to Finaet, and for a moment I could have sworn I saw fear in his face. Behind him stood several persons, but two in particular caught my eye. One was a thin dark man dressed in a long gray-white woolen robe, and wearing on his breast a strange lunate necklace composed of many carved and polished pieces of jet, as bright and as black as his eyes. The other was a tall woman in early middle age in a dark blue robe of fine-spun wool, thickly embroidered around cuffs and throat with a pattern of red and gold threads which shimmered like silk in the firelight. Unlike the rest, these two kept their gaze on us as we walked up and stopped behind the bearers of the ransom; nor did they look down except briefly as the packs were opened and their precious contents spread before the King.

"Three rods of gold as long as our King's arm, and as thick as his thumb; and nine times their weight of silver," said Talorc, speaking as before in Pictish and then in British. "Five hunting horns, mounted and stemmed with silver, and all with silver fittings on their straps. Five silver chains of office, each double-linked and as long as our King's forearm. And five swords with gold and silver and precious stones set on their hilts and scabbards, each as good as that carried by our King. This, and the cattle which are following behind us, is the ransom demanded for Neirin son of Cynfelyn. Is it complete?"

"It is," said King Mailchon in a thin, rusty voice. "You have discharged your duty." And his tongue came out for a moment and licked his lips, as if they were dry. "The debt which was owing to us for the blood shed has been paid, and that is good. But sorry I am to tell you that you have had your journey in vain: Neirin mab Cynfelyn is dead."

He had spoken, like Talorc, first in Pictish and then in British, but even before he translated I knew what he had said: it was in the tone of his voice, and his half-sorrowful, half-frightened expression. It struck me like a blow beneath the ribs, and for a moment I could not draw my breath. Then, even as my ears heard and my mind grasped the sense of what he had said, my heart rejected it. "No!" I said. "No! He cannot be! I will not believe it!"

The people on the dais looked at me with various expressions—surprise, curiosity, pity, incomprehension, and on Finaet's part even a sort of satisfaction. I stared back at them, my heart pounding loud in my ears. Then Talorc turned to me and grasped my arm in a strong clasp. "I am sorry, Gwernin," he said. "This is what I feared all along. I should not have let you come."

"Ask them"—I struggled to get my breath—"ask them, when did he die? Where is his body? I will not believe it unless I see him dead." There was some brief conversation in Pictish, to which I paid no heed. Then Talorc said, "They say that he died three days ago, after Finaet left for the border. They cannot show us his body; it is high summer, and they did not know that we would come so soon. They buried him with all reverence; he is in the dark earth now, under the ground. They will show us the place tomorrow. I am sorry, Gwernin; there is nothing left to see, nothing left to show."

The tall woman spoke from behind the King. "She offers condolences," said Talorc. "She will herself take us to our lodgings and send food and drink to us. Tomorrow, when we are rested, she will answer any other questions we have. Will you come with her now?"

"Yes," I said helplessly; there was nothing else to say. I realized that I was weeping, hot tears running down my face in streams. Half-blinded, I followed the tall woman out of the hall and across the courtyard to a wooden building inside the stockade. In the doorway I turned back to Talorc. "Who is she?"

A question, a response. "She is Inoide," said Talorc. "She is sister to King Mailchon."

"Thank her for me," I said, meeting the woman's eyes. There was sadness in them, and sympathy, but also anger. It seemed a strange combination, but my mind was too numb just then to puzzle out its meaning. Only later did I find the answer, and it came not a moment too soon.

But that, O my children, is a story for another day.

Galanas

I have known sorrow and heartbreak enough in my long life, but few nights as bad as that one in King Mailchon's *llys* in Cromar valley, after they told me that Neirin was dead. For a long time I could not take it in. I did not want food, I did not want drink, I did not want company; I only wanted to sit and weep, and my companions considerately left me to it. In so far as I had a coherent thought, it was to wonder what Taliesin would say when I brought him the news. He had sent me along to help Neirin, and I had failed: failed both of them, and failed myself as well. I should never had stayed behind at Caer Iddeu, I thought, forgetting that I had had no choice; although how I, as poor a swordsman as ever carried a blade, could have helped in that desperate fight, not even my guilty heart knew. At last I stretched out fully-clothed on top of my blankets, and eventually fell asleep from pure exhaustion.

Again I dreamed, but this time I was no eagle. Instead I was a drop of rain in the air, sparkling as I fell. Below me was a wide green countryside, lying cool and clean in the morning sun; I saw Cromar *llys* with its village and fields about it, and nearby on a hill a ring of tall gray stones. At the foot of that hill were graves: old grassy ones, and also raw new ones: half a dozen in one place, and in another, one large mound, as if for many people, and a single grave beside it. I fell toward the single grave, but before I reached it I heard a voice—Taliesin's or Gwydion's, I was not sure which— saying, "He is not there: he is under stone and under sod, sleeping in the darkness." And the dream dissolved into darkness in its turn, and I awoke in my dark room; only just for a moment the voice in my mind was Neirin's, sleepily calling my name. Then it was gone, and I lay on my blankets wide-eyed and awake, and unsure of the truth. After a while I got up and went out through the dawn-gray courtyard to the well, where I drew cold water to wash my hot face and stay my empty belly until breakfast. I did not hope, and I did not despair; I waited for what the day might bring.

Eventually it brought food. First there was the stirring of sleepy girls around the kitchen-place near the hall, then the smell of fresh wood-smoke as the ovens were heated, and eventually the wonderful scent of baking bread. In the feast-hall the *teulu* rolled out of their blankets and stowed them away, and wandered out into the early sunshine by ones and twos, scratching tousled hair and heading for the latrines. In the stables the horses neighed in anticipation of their morning feed, and the stable lads went back and forth with wooden buckets, whistling. In the huts around the walls of the *llys*, and in the village outside, I heard the shouts of children, awake before their parents and already at play. And in the guest-quarters behind me, my friends woke up, dressed and groomed themselves, and came forth with sad faces to see where I had gone. They seemed relieved to see me more myself, and joined me on my way to the hall, where the first food was now being set out on the trestle tables. None of us had much to say for ourselves, but sat in silence and ate a gloomy breakfast.

As we were finishing, Finaet Du came up to us, his orange and red clothes bright in the dim light of the hall. "Good day to you all," he said to us in British, and then something in Pictish at which Talorc frowned. I was happy to see Erp beside him keep a neutral expression, as though not understanding. The next minute, however, I lost any desire to smile. "Are you ready, then," asked Finaet, "to see the graves? I will have your horses saddled."

"Is it so far?" asked Talorc, still frowning.

"Not far, if you do not mind muddy fields," said Finaet, grinning. "I prefer to keep my boots clean. Will you walk or ride?"

"We will ride, then. You may," said Talorc smoothly, "tell the boys to saddle our horses. We will meet you in the courtyard when we have finished eating."

Finaet's eyes flashed and his mouth tightened, then he mastered himself. "That will be soon enough," he said, and grinning left the hall. Talorc reached for another piece of crusty bread and refilled his cup, although I knew he had been about to rise. Meeting my eyes, he said, "To hurry is not good."

"No, indeed," I replied, taking more cheese. Almost Talorc smiled.

When we finally came out into the courtyard our horses were waiting, held by two stable-boys, but Finaet Du was nowhere to be seen. He rode up as we were mounting. "Ha!" he said. "Are you ready at last? Come on, then." And without waiting for an answer, he turned his horse for the gateway and rode out, leaving us to follow as we would.

Catching up, I said to him, "I thought the King's sister—what was her name? Inoide?—was going to escort us this morning."

"She has other duties," said Finaet, showing all his fine teeth in what might have been a smile. "You will find me a better companion."

"Can you tell us, then, what rites were used to bury them?" asked Talorc on his other side. "Your people and mine, I know, worship the same gods, but Gododdin"—with a glance at me—"follows the Christus."

"We buried them all the same way," said Finaet shortly. "If a Christian priest wishes to say prayers here later, we will give him safe-conduct."

"That will be good enough," I said. My throat was tight, and I doubted my dream: why should these people lie?

"What of the mission on which they came?" asked Talorc after a while. "Eight young men's lives on our side, and—how many?—on yours? Are they to be thrown away?"

"I am not High King of the North, to negotiate with you," said Finaet brusquely. "Ask Mailchon when you see him. But I would say, lives have been thrown away before, and will be again. You have paid for the damage your eight did; for that, we will give you peace, for a while."

"And for their deaths? Who will pay *galanas* for that?" asked Talorc. "I say that what was done to them was as unlawful as what they did. Where is the balance?"

"Not with me," said Finaet, drawing rein. "Look, here we are now at the graveyard! Take up these matters with King Mailchon later; I have done my work." And turning his horse, he urged it into a canter back toward the *llys*, leaving us staring after him.

The arrangement of the graves was much as I had seen it in my dream, except that the six at one end and the shared grave at the other were covered with large stones. Two or three men were taking more stones from a cart and piling them on the last single grave, which must be Neirin's. *Under stone and under sod...* What of my dream now? I blinked back the tears that sprang unbidden to my eyes, and swung down from my pony. The laborers looked up incuriously, then backed away as I came toward them. "Whose grave is this?" I asked the eldest, pointing. "On whom do you pile the stones?"

He answered something I could not understand, and after a moment Talorc, coming behind me, translated. "He does not know, he only does the work he was told to do. He was not here for the burying; he lives across the valley and works at his lord's direction. Finaet is his lord."

"Thank you," I said numbly to Talorc, and to the workmen, "Thank you." They nodded, smiling. "Could you ask them if they would wait—if I might be alone here for a few minutes?" Talorc was already translating. The workmen's smiles vanished; they nodded and walked away. I stood for a moment, trying to clear my mind, trying to listen, but it was no good. I was too aware of my friends behind me, and of my own troubled heart; of the hot sun on my shoulders, and the smell of crushed grass and damp earth; of the fierce cry of the hawk circling overhead, and the beat of my own blood; of the thousand and one things that lay between me and Neirin, alive or dead. *He is sleeping in the darkness...* I shook my head and turned away, to meet Talorc's concerned and sympathetic gaze. "Let us go back," I said hoarsely, and he nodded. All the way back to the *llys* we spoke no word.

When we entered the courtyard, Finaet Du was sitting lazily on a bench in the corner, picking his teeth with a sliver of wood and watching two of his *teulu* square up at sword practice under the eye of their captain. They were using wooden practice swords, much like the ones Neirin and I had worked with earlier that summer: swords that could bruise but not kill. My heart hurt me at the memory. I wanted to scream, or fight, or drink until I was drunk, or sleep: anything to take away the pain. If I had brought my harp, I might have lost myself in music; but even that reminded me piercingly of Neirin. We had been too much together that summer, too much in each other's minds; it was like losing a part of myself.

"*Storyteller!*" I whipped around to see Finaet beckoning me. "Something for you," he said in a lower voice as I came up. And picking up a sheathed sword from the bench beside him, he tossed it at me. I caught it without thinking, then looked at what I held. It was Neirin's. I looked up again to meet Finaet's contemptuous gaze. "Keep it," he said, "in memory of your *friend*." He used another word than *friend*, a word I will not repeat here. My face slowly reddened; I grasped the hilt and started to draw the sword. Cenau's hand on my wrist stopped me. I struggled for a moment, but he was immovable as the mountains. "Not now, Gwernin," he said. Then looking at Finaet, who had not stirred from his lounging position, "Vengeance will come in its time. Come away."

Drawing a ragged breath, I sheathed Neirin's sword again, and turned to follow Cenau. Behind me I heard Finaet laugh.

The day seemed endless, but we could not leave until at least the next morning, after the cattle had arrived and been counted. Taking pity on me, Cenau took me aside for sword practice, and under his patient teaching I found in time a measure of calm, if not of peace. He worked me hard, himself barely raising a sweat. "You need to *do*," he said, "not think so much." Next he set Erp to partner me, while he stood by, coaching us both. Some of the *teulu* wandered past and stopped to watch, joking among themselves and making friendly bets on the outcome. When at last Cenau called a halt, my right arm was trembling with weariness; I still wanted to kill Finaet, but I was too tired to try.

The afternoon I spent in the stables, grooming my black pony until he shone like polished jet. This also was Cenau's idea. "Stable-boys are all very well for feeding and mucking out," he had said, "but they are not going to *ride* the horse, maybe into battle where you life depends on him. For that, you should know every inch of him, and he should know you." And by the end of the afternoon it was so. Good mindless work it was, steady and soothing, just what I needed. I had grown up with horses, and thought myself knowledgeable enough, but I learned some new things that day. Whatever Cenau did, he did thoroughly and well. I was to be glad of that later.

Coming back from the stables, I met Talorc, looking very sleek. His long face was as sad as ever, but there was a certain light in his dark eyes that I had not seen there before. Questioned, he laughed, and said that he had tried to speak to King Mailchon, to no avail, but had instead spent the afternoon talking with the King's sister. "She is a very fine woman," he said, "intelligent and forthright as a man. Pity it is that she is not King in her brother's place; she would do much better!"

"Do the Picts, then, have she-kings, as some of the British tribes once did?" I asked, remembering the legends of Boudicca.

"Na, but if a king has no living sons, the rule sometimes passes through the female line. And Mailchon, I think," said Talorc thoughtfully, "is childless. The man who married his sister would have a strong claim to the kingship."

"Has she not been married long since?" I asked; she seemed quite old to me.

"She has, but her husband died, and she had borne him no sons. She lives and travels with her brother now—and that is a great waste, for she is a very fine woman." There was a certain gleam in Talorc's eye that I was to remember later, but my mind was elsewhere.

"Was she there at the fight, when Neirin—when Neirin's men were killed?" I asked.

"She was. She it was who stopped it, she and Broichan the Druid, but too late. She told Finaet Du that to kill a Bard was the worst of ill luck, or he would have finished your friend then and there. And it is to her," said Talorc seriously, "that I owe my son's life. She and her people staunched his wounds and sent him back to the border as her brother's messenger. But Neirin she could not save; Finaet insisted that he stay here as surety for the ransom."

"Maybe," I said slowly, "he would have died anyway, but I wish—I wish … that I could have seen him once again."

"Indeed, our loss is great," said Talorc solemnly. "He borrowed a harp and sang for us, that one night at Dundurn before they set out. I have never heard a finer bard, and I have heard many."

I nodded silently, once more fighting my tears. After a moment I said, "Does the King sit in hall tonight?"

"He does," said Talorc. "You should go and make ready, for you and I will sit with him at table. Make yourself fine, in memory of your friend: that is the best way to honor him. I know: I have lost many a one in my time, my dear wife included. The pain does not diminish with custom."

I took Talorc's advice and dressed in my best that night. It was not much, nothing to compare with Neirin's red and blue checker, or his polished black leathers, but such as it was, I wore it: my brown and black patterned wool tunic, and Owain's best trews beneath it. I polished my belt and boots as well as I could, but they were old and scuffed; I should have to get myself new ones when I could. I looked longingly at Neirin's fine sword in its jeweled sheath, but that was no thing to wear at a king's table, and in the end I left it in my bed-place, covered by my blankets. My long hair—light brown it was in those days, and bleached pale by the summer sun—I tied back on my neck with a thong. Then I put on a bold face, and went out to join my friends in Mailchon's hall.

I would have liked to have offered to tell a tale at the feast, not least to occupy my own mind with my craft, but few of the Pictish court had any British; and though I might have borrowed a harp from one of their musicians, I had not Neirin's gift, to hold a hall enthralled by sound alone. Instead I sat quietly at Talorc's side,

eating and drinking what came my way, although with little appetite.
We were seated at Mailchon's left hand; on his right was Finaet Du,
and beyond him again the King's sister, Inoide—or at least that was
her place, for she came unaccountably late to dinner, and rose often
to deal with some detail or other of the feast. Beyond Finaet's bulk
I could see little of her, but I gained the impression that she was not
pleased with him. At one point I heard her loudly say something
which sounded like "No!" Startled, I looked at Talorc, and saw him
frowning. "What is passing there?" I asked him.

"Do not seem to notice," said Talorc quietly. "He has tried, I
think, to tell her her duties, and she has rebuffed him. It is not for
him to offer the guest-cup or to withhold it, here at the King's
feasting, however much this may be his Dun. Go on, eat, nothing
has happened, you have not seen it."

Frowning in my turn, I took a piece of deer-meat at random
from my bowl and chewed it thoroughly, then swallowed it. "What
are they not saying now?" I asked.

The corners of Talorc's mouth quirked up beneath his mustache, but he took a morsel from his own bowl in turn, inspected it,
and ate it. "They are not talking about a certain herd of cows, who
are not causing trouble. It could not be that three of those great
horned beasts did not wish to leave their homeland."

I did my best to suppress a laugh, and turned it into a cough.
"Such a thing would be most unfortunate and unlikely," I said when
I could speak.

"Indeed it would," said Talorc, but he was frowning again.
"Wait, be quiet, listen." Startled, I looked beyond him, in time to
see the lady Inoide, her face carefully blank but her whole body
expressing outrage, rise up from her seat and leave the hall. Beside
her Finaet Du also rose, but paused, and at a word from King
Mailchon took his seat again. His face was flushed, whether from
anger or mead I could not tell, but he did not look rebuked. Instead
he ran his brooding gaze around the hall, as one who counts his
allies and his enemies, and his mouth moved in a smile within the
frame of his black beard. Then he pulled his heavy silver cup

toward him and sat sipping his mead until King Mailchon rose and left the table.

That night in the guest-house I sat for a long time with Neirin's sword across my lap, stroking the sheath now and then as I might have fondled a harp. Over and over I vowed, by my blood and my gods and the *awen* I held sacred, that I would have Black Finaet's life in exchange for Neirin's, even at the cost of my own. Somehow, before we left this place, I would do it; I would take vengeance. At last, weary in body and mind, I lay down with the sword beside me and slept.

I did not, as it happened, carry out my vow. But that, O my children, is a story for another day.

The Earth-House

I am not sure how long I slept—it cannot have been long—before I became aware of a tapping on the door of my room. While I was still fighting my way up from the depths of sleep, the door opened quietly, and Erp slipped in, carrying a rush-light in his hand. Groggily I threw back my blankets and sat up, half-naked, on the edge of my bed. "What do you want?" I asked.

"To tell you what I have overheard by being stupid," said Erp. "Gwernin, I think—I *think*—there is someone being held prisoner in this place."

"What do you mean?" I asked, blinking. "What did you overhear?"

"It was one of the servants in the kitchen, asking another if he had yet taken the food to the *tŷ-deyerin*, the earth-house." Erp frowned, trying to make himself clear. "That is a sort of underground store-place we build here in the north. Food is kept in it, yes, but usually things like grain, or cheese, or—or other things which have not been cooked. And the word he used was the word for *some* food—a meal. The amount you would take to a person for his dinner."

"Did you see where he went?" I asked.

"Na, I could not follow; they would have noticed me. But I am thinking it would not be far."

I ran a hand over my face, trying to think; my head felt thick with weariness. "Is it late yet? I have been asleep."

"Na, people are still about. We will have to wait for a while and a while, before we can look. Cenau would not have had me tell you, in case it is not—not Neirin, but I said you should know."

"Thank you, Erp," I said, and touched his shoulder briefly. "I will dress and stay here for now, to keep out of sight, but do you let me know when things are quiet, and I will be waiting."

"I know it well," said Erp, and smiled briefly, and was gone, slipping out of the room like a shadow, and leaving me to try and make sense of what was happening.

It seemed a long time before he came back, but at last he came, opening the door this time without tapping first, and slipping quickly through. "Gwernin? Are you ready?"

"Yes," I said, just above a whisper, and stood up. Erp's hand closed on my arm in the darkness—he had not brought a light this time—and tugged gently. "Come," he said. "Cenau is waiting."

"Have you told Talorc?" I asked, following him to the door.

"Na, let the old man get his sleep. Time enough to wake him if we—have any luck. Quiet, now." And we went out.

Cenau was waiting just around the corner, his sword belted on as usual and a cloak slung over his shoulder. He looked me up and down in the faint twilight—there is not much real darkness in the high north at that time of year—and nodded. Quietly we made our way towards the rear of the compound, stopping now and then in the shadows to listen. A blink of firelight in the hall and one or two sleepy voices showed where the men of the retinue were bedding down. There was no proper watch kept on the outer wall of the *llys*, only a sentry or two by the main gate. Kitchen, store-houses, stables, all were quiet. A moving shadow caused us once to freeze, but he was quickly gone, stumbling back from the privy on his way to bed. We passed the stables, the well, and more storehouses, still with no success, and I wondered if Erp had misunderstood the servants. Finally in the far corner of the court we saw it: a pit with sloping sides leading down into the earth. At its deepest end was a stone lintel, and a door in the shadows beneath it. Farther back, closer to the stockade, a sort of small stone chimney rose from a low, wide mound. "Ah," breathed Erp beside me. "That is it."

Quietly we made our way down into the pit. The wooden door was closed by a bar, but there was no lock. Cenau started to ease it open, then paused and pointed. On the center of the door a symbol was roughly daubed, in mud or something darker—a mark like a crescent moon, horns up. We stared at it a moment and exchanged glances; then Cenau shrugged and opened the door.

Inside was utter darkness. A breath of chill air flowed out around us, smelling faintly of smoked meat, and apples, and earth. "We must all go in," said Cenau softly, "before I can strike a light. Gwernin, you first, and be careful."

I put one hand tentatively on the wall inside the door, but it was clean dry stone. The thought that Neirin might be a prisoner in this tomb-like place pushed me onward. I found myself in what seemed to be a stone-lined tunnel, leading gradually downward and bending slowly to the right. Under my feet the floor was hard-packed earth. Stepping cautiously forward, I stumbled over something by one wall which felt to my groping hand like curved wood. Then there was a flicker of light from behind me, and I blinked. The light flared up, almost died, and then steadied, and Cenau came up behind me carrying a rush-light. In its wavering brightness the tunnel was suddenly much smaller, the stone slabs of the roof close above my head. The thing I had stumbled over was a barrel of early apples. "Neirin!" I called softly. "Are you here?" No answer. "Go on," said Cenau from behind me. "Here, take the light."

With this encouragement I started forward again. The tunnel continued to curve to the right; and now and then there were wider spaces in its left side, where more barrels and crocks and chests were stored. I was afraid to call again for fear of getting no answer; instead I walked on through the chill, stagnant air. Suddenly around a bend the tunnel widened out into a circular room and ended. Here there was a series of wooden beams and posts, offering additional support to the low roof; also many more barrels and boxes, filling most of the floor space. I saw a small circular opening in the ceiling near the center of the room, probably leading up to the chimney we had noticed earlier: an air vent. I was picking my way toward it when I heard something move near the far side of the room, something that made a brushing noise, as of cloth, and a faint metallic sound. "Neirin?" I whispered, holding the rush-light higher.

There was another movement, another clink of metal, and a pale face rose out of a tangle of blankets, blinking in the light.

"Gwernin?" said Neirin sleepily. "*Hai mai*, I thought you would never come! What has been keeping you?"

"Only a small matter of a ransom," I said on a sort of laugh, dropping to my knees beside him and almost extinguishing the rush-light in my haste. "I did not know the King's sister was so stricken in years, or I would surely have made more speed." I grasped his arm hard to make sure he was real, and felt him flinch. "Are you hurt?"

"Nothing that will not mend now," said Neirin, twisting a little in his blankets as if to find an easier position. "But I thought at one time I had got my killing. What have they told you, to bring you here seeking me at midnight?"

"They told me you were dead," I said, suddenly remembering. "Neirin, what has been happening here? What are they about?"

"Gwernin," said Cenau behind me, "do we want to take him and try to leave tonight, or not? I ask purely for information, you understand."

"That might be better," I said. "Neirin, can you walk?"

"I—am not sure," said Neirin, shifting position again. "But there is—a small problem." And throwing back the blankets, he thrust out his bare right leg with a metallic clinking, showing me the chain which led from a ring on his ankle to circle one of the posts that supported the roof—a heavy, solid iron chain which there would be no breaking, and no silent cutting through. "Not easy, this," said Neirin, and faintly grinned.

Cenau dropped down beside me to examine the chain while I was still staring. There was a sort of lock holding the shackle shut at one end, and a heavier one fastening the chain to itself around the thick post. "Huh," he said, trying his strength on both with no results. "A file might take this off, but I have none with me, and it would need much time. Who has the keys?"

"The King's sister, Inoide," said Neirin. "She, or Broichan the Druid. Have you seen them?"

"The dark man in the white robe, and the tall woman?" asked Cenau. "Yes, I saw them in the hall tonight. But where to find them now, with the court all asleep, I do not know. What do you think, Gwernin? Can this wait until tomorrow night?"

"I think that it must," I said, "though I hate the thought of it." I had one arm behind Neirin's shoulders, easing him back on his pillow. Even by rush-light I could see his pallor and the bruised hollows around his eyes. Under his tangled red hair his face was thinner than ever, and his left shoulder was heavily bandaged. Otherwise he seemed to be sound enough so far as I could see, although I did not throw back his blankets to check.

"Na, it is no great matter," he said, smiling up at me in understanding. "I can possess me in patience for yet one more day. But what are you planning to do, friends, after you get me my loosing? If they have told you I am dead, they will hardly let you bear me peacefully away to give them the lie. Moreover, I would not wish to flee like a thief in the night, who came here as an ambassador."

"But what do you mean?" I asked, bewildered by this flow of eloquence.

"I need to have speech with King Mailchon before I leave," said Neirin seriously. "I have had much time for thinking, these last few days, and there are things I must say to him. His sister agrees with me, but he will not heed her; from me it would maybe come with more force."

I blinked at this, and Cenau gave a sort of snort. But Erp, who had knelt quietly down on my left side and was checking Neirin's bandages with quick, deft fingers, only smiled. "*Sa, sa,*" he said softly. "If that is what you need, *gwas*, we will try to get it for you. Is there more?"

"I am thinking that will be quite enough," said Neirin with a weary grin. "Na, na, let be, Pictling, I am well enough. It is only the shoulder, and the blood-letting: nothing to concern you. Gwernin, the gods know my heart is glad at the sight of you, but I think perhaps you should take our friends away now. I leave the rest to your arranging: I am tired." And he yawned, and changed the yawn into a sigh, and sighing, closed his eyes.

"Well," I said, tucking the good woolen blankets back around him, "I must do my best. Rest you well until tomorrow." And I briefly touched his sound shoulder; then getting to my feet, I urged my friends out of the earth-house ahead of me, and left Neirin to his sleep.

Much of the rest of that night I spent thinking, and as soon after dawn as was reasonable I went seeking Talorc. He had been lodged in another small room close beside mine, I think to give me privacy in my grief. If he was surprised to see me so early and in such improved spirits, this was as nothing to his surprise when I poured out the story of my nocturnal adventures. Indeed he stared at me at first as though I had run mad, but as the tale unfolded, his eyes narrowed in thought and he frowned. "This is indeed a puzzle," he said when I had finished, "and I do not see the key, but I am sure that Finaet Du is behind it somehow. He has been threatening to upset the balance in Ce for a long time, and now here he is, very much to the fore, and Mailchon is afraid of him." And he fell to stroking his grizzled beard. "What do you plan to do?" he asked me suddenly.

"Get Neirin out of the *tŷ-deyerin* tonight, for a start," I said. "It is as being on thorns to me, to wait even that long. I do not trust these people, not any of them!"

"And you have reason," said Talorc. "Well, and then?"

I shrugged. "Find some way for Neirin to have speech with King Mailchon. If he says it is necessary, then so it is."

Talorc shook his head, but he was smiling. "Such faith the two of you have in each other! And after that?"

"Go south," I said firmly, "by whatever road we can." And suddenly in my mind I heard the voice from my dream—was it only three nights ago?—saying, *"Take the Eagle's Path!"* But what that meant I still did not know, and had now no time to ponder, for Talorc was speaking.

"I had better hold myself ready, then, to go with you," he was saying, still smiling faintly, "for I do not wish to stay on in the hornet's nest you will certainly leave behind you!"

My next task was to speak with the King's sister, but this must perforce wait until later in the morning. In the meantime, I had hard work at first to keep my demeanor appropriately gloomy, now that I knew Neirin was alive; but thinking on what he must have suffered in that hole in the ground soon made my face grim enough. In the event, it was easy to get speech with the Lady Inoide: she herself came up to me in hall, where I sat eating thick oatmeal porridge from a wooden bowl. "I would wish you good morrow, Gwernin," she said softly in the British tongue, "but I know it is not good, not to you. I promised the other night to answer any questions you still have about Neirin mab Cynfelyn and the way of his dying."

"I thank you, Lady," I said, abandoning my porridge without regret. "Might we go somewhere apart? I would not shame myself again by giving way to my grief in open hall."

"It was no shame," she said, smiling slightly. "But come with me; we can be private enough in my chamber." And she led me through a maze of hallways to a good-sized, wooden-floored room whose casement opened out over a small garden. "This is Utha," she said, nodding at an elderly woman who sat sewing by the window. "She helped to nurse your friend; I have no secrets from her. Sit here"—indicating one of a pair of stools, and seating herself on the other—"and ask me what you will."

I sat as she requested, but did not immediately speak. Instead I looked thoughtfully at her. She was dressed that day in brown, a deep russet brown like ripe chestnuts, which called out matching highlights in her still-dark hair. Her eyes were more hazel than green, changeable brook-water eyes, with a network of fine wrinkles at their corners. She was tall for a woman, taller than I was, and graceful with it; and it passed through my mind to wonder why she was, as it seemed, unwed; but I remembered Talorc saying that she was recently widowed and returned to her brother's house. She met my gaze squarely, and after a moment the corners of her mouth moved again in that slight smile. "Come, Gwernin, ask freely; or shall I begin? I know this is hard for you."

"I have only two questions to ask you, Lady," I said, reaching a decision. "First, why did your brother the King say that Neirin mab Cynfelyn is dead, when you know it is not so? I found him and spoke with him last night, after you were sleeping."

Her eyes widened, and she gave a small gasp of surprise, a slight, involuntary indrawing of the breath which said more than words. Then she smiled. "I did not think it would work," she said. "I told them it was not wise to play such tricks with bards, even bards so young as you yourself. Yes, my brother lied, but his reasons were not simple, and are not for me to tell. Your friend is in more danger than he knows." She frowned. "What will you do now?"

"Leave, as soon as I can manage it," I said frankly, "and take Neirin with me. And that brings me to my second asking: is it you or Broichan the Druid who keeps the keys to my brother's shackles?"

Involuntarily she laughed. "I suppose he told you himself to ask me that? It has the very flavor of his voice. Well, and it is Broichan. What else?"

"Neirin wants to talk with your brother before we leave," I said. "About what, he did not tell me, but I think you know. Can this be arranged?"

"Yes, I do know," she said, and sighed. "It will have to be in secret: sometime late tonight." She thought for a moment. "All five of you will be going, after that? What of the ransom, the gold and steel and silver, and the cows? You will not try to take it back with you?"

"Gold and steel and silver are of little account to me, beside my brother's life," I said. "And as for the cows"—I smiled a little, remembering our northward journey—"I would not lift a finger to retrieve them, even were they mine, which they are not. Keep them with my good will! But it would be well to take as much of Neirin's clothing and gear as might fit behind a saddle. Is his pony still in the stables?"

"The dappled gray? Yes, I think so. As for the clothes and gear, Utha shall bring them to your room openly this afternoon; it is only right, and no cause for wonder, that you should take your friend's belongings." She sighed. "I shall be sorry to see him go, but glad to have him out of danger. Even when he was in fever, and we were tending him, he would joke with us so! Utha shall take you to speak with Broichan now, and tell me what is decided. I will leave it until evening to talk to my brother; what he does not know, he cannot give away! Is there anything else?"

"No, Lady," I said, rising. "I thank you for your frankness, and all you have done for Neirin." And I smiled involuntarily at a memory.

"It was no hardship," said Inoide. "But what amuses you?"

"Before he left on this journey," I said, still smiling, "I teased him that I should need to come with him, to keep the King's sister from his bed, for he is a great one for the women; but I am glad I could not do so, though it was not a sick-bed I was meaning."

Inoide's answering smile sparkled in her hazel eyes. "Na, I think he would have been in no danger from me; but had I been twenty—or even ten!—years younger…" She laughed. "Away with you, you are as naughty as he! I will see you tonight in the hall; go now with Utha." And I followed the old woman out of the room.

Broichan the Druid lived apart in a small boothy towards the back of the compound and possibly older than it, a stone-and-thatch mound of a house half-sunk in the earth, and not far from the *tŷ-deyerin*. He was sitting on a bench against the house-wall when I came up—Utha had pointed out his dwelling to me from a distance and gone on about her business—and at first I did not see him, for instead of the long white robe of two nights before, he was wearing an ordinary woolen tunic dyed the same blue-gray as the stones behind him. Looking at him now in daylight and with my full attention, I realized that he was something new in my experience: an actual painted Pict. On both of his cheek-bones above his beard thin blue lines of tattooing formed the same up-turned crescent pattern as the jet necklace he had worn two nights before—the same pattern I had seen daubed on the door of the *tŷ-deyerin*. These, together with his strong, dark eyebrows and rather large nose, gave him somewhat the appearance of a startled owl, roused untimely and resenting it. The blue design was repeated on the backs of his hands, but nowhere else so far as I could see. He greeted me in very fair British, but with an Irish twang to it: "The light of the day on your path, Gwernin Storyteller. What is it that you are you seeking?"

"Knowledge, Lord, for a start," I said. "How shall I address you?"

"Oh, Broichan will do, lad." His manner was genial enough, but his eyes were watchful. "Or Brocc, as your people would have it. Knowledge, is it? Of something besides my calling-name?"

"Of something else indeed, Lord," I said, standing before him and blinking uncertainly in the bright sunlight as he sat at his ease in the shade. I was suddenly reminded of my first interview with Talhaearn, a year ago in Caer Deganwy. "May I sit down?"

Broichan smiled thinly. "Yes, sit and be welcome." And he nodded at the bench beside himself, and half turned to face me as I sat. Close up, his resemblance to an ill-tempered owl was even stronger. I reminded myself again that I had been stared down by better men than he, and met his gaze squarely. "I have come from the Lady Inoide," I said.

"Have you, now?" said Broichan. "And what brings you here to me?"

"Two keys that I need, and which she says you hold."

"Hmm," said Broichan, but I thought he blinked. "Keys, is it?" And he put up his left hand and stroked his short beard, much as Talorc had done earlier that morning. "And why should I give them to you?" he asked after a while.

"Because—" I said, and paused. It was a good question. Various answers trotted through my mind: threats of violence; offers of payment; appeals to sentiment, to honor, to the gods we both served in our own ways… "Because I need them to free my friend Neirin and take him home, and if I cannot get them I shall have to stay here with him, and maybe die with him, which I think will benefit no one. Will you give them to me?"

Broichan stared at me without moving for a moment longer, then his face relaxed into a smile. "And that is the truth, and the right answer," he said. "Yes, I will give them to you." And he stood up and went into the boothy, and came back in a moment with two iron keys in his hand. "When will you be planning to loose him?" he asked, giving them to me.

"Tonight, after things are quiet," I said, hardly able to believe in my success—but here the keys were, cool and heavy in my hand! "After that we will leave as soon as we can, as soon as Neirin has had speech with the King."

"Hmm," said Broichan again, sitting down beside me, and his eyebrows drew together in a frown. "Yes, it is probably better if he does, and yet…" He sighed, and looked sideways at me. "Which way are you going?"

"I—had not thought," I said slowly. "Broichan, I am thinking you would know: where, or what, is the Eagle's Path?"

"Ah," said Broichan. "How did you hear of that?"

"In a dream. Someone told me to take it, that it was the only way home. You know of it, then?"

"Yes." Broichan stood up and started around the boothy to the left. "Come here." I came. He pointed at the mountain above us. "Do you see it?"

I looked up at a thin line, lost and then found again, which wound back and forth across the face of the mountain. "*That*—is the Eagle's Path?" I asked, feeling my breath come short.

"The start of it." Broichan looked slyly sideways at me, the tattoos moving on his cheeks as he smiled. "Will you take it?"

"If I have to." I took a deep breath. "The moon is nearly new; I am thinking it will be dark tonight."

"Sure, it is dark the moon will be entirely." Broichan was still looking at me. High up the mountain I saw an eagle circling, his wings showing dark and golden by turns as he banked in the sunlight. Beyond the mountain face the peaks went on, soaring one after another into the west.

"I will take it, nevertheless," I said, "if that is the way home."

"That would be well," said Broichan, still smiling. "Who knows, I might even come with you for a while, to set you on your way." And he nodded once, and went back to his bench, leaving me still watching the eagle. "I will take it," I said again to the eagle, to Gwydion, or Taliesin, or whoever had spoken in my dreams. And I did.

But that, O my children, is a story for another day.

The Eagle's Path

It was a long day, and it was a short day, the day I had to get through before we freed Neirin. That is the way with waiting; and the more important the occasion, the worse the wait—or so it has always seemed to me. After my interview with Broichan the Druid, I talked with Cenau and Erp, and we made our plans as well as we could. Utha brought me Neirin's clothes and gear, and I rolled the most of it into a neat bundle, making sure I included his rain cape; I had a feeling it might be needed on this journey. I packed my own gear likewise, unpacked it to check I had forgotten nothing, and packed it again. Then there was nothing to do but wait until evening. After a while I lay down on my bed, and against all expectation fell asleep.

It was Erp who woke me, tapping on my door lightly and then slipping inside. "It will be time to go to the feast-hall soon: I came to see if you had any more orders," he said. "It is good you were sleeping; Cenau and I also napped this afternoon, for we will be needing all of our strength tonight."

I sat up and yawned. "That was in my mind also. Have you made all ready?"

"*Sa*, we have. The horse-gear is ready, and the ponies well-fed. I have found Neirin's gray—he is stabled not far from ours, and looks eager for work. I have taken the baggage-rolls over there already, except for yours and Neirin's. Cenau thinks we should take one of the pack-string with us as well, if we can, for a spare—this will be no trip for leading a lame horse!"

"That sounds good," I said, combing my fingers through my tangled hair. "Let you take my gear and Neirin's over to the stables now as well. If anyone asks, we are planning to leave tomorrow morning, as our mission here is done—or will be as soon as those god-cursed cows arrive!" And straightening my clothes and belt, I went out and left him to it.

The feast-hall that evening was crowded, and loud with voices and the sound of music. Talorc and I were seated at the high table again, in honor of our mission, and I gazed thoughtfully at the Pictish harper who sat playing for us nearby. His harp was larger than any I had ever seen before, and he held the base between his knees while his fingers danced on the strings, making a music intricate and interwoven as the carvings on the harp herself. I thought of my own dear harp and Neirin's, left behind in Manau with much of our gear, and I hoped that they were safe: but the Eagle's Path would be no place for them.

Talorc was seated again at the King's left hand, and I on Talorc's left. On Mailchon's other side, and seeming by his size and vibrant presence to make it the center of the table, sat burly Finaet Du, bright in his robe of red and orange checker, his thick arms heavy with gold and silver bracelets. His voice was loud and his manner tonight triumphant; beside him Mailchon looked small and old and of little account, despite his fine clothes and golden circlet. His thin face was mostly turned toward his bright neighbor, but the set of his head and shoulders spoke of nervous tension.

Presently Inoide the King's sister came to bear the guest-cup to us, as there had been no proper offering of it the night before. "Be welcome, Gwernin," she said to me; then more softly, under cover of the noise and music in the hall, "Broichan will bring you to the side door when the time is right, and I will be waiting. Only beware Finaet's soldiers—there are too many of them here, and too many of his men in our *teulu*."

"Thank you, Lady," I said aloud, and drank from the cup she offered—pale heather-honey mead was in it, sweet and bitter together, all of life mingled in one cup. I handed it back with a brief smile, and put on my somber expression again. I had constantly to remind myself that evening that I was the one on display here, not sitting unseen somewhere in the hall, and that my face and body should tell the right tale to any who saw me. It was an aspect of my craft which had not occurred to me so strongly before, but has been of value to me since.

The feasting seemed long that night, but at last it was over.
Walking back to our lodging through the soft twilight, I said to
Talorc beside me, "Are you ready?"

"I am," said Talorc. "Am I to come with you to the earth-
house?"

"I think not," I said. "Better you go to the stables and wait
with the horses; you may find Broichan there already. I will send
Erp to you once Neirin is free. Too many people moving in a group
so late at night would be strange."

"I am thinking this will all be strange," said Talorc on the ghost
of a laugh. And with that we went into the lodging to wait for
Cenau's signal.

This night was darker than the one before, with high cloud
dimming the afterglow in the north. Once more the three of us
made our way through the sleeping *llys*; once more we entered the
earth-house and Cenau lit his rush-light; but this time it was eagerness rather than fear which drove me down the tunnel. Neirin was
awake, sitting propped against the wall with his blankets around
him. His face still looked pale and ill under its thatch of dark red
hair, but he greeted us merrily. *"Hai mai,* brothers, I am glad to see
you! It is dull work waiting in this place. Have you brought the
keys?"

"I have," I said, dropping down beside him. Neirin obligingly
thrust out his foot from the blankets, and in a moment, with Erp
holding the rush-light, I had unlocked the shackle. Neirin sighed in
relief.

"Glad I am to be free of that! Now before we go further,
friends, help me on with my trews and boots. Utha brought them,
and got me into this tunic, but you cannot put on trews with a chain
on your leg, and I would not wish to come before King Mailchon
looking like a bare-breeched Irishman in my shirt!"

"Only hold out your leg, then—so," I said, laughing. "Erp, do
you put on his other boot. Now, Neirin, can you stand?"

"I can—but—lend me your shoulder, Gwernin—a moment,
now—my head is spinning!"

"Easy, easy, I have you. Pull up his trews, Erp. Is it better, brother?"

"It is," said Neirin, gasping and clinging to me with his sound arm. "It is only that I have not—stood on my feet—in so long. Erp, if you could straighten my belt—ah! mind my arm! This sling is— not all that it might be."

"We will fix it, *bachgen*," said Erp. "There, now. Can you walk? I would help you, but there are too many barrels in this room."

"Na, it is no problem," said Neirin. "Only bring my cloak—it was with the other clothes. Now, Gwernin, I think we should go. I have been long enough in this place—like Taliesin, I need fresh air!"

Between us we got him down the passage and out into the night. Cenau had been standing guard at the door, and now barred it again behind us. "What did you do with the keys?" he asked.

"Brought them with me, to give back to Broichan," I said. "I re-locked the shackle—maybe they will think he left by magic."

"Hmm," said Cenau. "Somehow I doubt it, but we will see. Erp, I can help them now if they need it; do you go and hold the horses ready. Now, where is Broichan?"

"Right beside you and waiting, lad," said the Druid, seeing to appear out of nowhere at my elbow. "Only keep your voice down, do. Not everyone in this court is asleep. Neirin, well met to you."

"And to you, friend," said Neirin on a laugh. "Are we all ready, then? Good. Now let us go to the King!"

Seldom have I seen a man so surprised as King Mailchon was that night, finding himself being visited at midnight by his sister, two bards, a soldier, and a Druid—for Broichan had decided to accompany us. The King's chamber was spacious, but we filled it up and took it over. Neirin lowered himself into Mailchon's high-backed chair with a sigh of relief, leaving the King to perch on a stool in front of him. The rest of us stood wherever we could— Cenau on guard by the door with a drawn sword, Inoide beside her brother, and the Druid and I behind Neirin. "Now," said Mailchon, trying to regain control and failing, "what is this all about?" It is

difficult to look confident when faced with a man you have de-
clared dead only two days before, let alone an ambassador who has
just been released from a *tȳ-deyerin*, and you a king in your night-
robe.

"A little matter of formality, first," said Neirin, in his Bard's
voice. "You will remember, Lord King, that I was presenting my
credentials to you when the—dispute—broke out. I am Neirin, son
of Dwywei and Cynfelyn Eidyn, come from Nechtan son of
Drustan of Dundurn to arrange a truce between his people and
yours. Now, I understand this will be difficult to manage at the
moment"—and here he grinned—"but I would urge you to follow
up on this course so soon as you may, for it is in the best interests
of you both."

"I—yes," said Mailchon, looking rather stunned. "Yes, you
speak truth. Such was my wish as well, only—"

"Only for the small matter of Finaet Du, your sub-king here in
Cromar, who does not share your wishes," said Neirin. "Forgive me
if I speak bluntly, Lord, I have not much time. Finaet does not wish
peace—he prospers by raiding, under cover of blood feud. Finaet's
men are in your retinue, and around your house with sharp steel.
Finaet it is who would wed himself by force to your sister, and
make himself King by her right in your chair—you who have no
sons, Lord, to come after you! Finaet it is who started the fight in
which all my retinue were slain, and would have killed me myself,
had Inoide and Broichan not stopped it—for even Finaet Sub-King
hesitates to kill a Bard in cold blood. King Mailchon, I said I have
not much time to speak to you tonight, but I think that you have
even less time than I. In the long-ago-years, the Feast of Lughnasadh was the Feast of the King-Making: my *awen* tells me that this
year it will be so again, if you do not move against Finaet now."

"But what can I do?" asked Mailchon, and all at once his reedy
voice was stronger. "I have eyes, I do see that I am as much a
prisoner here as you are. But how can I escape? I must go slowly
and cautiously, not to provoke Finaet's ire, until I can see my way
clear."

"That is the strategy of the mouse who fears the hawk," said Neirin, his own hawk-eyes blazing. "How many mice has it ever saved from her claws? I am no whole man, but I will take horse tonight, and ride. Can you not do as much? I know you have supporters farther north, if you can but reach them."

Mailchon sighed, and looked up at his sister. "You have told me this before; I should have heeded you."

"True that is," said Inoide, smiling down at him. "But after to-night, my dear, you will have no choice: once these men are fled and the tale of his treachery is out, Finaet will have no cause to hold his hand. What will you do then? For I tell you true, I will cut out my own heart before I will marry with Finaet Du."

"Lords," said Cenau abruptly, "there are men outside this door, and I do not think they are friendly." He was silently fixing a bar across it as he spoke. "Is there any other way out?"

Broichan was already at the window, peering through it. "They are not in the garden yet," he said, and without more ado hoisted his leg over the sill and climbed out. "Close it behind me," he said, and was gone. Inoide pulled the shutters to and latched them; they were heavy and fitted snugly, but like the door they were only wood. There was a moment of silence, in which we could clearly hear the shuffling of feet in the hallway.

"Are there weapons here?" Neirin asked.

"Yes," said Mailchon, and went to a chest at the foot of his bed, and opened it. "I have not used the King's Sword in too long," he muttered to himself, pulling a blue blade from its sheath. "Sister, give the others to the young men, and take one yourself—I know you can use it."

Inoide brought swords to me and to Neirin. He unsheathed his eagerly, then looked up at me, grinning. "Am I safer with you beside me or apart, brother?" he asked, his amber eyes dancing.

"Beside you, of course," I said, grinning back. "I have taken lessons from Cenau since you left—I am now a good fighting-man!"

"Yes, he is almost as dangerous to the enemy as to himself," said Cenau dryly. "Be quiet now, all of you, I need to listen."

Suddenly there was a pounding of fists on the door. "Open, Mailchon who was King, for Finaet son of Girom," cried a great voice. "Open now, or be dragged out to die!"

"Let them break their way in," said Cenau. "It will give us more time, and hinder them. We can die bravely soon enough, if we must. Gwernin, stand on my left side here; Mailchon King, on my right. Neirin, stay where you are, and watch the window; Lady, stay beside him. Now then, we are ready, and two of us are bards: can either of you give me a battle-song?"

There was a crashing against the door, as of axes. "I do not think there will be time," said Neirin dryly, "but if we live out this night, Feeder of Ravens, I will make you a praise-song the like of which the North has never heard!"

"That will be payment enough," said Cenau with a grim smile.

The ax-blades were coming through the door now; it could not be much longer. I took a better grip on my sword, and tried to steady my breathing. This was not like riding into clean battle, this waiting in a trap for death to come and take us. "Neirin," I said, "I am sorry: I have failed you."

"Na, na, brother," said Neirin, and I could hear the laughter in his voice. "You have done all a man could do, and brought me a fine company for my ending. Better to die fighting if we must. Watch the door!"

The axes crashed through the bar, and the door burst open, and Finaet Du stood framed in it in all his red and orange glory. Cenau did not pause to admire him, but struck at once like an adder. There was a clash of steel as Finaet blocked the blow, and the fight was underway—two superb warriors in their prime, neither yielding ground to the other. As long as Cenau could hold his opponent in the doorway, no one else could enter, and Mailchon and I had nothing to do. Then came a beating at the window. "Gwernin," gasped Cenau, "over there!"

"I go!" I cried, and turned. Inoide was ahead of me with a naked sword in her hand, and Neirin braced against the wall beside her. "*Hai mai*, brother," he said as I joined him, "now we will stand together!"

"Glad I am of it," I said, "but do you watch the door behind me. I am no Druid, to see both ways at once."

Suddenly there were screams in the hallway. Whirling around, I saw Cenau take advantage of that slight distraction and strike. Finaet's sword rang on the floor as he staggered back, blood bursting from his right shoulder, and vanished into the crowd of men behind him. Cenau struck at the next man without a pause, taking his hand off at the wrist, and more blood sprayed us all. I saw him kill three, one after another, before the survivors in the hallway turned from him as one man and fled.

"Gwernin!" cried Neirin. "The window!" And I turned back to my own duty, but Inoide again was before me. The first man to push open the shutters got her sword-blade in his throat and fell back gurgling. After that his fellows were less eager. Then I heard shouts in the garden as well, and the soldiers vanished.

Suddenly Broichan's owl-face appeared at the window in their stead. "Come on now, all of you," he cried. "The way is clear, and the horses are waiting. Inoide, Mailchon, you had better come too; the battle is not over, and I cannot predict the outcome. Your men are holding your horses outside the gate; you must ride for the north tonight."

The hardest part after that was getting Neirin through the window. In the end Cenau simply picked him up over his shoulder and climbed out carrying him. "Follow me," he said, and took off at a lope through the garden with Neirin still in his arms. The night around us was loud with confused shouting as we ran, and now and again we heard a clashing of steel. Broichan led us to the torch-lit back gate of the *llys*, which was held by some of Mailchon's *teulu*. Beyond in the darkness were many more men holding horses.

"This way," said Broichan, and took us to where Talorc and Erp waited with our ponies. Cenau dumped Neirin down beside his dappled gray and helped him mount.

"Are you well, brother?" I asked, ranging alongside him on my black. "I am afraid we have treated you rather roughly tonight."

"Na, na," said Neirin, laughing. "I am only—a little shaken! Which way are we going?"

"After Broichan," I said, as the Druid appeared on the back of another gray pony. "We are taking the Eagle's Path. It is the one way no one will be watching—and I do not blame them!"

Craig yr Eryron rises one thousand feet above Cromar valley in less than a mile, and too much of it is sheer. In the darkness, on a nervous pony, the trail up its face seemed to me no wider than a sword-blade, and I do not like heights. It is one thing to have your own feet on the rock, and your fingers tight on its hand-holds if need be; it is another thing entirely to depend on the mount between your knees to be brave for both of you. More than once I found myself clinging to the saddle-horn, as if that would make me safer. My mouth was dry with fear, and my heart was in my throat every time Du pecked at a stone, or scrambled around the switchbacks kicking pebbles into the void. If it had been only my life at stake, I think I would have turned back, or at least got down and led my pony; but where all the others could ride, I must go also. How many things men dare, rather than be called a coward!

Nevertheless, I was too worried for Neirin that night to have over-much concern to spare for myself. He was holding up wonderfully, but he was a man newly risen from a sick-bed, and there must be an end to his strength. Mind you, there was nothing I could have done to help him if he had started to fail—the trail was too narrow for rescues—but still I kept my eyes on him so far as I might. Only gradually, as the gray light strengthened toward morning, did I realize that there was no longer an immense drop beside me, but only a shallow valley; we had turned the corner of the mountain, and for the moment we were safe. I sighed in relief for us both.

Sometime after daybreak we stopped for a while for rest and food—Cenau and Erp had seen to it that we were well provisioned, both in our saddlebags and on our one packhorse. Neirin was drooping in the saddle by then, but his good humor had not left him. I think it was partly sheer joy at his escape, first from the *tỹ-deyerin* and then from Finaet's trap. Sitting on a saddle-pad and leaning back against me while Cenau and Erp did something around a campfire, he told me a little more of the fight which led to his being held hostage. "In truth, I thought I had my killing then," he said softly. "All the others were dead, and I was fighting alone. Red swords, and bright pain, and my own blood flowing—so much blood, and I could not stop it!—and a falling into cold darkness: death must be like that! I tried to reach out to you, but the strength was not in me, not in me at all."

"You reached me in dreams," I said, remembering. "But when I woke I could not find you."

"Na, that is not easy for the waking mind: it takes a sort of sideways-looking. Taliesin can do it, sometimes, and I have done it once or twice, but my concentration was not at its best." He sighed, and moved to settle his head more comfortably against my shoulder. "Here comes Cenau, I *think* with something warm to drink, which will be good: I am still cold from last night."

"Warmed wine with water and honey," said Cenau, handing me the cup. "And cold barley-bannock: the best I can do here. We will do better tonight, but we have a long ride yet before us; Broichan has told me the way of it. He will lead today, but tomorrow we must go on without him."

"And you are in haste to press on: I know," said Neirin, taking the cup from me one-handed, and drinking. "Gwernin, do you eat something as well; you cannot only tend to me."

"Na, I can eat as I ride," I said. "And that, I think, will be with you before me in the saddle; we cannot have you falling off, and so wasting time."

"When I get my strength back," said Neirin, "I will show you who is wasting time! I am in charge of this expedition, remember!"

"Always," I said, laughing. "Now drink your wine, so I can the sooner obey you—or Taliesin will hear of it!" Neirin gave a sort of snort, but he drank it all, and ate most of the bannock as well.

The rest of that day we rode among giants, over steep saddles where the ponies must sometimes be led, then dropping past deep blue lakes into lost valleys fragrant with pines. We took turns putting Neirin up before us—fortunately he was a light-weight yet, though taller that I—and I think he slept most of the day. Now and again we saw eagles—one in particular seemed to follow us, and I regarded him thoughtfully; but if he was Gwydion mab Dôn, he did not speak to me. That night we camped beside another lake, and Erp conjured a number of small trout from its depths, which we cooked on hot rocks beside our pinewood fire. Afterwards Broichan the Druid showed me how to dress Neirin's wound—a wicked slash across his left shoulder, which would have killed him if it had landed squarely—and gave me a pot of the dark, pungent-smelling ointment he made himself and used for such injuries. And the following morning he left us, after pointing out our next set of landmarks. Before he went, he gave me a token: the same sign he wore tattooed on his cheeks, scratched on a piece of gray slate from beside the trail. "This will let you pass through many gateways," he said, "and get you help when you need it." And he clasped hands with Neirin, and said something to him in soft Pictish.

"Na, na," said Neirin, smiling. "The next time we meet will be soon enough for that; and you know the way of it as well as I do. But in the future, beware of Irishmen!" And they both laughed, and so parted.

The rest of our journey went well, if not always easily; but every time we needed it, some wandering hunter or some wild beast would appear to help us or to set us on the right path. And well I remember the morning when I awoke early, to find an eagle sitting in a pine tree above me, regarding me with interest. "Neirin," I said softly—we had been sleeping side by side for warmth in the cold mountain nights—"I think we have company."

Neirin yawned, and look up at the bird. It ruffled its feathers a little and eyed him expectantly, then opened its mouth and made a *craik*-ing noise. "Na," said Neirin, and I was not sure if he spoke to the eagle or to me. "I do not think so." And with that the bird took wing and flapped heavily away. "Only curiosity," said Neirin, and yawned again, and went back to sleep.

It must have been about five days after leaving Cromar *llys*—I mind the moon was showing her new crescent by then—that we came at last into a south-trending valley, and followed it down to a village, and found that we were in King Nechtan's hunting runs once more. And two days later we rode into Nechtan's fortress of Dundurn, and were greeted there in the courtyard by the King himself. He feasted us like heroes and loaded us with gifts, and thanked Neirin again and again for his efforts. While we were riding the crests of the mountains, news had come from the north: Finaet Du had died of the wound Cenau gave him, and Mailchon was once more King in truth of Ce, and was suing for peace and offering reparations—including the same three hundred cows and three bulls, now on their way back south. As I said to Talorc when I heard it, at least this time we did not have to ride behind them.

Talorc also had one other piece of news, and looked a little sly when he told it to us: as token of the new peace between Ce and Dundurn, King Mailchon was offering his sister's hand in marriage, and as King Nechtan already had a wife, some other suitable noble must be found to partner her. "And I," said Talorc, grinning, "am Nechtan's close cousin, as high-born as any in this land, and a widower of many years." And he laughed, and we laughed with him. He had not wasted his time in Cromar after all, had Talorc.

After several days of Nechtan's hospitality, Neirin and I felt the need for rest, so a few days before Lughnasadh we loaded our presents on the two pack-ponies which were part of the gifts, and rode south toward Manau and Dun Eidyn, and the great Contention of the Bards which was soon to be held there.

But that, O my children, is a story for another day.

The Contention of the Bards

The difference between bards and harpers goes as far back as the invention of the harp. Underlying it is a fundamental distinction between those who work with sense—with words—and those whose primary tool is sound. And yet there is not all that much difference between us: harpers also may sing, and bards make music; indeed, the best poetry has a music of its own. To be equally good at both, however, is a gift given only to a few.

"Na, I cannot do it!" said Neirin, putting his harp down on the bed-place beside him with a gentleness which belied his suppressed fury. "I am not good enough, and I will not show myself as less than my best!"

"You sounded good enough to me," I said mildly. We were in a room in the guest-house of Clydno's court at Dun Eidyn, and it was the day before the competitions for bards and harpers.

"Na, but my left hand has lost its cunning." With his tunic stripped off, Neirin was wincingly kneading his left arm and shoulder, where the long scar of his barely-healed wound still showed lividly red against his white skin. "It will not—move—as it should!"

"Well, do you let it rest, then," I said, setting down the sword whose scabbard and hilt I had been polishing. "You will not mend it overnight by mauling it about like that. Let you enter the poets' competition instead; there is nothing wrong with your voice."

Neirin sighed. "*Sa*, you are right. Only I had wished—well, no matter. But what shall I sing? I have not thought."

"You still owe Cenau a praise-song," I said, getting up from my seat and straightening my belt. "Make him one now: will that not be good enough?"

"*Sa*, it might be," Neirin said, stretching himself out on the bed and yawning. "Where are you going?"

"Down to the fair," I grinned, with my hand on the door-latch. "In a moon or so we will be home again, and I need a present for my woman. And here I am at the greatest fair in the North with silver in my pouch—it will be strange if I cannot find something suitable!"

"Do you go, then," said Neirin, and closed his eyes. "I will stay here, and think on my singing. It will be well for me to do a good job of it: I have need…"

Indeed, and he had: I thought about it as I went down the hill toward the fair. Neirin's reception by his half-brother Clydno Eidyn at Caer Iddeu had been as cool as his seeing-off. "So, you are here again; I heard you had some trouble," had said the King, and "*Sa, sa*, but nothing to matter," had said Neirin.

"That is good," Clydno had said. "Let you come with me to Dun Eidyn tomorrow, then; any later and you would have missed the Contention." And with that he had turned on his heel and gone about his business, leaving us to make our own arrangements. No questions or praise about Neirin's mission in the North; no interest at all, one would have said; and yet he had still been waiting for us at Caer Iddeu. Then and later, I was always in two minds about Clydno Eidyn.

Once I reached the fair, however, I soon forgot Neirin's troubles. The merchant-kind had gathered from all the North and beyond for this occasion, and their tents and booths stretched across a large swath of the foreshore between Dun Eidyn and the sea. Everything I could have imagined buying was there—blue-bladed swords and bronze-hilted daggers, jewel-bright bolts and bundles of fine woolens and silks from over the sea, heavy silver arm-rings and enameled shoulder brooches, and cunningly-carved leatherwork of all kinds; foods, too—huge brown clay amphorae of precious olive oil and red Falernian wine for the tables of rich lords, and well-wrought wooden barrels of lesser wines from Gaul; fruits dried or preserved in clear honey, and strange pungent spices, their scents mingling oddly with the more homely aromas of wood-smoke and roast meat, beer and sweat and horse-dung, fish and seaweed and human-kind on the warm summer breeze.

For those less lordly of purse, there were other temptations: clothing and belts, boots and shoes and weapons, woolen narrow-wares and skeins of bright silken thread, bronze pins and brooches, and jewelry: necklaces of jet, of amber, of river pearls cunningly pierced and strung, of bright-colored glass or strange polished gem-stones; and bracelets and ear-drops and rings to match them all. That was my fancy, and I wandered from booth to booth, looking, touching, comparing, seeing this necklace clasped around Rhian-nedd's slender throat, that bracelet adorning her slim brown wrist, those ear-drops gleaming in her thick dark hair. After so long a time apart—during which, I admit, I had mostly had other matters on my mind!—the thought of her now was an ache in me, the days and miles before I could reach her again an endless gulf. I settled at last on a necklace of bright polished amber and red and blue glass beads, with a bracelet to match: it took a good part of the silver I had earned that summer, but I did not grudge the price. I bought a few other things as well: a carved leather belt for Talhaearn, a new knife-sheath and a plainer belt with a bronze buckle for myself, and a few strands of the gray river pearls and carved jet beads common in the north in case I had need of other presents. It was all joy to me, even the looking; never before in my life had I had such treasure to spend, and I spent nearly all of it. My pouch was lighter by far when I went back up the hill that evening, but my heart was full, and my memory, with the delights of the day.

Five days now the fair had been going on, and it had one more to run: that was the evening for the bards' contention, the highlight of the feast. Two days before I had stood up with a dozen other storytellers to contend for a prize, and though I had not won it, I was satisfied with my performance: others had merely been better. I had learned new stories, and made new acquaintances among the performers, and generally enjoyed myself: what a difference, I thought, smiling inwardly, from last year at Caer Seint! I hoped Neirin would do well in his competition; I knew he still felt the effects of his ordeal in the Pictish lands, though he did not say so, and tired easily. And singing before his brother as he would be, he had need to excel.

I found him still stretched on his bed, but not asleep: he greeted me absently, but was obviously involved in composition, a frown on his brow and an inward-looking expression in his amber eyes. Nor would he come with me to dinner in the fire-hall that evening. "Na, na," he said, running his fingers distractedly through his red hair, "I have more need of thought than of feasting tonight; I must not lose the thread of this, it is still too new. Bring me back something if you will, brother; only go away now and let me think!" So I grinned and left him; after my day at the market I had appetite for two.

In the feast-hall, to my surprise and delight, I found Talorc of Dundurn, dressed in a long robe of wine-red wool, and with a fire-new silver chain of office on his breast. "Gwernin," he said when he saw me, his dark eyes sparkling and his long face relaxing in a smile, "I have been looking for you and Neirin since I arrived. How do things go with you both?"

"Very well, Lord," I said, smiling back at him. "But what brings you here?"

"A desire to see the ending of a story," said Talorc. "For it is tomorrow when they hold the Contention of the Bards, is it not? And Neirin will be singing?"

"Yes, and yes," I said, "or rather, yes, and I hope so: he is still composing."

"That is like him," said Talorc, nodding. "But I think he will be ready; it is not in that one to fail."

"*Sa*, I hope you are right," I said, and we fell to talking of the festival, and of other people, and spoke no more of Neirin that night. After a while Talorc went to take his place at the high table beside Clydno Eidyn and his Queen, a slender red-haired lady with skin like heavy cream and eyes as green as the waves I had watched breaking that afternoon on the beach. I had seen her at the story-telling contest two days before with her elder son, a dark-eyed, red-headed child who could have been Neirin's younger brother; it seemed the line of Cynfelyn bred true. Even Clydno, for all his darker hair and complexion, had the same thin face and strong cheek-bones, the same wide mouth as my friend. Only the spark, the brightness that burned so high in Neirin, was missing: closed, and careful, and cold was Clydno, then and always; only once in the long years I knew him did I see him give way to emotion, and that was a bitter day.

Neirin seemed asleep when I got back, but sat up after a moment, yawning and blinking in the light of my lamp. "How is the song coming?" I asked, handing over the food I had brought him.

"Well enough, I am thinking," said Neirin, stuffing bread and pig-meat in his mouth. "There is a little trouble with the ending, but I think I can fix it."

"That is good," I said, yawning in my turn as I pulled off my boots. "Talorc is here, by the by: he has come to see the Contention."

"Good! Then he can be taking the song home with him; it was sorrow to me that he would not hear it." Neirin licked his fingers, looked around, and sighed. "*Hai mai*, is that all that you have brought me?"

"Go yourself next time, then," I said and laughed. "You will not starve tonight!"

"Na, but I am still hungry. This thinking is hard work." Neirin lay down again and closed his eyes. "And I must have a song ready before the next day dawns…"

The next day dawned fine and clear. I woke early and went out quietly, leaving Neirin asleep; presumably he had finished his composition. For myself, I was restless, with the sense of some impending excitement. I found cold meat and bread in the feast-hall, and went to the stables to see to our horses: we had five now, including the two King Nechtan had given us, more than we needed. On the other hand, Du, the black pony I had been riding all summer, was Taliesin's, while the sturdy little red mare I had been given in Dundurn was mine: another first in my life. She was not broken to the saddle, but that could be altered, if Prince Cyndrwyn did not mind me adding her to the horse-herd when I got home. From there I went on to think of Rhiannedd, and my restlessness increased. After a while I went down to the fair again, and in looking at the wares, and talking to some of the merchants—there was a fine little yellow-haired girl working the cobbler's booth!—I managed to pass the day pleasantly enough. But all the same I was glad when evening approached and I went back up the hill.

Neirin was dressing when I came in. His favorite red and blue checked tunic having been lost in Ce, he was wearing instead an even finer garment which King Nechtan had given him, its rich woolen folds bright in green and blue and gold, with narrow bands of red silk gleaming at neck and shoulders. His hair was pulled back and tied with a thong at the base of his neck, and all his leather and bronze fittings gleamed with polishing. The young beard of which he was so proud made a neat line at the bottom of his jaw. "Are you ready, brother?" he greeted me gaily, his amber eyes sparkling. "You look dressed more for the stables than for the mead-hall."

I looked down at myself and brushed some straw off my brown tunic. "Ready enough, if you are not too fine now to be seen with me. Are you bringing your harp?"

"Yes, for accompaniment only." Neirin grimaced. "My playing at least is still good enough for that. Let us be going, then; to be late would be bad."

"Indeed, and it would," I said, taking the harp from him and matching his stride. "Have you had anything to eat today?"

"I am not remembering. It does not matter; I will eat later. There is no room in my belly for food until this thing is done." I nodded, knowing what he meant; I too with less reason had been unable to eat before a contest.

In the hall the bards were already gathering, many of them even more brightly dressed than Neirin, one or two in the multicolored cloaks beloved of the Irish. There were perhaps a score of them, ranging from boys to gray-beards. Looking at them, my confidence was shaken: some of them looked very experienced; very successful too, for three or four were wearing silver circlets like

Taliesin's, the mark of a master who had won a contest. I hoped Neirin would do well.

He was exchanging words and smiles with a few of them. Looking more closely, I saw some faces I recognized from Alt Clut; one or two even from last summer. A tall gray-haired man with a fine bushy beard seemed to be asking him questions; Neirin replied with a shake of his head, and words I could not catch. Some of these men, I realized, must be acquaintances of Taliesin's, familiar to Neirin from past contests where he was an onlooker, not a participant. Bards travel: it is our need and our nature. For this competition, many must have traveled far.

After a while a clerk moved among them, noting down names on a wax tablet. Whether by chance or not, he came to Neirin's clump almost last. I did not know the custom—storytelling competitions were less formal—but if this was the performance order, we would have a long wait. Meanwhile people were taking their seats; I found a space on the benches half-way down the hall, and saved room for Neirin.

Presently he came to join me. The King and his followers had taken their places; the servants were bringing the first platters of food to the tables. The rich smell of roast meat filled the hall as the first performer took up his stance in the center. The competition would run throughout the feast; only the best, I thought, as a babble of conversation broke out around me, would be able to make themselves heard and noticed. If nothing else, it would make the judges' job easier; anyone they could not hear could be safely ignored. Beside me Neirin sat listening intently, slowly crumbling a piece of bread into fragments but eating nothing, the cup of wine beside him untouched. With a slight sense of disloyalty but good appetite, I helped myself to a dripping chunk of cow-meat from a platter and began to fill my own belly.

Despite the noise in hall, some of the performers had the wherewithal to make themselves heard. Several had striking songs, all dealing with battle, many praising Clydno Eidyn and his retinue. One of the best was a piece by the gray-haired bard, whose brisk battle-song, done in a strong Gwynedd accent, had us all beating the tables in time. "Who is he?" I asked Neirin when it was over.

"Ugnach mab Mydno, of Caer Sëon, near Aber Conwy," said Neirin quietly. "He contended against Taliesin last summer at Caer Seint, and almost won: were you not there?"

"No," I said slowly, "but I heard something of it later. They exchanged *englynion*."

"Yes, beforehand. What came after was more serious. Hush, the next man is starting."

More inadequate performances followed, interspersed with one or two of note. A striking piece by one of the Irishmen, a red-gold man with a strong baritone, held the hall silent. Then the noise surged up again, and it was Neirin's turn. He stood, drank a few swallows of wine to wet his mouth, took his harp from me, and walked into the center of the hall. He took his stance; I even saw him draw a deep breath to begin. Then there was a burst of snarling and barking, and almost under his feet a dog-fight broke out, three great hounds contending loudly for a single bone. Neirin took an unwary step back, tripped on something hidden in the rushes, and started to fall. Twisting instinctively to protect his harp, he struck his left shoulder on the trestle table beside him. I saw his mouth open; I saw the spasm of pain go through him; but he made no outcry. Before I could move to help him, he was on his feet again, the harp clutched clumsily against his chest. Someone had kicked the dogs away; it was time to begin. He tried to adjust the position of his harp on its sling, shook his head, and slipping off the instrument, set it on the table-top beside him. Then he stood up straight and began to sing, alone and unaccompanied, and the hall grew quiet to listen.

> "I sing a great deed—the North has known it—
> High will I sing it here in the King's hall!
> I sing seven warriors in harsh battle fallen,
> seven bright swords, blood-bordered and keen—
> Taran and Talogan, Galan and Drest,
> Buan and Llif, and Arthnac the Tall—
> riding swift horses you went to the North:

may the green earth above you lie light!
Bold you went forth from the courts of Dundurn,
with no concern for the end that awaited;
on that day red, though your own blood was flowing,
ravens you fed—you deserved well your mead!
Dauntless, undoubted, you slew as you fell—
one man alone came back from that slaughter:
Anile mab Talorc, defending me dearly—
and I, streaming blood, for the sake of my song.

I sing a great deed—the North has known it—
high will I sing it here in the King's hall!
I sing three strong friends who brought me my ransom:
Gwernin and Erp and Llywarch's bold son.
With fine steel and silver, with gold and black cattle,
ready for battle they rode from the south
to buy my way free with bleeding or blood-price,
with high hearts, hurt-heedless, they came like fierce hounds!
A green mound above me, beyond daylight's candle
in darkness I lay with cold stone for my bed;
men called me dead then and laid in my grave there,
but chained like a slave, I still waited alone.
In the dark night then, unfrightened and fearless,
my friends found me there—they broke my iron chain!
They brought me to freedom from out my cruel prison,
from my death risen—my *awen* their gain!

I sing a great deed—the North has known it—
high will I sing it here in the King's hall:
how we met Finaet, False-King, in fair fight—
Cenau mab Llywarch put flight to his pains!
Feeder of Ravens, fierce, first in slaughter,
blood flowed like water when Cenau came near:
strong door of battle, he stood in the gateway—
gave men their fate: he filled many a bier!
I saw blue blades bloodied,
I saw red blood spurting,
I saw white bones shattered
by strong Cenau's hand;
I saw brave men fleeing,
I saw bodies broken,

I saw a strong troop routed
by one savage man!

I sing a great deed—the North has known it—
high will I sing it here in the King's hall!
I sing of bright swords, blood-streaming in battle,
of red-bordered saddles, and fire in the night!
I sing of swift Cenau, who saved me from harm,
his strong arm around me—the warrior was bold!
Over cold hills they found me my freedom;
on eagles' wings my friends bore me home.
Now can I sing them the song they deserve—
fierce and unswerving in that my sore need!
I sing a great deed—the North has known it—
high have I sung it here in the King's hall!
May all who hear it remember these names:
grant them true fame: they deserved well their mead!
Taran and Talogan, Galan and Drest,
Buan and Llif, and Arthnac the Tall—
Anile mab Talorc, defending me dearly—
Gwernin and Erp, and Llywarch's bold son."

When he was finished, there was a long silence; then the cheering began. I found my cheeks were wet with tears, and I know I was not the only one weeping, not the only one exalting. Neirin stood in the midst of it, smiling faintly; then he picked up his harp with his right hand—he had tucked his left thumb in his belt while he sang—and came back to join me at the table. And at last the storm of applause died away.

"Drink this," I said, pushing a cup of wine in front of him and taking the harp. "How badly are you hurt?"

"Only—bruised, I think," said Neirin, fumbling inside his tunic right-handedly. "Na, there is no blood. Gods! but it hurt—I thought for a moment I would faint, and that would have spoiled everything." He took the wine-cup in a shaking hand and drained it. "*Hai mai!* At least that is over, and I can eat; it is starving of the hunger that I am!"

Food and drink was passed his way down the table, while I put his harp in her case and slung her at my back. The next contender was trying to perform, and making heavy going of it. I am not sure if it was two or three more that came after him; I did not notice, and I doubt many others did either. Neirin's song had broken their battle-line, and there was no confidence left in them.

After a while a herald called for silence, and summoned three men to the front of the hall: Neirin, Ugnach, and the Irishman with the golden voice. I slipped along at the side of the hall behind them, uninvited, to see what passed.

Clydno Eidyn stood up to greet them. "My judges and I are agreed," he said smiling, "that you three gave the best performances tonight, and it is my honor and pleasure to reward you. For Fergus of Ireland, gold to match your voice," and he handed the man a gold bracelet.

"My thanks, Lord King," said the Irishman, smiling. "A joy it is to me to be in your court, and to praise your generosity."

"For Ugnach of Gwynedd, whose song was like a sword in the hand, this weapon," said Clydno, and he handed the man a long blue blade in a jeweled sheath, a weapon fit for a king.

"My thanks, Lord King," said Ugnach, grinning. "As it shall defend my life, so shall I defend your honor."

"And lastly, for my half-brother Neirin," said Clydno, and he was not smiling now, "three things that are owed to you. First, because I have not forgotten what day this is, a present." And he picked up a small carved wooden box from the table, and held it out to Neirin, who took it clumsily in his left hand and opened it. He stared at what lay inside, then looked up to meet Clydno's eyes again. "Where did you find this?" he asked softly.

"In the treasury," said Clydno. "I thought you might like to have it for a name-day gift. It is twice nine years today, is it not, since you first saw the light of morning, and set up a yelling fit to wake the whole *llys*?"

"It is," said Neirin, and smiled a little, and closed the box. "I thank you."

"Secondly," said Clydno, "for the songs you have made for me this summer, and those I hope you will make in the future," and he stretched out his right hand, and in the palm of it I saw a gold ring. "Will you take this from me, and be my Bard?"

Neirin looked at the ring, but made no move to touch it. "Na, I may not," he said. "I am yet bound to my master, and will not be leaving him for a while and a while. But again I thank you."

Clydno nodded, and closed his hand on the ring, and set it aside. "I expected that," he said, "but you deserved the offer. Finally, then, for your performance today." And he picked up from the table a heavy leather bag which clinked as he lifted it, and a silver circlet such as the other two bards wore, and held them both out to Neirin. "My two judges tell me, and I agree, that your singing was the best in this contention. Take the prizes that you have won, and wear your crown in good health"—and faintly he smiled— "brother."

Neirin took the circlet in a hand which was not quite steady. "For the third time, I thank you, brother," he said, and smiled like the sunrise. And the two bards beside him took the circlet from him and placed it on his head, and behind him the listening silence of the hall broke up in cheers.

Later in our room I asked him, "What was in the box?" and he took it out of his pouch and showed me: a slender silver ring of a size to fit a small woman's hand, engraved with the twisting designs beloved of the Picts.

"It was my mother's," said Neirin, smiling—he was still glowing with happiness. "I thought it went into the earth with her, but my father must have kept it. I am glad"—and he put it carefully on the little finger of his left hand, where it almost fitted—"to have it back, and on such a day!"

"You never told me it was your birthday," I said.

"I am thinking I had forgotten," said Neirin, and yawned hugely. "Gods! I am tired! But this has been a day to remember, one I will not be forgetting again!" And that was a true word, in more ways than one.

But that, O my children, is a story for another day.

The King's Sister's Wedding

Like the Britons to their south, the Picts are warriors, herdsmen, and farmers, and at all of these things they are good. But in one thing and one thing only they surpass us, and that is in their use of the sea. Everyone knows of the Saxon sea-raiders who harried our eastern and southern coasts in the past, before they drove us out and settled there, and of the Irish who harry our western coasts today. But the Picts were here before either of them, and in the islands of the West and North they came to their mastery of the sea, and hold it still.

Talorc mab Uoret, who had been in the hall to hear Neirin's singing during the Contention of the Bards, had barely been able to restrain himself until the judgment was over before coming to embrace us both. He had insisted on taking us back with him to Dundurn, so that everyone there—not least his son Anile, the only survivor of Neirin's ambassadorial retinue—could hear Neirin's song from Neirin himself. Once there, of course, we had to stay for several more days of feasting and entertainment. Then it developed that the wedding between Ce and Dundurn would be soon—King Mailchon was in haste to cement the alliance, and also to get his sister safely out of reach of any other of his fellow-countrymen who might wish to claim his kingship through her right—and so we must stay on for that. It was no hardship, for King Nechtan's hospitality was most generous, and the dark-eyed Pictish girls very friendly—so friendly that I almost forgot my desire to hurry south again to Rhiannedd!

Thus it came about that Neirin and I found ourselves standing with Talorc and a host of others on a low hill beside the river Tay, waiting for the ship that would bring Inoide, sister of the King of the Northern Picts, to her wedding. It was ten or twelve days after the Contention of the Bards, and the moon which had been new when we left Ce was waning toward new again. The afternoon sun shone hot in a cloudless blue sky, and I was glad for the breeze from the estuary to the east, heavy though it was with the sea-scents of fish and seaweed, mingling with the smells of mud and marsh-water from the saltings across the channel. I could feel runnels of sweat trickling down my ribs under my new woolen tunic—bright red it was, and banded at throat and cuffs and shoulder seams with blue!—and though I was outshone by half the men around me, still I felt fine as a fighting cock, and smiled every time the color caught my eye. After my make-shift appearance at the Contention, Neirin had made sure I dressed for the occasion this time. He himself was arrayed with all his usual care, and his new silver circlet glittered on his dark red hair. Beneath it his expression was abstracted, his hawk-eyes narrowed against the bright day.

"How much longer do you think we will be waiting?" I asked him. It had been late morning when the scouts had arrived to tell us the fleet was on its way. Talorc in his eagerness had swept us all down to the docks to wait—and wait, and wait. It was a long time now since breakfast, and my belly was growling with emptiness.

"Na, I am not knowing," said Neirin. "But I think—" Even as he spoke I heard the stirring in the crowd around us, and the distant calling of voices. Talorc, standing a little way from us and convers-ing quietly with King Nechtan and two other bright-clad Pictish nobles, heard it too; his dark head went up, and he raised a hand to silence one of his companions. "I think," said Neirin, grinning, "they are here."

I worked my way sideways through the crowd, most of them taller men than I, until I could see the oncoming ships. In those days the Picts used blue or green sails, to pass unnoticed at sea; but Inoide's was a royal ship, and her wide sail shone a clear fire-red in the sunlight, in contrast to those of her escort. She was standing straight in toward us with a light breeze behind her, and the white water showing now and then at her bows as she came. Then as she drew close the sail came down with a run, and the steersman turned her in a long arc that brought her neatly against the dock with hardly any use of her oars. Her escorting ships followed, mooring here and there along the shore as their fancy took them. The crowd surged eagerly forward around me, and I lost the sight of them all for a moment, but Talorc cleaved a path through his fellows, and Neirin and I followed him.

Besides the sailors and fighting men on the ship, Inoide had brought her own escort, and one of them, I saw with pleasure, was Broichan the Druid. Both of them were wearing long cloaks against the sea-spray, Broichan's pale gray and Inoide's a clear forest green. As I watched she pushed back its hood, exposing her dark hair to the sunlight, and smiled. The sailors put down a gangway, and without waiting for aid she stepped across it and onto the dock, to where Talorc and the King himself stood waiting for her. They exchanged a few sentences in soft Pictish, formal-sounding words of greeting and welcome. Then Talorc, seeing us out of the corner of his eye, turned and motioned us forward.

When she saw the two of us, Inoide's smile grew wider still. "Oh, this is good," she said, switching to British. "Neirin and Gwernin as well—I was so glad to hear you all came safely home. My brother sends his greetings and regrets—he is still busy putting down the last of Finaet's rebels, and sorting out the succession there in Ce. Broichan is here to stand in his place at the wedding."

"And glad I am to do it," said the Druid, the tattoos on his cheeks moving as he spoke.

"Then he is doubly welcome," said King Nechtan, smiling down at her—for tall woman though she was, he was taller. "But you must be tired after your journey."

"Not at all," said Inoide. "We had a good following wind, and the sea was not too rough. All the way from Inverness we came in three days!"

"Come, then, both of you," said Talorc gaily. "If you are not tired, I know you will be hungry—I have been at sea once or twice myself. Never a bite could I eat until I came safe again to land!"

The fortress of Dun Moreu stands on a hill overlooking the joining of the Rivers Tay and Earn with the sea. On the south side the land drops steeply, but the north and east sides are more gentle, and it was up that slope we rode from the harbor. The King had provided a gray gelding for Broichan, and a beautiful little white mare with a gold-fringed saddle-cloth for Inoide. She mounted it gracefully and we set off, Neirin and I dropping back in deference to her royal escort. It still seemed strange to me sometimes to be riding in such company, I who a year before had been leading my master's pack pony on foot in Prince Cyndrwyn's train. I said something of this to Neirin, who first looked surprised, and then nodded in understanding. "*Sa, sa,*" he said, "I forget sometimes, brother, the changes you have seen. Well, well, a bard's life has its moments. By the *awen* that is in me, I prophecy that we may yet find ourselves horse-holders again someday, before the end." And that was a true word, though not as I thought it then.

For the next few days Nechtan's fortress of Dun Moreu was as full as it could hold with kings and nobles—for Clydno Eidyn was there himself, being a near neighbor, and many of the other kings of the North sent representatives. Owain of Rheged, Urien's eldest son, had come in his father's place, and I wondered, seeing his lofty head with its mane of pale hair, if Neirin was reminded as I was of his twin sister Morfudd; but Rhydderch Hael had stayed at home with his new bride. Such was the crowding that we were lucky to find bed-space in the feast hall, and most of the retinues were reduced to camping on the slopes of the hill itself, along with such of the Pictish seamen as did not sleep on board their ships. In the fine warm harvest-tide weather, this was no hardship: strings of pack-ponies brought in firewood, and cattle were driven in from the countryside, and the savor of roasting meat went up from the cooking fires at all hours. The camps were bright with banners, and loud with the neighing of horses and the voices of men. Minstrels and merchants came also to play and to sell, until the place seemed almost like a second Lughnasadh Fair.

At our hosts' bidding, Neirin and I performed first at the feasting most nights, and the silver in my purse began to grow again. From Inoide, too, we had presents, though they were not given in hall. Three days after her arrival she called us to her room, where we found her surrounded by chests and boxes, bales of fabric and piles of clothing. "Come in and sit, if you can find a space," she said, smiling. "Mailchon has sent me with a queen's dowry, and there is no storing of it here. Utha, do you find them stools—ah, Eithne has them. Do you bring them here, child. Now sit, friends, and be easy."

I sat, but looked at the child who had fetched the stools. Eight or nine years old, she was, but tall for her age and slender, with a cloud of dark hair and brown eyes. "Who is this, then?" I asked, but I knew the answer already: the likeness was there, in the long oval of her face and the shape of her generous mouth.

"My daughter," said Inoide, holding out her hand to the child. "She was not with me at Cromar, and that was well; but my brother let me bring her south with me. Eithne, this is Gwernin and Neirin: you have heard me speak of them."

"Greetings, Eithne," said Neirin, and he smiled at her. She looked solemnly back at him for a moment, and then smiled in her turn: her mother's sweet smile. "Neirin," she said in a lilting voice, tasting the name. "Yes, I have heard of you: Mother told me stories."

"Eithne, find the red box for me," said Inoide. "There is something in it for Neirin." The girl ran to get it, and came back carrying it carefully: a wooden chest perhaps four hand-breadths square, carved and painted with birds and animals in the Pictish style. Inoide took it on her lap and raised the lid. From inside it she brought out a piece of flame-red silk, and unfolded it and held it up for Neirin to see: a woman's scarf, cut and frayed at one end, and with darker patches on it like bloodstains. "You were wearing it when you were wounded," said Inoide. "I thought it had some meaning for you, and you might wish to have it back. I am sorry about the stains: we could not wash it all out."

Neirin had recognized the scarf instantly while I still sat staring, and his hand went out for it, but the girl took it from her mother and brought it to him. He ran it through his fingers, his eyes narrowed and his smile a little twisted as at a bittersweet memory;

then he looked at Eithne and his face relaxed. "I think it should stay in Alba," he said. "Would you like it, Eithne?"

The child looked at him wide-eyed, and nodded. "Come here, then," said Neirin, and reaching out, he put it around her slender neck under her dark hair. "Take care of it for me, until someone brings you a better one. Then you may gift it where you will: to your first daughter, if you like."

"Thank you," Eithne said softly, stroking the ends of the silk, and then broke into a torrent of Pictish words I could not understand, though Neirin seemed to. "Na, na," he said. "It is not magic, but it *is* from very far away: a princess gave it to me, for a song I made her. Do you wear it in your turn; it goes better with your hair than with mine." And he laughed.

"Ah," said Inoide, "I thought that might be the way of it. Are you sure you want the child to have it?"

"*Ie*, I am," said Neirin, and nodded. "But thank you for bringing it."

"It was no trouble," said Inoide, turning over things in her box as if searching for something more. "Now where—? Ah, here they are." And she sat for a moment cupping two hidden objects in her hands. "You two are young, and no man's bard as yet," she said, "and so you have no bardic rings. Do you wear these from me until that day comes." And she opened her hands to show us two silver rings, made in flat triple spirals like miniature arm-rings. "Eithne, do you take them."

The girl took the rings and brought them to us. Mine she placed in my palm, and I put it on; but when Neirin would have done the same, she took his hand in her small one and solemnly slipped the ring onto his second finger. And he let her do it, but with a frown. "*Hai mai*," he said ruefully, looking up to meet her mother's eyes. "I hope this is not what I think."

"She will grow out of it," said Inoide, amused.

"She will have a long time to do so," said Neirin. But looking at Eithne's determined face, I wondered how long would be long enough.

Three days later, at the new moon, Inoide and Talorc were joined in marriage. The ceremony was long, and of course all in the Pictish tongue, so that many of the details blur in my memory after so many years. There were sacrifices, and processions, and garlands of barley-corn and flowers, as at any such wedding; a binding of their hands together with a red cord, symbolizing the joining of their blood; an invocation chanted by Broichan and another Pictish priest, presumably calling down the blessings of the gods on this union; and a long feast with much drinking of mead and ale and wine, and singing of praise, during which the two of them sat side by side at the high table, eating little but stealing glances at each other, for all the world as if they were still in their first youth and not on the threshold of old age. At last, as the pale northern twilight was fading into night and the torches flaring red and gold in the smoky hall, Talorc stood up, and pulling Inoide to her feet, picked her up over his shoulder and carried her out of the hall to general applause, leaving the rest of us free to drink and sing and carouse until the dawn.

The next morning the *llys* was quiet, and I had a headache. Neirin had disappeared somewhere—I think with a girl—and I was able to have my sleep out in peace in a dim corner of the hall, which was filled with enough prone bodies to resemble a battlefield—though there is usually less snoring there! Toward afternoon Neirin reappeared, yawning and combing straws out of his hair with his fingers, and settled down with his harp to tune and play. I lay watching him lazily for a while, and thinking of nothing in particular.

Someone crossed the doorway to the hall, blocking the light for a moment, and I recognized the lean tall shape of Clydno Eidyn. Frowning, I remembered noticing him the night before, relatively sober when all about him were drunk, and talking—or rather listening—earnestly to Rhydderch Hael's representative, who seemed to be directing a stream of complaints into his ear. I wondered now what it had been about; but kings and kings' representatives often have business to transact, and where better than a crowded hall, where the noise is such that no one can overhear you, or even wonder at your shouting in each other's ear? Not like the quiet hall where I was at the moment ... so I said nothing to Neirin at the time, and presently forgot it.

After three more days of feasting, the celebrations came to an end, and the visitors dispersed. The Pictish ships which had come with Inoide spread their sails and headed north again, King Nechtan and his court and his retinue set off on their interrupted circuit up Dyffryn Mawr, and Talorc gathered up his new wife and her daughter and his own small *teulu*, and took them across the River Earn to his home at Forteviot. Neirin and I stopped the first night with them there, and then continued on toward Caer Iddeu and Dun Eidyn on the first leg of our long journey south.

I took away with me the memory of a happy couple, and the conviction that whatever else might be coming to the boil in the North, Pictland would be at peace for a while. Neirin, I think, took away with him a whole heart at last, and a fate which would be many years in the making. And Clydno Eidyn, traveling a day ahead of us, took with him his own plans for the breaking of peace and the rearrangement of kingdoms.

But that, O my children, is a story for another day.

The Road South

Hir pob aros, says the proverb—all waiting is long. So indeed for me was the time between the end of the Lughnasadh Fair at Dun Eidyn and our setting off again on our travels. Longer still, however, was to be our journey home.

The first delay, of course, was our visit to Dundurn. Then, once we had won our way back to Dun Eidyn, I found that Neirin was in no hurry to leave. Being on good terms with all his relatives was a new experience for him, and he wanted to savor it. His brother Clydno, moreover, kept coming up with reasons to delay our departure: yet another day's hunting, the possibility of bad weather on the morrow, a visit to one of his nearby courts to see new improvements or fine horses. Our entertainment was good and our lodging princely; but it was not for this, I thought, that Taliesin had sent us to the North.

One of Clydno's expeditions took us a day's ride to the south and west, along what should have been our road home. All that day a restlessness was on me, but Neirin was talking with his brother, and there was nothing I could do. It was only when we reached our destination and there encountered Elidyr Mwynfawr, the King of Aeron, hunting with a few companions and far outside of his own lands—a surprise to me, though I think not to Clydno—that I realized there was more to this than there seemed. Clydno straight-way invited him to stay and feasted him well, but though Neirin and I sang and told tales for his entertainment, and he rewarded us generously, he did not look much diverted.

Three nights we stayed at that forest court, kicking our heels while the Kings conversed in private, and I would have given much to know what they discussed. Neirin, who overhead some of it, told me afterwards that they mentioned Rhun mab Maelgwn Gwynedd, the King of North Wales, more than once. "Rhun?" I said frowning. "That is odd; are you sure you heard properly? What would the Kings of the North be having to do with him?"

"Na, I am not knowing," said Neirin. We were sitting in a sunny patch against the stable wall, eating ripe apples from the nearby orchard. "But sure I am, that is what I heard. Maybe it was in the way of family; Elidyr's wife is Rhun's half-sister, Maelgwn's daughter by another of his women."

"It is a long ride from Aeron," I said yawning, "only to talk of family. And I am not believing that this meeting was an accident."

"Sa, I agree," said Neirin, setting aside the core of his apple and starting another. The sweet juice of it ran down into his young red beard, and he wiped it away, then licked the back of his hand. "But I would not say they were only talking; arguing is closer to the mark. I wish I could have heard more, but when they saw I was listening they stopped." He finished the apple in three crisp bites and stood up. "I am for giving these to Brith. Na, I do not know what they are talking about, but I am ready to ride back to Dun Eidyn: there are no girls here, none worth the bedding, and I did not bring a harp."

"You are grown very nice," I said, standing up as well. "I remember when you were easier to please."

"Na, but when I ride with my brother the King, I must keep up my standards," said Neirin, and smiled. And I laughed and followed him into the stables, and forgot the puzzle we had been discussing; and the next day Elidyr took his departure, and we all rode back to Dun Eidyn.

So the days went by, and the Lughnasadh month reached its end, and the Harvest month began. I suggested once or twice to Neirin that we should leave, but he put me off—I suspected him of having found a girl more than usually to his taste—until I began to despair of reaching home before winter. At last even Clydno could think of no more reasons to delay us, and we began our preparations for departure.

Neirin had considered selling the extra pack-pony given to him by King Nechtan, on the grounds that two were quite enough for

the two of us to manage. In the event, however, we acquired some
help instead in the form of a young man called Bleiddig, recom-
mended to us by Clydno, who wanted to travel and see the South.
He would come with us at least as far as Elmet to help with the
horses and provide an extra spear in case of trouble; in return we
would pay him in silver and give him a good recommendation on
our arrival.

The reinforcement was welcome, for we not going back the
shorter, safer way through Luguvalium and Rheged, but instead
would be taking the old Roman road called Dere Street which
followed the east slope of the Pennines, close to the Saxon kingdoms of Bernicia and Deira. This also was Clydno's idea, suggested
as we sat at meat one evening. "Which way will you be going, when
you go south?" he had asked, as it seemed idly.

"I had not thought," said Neirin, smiling—he always seemed to
be smiling in those days. "Through Rheged, I suppose—unless it is
that you have some other suggestion?"

"Let you be thinking of it now," said Clydno. "I have heard
that the old eastern road through Trimontium is still clear. It would
be good, maybe, for both of us to know how far into the hills the
Bernicians are building nowadays since Ida has set up his court in
Bambaugh—but I would not be for sending you into any danger!
Not that I think that it would be very great, for two or three men
moving swiftly, but still…"

"As to that," said Neirin, his eyes sparkling, "I would not be
minding the danger, and I should like to see that high road over the
moors. What do you think, Gwernin? Shall we go that way?"

"Why not?" I said lightly, and so it was settled. But I remembered afterwards the look of satisfaction in Clydno Eidyn's dark
eyes.

I was thinking of that conversation a few days later, as we
crested the high ridge to the southeast of Dun Eidyn and paused to
look back one last time towards the Sea of Iddeu, pale in the
afternoon haze. A fine, warm day it was, with harvest underway in
the corn-lands below us, and the still-uncut grain standing pale and

golden in the fields, ready for the scythe. Away over to the north-east we could see a blue feather of wood-smoke rising from the old settlement at Traprain Law, though Neirin said that few folk lived there anymore since his grandfather's grandfather had moved the Gododdin court west to Dun Eidyn, back when the first Saxon federates began settling along the eastern coast. Mixed peoples it had been there in those days, Britons and Saxons living intermingled and at peace, and sometimes Saxon lords ruling British villages under a British king. It was all Saxons along that coast now, or rather Bernicians, under their own King Ida, and how much longer the peace would last was an open question.

"A fine day to be up here," said Bleiddig beside me with a grin. "Not like last winter when we were riding patrols in the sleet and snow!"

"Have you been patrolling this road often, then?" asked Neirin curiously. "My brother did not mention that."

"Sa, as far as the Three Hills," said Bleiddig. "Mostly just scouting parties, though. The King your brother was sending us out often last winter and spring, when rumor said Ida was planning a raid; but it all came to nothing, as it usually does. The Saxons know when they are well off!" He laughed. "To tell the truth, I got a belly-full of it; that is one reason I am leaving. I like a fight as much as the next man, but lying out in the heather in the rain is not my idea of a good time—give me a full horn of beer in a warm hall any day; sa, and a willing girl beside me!" And he laughed again loudly, and we laughed with him; and with that we turned our ponies to the south, and rode on.

Glancing sideways at Bleiddig as we rode, I thought that he would be good at hiding in the heather, despite his reluctance. A sturdy brown young man he was—brown-haired, brown-eyed, with a copper-brown skin from being out in all weathers, and a fine brown mustache and short beard. A few years older than Neirin— perhaps two-and-twenty—he seemed a solid, dependable sort; his bay pony looked healthy and well-groomed, and his gear in good condition. Though he was no Cenau, I reckoned that we could have done much worse in our companion and helper. Only slowly did it become apparent that Bleiddig was not of the same opinion.

It was as well that we had his help, for we were going to need the extra pack-pony. Horses ridden all day, and day after day, as ours would be, cannot exist on a mouthful of grass snatched by the wayside: they need grain as well. Moreover, we would not be stopping for hospitality with the Saxons of Deira and Bernicia, and so we were carrying extra food and gear for ourselves. This, I am glad to say, came by Clydno's donation, and not by our own purchase. He had been generous, and more than generous, to us both, as his title—*Mynyddog Mwynfawr*, the Generous One of the Mountain Court—implied; why then did I mistrust him so? I mulled it over as I rode, but did not find an answer.

We stopped that evening on the south side of the divide between Iddeu and Dee, at the place where the Romans once had a marching camp. A rough set of wood and stone buildings occupied one corner of it now, where a couple of farming families kept a way-station for Clydno's scouts. There was plenty of stabling and hay for our horses; plenty of room for us as well in the wooden bunkhouse beside the stables. The farmers' wives provided us with a generous meal of stew and barley-bannock that night in the big, warm kitchen of the stone-walled farmhouse, where the drifting wood-smoke under the high thatched roof had its way with the hanging slabs of bacon, and the dogs and children rolled together in the rushes beside the fire. Afterwards they asked for a story, and I gave them one—one I shall never forget, because of what came of it afterwards.

"This is a story," I said, "which I learned in Aeron, while my friend Neirin and I were making our way north in the early summer of this year. I heard it from a storyteller at King Elidyr's own court, and where he got it, I do not know. But this is the tale as he told it.

"Once there lived two brothers, and they were princes. Twins they were, born in one birth, and yet they were not alike. One had hair as golden as the sun at midsummer, and the other one, black as the sky on a midwinter's night. And it was the black brother who was born first, and the golden brother second.

"When they came into their manhood, the people asked their father the King to name one of them as his heir: for in that country, primacy of birth was not the only factor in determining who should rule. And the King, not being a very wise man, determined to send them both into battle, with the one who did the most feats to be named as his heir. 'For,' he said, 'a King must be first among his people in strength of arms.' "

As I looked around at my audience, I happened to notice Bleiddig, sitting on a bench against the wall and staring at me as if I were a ghost. His brown face was white as milk under his tan, and his eyes wide and dark, and I wondered if he was ill. But it did not seem the moment to inquire, and I went on with my story.

"Now the brothers, despite their differences, were good friends, and they did not like this way of pitting the one of them against the other. So they determined that each of them would match anything his brother did, and neither of them would do anything that the other could not do. And so they prepared themselves to go into battle together.

"Now their country lay at the edge of a land of wild mountains, the men of which would come forth every summer to raid. The two brothers—I will call them Gwyn and Du—expected this, and set scouts to report to them privately; and when the first raid occurred, they were ready. Before their father could send them into battle, they took their chariots and their picked followers, and rode out in pursuit of the raiders. Just below the hill-face they caught up with them, and there the battle was joined."

I looked over my audience again, and saw that Bleiddig had recovered some of his color. Somewhat reassured, I went on.

"The battle was joined, and the brothers began to perform their feats. Each of them charged an enemy chieftain, and running out along the chariot pole between the ponies, struck off his head with a single blow and caught it before it reached the ground. Again and again they did this, until each chariot-rail held a dozen heads tied by the hair, with their blood painting the wheels and the sides of the car. Then the brothers leapt down from their chariots, and charged the dismounted enemy on foot; and for every man that Gwyn killed, Du slew another. And so they kept it up, until the raiders were nearly all destroyed. But they reckoned without the ties of blood on the opposing side.

"There was one man of the raiders—in truth, he was only a boy—who saw his friends and cousins falling before the brothers. Rather than flee when the battle was lost, he vowed in his heart to avenge them. So he took his spear, and he set his horse toward the nearest brother—and that one was Gwyn—and he rode headlong without regard to himself, and when he came close, at the last moment he threw his spear toward his opponent. And Gwyn's spear took him in the chest, and pierced his heart, and he fell: and the darkness of death rolled over him. But his thrown spear struck Gwyn in the right eye, and bore him down to the black earth.

"When Du, the dark brother, saw this, he let out a great cry, so that all men stopped on the battlefield, and some fell senseless to the earth from the very sound of it. And he knelt down beside his brother, and lifted him up: but Gwyn's spirit had fled already, and there was no life left in him.

"Du placed his brother's body in his chariot, and bade his brother's charioteer guard it with his life. Then he mounted in his own chariot, and urged the horses forward himself; and all that he could come at, he slew, so that there came of his enemies not three men alive from that battlefield.

"Then he took his brother's body, all bloody as it was, and placed it in his own chariot, and drove back to the court. And when he came within it, his father the King was there waiting. 'Ah,' cried the King, 'I see you are back, and the winner of this contest. I name you then my heir, to rule over this land after me.'

" 'Na,' said Du, standing before his father in all the blood and filth of the battlefield. 'My brother has outdone me in feats, for he died bravely fighting, while I, alas, am still alive. Let him be your heir, and much joy may you have of him: I will go to another land,

and find another fate.' And leaving his father staring, he mounted a fresh horse, and rode out of the court; and he was not seen in that country again. And the King, who had foolishly meant to choose an heir by feats of combat, was left without any heir at all; and after his death his enemies came, and ripped his land asunder. And the name of that King and his people are nowhere now known on the earth." I looked up to meet Bleiddig's eyes, still fixed upon me; but he had recovered his color, and I could not read the meaning of his gaze.

After the applause for my tale had died, the farmer went out and returned with a pitcher of his better ale, a definite improvement on the stuff he had given us earlier. Then Neirin gave them a song as well, and at last we turned in, stumbling back across the dark courtyard to our beds. Above us as we went, the high, cold stars of early autumn burned bright in the moonless sky. The next day we would stop at the village Bleiddig had mentioned, in the shadow of the Three Hills, and after that it would be rough camping for us on the fringes of the Saxon lands, with hardly a welcoming hearth until we came to Elmet.

But that, O my children, is a story for another day.

Trimontium

The next morning we were off in good time, having a long ride ahead of us. The sun shone bright in a clear sky, but the air had a crispness in it that spoke of coming frost. All that day our road followed the gentle west side of a gradually widening valley, above the hazel and willow brakes that bordered the little river Leader. The hills across the river were steeper, cloaked thickly with a mixed forest of oak and ash—a good place for deer, or for the wolves that hunt them. Now and again we passed homesteads—clusters of thatched buildings, often with a turf bank around them to provide some slight defense—or saw grazing flocks of sheep or herds of black cattle, but for the most part it was a lonely countryside, shadowed as it seemed by the unseen presence of the Saxons to the east. I was glad when towards sunset we came to the ford on the larger River Tweed, a little upstream from its confluence with the Leader, and saw blue hearth-smoke rising from the farmsteads a couple of miles up-river to the west.

There we left the trace of the Roman road for a while and turned toward the smoke. Our track skirted the ruined fort of Trimontium on its steep bank above the stream, a brooding pile of broken stone walls and gate-towers, overgrown with alder scrub and the seeding stalks of willow-herb, white-tufted now above their yellow leaves. The local people had robbed the place of stone for their building, but showed no inclination to live near it, and I wondered why, for it was surrounded by good flat tillable land. Maybe, I thought, they were afraid of the Romans' ghosts. The stains of an old burning still showed on the walls; Trimontium had not fallen easily, and the memory of it lingered. To our left as we passed, the three hills stood silhouetted darkly against the evening sky, with the remains of a signal-tower on the nearest. "There should be quite a view to the east from up there," I said to Neirin, pointing.

"*Sa, sa,*" he said, looking up at it. "Indeed and there should be! I am thinking we will climb it tomorrow. We might have gone up there today if we had started sooner, but it would be dark now before we reached the top, and nothing to see. It could be worth staying on here for a day or two; there is something strange about this place."

I nodded. "*Sa,* I feel it, too. Well, tomorrow will be soon enough; I am for my dinner now!"

We got a good welcome that night in the hall of the local chieftain, Rhys mab Pedr by name. His *llys* was a cluster of well-built stone and wooden structures within an earth and timber wall, and if the gates to his courtyard stood hospitably open, it was clear that they were in good repair, and could easily be closed. A straggle of farmers' huts and barns surrounded the walls of the *llys*, with fields and pastures beyond. Altogether it seemed a prosperous place, and a pleasing sight after the empty countryside through which we had ridden most of that day.

Rhys and his people were glad to have company, for this was a seldom-used road, seeing few travelers aside from Clydno's patrols. Neirin and I were honorably lodged with his *penteulu*, the chief of his retinue, while Bleiddig bedded down comfortably enough in the hall with the other young warriors. Even here, two days' ride south of Dun Eidyn, the story of Neirin's singing at the Contention had spread, brought by folk returning from the Lughnasadh Fair, and everyone was eager to hear his winning song. My stories, too, found favor, being tales not heard before in these parts. I gave them *Arthur and the Three Truths*, and Cuchulainn's weapon-taking, and lastly the tale of Gwydion the Magician and Blodeuwedd, the woman who became an owl. In consequence we went very late to our rest that night, and we did not go sober, so it was well into the afternoon before Neirin and I set off up the lower slopes of the Three-Headed Hill. Bleiddig had stayed behind in the *llys*, having seen, as he said, enough of the countryside around here already. We left him in the stables, polishing our horse-trappings and whistling as he worked.

"What exactly do you expect to see from the top?" I asked Neirin as we climbed. "Wood-smoke looks like wood-smoke, whether it comes from a Saxon fire or a British one." Truth to tell, I was still feeling a bit unwell from the previous night's excesses, and less enthusiastic about hill-climbing than I had been the day before.

"Na, I am not knowing," said Neirin shortly. He had drunk as much heather-beer the night before as I had, or perhaps somewhat more—singing takes less time than story-telling!—and he was still a little pale as a result. "It is only that it seemed a good idea at the time. We can always rest for a while at the top, and it will be quieter there than in the *llys*."

"That is a true word," I said, and returned my attention to the thigh-high bracken and the heather roots which kept trying to trip me as I climbed. The slope was growing steeper as we went up, and not only because we were tiring: all three of the hills rise into a rocky point at the top, although the crown of the northern one had been somewhat flattened by the Romans in building their tower. I wondered fleetingly why there was no clear path to the top; it was an obvious place to post a lookout, but the local people seemed to avoid the hill, just as they avoided the fort, and had looked dubious when we mentioned our objective.

By the time we reached the ruined signal station, Neirin and I were both glad to stop and catch our breath; but the view was worth the climb. To the east the land stretched out in what seemed a level plain, centered on the course of the River Tweed and heavily forested with oak and alder and ash, still in their summer glory. Far in the southeast it rose again in a range of rugged hills, blue with distance—the Cheviots, as I later found they were called. Here and there I saw a smudge of what might have been wood-smoke, but on the whole the country seemed empty of settlements, a wild unin-habited land, and I said as much to Neirin.

"*Sa*, it is border country," said Neirin. "A no-man's land now between us and Bernicia. Our road goes that way"—and he pointed toward the distant hills—"but I do not think that we will be seeing much along it other than trees, and perhaps a few deer. The Saxons stay closer to the coast."

"Ah, well," I said, sitting down on a patch of smooth turf in the shelter of the wall, "it is quiet up here, as you said, and I am for a nap before we go down again. They will be wanting us to entertain again tonight, and in the morning we ride on." And I yawned.

"There is much in what you say," said Neirin, sitting down beside me. "Let you move over a little, brother, you are taking all of the level patch for yourself."

"As to that," I said sleepily, stretching out on my back in the sunshine, "I would remind you that there are other level patches here, and I saw this one first. Let you go and find another for yourself." And I closed my eyes. I heard Neirin laugh; I heard the crunch of his feet on the gravel as he rose and retreated along the wall; but what happened after that I do not know, for I was asleep.

It was the chill that woke me. I sat up, blinking, to find the sun balanced on the western horizon, and the evening shadows already thick around me. The land below seemed to swim in a blue haze of twilight. It was very quiet, and I was alone.

"Neirin!" I called, standing up. "Where are you? Better we should go down now, while we can still see." I got no answer, and even as I stood there the sun blinked out of sight. Shrugging, I turned and started left-hand-wise around the wall, in the direction I thought he had gone. Three-quarters of the way round, I came to a gateway and paused. It seemed unlikely that Neirin would be inside the wall; on the other hand, where else could he have gone?

Within its compound the signal tower rose to more than twice my height, crowned with broken battlements which showed dark and jagged against the paler sky. The door in its side was a black mouth, which could hide anything or nothing. Seeding grasses and willow-herb filled the enclosure in a shadowy waist-deep sea, threaded here and there by a few game trails. The only other structure still standing was a roofless building against the back wall of the place, which might once have been a thatched stable. I went to it first, but a quick glance inside showed it empty of life. That left only the tower. "Neirin?" I called softly from outside its door. "Are you there?" No answer. Before I could lose my nerve, I went in.

At first it seemed utterly black, with a musky smell as of some wild animal's lair. I stood still and waited; and after a while, as my eyes adjusted, I could see faintly by the twilight filtering down the stairwell against its back wall that the inside was all one large single room, and empty. Near the doorway a few plants had rooted in the wind-blown dust of centuries, but farther back the floor seemed clear. The roof above me went up into darkness; I could not see how it was built, but the stairs were stone, and from a distance looked sound enough. Cautiously I made my way to them across the stone-flagged floor. Once my foot struck something light and pale, which rattled away into the deeper shadows. Then I came to the stairs and began to climb. At their top was only the stone-built signal platform with its broken parapet, and a wide view of the darkening land below, nothing more. I was alone on the hill, and above me the stars were coming out.

"Neirin!" I called again. Behind me there was a rush of air, and a sound as of pinions. I turned quickly and saw a man-shaped shadow standing there, where no one had been a moment before.

Perhaps a finger's breath taller than I am, he was, and I am not tall. His long hair looked black in the twilight, and the heavy cloak just settling around him wrapped him like folded wings. His eyes glittered with star-light, and I knew that if I could see them they would be green. "Well met again, Gwernin," he said in a familiar voice, and yet I felt the hairs on my neck stand up, and a cold shiver went down my spine.

"Good evening to you, Lord," I said, trying to keep my voice even. "It is a long time since we met. You are far from home, are you not, Gwydion mab Dôn?"

He laughed; it should have been a cheerful sound, but it was not. "I could say the same of you, Gwernin. But whatever are you thinking, to be up here alone, and on such a night?"

"I was not alone when I came up," I said. "But what is it you mean?"

Gwydion cocked his head at me like a curious raven. "I cannot believe you do not know. The dark of the moon, and on the Triple Hill—! Look over there," and he pointed behind me.

Unwillingly I turned and looked where he pointed, to the middle of the three peaks. It was the tallest of the three, and I wondered in passing why the Romans had not built their tower there, rather than where I stood. "I see nothing but the hill. What is there to see?"

With a sound of impatience Gwydion stepped nearer to me and waved his left hand before my eyes, so close that I blinked. "Look again."

This time when I looked at the middle peak, I saw a haze of silver light around its summit, brightening slowly as I watched. "What is it?"

"If you really want to know," said Gwydion dryly, "stay where you are for an hour, and you will see. I would not, myself, recommend the experiment, but it is your choice. Or you might come down the hill with me now—walking, I mean," he added as I looked at the drop beside me.

"I must find my friend first," I said. "Do you know what has happened to him?"

"That is two questions," said Gwydion, and he sounded amused again. "The first answer I gave you for free, in simple goodwill for our past friendship; there will be a price for the second. Will you pay it, or will you take back your question, and come with me now?"

I looked at him in silence for a moment, trying in the darkness to see his face. "I do not trust you, Lord."

"Of course you do not," said Gwydion, his voice cool and smooth as silver. "In that, if in nothing else, you are wise. Come, Gwernin, what will it be? The answer, for an unknown price? The walk down the hill? Or will you stay here to meet what is coming? I will not!"

I closed my eyes for a moment, trying to think. If Gwydion the Magician himself feared the thing now shining ever brighter on the middle hill, I did not want to meet it. But where was Neirin? I could not leave him to his fate, supposing he was still here. Somehow I must find him...

...it takes a sort of sideways-looking that is not easy for the waking mind... Neirin had said that, or something like it, when we rode the Eagle's Path. But how did one look "sideways"? Then I remembered standing the wolf-guard last winter, when I had found myself seeing the fire beside me through the eyes of the pack. Without pausing to think, I opened my eyes, closed them again, and saw before me for an instant the silhouette of the tower on which I stood: saw it from the outside, and from a distance, through other eyes than my own. "I will go down now," I said, hoping it was the right choice.

Gwydion chuckled. "By my own name, Gwernin, you grow more interesting every day! We had better go, then—you first!" And he gestured to the stairs.

Having made my decision, I did not hesitate. Step by step, down into the musky-smelling darkness I went, all too aware of Gwydion at my back, and across the stone-flagged floor that echoed hollowly underfoot. Once or twice I stepped on some small brittle thing that crunched beneath my boot, but I did not pause to inspect it. Then I was in the doorway, with the gate-way before me—and in it, suddenly, the shape of a man. I stopped abruptly. "Neirin?"

For a long moment there was no answer. Then the shadow spoke, and not in Neirin's voice. *"In the Emperor's name, who goes there?"* The words were strange, but their meaning was clear enough. I heard the snick of a sword being drawn from its scabbard, and the jink of mail. There was a pale glow in the air, like torches in mist, although the night had been clear. By its light the man before me and the sword he held were becoming more and more solid. "Gwydion," I said over my shoulder, "is this some magic of yours?"

"Not mine, Gwernin," said Gwydion's voice behind me, and he sounded amused again. "And therefore not mine to undo. I think this problem is yours to solve. What are you going to do?"

I took a deep breath. I could see the soldier's eyes now, shining in the light of the phantom torches, as he took a step toward me. I knew if I turned I would see the tower whole again, and maybe manned. The mist was growing thicker, too, and moving in a wind I could not feel. It blew the soldier's red cloak sideways, showing the armor he wore, a suit of silver scales shining in the light like the skin of a fresh-caught salmon. Outside the walls I thought I could hear shouting, and the distant sound of a horn. The tribes had risen, and the fortress below was under attack. Why had we not given them warning? We could have seen the attackers massing; the night was not that dark. We must go down and join the fight, before our men were overrun. We must go down—!

I opened my mouth to say it, to say words in a tongue I did not know. I could feel the weight of my armor, the weight of the sword by my side, and my vision was blinkered by the helmet I wore. Who was I? Uerninos?—Cernonos?—something else…

"Gwernin!" It was a shout in my mind, not in my ears, but it echoed through my head. I blinked, and knew again who I was. Behind the soldier in the gateway stood another figure, one which shone in an aura of red and amber fire. In its light the figure of the soldier wavered and dimmed and disappeared, taking the light with it, and leaving darkness and silence behind. "Gwernin," said Neirin's voice from the gateway, "I am thinking we should go down now; this is not a good place to be after dark."

Behind me I heard a chuckle, and then the sound of wings as something took flight back up the tower. I ignored it. Stepping forward, I held out my hand gropingly, and it met Neirin's, hard and warm and real. "I agree with you, brother," I said. "Let us go down—and let us go down *now!*"

"The path to the fort is just here," said Neirin, going before me. "But what is your haste? Whatever was here has gone, at least for the moment. Do you know what it was?"

"I do not know," I said, looking back toward the south over my shoulder. "And I do not think I want to know!" The silver glow around the middle hill had vanished; maybe I had imagined it—and maybe not. But above the signal tower something dark moved for a moment against the sky, as if a large bird had suddenly taken wing.

We made very good time coming down the hill, despite the darkness, and we gave the ruined fortress at the bottom a wide breadth for good measure. We did not talk much as we came, but saved our breath for walking. The path was steep and rocky, and would have been treacherous even by day, but Neirin seemed to see his way clearly enough in the starlight. Now and then he reached back a hand to me, and I thought I saw a flicker of light around it, red and amber, there and gone again. "What was it you were doing, inside the tower?" he asked me after a while. "And who was it that was with you? I do not mean the ghosts—the other one, the strange one."

"I was looking for you," I said. "Where were you?"

"I went to see—what there was for seeing, on the middle hill," said Neirin, and there was a smile in his voice. "But the people there would have been for keeping me too long, and I have not the time, not yet. Besides, I heard you calling me … so I came back. And who was with you? I could not see him clearly, and then he— left."

"A friend from Gwynedd," I said, and laughed. "Na, I will tell you the tale, one of these days, but not now—I would not be saying his name, here in the darkness: he might come back." And I glanced up for a moment at the star-spangled sky above us, and the dark shadow of the hill.

"That," said Neirin, "is probably wise. *Hai mai*, it is glad I will be to reach the hall again; it is starving of the hunger I am!" And with that we said no more for a while.

When we came at last to the village, all the dogs there set up a great barking and snarling as if we had been a pair of wolves, and then shrank away from us as we came closer. I looked sideways at Neirin in the torch-light, and saw him looking sideways at me, and we both laughed. But the songs and stories we performed that night in the hall were more than a little strange, and no one asked us to bide a day longer; and I was not surprised.

It was only late that night, when I was stripping off my boots and belt and tunic in the *penteulu's* lamp-lit quarters before lying down on my pallet on the floor, that I noticed the odd thing. I had opened my pack to put away my belt and pouch, when I saw that my belongings were not quite in the order that I had left them. In particular, the soft cloth bag which held Rhiannedd's necklace and bracelet, and which I had thought packed in the middle of my clothes for protection, was on top. Not much difference—and I had not been at my best when I had last opened the pack that morning!—but a traveling man, if he is careful of his gear, knows exactly how he has packed it. I poured out the necklace into my hand for a moment, admiring again its shimmer of jewel-bright colors, then quickly checked the rest of my gear. But nothing seemed to be missing, so I concluded I had been mistaken, and went on with my making ready for bed. And what with the much greater strangeness of our earlier adventure on the hill, and my own readiness for sleep, I forgot the incident, and only remembered it when the next thing happened—and by then it was too late.

But that, O my children, is a story for another day.

The Long Straight Track

The old Roman road which some are nowadays calling Dere Street, after the Saxon kingdom of Deira through which it runs, is a long, straight track. Stone-built it was when it was new, and wide enough to take a company abreast; and even now, after many generations of men, you can follow the stone paving for much of its length, especially where it crosses high country. All the way from Dun Eidyn in the North to the gates of Londinium it runs, though it changes its name along the way, or so I am told—for it is only the northern half I have traveled myself; the rest of it runs through lands now held by the Saxon kind, and no safe place for a Briton. Not that the northern half was without its perils, even in the days when I traveled it with Neirin, as I found to my cost.

The first day after we left Trimontium, though, was easy enough traveling. Once we passed the Three Hills—and that we were happy to do in daylight!—the road ran straight as a stretched string for mile after mile, across gentle country heavily timbered with alder and oak and ash, avoiding the marshy areas that lie here and there in that plain. We reached the ford on the Teviot River in late morning and paused there for a bit to rest the ponies; when we went on, we found the road less level, through still straight as ever, cutting across hill and valley with a fine disregard for the slope. In the green shade of the trees we saw no signs of man, but we flushed a number of deer, many of them does accompanied by their half-grown, spring-born fawns. Pig-sign was abundant, too, in the black leaf-mold beneath the oaks, although we saw none of them, and for this I was glad: pigs, as I have said before, are not my favorite animals. Above us squirrels leapt from branch to branch, chittering at us as they ran, and all the woods were loud with bird-song.

Toward late afternoon the road began to climb more steeply, and the forest to thin out, until quite suddenly we broke free from the trees and found ourselves on the edge of a high moorland, with the rugged slopes of the Cheviots rising ahead of us to the south and east. "This is fine country," I said to Neirin then. "Almost it reminds me of Powys."

"Cruel country in the winter, I am thinking," said Neirin, but like me he was smiling. After the long day in the close quarters of the forest, it was a relief to see clear distance, and feel the fresh wind on your face, and its touch in your hair. "Bleiddig, have you been this way before?"

"Na," said Bleiddig from behind us, where he rode leading the pack-ponies, "we did not patrol beyond Trimontium. I am thinking this land is too close to the Saxons—too close for my taste, at any rate!"

"*Sa, sa,* that may be so," said Neirin, "but it is Gododdin land all the same, or used to be. By what Rhys told me there are still shepherds in this country, if no one else."

"Where will we be staying tonight?" I asked Neirin. The day was clear and warm, and camping would be no hardship, but I was curious to know his plans.

"In two or three miles," said Neirin, "we should come to an-other of the Roman marching camps, where there is some sort of shelter. Pen-y-muir, they call it now: the Head of the Moor; the Roman name is lost. Tomorrow we will have some steep country, and a short day in consequence. After that the road should be easier; but it will be rough camping for us, with none but Saxon hearths in the land, until we come to Elmet."

"Did you get all this from Rhys?" I asked. "You did not talk with him for very long."

"Na, some of it I had from Clydno, and some from Taliesin: he rode this trail once, long ago." Neirin was silent for a bit, and a little smile played around the corners of his mouth. "It will be good to see him again," he said at last. "It seems a long while now that we have been gone."

"Indeed, and it does," I agreed, and fell to thinking in my turn of Rhiannedd, and my master Talhaearn, and all the life I had laid down so lightly in the spring to come on this adventure. "Five moons it is now, since we tòok the road north. It will be good to be home again."

"Home…" said Neirin thoughtfully. "Where is that now, though, for you? Pengwern, or Llys-tyn-wynnan?"

"I … had not thought," I said slowly. "But … it was not of Pengwern I was thinking, and that is strange, after six seasons away."

"Not so strange, maybe," said Neirin. "You told me once, I think, that you left because your folk would not let you study to be a bard?"

"*Sa*, that was not their idea of a proper life." I frowned, re-membering my long-ago frustration. "They had listened to a priest once who traveled through that country preaching—a Christian priest of some renown, I think he was, though I cannot now remember his name—and they would have had me follow his calling instead, as being more pleasing to their God. That was how I came to get me my letters, a little … but it did not suit me at all. It is such a narrow little room that you must live in, to be a Christian, with so many things forbidden—the thinking of them as well as the doing! So when I was old enough, I plagued Ieuan until he agreed to take me with him, and came away to find my own road. And I have not regretted it."

"Na, you would have made no sort of Christian priest," said Neirin, grinning. "You are too much of a man for the girls and the beer—you are better out here with me in the free air and sunlight, serving the *awen* as the gods send it and taking their rewards."

"That is a true word," I said and laughed. "And the rewards have been good enough this summer—how much silver did you get for winning the Contention?"

"Na, I forget," said Neirin. "It is in my pack somewhere—a tidy bagful Clydno gave me, and half of it gold! For me it was the winning that mattered, not the silver…" And he smiled to himself again, and fell silent; and slowly the miles passed by on the long straight road, which bent now and again as the mountains bend, but never curved.

Not long before we reached our camping place, we saw a stone circle, five dark stones set on a high point of the moor a little to the east of our road. As we came closer I could see the shapes of one or two more lying in the bracken where they had fallen. Open, empty, the circle stood, bare to the pale autumn sky. Neirin and I stopped our ponies and got down, and walked into its center, but here was no residual magic, no lingering enchantment. No one had worshiped here in a very long time. After a while Neirin shook his head, and we remounted and rode on. And presently, as the sun was dropping low in the west, we came to Pen-y-muir.

We saw the hearth-smoke from the houses first. Perhaps a mile south of the five stones, the high moorland we were crossing reached a crest and began to descend. As it did so, the view opened out wider and wider to the south, to the broad saddle between two drainages where the low earthen ramparts of the old Roman camps—there were several there—showed clear under the bracken and heather, picked out by the low angle of the westering light. In the corner of one of these enclosures the shepherd folk had built their summer huts, a few more sod-roofed mounds among the heather, which would have been unnoticeable except for the blue feathers of peat-smoke rising from them to scent the warm evening air. The gray-white dots of the sheep were easier to see, and the occasional calls of the men to their herd-dogs as they gathered their flocks for the night rang clear across the distance. A homely sight it was, there in the great emptiness of the hills, and a welcome one; I said as much to Neirin, who nodded. "*Sa, sa,*" he said, "and I am thinking we will be as welcome a sight to them. We will earn our suppers tonight, ours and Bleiddig's."

"Will you sing for such poor folk as these, Lord?" asked Bleiddig in astonishment. "Surely they should give us whatever we want, and expect nothing back!"

"Why should we not sing for them?" I asked. "We entertained the farmers at Headshaw, and Rhys' folk at Trimontium."

"The Lord Rhys has a proper court, and a war-band; it was right for you to sing for them," said Bleiddig. "As to the farmers, I did wonder at it, but at least they are free land-holders, and the King's men. But what are shepherds, living wild in the wild hills? To sing for them would be to lower yourselves to their level."

"*Hai mai*, you are very nice in your ways," said Neirin lazily. "Where are you from, Bleiddig, and what was your raising, to be so careful of your company?"

"I got my birth in Aeron," said Bleiddig, a dull flush darkening his brown face. "I am the second son of Eulad Hir, who is the son of Cynrain, son of Cadlew, son of Dyfynwal Hên; my father is third cousin to Elidyr Mwynfawr himself, and *uchelwr* under him at Buiston *llys*. Three years I was in Elidyr's *teulu*, and three with Clydno Eidyn."

"And now you are on the move again," I said, and laughed. "You are a restless fellow, Bleiddig."

"Na, maybe I look for better hunting," said Bleiddig, frowning. "Clydno Eidyn does not lead many forays; there has not been much plunder for the war-band this past year and more. Riding border-patrols in the heather is no work for a warrior."

"Yet I do not think many others are leaving my brother's *teulu* for want of work," said Neirin quietly. "Cenau, for example, is not known for the seeking out of peace."

"It is well enough for him," said Bleiddig. "His is the captain's share of the plunder, and of the praise! Na, na, I know that he is your friend—forget that I spoke! We must ride a long trail together; better it is that we do not quarrel. Let you sing for whom you will; it is none of my business."

"That," said Neirin carefully, his own cheeks a little flushed and his eyes sparkling dangerously, "is a true word, and well spoken; do you keep to that, Bleiddig, and all will be well between us. Gwernin, let you ride ahead a little with me; I would show you something before we come to the camp." And urging his pony to a trot, he rode on a little faster, leaving Bleiddig some distance in the rear.

"What is it that you would show me?" I asked him after a few minutes.

"Nothing: or rather something in my mind; but mostly I was wanting to get away from Bleiddig," said Neirin quietly. "Gwernin, I am remembering my last conversation with Cenau, before we left Dun Eidyn. I mentioned that we were for taking Bleiddig with us, and for a moment he frowned and looked as if he would speak, and then stopped himself. I had not thought of it before, but now I wonder…"

"Well, if Bleiddig thinks too well of himself, and is touchy because of it, it might explain his moving on so often," I said. "I am not so high-born myself that I need take offense."

"Na, you need not worry," said Neirin, smiling. "You are secure in what you are. Neither of us will draw all his status from his lineage, but from what he can do: so it is with all bards. If Bleiddig is less happy, it is his affair; we will not be together long."

"Likely you are right," I said. And at that point the sheepdogs began to bark at us, and we said no more.

As Neirin had prophesied, the shepherd folk were pleased to see strangers, if somewhat shy of us at first, and gave us freely of their best. Sitting that night on sheepskin-draped benches by the central fire-pit in their chief's house, we ate rich mutton stew and barley-bannock from new white birch-wood bowls, and drank pale heather-honey mead from ancient use-polished clay beakers with Roman designs stamped on their sides. All the while the entire encampment—those not attendant on the sheep—sat around and watched us, from gnarled brown men and gray-haired women down to the smallest children. There were flax-pale heads among the dark ones there, and blue eyes as well as brown, the mixed blood of the borders showing clearly. Even the dogs sat and watched, eyes glowing green and gold in the firelight like those of the wolf-kind their brothers, now and then growling softly—the taint of the Three-Headed Hill had not yet worn off us—but slapping their tails against the ground as well, to show that they meant no harm.

Afterwards we sang for them all, and Neirin brought out his harp—the first that the children there had ever seen!—and made for them a strange dark complex music like to that I had heard in

King Mailchon's hall in Ce. At the end of it he looked up and met my eyes, and grinned. "Na," he said, "I did not spend the whole of my time there in the earth-house: only the last part of it. But it is your turn now, brother—what will you give them? A tale of magic would go well, after that."

"Na," I said, thinking of the Three Hills and my meeting with Gwydion, "something different, tonight." And I told instead a tale I had heard at the storytellers' competition in Dun Eidyn, about a boy who went looking for the secret of courage, and found that there was none, only the doing of whatever had to be done. Toward the end of the tale I caught Bleiddig's eyes fixed on me strangely, and when I looked back again he was gone; but the hour was late, and we had drunk much mead, and I thought nothing of it. After that Neirin gave them his Lay from the Contention, and at last we went to our blankets in the smoky turf-roofed hall. And if, when we rode on the next day, Bleiddig was more than usually silent—why, he was not the only one with a headache that morning!

That next day's ride started easily, dropping down to ford a little river east of Pen-y-muir, but after that our way climbed relentlessly through some of the steepest country I had seen since I rode the Eagle's Path in the Pictish mountains. One sheer precipice after another we skirted, looking down on the backs of the hunting hawks wheeling in the coomb below us, and each ridge-line we reached was only the bridge to another mountain face rearing above us. I thanked the gods that the weather was good, and our ponies mountain-bred for the most part and well seasoned, but I found myself sweating and dry-mouthed more than once before we reached the top, and not only from the after-effects of the mead.

Finally, when we had climbed so high that the eagles below us looked like wrens, we reached the summit ridge. Glad I was that it was a clear day, and gladder still that it was a warm one; but the wind that blows across those peaks is never really warm, even in high summer. I could not imagine traveling that road in winter, though Neirin assured me it had been done. He seemed to be enjoying himself, his amber hawk-eyes sparkling and his red hair blowing loose in the wind like the hawk's tail behind him; but anything that smelled of difficulty or danger was always his meat. Bleiddig, on the other hand, was more silent even than I myself, and once or twice I thought his brown complexion had a greenish tinge. I certainly could not blame him.

The view, however, was incredible. Far off to the northwest across the hazy lowlands I could see the triple peaks where we had stood two days before, and beyond them the ridge that lay between us and Dun Eidyn. To the northeast the high bulk of the Cheviot hid from us the sight of the Saxons and the sea, but all around us in every other direction the land fell away. In the west it rose again to the central spine of Britain, but to the south the country dropped faint and blue as far as the Wall, three days' march away, and beyond.

Around midday we stopped beside the ruins of a Roman signal station to rest the ponies and eat the food the shepherd-folk had given us: salty white ewe-milk cheese, and strips of smoked mutton, and barley-bannock sweetened with wild honey. I noticed that Bleiddig, despite his expressed distain for them, ate his share of their food with good appetite, but I said nothing. Afterwards I decided to climb the tower, which was much like the one above Trimontium except for being built against the back of its enclosing wall, so that it perched on the edge of a cliff rather than in the center of a courtyard.

"Do you go on up," said Neirin, who was checking his gray pony's hooves for stones and fending off its switching tail. "I will be with you as soon as I have finished—na, na, Brith, stand you still!"

"I will come with you," said Bleiddig, rather to my surprise. "I would not mind seeing how such towers are built."

"Mind the stairs, then," I said, starting up. "Some of these stones are loose." One of the treads had shifted under my foot as I spoke. I went on carefully, feeling my way, but the rest of the steps were sound enough. At the top I stood well back from the breast-high parapet, not liking its looks: the view was just as impressive from the middle of the tower, after all.

"Gwernin," said Bleiddig, coming up close behind me, "I have a bone to pick with you."

"Why, what is that?" I asked, looking around. "How have I offended you?"

Bleiddig was frowning, his dark brows almost meeting above his straight nose. "I did not like your choice of stories last night. Who are you, a beardless boy and no warrior, to make jests about courage, or deny its existence?"

"I did not deny its existence, but only that there is any magic to it," I said, astonished at this challenge. "And as for being no warrior, I have carried my sword in battle, and have the scars to prove it. Can you say as much?"

Bleiddig took a hasty step toward me, his face darkening with anger, and I backed up instinctively, for he was at least a hand's-breadth taller than me and broad in proportion. "Are you calling me a coward?" he cried. "You half-grown puppy! You peasant trash! Where did you get that sword you brag of? Not honestly, by God!"

"I got it from Gwallawg Elmet himself," I said furiously, "for the telling of those stories you dislike. He is maybe a better judge of their worth, seeing that he is a King, and you are only a spearman. Where is *your* sword, Bleiddig?"

With an inarticulate cry, Bleiddig grabbed me by the throat and shook me, his height and anger making a joke of my strength. I clawed at his hands and tried to strike him in the face, but he lifted me off my feet and slammed me back against the stone parapet. "Look out!" I choked, struggling and feeling the blocks start to give way beneath me. I caught at his wrists in a vain attempt to thrust him off and yet keep my balance, but he leapt back, breaking my grip. Just for an instant I tottered on the edge, seeing the anger in his face turn to horror. Then the stones under my feet crumbled as well, and I was falling.

If the signal tower had been built only a little closer to the edge of the cliff, or if there had been clean rock below its walls rather than three centuries' accumulation of bracken and heather, I would not be telling you this tale today. As it was, the next thing I was aware of was pain, a great deal of pain, and Neirin's voice repeatedly calling my name.

"What?" I said, or tried to say; I think it came out as a groan. I opened my eyes, but the light was too bright and made the pain worse, so I closed them again. "What … happened?"

I heard Neirin sigh with relief. "Let you lie still, Gwernin. You fell off the tower. Can you move your legs? Na, that is enough. Do not you be moving too much, brother, this is not a good place. Lie still!"

"I need—to turn over, Neirin," I said, rather indistinctly. "I am going—to be sick."

"This way, then—easy, easy!" A strong hand grasped my shoulder and turned me onto my side, while its mate supported my head as I retched. "Now, lie still! Bleiddig, the rope—na, I cannot reach it, I must hold him—come closer! Now! Gwernin, hold on to this, can you? That is good—that is good—bravely done!" I felt myself raised a little, and a rope was passed under my ribs. The pain in my head was worse, and something warm and wet was running across my face. I thought that I would faint, but still I clung as hard as I could to the prickly stems of heather which Neirin had thrust into my hands. I could feel him tying the rope around me, and I had suddenly a very clear idea of where we were. I concentrated on lying entirely still.

"That is better," said Neirin. "Bleiddig, take up the slack. Gwernin, we are going to pull you up now. Can you crawl? Na, it is no matter—I have you. Let go of the branches now—gently, gently! Bleiddig, do you keep pulling—slowly! Gwernin, hold on to the rope—here—and here—that is good. Turn your head, so, on your arms—now, Bleiddig, pull!"

Somewhere in the middle of it all I think I fainted. The next thing I was aware of was darkness, and wood-smoke, and the flickering of firelight on a stone vault somewhere above me. My

head hurt, and my back, and too many other parts of my body. I
tried to move, and groaned.

"Gwernin?" said Neirin's voice nearby. "Are you awake now,
brother? How do you feel?"

"I think," I said slowly, "that I must be alive—I hurt too much
to be dead. What happened to me?" I gradually realized that my
head was bandaged, and my left arm, but it seemed too much
trouble to ask why.

Neirin laughed, and then sobered abruptly. "You fell off the
tower. Do you not remember? You leaned against the parapet and it
gave way. Bleiddig tried to catch you, but he could not. Do you not
remember anything?"

I sighed. "Na, I cannot. Maybe when my head stops hurting…
Is there anything to drink? I am thirsty." My mouth was dry, and
tasted of blood and sickness.

"Yes, there is water. Easy—let me help you." Neirin's arm was
behind my head, lifting me; a cup clinked against my teeth, and I
tasted cold spring water, sweet and delicious. He held me while I
drank, then eased me back on my bedding. "There. Sleep now,
brother, it is the best thing for you. I have sent Bleiddig back to
Pen-y-muir for supplies—he should be here again sometime
tomorrow. Then we can take better care of you. Rest you now—all
will be well with you soon."

"Bleiddig…" I said sleepily. "Bleiddig … something I should
remember, but I cannot, my head hurts too much…" I sighed.
"Maybe I will remember it in the morning." And I closed my eyes
and drifted off into the darkness around me. Later I woke to the
touch of Neirin's shoulder against mine, where he lay sleeping
beside me to give me his warmth as I had done for him in the
mountains. At that moment the sound of his soft breathing was the
most comforting thing in the world to me; I sighed, and slept again,
and did not wake until morning.

I do not remember much of the next few days; I think I spent
most of them sleeping. Sometime during that first day Bleiddig
reappeared, bringing not only provisions but help in the form of

one of the women from the camp, an elderly gray-haired dame with a kind eye. With her came her youngest son, a slender coltish boy just out of childhood, pale-haired and dark-eyed, a true borderer. He had come up, it seemed, trotting beside her pony like a hound, ready to help her or guard her as the case might be, with a Saxon knife half the length of his arm thrust casually though the belt that gathered in his oversized tunic.

The first I knew of this was when they all burst together into the big room at the base of the signal tower where I had been lying half-asleep. Bleiddig was trying to explain himself loudly to Neirin—I gathered the additional company had not been his idea—but Neirin put him firmly aside, and taking the woman by the hand, brought her to my bed-place. "Ah," she said, "I see that I did well to come. Harper dear, do you put the loud one outside"—here she pointed at Bleiddig, red-faced and still trying to explain himself— "and show my boy where he can fetch water. Then we will do what we can for your poor friend." And kneeling down beside me, she began to ask me where I hurt, ignoring the rest of them.

Before long Neirin came back, and between them they soon had me out of my blood-stained tunic, my cuts and gashes cleaned, anointed, and rebandaged, my broken ribs strapped up, and a pot of broth heating on the fire to spoon into me when they were finished. I ended feeling much better, but also exhausted, and very glad to go to sleep again afterwards; that was generally the effect Greta Ædricsdottir had on people.

She raised her eyebrows in surprise when Neirin showed her the pot of ointment he had used on my injuries. This was the same stuff Broichan the Druid had used on Neirin's own wounds—I had recognized the pungent scent of it without remembering the source—and between that and her remedies, my cuts healed cleanly and well, even the crushed and broken bruises on my left arm gradually scabbing over. The bones, she thought, were cracked but not broken; they ached for many days, but healed in their time. She stayed with us until I was recovered enough to travel, and then she left us as casually as she had come, setting off back down the mountain to Pen-y-muir on her small shaggy pony with the boy loping at her side. I never saw her again, but I remembered her with gratitude, and many years later I met her daughter.

While she was with us, however, she gave us much pleasure, and also much to think about—how much, I did not realize for some while, although Neirin of course did.

But that, O my children, is a story for another day.

Mixed Blood

Great troubles may grow from small mistakes, and deeds done in anger can lead to bloody outcomes undreamt of by the doer. So I have known it in my own life; so I have seen it in the lives of kings and princes. A wise man thinks before he acts: but who among us is always wise?

The first few days after my fall from the tower are blurred in my memory. I had taken a hard blow to the back of my head on landing, and my wits were slow to settle. Greta and her son I remember clearly, but it may be I have pieced later memories of them over the splintered picture of their arrival. One thing, however, that sticks clearly in my mind—as it did in Neirin's!—was a comment which she made the first evening she was with us. Without it, who knows what fate might have overtaken us? I do not.

It was on the edge of twilight, and the small flames of the cooking fire lit the cavern of the tower's base with a warm flickering light. Greta and Neirin were helping me to sit up in my blankets, the better to drink the gruel she had made for me. She was directing their efforts from in front, and Neirin was lifting and holding me from behind. Once I was more or less upright and leaning back against his shoulder, she turned for the wooden bowl she had prepared; then, turning back again, she paused, frowning. "Was it fighting you were, my dear, before you fell?" she asked me.

"Na, old mother," I said, "not that I remember. Why do you ask?"

"Because of these," said Greta, tracing a line across the base of my neck with a warm finger. "These bruises look as if someone had been trying to rip the throat out of you with his bare hands. I cannot think how else they could have been made."

"*Sa*, I noticed them also," said Neirin quietly from behind me. "It may be that we did it somehow, hauling him back from the cliff edge yesterday. I am thinking it is not a thing to concern us now."

"Na, I daresay you are in the right of it. I was only curious," said Greta, settling the bowl comfortably in her left hand and offering me a spoonful of its contents. "Do you drink this down now, my dear, and then you can sleep again. Rest and sleep is the best thing for you."

I swallowed the thin porridge of barley-meal and water she fed me—a food which took me back to my early childhood—and was warmed and comforted by it. It was only when she turned away with the empty bowl that I saw Bleiddig, seated across the fire and watching us intently. What thoughts were going on behind his dark eyes I could not tell, but his expression was somber. Then Greta and Neirin were laying me down, and in a little while I lost that image and all others in sleep; and if Neirin slept beside me again that night, I did not know it.

During the days that followed, however, he was seldom far away from me, and never when Bleiddig was there. He went out each day to do his share of caring for the ponies—grooming and feeding, watering and exercise must go on regardless, and there was little enough good pasture on that stony ridge. Other times, though, he sent Bleiddig off on one errand or another—to fetch firewood from the coomb to the east, or to search for small game for the pot—while he himself stayed behind in the tower. Sometimes Greta's son Grimm went along as well, borrowing my black pony to speed him on his way, but she stayed with us, tending the cook-fire and baking barley-cakes on the hot stones beside it for the hunters' return.

We needed that fire for more than cooking now, for autumn was well upon us, and the nights on the ridge were growing cold. Neirin and Bleiddig had taken from our gear a sheet of woolen sail-cloth—meant to serve us as a tent at need—and hung it across the doorway, and had blocked up the stairway to the top of the tower as best they could with branches from the coomb and the leather pack-covers from the ponies' gear. It made the place somewhat warmer, but it also kept out the light and made a smoke-house of our quarters, while nothing could entirely stop the icy draft which crept along the floor at night, especially when the wind was in the east.

It was on one of those evenings, with the east wind gusting around the tower and making the firelight jump and flutter on the walls, that Neirin looked up from his harp with the harp-key poised in his hand—he seemed to spend more time tuning than playing in those days—and smiled at me. "Gwernin," he said, "I am thinking we have missed your name-day. Did you not tell me once you were born at the half-way point of autumn, when the days and nights are equal? Unless I am out in my reckoning, we must be a few days past that by now, for the moon has turned half-full again."

"Indeed and it has," said Greta, from where she sat spinning her orangey-gold, crotal-dyed wool by the firelight. "The sun moved past the mark-stone to the east of our camp on the morning of the day I rode up here—the nights are longer now than the days. Our folk will be driving the sheep down into the valley soon, before the autumn rains set in."

"Then you must needs be leaving us, mother," I said. "I am well enough now—I made it to the door-place by myself today!"

"Na, there is no such haste as that," said Greta, smiling. "It will not hurt me to stay a few days longer, and I am enjoying the harping. But we must make some celebration for your name-day just past: how many years do you have now?"

"Seven and ten," I said. It seemed a great number to me then, who had left home at fifteen. "Almost I am an old man."

"Na, that cannot be, brother," said Neirin, grinning. "For I am one year older than you, as well you know, and old age is not yet upon me!"

"Ah, you are both still boys," said Greta, and Bleiddig beyond her gave a short, sharp laugh. "Na, but I forget—I was wife and mother at your age, and had left my birth-people and come to live among strangers, for the sake of my man..."

"Would you be telling us that tale, Mother?" asked Grimm from his side of the fire. "It is a long while now since I heard it, and these men have not heard it at all."

"*Sa, sa,* do tell it, if it please you," said Neirin. "Gwernin and I, being tellers of tales, are always glad to hear new ones." I added my entreaties to his, and after a moment Greta agreed. Laying down her spindle, she sat looking into the flames for a bit as if marshaling her thoughts. Then, with a sudden private smile, she began.

"I was born on a farm close by the eastern shore, near Bamburgh, as they call it now, and not far south of Metcaud Island. In those days the burgh had still its British name, which was Din Guoaroy, and many British people lived there. Nowadays, or so I hear, it is all Saxons—*Englisc* in their tongue. Na, 'their tongue' I say, as if I were not one of them, by blood and by birth … but it is many years now since I left that country.

"My father Ædric was a small-holder there, one of our King's war-band who had been settled on the land when he grew too old to fight. He took a British woman to wife—Efa, her name was— and got me on her, and three sons besides. She was a healer, a *læce* as the Saxons say it, and all her skill and learning she taught to me. We treated all the people round about: not only those on our farm, but all who were in need. And so when the half-drowned man was found on the shore, it was to us they brought him.

"I was a young maid then, no older than Grimm is now, and not yet pledged, though I knew my father was meaning to give me to the only son of his cousin Godric the following spring. I liked the young man well enough, and was content in my fate. Our steads lay close together, and I would be near my kin; this is a good basis for marriage.

"It was about this time of year, and the east wind blowing as it is now, when the first thing happened. Two of Godric's thralls, walking the beach for sea-wrack on the morning after a storm, found the remains of a boat, high up on the rocky strand where the waves had broken and thrown it. When they came near, they saw that what they had taken for a tangle of ropes and sailcloth was a man, bound by his leather belt to the stub of the mast. Cold as a corpse he was, and his dark hair and beard full of the sand and the sea-weed, but when they unbuckled his belt for the fine-wrought clasp that was on it, he moved and drew choking breath, and they saw that he lived. So they wrung the salt-water out of him as well as they might, and put him on a hand-cart with the rest of their gains; and by and by they brought him to us, for saving or burying—and the latter seemed the more likely."

Greta paused for a moment, and the same private smile came and went on her weathered face, and the wind sounded loud in the silence. Then she went on.

"We warmed him and dried him, salved his cuts and bruises, and put him to bed. Presently he began to toss and mutter, and we knew then by his speech that he was British, and none of our folk. But that had seemed likely enough already, by the color of his hair and the cut of his good clothes—for he had the clothing and gear of a warrior, not of a fisherman. And though his beard had grown, he was not old, but a man in the flower of his young strength.

"He needed that strength, for the sea had dealt harshly with him. Three or four days he lay, out of his wits and wandering, and my mother and I tending him, until at last the fever broke and his hurts began to heal. My father and Godric came to some agree-ment—for if he was Godric's prize by the finding, he was ours by the saving—and when he could stand and work, our smith put the iron thrall-ring on his neck, and he went to sleep in the byre with the other British farm-hands. They called him Orkney, for he came, as he told them, from the Orkney Islands; but what his name was he would not say, nor the fate that brought him to be shipwrecked on our shore. He was good with the beasts, and especially with the horses, so my father set him to work with them; and so the winter passed.

"That winter I had other worries, for there was a coughing-sickness about which struck many down. Some few died of it, and one of them was Efa my mother. I had not expected it, for she was younger then than I am now; but her health had begun to fail after my last brother was born, and in three days the fever took her. We buried her in the old church-yard, for her people had been Christian, and I was left to be the lady of the place until my eldest brother wed. And that would not be for some years yet: so my hand-fasting was put off, even though everyone knew by then that I was promised to Bjorn.

"The next time that I saw Orkney to notice was late in the spring, when he came to me again for salving. One of the horses had bitten him while he was helping to hold it for the smith, and the wound had turned ugly. I cleaned and bound the place—it was high up on his right arm—with the ointments I had by me, but it was stubborn to heal, and needed many dressings. Each time he came to me we talked a little, for he was learning my tongue, and I was glad of it; my mother had been my best friend on the steading, and I was missing her sore. So I began to see him, not as a thrall only, but as a man, and in some sort a friend.

"He would not speak much of himself, but rather asked me halting questions, frowning as he tried to understand my answers in a way that set a crease between his black brows. His eyes were darker than any I had ever seen before; and though he slept in the straw of the byre with the other thralls, and wore a laborer's rough tunic—his own good cloth and fittings had gone to Godric's share—he kept himself cleaner than the rest, and seemed no common man. I was almost sorry when his wound healed, and he needed come no more to me for tending. But thereafter if our paths crossed about the place, we would smile, and sometimes stop to share a word or two.

"So spring turned to summer, and summer to harvest; and Orkney had been for a year upon our stead. Looking back, it seems a marvel to me that he did not take his chance and run, for he was young and healthy, and the hills not far away: the high peaks showed clear in the west every evening, and every morning they caught the rising sun. The truth was he was caught between rock and headland, and did not know what course to steer. But that I did not learn until later, when he told me who he was.

"That autumn when the crops were in our King called a thing-moot, to put certain matters before the free men of the folk. I stayed at home, of course, with the other women and children and my younger brothers; but my father and Godric went, and took their eldest sons. Up by Metcaud, the moot was held, at a royal farm the King had there, and five days and nights they would be gone. Meanwhile the rest of us got on with drying and storing the corn-crop, and picking the last of the sweet apples, and making ready for the Blood Month slaughter and the salting and smoking that goes with it. But before then, my fate came upon me: and this is how it befell."

Greta paused again, looking into the fire, and sighed. By its leaping light her hair seemed barley-pale, not gray, and her face had the flush of the youth she was remembering. After a moment she shook her head, and went on with her tale.

"Three days it was they all had been gone, when in the after-noon we heard the drumming of hooves in panic flight, and my brother came riding into the yard like a madman and almost fell from his horse. 'Greta, call the thralls in and arm them. Father is dead in a fight, and Bjorn Godricsson with him, and Godric has sworn to have all of our blood in payment. He will take no wergild; they will be here soon, for he was not far behind me. Run, call the thralls, or we are all dead!' And he staggered and went to his knees, clutching his left sleeve which was sodden-red and dripping with blood.

"Torn between two needs—to call the thralls, and to tend my brother's wounds—I looked round the yard and saw Orkney, standing by the doorway of the byre with a basket of apples in his arms and staring at us. 'Run, Orkney, fetch all the men from the orchard, and quickly!' I cried. Without a word he dropped the apples and took to his heels, and I bent over my brother.

"By the time I had torn open his sleeve and bound the sword-cut on his arm, Orkney was back with the thralls. 'Where are swords?' he asked, and I cried, 'In the kist by my father's bed.' Then he was off with the other men behind him, while I helped my brother to his feet. 'Na, na, Greta,' he said, 'I am well enough; a little blood-letting will not kill me.'

"Before I could answer, there were more hoof-beats, many more, and Godric and his men rode into the yard. My brother lunged for his saddle where his sword still hung sheathed, but they cut him down before he could reach it. Leaning from his horse, Godric grabbed my arm before I could run, and pulled me up and across the horse's withers before him. 'Lie still,' he said, 'or you die now.' And to his men, 'Kill them all and burn the steading. If this girl cannot be my son's wife, still she will go to the gods with him on his pyre.'

"The men ran into the house, and I heard screams. Despite Godric's warning I struggled, until he struck me on the head again and again with his fist. Half-stunned, I lay helpless and heard my kinsfolk die. Then there were more shouts and the clash of steel, and the cries of dying men, and after that, silence.

"Godric sat his restless horse holding me, and waited for some time. I think he was uncertain whether to dismount and seek his men, or simply ride away. Suddenly he gave an exclamation. Twisting my head for a sight of the house-place doorway, I saw Orkney, standing alone with a bloody sword in his hand and an expression on his face I will never forget. His strong teeth showed white in his beard, and his eyes seemed to burn; there was nothing of the thrall about him in that moment; he looked like a warrior-king. Then I lost sight of him as Godric spurred his horse forward, meaning to cut the thrall down. But Orkney dodged the blow and threw one in return that almost struck Godric's sword from his hand. 'Come down and fight, big man,' he cried mockingly. 'Coward who shields behind women!'

"Whirling his horse, Godric laughed. 'I do not fight with thralls! Stay here and rot if you will: I will take the girl home with me. Half-blood though she is, she can warm my bed before my son's death-fire warms hers.'

"Even as he turned away, I heard running feet, and Godric gave a shout and rocked in his saddle. Then he was falling forward across me, and the hot stink of blood was in my face. Reaching sideways I caught at the reins, and my clutching pulled at the horse's mouth so that he turned and stumbled. Godric's body fell off of me, and the plunging horse trampled it. Then Orkney was there, catching the horse and lifting me down.

" 'My brothers,' I gasped. He shook his head.—'Dead, and most of your men and women with them. But we killed all of his, and him.' And he set me on my feet. Looking down, I saw Godric's body, lying motionless in a widening pool of blood. Instinctively I started to go to my knees beside him, but Orkney pulled me back. 'Na,' he said, 'let him lie. He is food for ravens now.'

" 'Then you must run,' I said. 'Take his horse and go quickly, before anyone misses him. For a thrall to kill a free man means death, and a hard death, too! Go, you can reach the hills before nightfall! Why do you stand staring?'

" '*Sa*, I will go,' said Orkney, and incredibly he smiled. 'But only if you come with me. Will you come?'

"I put both hands to my head as if to steady my wits. There was blood in my hair where Godric had struck me; blood—his or mine—was running down my face. Orkney was bleeding too; all the world was red. 'I do not know,' I said. 'I do not know what to tell you. I should be here to lay my brothers out, and weep at their burning. I should be here to serve the funeral meat and the ale.'

" 'Greta,' said Orkney, and his voice was unexpectedly gentle, 'if you do not come, I will stay here with you and die. Do you want that?' And he put his left arm around me; his right hand was still holding the sword. 'You gave me life: now I give it back,' he said. 'I am outlaw and exile, for a killing done in the North. I have no name, and no home to go to; and now you have lost yours as well. Come with me to the hills, and we will make a new home together.' And after a moment I nodded, and we gathered what we needed, and came away."

In the silence that followed her words, only the wind spoke, and the fire. Then, far-off, I heard a long-drawn-out wail, like a keening. It rose and fell on the wind, and then ceased: the wolf-kind also felt the approach of winter. It was time for us to go home…

Then Greta gave herself a little shake, as if shaking off the past and its memories. "I am for bed now, my dears, and you should be, too." And she smiled.

"What was the end of the story?" I asked her from my blankets. "Is Orkney still at Pen-y-muir with you and the sheep?" For I had not seen such a man in the summer camp that I remembered.

"Na, he is down in the valley now, in the church-yard," said Greta quietly. "Five winters it is now since he died, and I still miss him sore. But thirty good years we had before that, and I have his sons and daughters to keep me company, and mix his blood and mine with the blood of the hills. Who could ask for more?" And smiling she went to her own cold blankets, and with her mixed-blood son beside her she slept sound.

It was many years before I heard the other half of Orkney's story, and knew who Greta had married.

But that, O my children, is a story for another day.

Bleiddig's Hunting

A broken head does not heal in a handful of days, and broken ribs take even longer. By the time I could sit a horse unaided, the moon which had been new when we left Trimontium was full, and the Harvest Month had slipped away. Still, it might have been worse, as Greta pointed out to me when I became impatient with the slow pace of my recovery. "It is lucky you are, my dear, to have landed as you did," she had said, parting the hair on the back of my head to come at the clipped patches where the gorse-branches had torn my scalp. "Your hair will grow again and hide this in a few months, but if you had fallen face-down, you would not be a pretty sight—let alone you would probably have broken both your arms, trying to catch yourself!"

"That is true," I said, wincing as she pulled at a tangled clump of hair, "but happier I would be not to have fallen at all. And *still* I cannot remember how it happened, when I knew beforehand from looking that the wall was unsound!"

"Likely you will remember it one of these days," said Greta wisely. "Folk generally do—but it may take a while."

"Ah, well," I said and sighed, "it is not important, after all—only that I would like to know how I came to be such a fool."

"Na, there is no accounting for the things that folk will do," said Greta. "This is looking very good, my dear. I think tomorrow I can be on my way, as you can be on yours. Only do not overtax yourself at first, mind!"

"Na, I will see to that for him, mother," said Neirin from across the fire, where he sat idly plucking runs of notes from his harp. "But I thank you, both for your care of him, and for the warning." And I noticed that as he said it, he was not smiling, but I thought nothing of it at the time.

The next day dawned bright and crisp and clear after a night of hard frost. We did not make an early start, for there was much gear to repack; six ponies, moreover, take some time to feed and harness and load. I was sorry to see Greta go, for she and Grimm had been good company. Neirin tried to offer her silver for the help and provisions she had given us, but she waved it away. "Na, na," she said, "we are not such poor folk here in the hills that we cannot gift to friends. You did not ask payment for your harp-song and stories when you stayed in our camp."

"Take this, then, for remembrance," said Neirin, and choosing out the finest of the bracelets in his purse, he slipped it onto her sinewy brown wrist, then stooped and kissed her wrinkled cheek.

"*Sa*," said Greta, smiling, "for that I will take it." And after embracing us both as if we had been her children, she mounted her small shaggy pony and rode away, the boy Grimm loping beside her like a hound. I watched them out of sight, and then turned back to our packing, and it was only later that I realized she had offered no farewell kiss to Bleiddig. But then, I thought, he would hardly have wished one; he thought far too well of himself to give it any value.

That first day back on the road, the three of us made only five or six miles before Neirin called a halt, and to tell the truth I was glad of it, for my headache had come back, and my ribs were paining me more than I had expected. That afternoon we camped in a tree-sheltered valley above a waterfall, and while I rested Neirin sent Bleiddig out hunting, for the supplies Greta had brought us were nearly exhausted, and we would soon be down to barley stir-about and dried deer-meat, and not much of that. While Neirin gathered wood and built a fire, I lay on my back in the grass, looking up at the birch leaves spinning in the wind above me and waiting for my head to stop hurting. Most of them were yellow already; winter was not far away. Time for birds to be flying south-ward, and wanderers to be heading home... I fell asleep thinking of it, and did not wake until the scent and sizzle of cooking meat informed me that Bleiddig was back, and not empty-handed. A young hare and two grouse, roasted over the camp-fire, were not much among three hungry young men, but they served to flavor the stir-about. Neirin and I praised Bleiddig's success, and for the first time in many days he smiled. "Na, na," he said, "it was no great thing; I will do better when we get out of these barren hills. Wait until we reach the forest again—then I will get us some deer-meat."

When we bedded down that evening Neirin put his blankets next to mine, as he had done the first few nights after I was injured. "What is this?" I asked him when I saw it. "I am well enough now, and you will be warmer beside the fire."

"Na, humor me in this, brother," said Neirin quietly. "It is a fancy of mine, nothing more; we will not have so many more nights together on this trail. Look, the moon is rising, and she is full tonight."

"Indeed, and she is," I said, yawning. "Well, do you have it your way: you are the leader of this expedition."

"Indeed, and I am: let you not be forgetting it," said Neirin, lying down beside me, and I could hear the smile in his voice. But his face in the moonlight was thoughtful; and he was not looking at the moon, but rather at the dying embers of the fire and beyond, where Bleiddig lay wrapped in his own blankets and already snoring.

"What are you thinking?" I asked him softly.

"Na, brother, I do not know myself: only that one or two things about our friend do not make sense. Do you sleep now; maybe I will have more to tell you by and by." And with that he yawned, and turned his back against mine, and we slept.

We made about the same distance the next day, or perhaps a little more, easy riding on a long straight road over gentler hills, for the country was changing. In the afternoon we came to the ruins of another Roman fort—Bremenium, I think its name was—on the east side of a broad river valley. Outside the broken Roman walls there were other ruins, newer ones: the burned-out remains of a British village. The damage was not fresh; wind and rain, ice and sun, had long since removed the stench of burning, and time and scavengers had cleaned the white bones which still showed here and there through the brambles and willow-herb that had grown up in the place. Saxon bones, or British? There was no way to tell. "Let us ride on," said Neirin, looking at them with distaste, and we did, down the valley for another couple of miles and across the river to a place where more Roman walls offered a partial shelter from the wind. That night we all slept with one eye open, as the saying is; but nothing troubled us, not even ghosts, and in the morning we felt a little foolish. "*Hai mai*," said Neirin, looking at us around the breakfast fire, "we are brave warriors, afraid of a few bare bones! We will have to do better than that, my friends, when we come within sight and smell of the Saxon settlements, as we may yet do on this road."

"Maybe," said Bleiddig, slowly and it seemed reluctantly, "we might do better to take a more westerly path."

"Na, na," said Neirin, "I have said I will ride this road to its end; moreover, we do not know the paths through the hills, and are as like to come on trouble there as elsewhere. But you may leave us freely, if you so will it."

"Na," said Bleiddig shortly, "I will ride with you; I only offered counsel."

"Let us go on, then," said Neirin. "Another short day to Habitancum, and there I think we will lie up for a day to let Gwernin rest while you hunt the river valley for that deer you promised us, Bleiddig."

"I do not need to rest," I protested. "I am much better now; I can go on as long as you can."

"I am sure you can, brother," said Neirin, smiling at me, "but there is no need to stretch yourself to your limits: not yet. Besides, we are not likely to find a welcome at any hearth in this land, and we need the meat; our meal-bag is too light, too light by far, for the distance we have still to go."

We discussed it a little more as we rode, but Neirin's logic was sound, and our empty bellies knew it. And so, having made a good camp and had a quiet night in the courtyard of the old sandstone fort at Habitancum, Neirin and I saw Bleiddig off to his hunting the next morning. "Why did you not offer to go with him?" I asked Neirin afterwards. "I could have stayed here well enough by myself."

"*Sa*, I know it," said Neirin, with that slight frown he had been wearing so often lately. "But he will hunt well enough by himself. In the meantime, let us go down to the river and try for some fish; that should not tire you out too much."

At fishing I had the advantage, having grown up beside the Severn, which is a big river. The River Rede at Habitancum was of no such size, but the water was clear and swift-flowing, and of fish there were plenty. We cut wands from the willow and hazel thickets along the banks to improvise weirs and traps, and with two of the heavier branches we made ourselves fish-spears. It was a warm, bright day, more summer than autumn, and no hardship to go wading barefoot through the cold water in search of our prey. By mid-afternoon we had a good rack-full of fish, split and smoking over an alderwood fire on the riverbank, and were feeling pardonably pleased with ourselves.

When we were done with our fishing, we pulled out our traps, then washed ourselves and our clothes in the river and hung our tunics to dry on bushes upwind of the fire. After that I stretched out to sleep for a while in a patch of sun-warmed grass while Neirin tended the fire and kept watch. Towards evening we dressed and took our catch and our ponies—who had been grazing peacefully nearby while we fished—back up to the fort. There we built up our banked fire from the morning, and settled down to wait for Bleiddig.

He came riding into the courtyard soon enough, bringing the promised deer with him, but he did not come alone. He was carrying the stag's body slung over his pony's withers before him, but there was something else slung there as well—something that looked like a bundle of rags until it moved, and I saw it was a girl.

"What is this?" said Neirin, looking where I looked. "Bleiddig, what have you done?"

Bleiddig reined his pony to a stop near the fire and swung down, lifting the girl down after him. Young and slender she was, just ripening from child into woman, with a faded, sleeveless dress of blue homespun, torn at the bottom, and a cloud of pale hair escaping from ragged braids: Saxon hair. Her wrists and ankles were tied with strips of her dress, and there was a gag in her mouth. "Congratulate me, friends," said Bleiddig, grinning widely. "My hunting has been twice lucky today, and I have brought back both of my prizes to share."

"Where did you find her?" asked Neirin, and his voice was not friendly. The girl's eyes were wide and dark in the firelight, and the left side of her face showed a purpling bruise.

"A few miles to the east," said Bleiddig, still grinning. "I had just killed and was gutting out my deer, when I heard a noise in the bushes nearby. When I went to see, this one broke cover almost under my feet. She will not tell me where she comes from, but it cannot be far away; we will want to ride on at first light."

"Why did you bring her here?" asked Neirin, still in that hard-edged voice. "That is to draw pursuit down on us all the faster."

"Should I have knifed her and left her there, or let her go to sound the alarm?" asked Bleiddig, no longer grinning. "They cannot find my trail before daylight, and in the meantime we may have our way with her. It is a long time since we left Dun Eidyn: I need a woman, if you do not."

"Let her go, Bleiddig," I said, and my voice sounded hoarse in my own ears. I was remembering the little dark girl in Olenacum, dead at the Saxons' hands back at the beginning of the summer, and I felt sick.

Bleiddig flicked a glance at me; bit by bit his confidence was draining away, and now he looked merely sullen. "Na, na," he said, "I do not take orders from *you*; if you want her, you can wait your turn." And he began to fondle the girl's small breasts with his free hand while she tried to squirm away from him.

"There will be no turns," said Neirin. "We are riding out of here at moonrise. Give me the girl now, Bleiddig, and pack your gear."

"Na, why should I?" said Bleiddig. "It was I who caught her, and I will have my rights. It will not take long. Pack your own gear, boy, if you are afraid."

"You fool!" said Neirin. "Boy or man, you took service under me: is this how you earn your mead?"

Bleiddig's face in the firelight was dark now with anger. "If you are a man, I have seen no signs of it, for all your beard has grown. Run now if you will—I am not worried!" The girl began to struggle in his arms, and he struck her. "Be still, you!"

"Bleiddig," I said, "I think you *should* be worried." Bleiddig looked around in surprise, and his eyes widened: I had drawn my sword, and its bright blade gleamed in the firelight. "Give the girl to Neirin," I said, "and pack your gear."

"You will not use that on me, puppy," said Bleiddig contemptuously. "Why all this concern about a piece of Saxon trash? Is it fellow feeling?"

Somewhere in my head his words echoed, touched a memory. Just for a second I saw two Bleiddigs—one of them in flickering firelight before me, the other in bright daylight atop the Roman signal tower—and both of them were angry. I opened my mouth to speak, but Neirin forestalled me, stepping forward to grasp the girl's shoulders. "Let go of her now, Bleiddig," he said, and there was nothing of the boy left in his face or in his voice. "Otherwise, if Gwernin does not kill you, I assuredly will. You may believe me."

Bleiddig looked from one of us to the other in frustration, then suddenly shoved the girl into Neirin's arms. "You fools!—Take her, then," he said bitterly, and turned away to pack his gear. Neirin lowered the girl to the ground and knelt beside her. Drawing his belt knife, he began to cut the tight-knotted strips of cloth which bound her wrists and ankles, saying a few soft words to her as he did so. I stood for a moment watching all three of them, then slowly put my sword back in its sheath and turned to my own bedroll. I remembered now what had happened on top of the signal tower, but this did not seem the moment to discuss it.

Neirin was still talking softly to the Saxon girl, who lay tense as a frightened animal beside him, her wide eyes fixed on his face. When he took the gag out of her mouth, she turned her head suddenly and bit him with her small white teeth. I saw the wincing in his face, but he made no movement except to grasp her shoulder firmly with his free hand, and after a moment she let him go. "*Eala, ic bidde þe, alies mec!*" she said in a small desperate voice.

"*Na, ne geat,*" said Neirin. "*Wes stille, bida, deor! Froend ic beo.*" And over his shoulder, "Gwernin, let you be packing my gear as well as your own, please. I am not wanting to frighten this one more than I need, but I do not want her to run away from us just now."

"Gladly," I said, with a glance at Bleiddig, who was loading the deer carcass onto one of the pack-ponies. "But what are you going to do with her?"

"Na, I am not knowing," said Neirin, touching the girl's wrists gently where the ties had bruised them, and ignoring the blood on his own hand. "How can we call the Saxons barbarians, if we act no better?—*Sa*, but I do know! Look in my gear, and find me a silver bracelet, and bring it here." And to the girl, "*Hwaet ðu hattst?*"—"*Ic hatte Ælfgifu,*" she replied.

Neirin's packing was not so neat as mine, but I found what he wanted without much trouble, and took it to him. When she saw me coming, the girl Ælfgifu gathered herself as if to flee, but Neirin tightened his grip on her and hushed her with a word or two. As he took the bracelet from me, I saw that she was even younger than I had thought, her skin a smooth summer-gold and her eyes as blue as old Greta's, and the anger I felt toward Bleiddig grew.

By the time that our food and gear were loaded on the ponies, Neirin had eased himself to a sitting position beside the girl, his left hand still gripping her shoulder. "We are ready," I said to him. "What would you have us do?"

"Let the two of you ride down as far as the river," said Neirin. "Take my pony with you; I will join you there soon enough. And Bleiddig, let there be no accidents: are you understanding me?"

"I hear," said Bleiddig grimly, and with a shake of the reins urged his pony forward, leading the pack string. With one more glance at Neirin, who was carefully fitting his silver bracelet onto the Saxon girl's bruised wrist, I followed them into the darkness. "Ælfgifu," I heard him say behind me, "*þes is forðæm ðe...*"

It was not long that we had to wait; the moon was just topping the trees on the hill behind the fort when Neirin came, walking quietly down the dark road toward us, one more shadow in the shadows of the night. Taking the reins of his gray pony from me, he mounted. "Let us ride south now," he said. "I want to be well away from this place by daylight." And so we went.

Even with the moonlight and the good straight Roman road, it was not an easy ride we had of it that night. The trees cast too many shadows, hiding too many rocks and holes, and we could not afford a lame pony, so we went at a walking-pace despite our need for haste. The night was very still, and quiet except for the ponies' hooves clip-clopping on the stones. The occasional hoot of an owl in the deeper woods sounded loud, and once, far-off, I heard the eerie cry of a vixen seeking her mate. We did not talk much; Neirin had ordered Bleiddig to go ahead of us this time, where we could watch him, while I followed with the pack string. I knew there was a reckoning coming soon between us, but I hoped it would not be tonight.

Just before dawn we reached the Wall. By then I was riding half-asleep, concerned mostly with the ache in my ribs, and Bleiddig was leading his weary pony on foot. Only Neirin still seemed awake and alert. "Look!" he said softly to me, and I looked up, to see the ruins of the gate-house silhouetted black against the brightening eastern sky. Something about its shape stirred a memory deep within me; it looked like a refuge: it looked like home. But home, as I knew, was still far away.

In the crumbling buildings of the mile-castle we found a shelter of sorts, in what might once have been a stable, and when we had fed and watered the ponies—fortunately the well there was still in usable condition!—we ate some of the previous day's smoked fish and turned in. There was no suggestion of setting a watch; we were all too tired. Better to get some rest while we could, Neirin thought, and trust in our luck; we were going to need it. As it happened, he was right, but not for the reasons he expected.

Sometime in the afternoon I woke to sunlight and the sound of raised voices. Neirin's blankets beside me were empty and cold; he had been up for some time. Yawning and rubbing my eyes, I dragged myself out of my own bedding and stumbled to the door: the voices were coming from the courtyard outside, and they were angry.

"Na, I am not for caring," Neirin was saying. "Let not you be giving me any more reasons or excuses; I do not want to hear them. There are two choices for you now, Bleiddig, and two only. One is to kneel here in front of me, and swear by whatever god you swear by that you will do my bidding—and Gwernin's as if it were mine!—without question or hesitation, until we come to Elmet and release you. If that choice does not please you, then saddle your pony now and leave us. You need only follow the Wall westward, and in two days—three at the most!—you will come to Luguvalium, where Urien is always needing soldiers. These are your choices, and no others."

"It is a hard choice you are giving me," said Bleiddig after a moment. He was standing by the side of the well in the middle of the courtyard, holding a dripping leather bucket which he had just drawn up by its rope, and Neirin was somewhere across the courtyard from him, out of my sight. Bleiddig looked unkempt and weary, and his face wore a familiar frown. "Your brother Clydno found no fault with my service," he said. "What grievance do you have against me, aside from our quarrel last night?"

"You are knowing that better than I," said Neirin. "Let you tell me again how Gwernin came to fall off the signal tower, and let me hear the truth from you this time."

"But—I have told you," said Bleiddig, surprised. "He leaned against the wall, and it gave way under him. I called out and tried to catch him, but I could not. What else can I say?"

"That is a lie," I said, coming forward into the sunshine. "Try again, Bleiddig, try again: I have got my memory back at last; I remember what you said, and what you did."

Bleiddig swung toward me, startled; then his face set in an anger to match my own. "You!" he said, throwing down his bucket. "You Southern trash, with your stories, and your boasting, and your *sword*—! I should have pushed you harder, or throttled you first! I should have beaten your head in! Then I would be in Elmet by now, and free of you both!"

"That is enough!" said Neirin. "Saddle your pony, Bleiddig, and ride out now, while you still can! And let me not be seeing your face again—you would not be liking the word-fame I would give you with my song!"

Bleiddig's hand went to his knife-hilt, and for a moment I thought we would have bloodshed, but Neirin stared him down, and after a moment he swung away with a curse. While he was rolling his blankets a thought occurred to me, and I went to check my own pack; but Rhiannedd's necklace was still where I had hidden it, rolled up small in my oldest trews. Bleiddig's eyes followed my movements, and he looked for a moment as if he would have said something more, but then he set his jaw and worked on.

Earlier that day he had dressed out the carcass of the deer ready for smoking, and he now proceeded to load all the best cuts on his saddled pony. My empty belly rumbled at the sight, and I sighed; I had been looking forward to that meat, but I would not have asked for it now had I been starving. When all of his gear was loaded he mounted, and sat for a moment staring at us, his mouth a little open as if about to speak.

"Go on," said Neirin. "What is keeping you?"

"Your brother Clydno—" said Bleiddig, and stopped.

"My brother Clydno is not here," said Neirin. "What of him?"

"Na, forget that I spoke," said Bleiddig. And with that he spat on the ground at our feet, and turning his pony's head, urged it toward the gateway.

We walked after him as he rode out of the fort, and stood to watch him as he took the stone-paved road to the west that runs along the Vallum-ditch behind the Wall. We watched until he was small in the distance, until at last he dropped below a rise on that long straight road, and then Neirin sighed. "Sorry I am to say it," he said, "but better it is that we pack now ourselves, and ride south. I am not for trusting him not to double back tonight and knife us while we sleep!"

"*Sa*, I agree with you," I said. "I wonder what it is that makes him so touchy? Though I doubt me I shall ever find out."

"I am not knowing," said Neirin, and grinned wearily. "*Hai mai!* But glad I am to see the back of him, even if it means we must do all the work ourselves from now on."

"That is a true word," I said, turning toward the stables. "But at least we can sleep quiet tonight, wherever we camp." And a little while later we too rode out of the old Wall fortress, heading south for Corstopitum and the River Tyne, and the Saxon land of Deira that lay beyond it.

But that, O my children, is a story for another day.

The Gates of Annwn

Summer days seem to last forever, but once the tide of the year has turned toward winter, it is amazing how fast the light drains away. So it was for us on that lonely ride through the fringes of Deira. Each day the sun rose and set a little farther south; each day it seemed to lose a little more of its heat. The trees, though still in full leaf, had begun to wear a weary, jaundiced look as their summer's green faded through yellow toward brown. Nuts hung heavy on the branch, and bramble-fruit dark and ripe on the vine; every morning the rowan-berries showed a brighter red along the wood-shore, and their leaves a brighter gold. The nights were colder now, so that Neirin and I spread our blankets side by side for warmth as well as safety. We could not escape the thought that Bleiddig might be somewhere on our back-trail with his grievances still burning in him: having him out of our sight was no comfort, after all.

We were five days south of Corstopitum when the rain began, five days of hard traveling through a darkly forested land of low hills and boggy streams and sudden cliffs and marshes. Here even the Romans' road must sometimes twist and turn, half-hidden beneath the fallen leaves of uncounted autumns and dwindling to a game trail, so that more than once we lost our way and struggled to regain it. Neirin was concerned to pass through these western fringes of Deira as fast as we might, and not only for fear of meeting hostile warriors: the grain ration for our ponies that enabled such a pace was dwindling fast, and our own food supplies faster still. Bleiddig's departure, it was true, had lessened the drain on our meal-bag, but he had taken his deer-meat with him, and the fish we had caught and smoked at Habitancum was almost gone. We foraged now and then as we could, when an occasional clearing in the forest offered a chance for the ponies to stop and graze, but hazelnuts and blackberries do not stay the belly like red meat and barley-bannock, and we had none of those, nor were like to get any soon.

It was early afternoon when the rain began, as well as I could judge—for it was already dark enough for evening in the green gloom under the trees. It came at first as scattered drops, falling from the canopy of the forest high overhead, but soon it grew heavier, so that we must stop the ponies and get out our leather rain-capes, little used in this past month of dry weather. I put mine on with pleasure, remembering the giver, and was glad of its warmth, which seemed to soothe a little the ache in my still-healing ribs. But a wet camp in the cold wet forest was not an appealing prospect. "Neirin," I said as I remounted my black pony, standing patiently beside me, "are we likely to see any shelter soon? If so, perhaps we should stop then."

"Na, I am not knowing," said Neirin, frowning as he dug through one of the ponies' packs in search of his own cape. "This gear is not as I remember stowing it. I am wondering—ah, here it is." And saying so, he pulled out the object of his search from the bottom of the pack. As he did so something dropped from its folds, something that struck the ground with a slight metallic clinking and lay still. Bending, he picked it up: a leather bag, half-full of something heavy. "*Hai mai,*" he said, "so that is where it was!"

"What is it?" I asked, curious.

"My winnings from Dun Eidyn. But…" About to put it back in the pack, Neirin paused and hefted the bag, then began to untie the thong that closed its neck. Rings, bracelets, and heavy silver coins spilled out into his waiting hand, but not many of them. "But…" said Neirin again, staring at his treasure in amazement.

"That is not much of a prize, for the Contention," I said. "I did not think Clydno was so mean. Or have you been spending it while my back was turned, brother?"

"Na, na," said Neirin, pouring the silver back into the bag, and tying the thong. "I have not spent it; there was nothing I was wanting. I have not seen it since we left Dun Eidyn: but half of it, at least, is gone—and that half was gold!"

"Bleiddig?" I asked after a moment, remembering the disarrangement of my own gear.

Neirin shook his head doubtfully; he was re-closing the pack and tying down its cover to keep out the rain. "It might be so. But in that case, I am wondering…"

"What?" I asked.

"I am wondering what else may be missing," said Neirin. And pulling on his cape, he remounted his gray pony, and we rode on very thoughtfully through the rain.

The light was almost gone, and the rain was getting heavier, when we broke out suddenly from beneath the trees, and found ourselves riding between the sort of grassy hummocks that we knew well by now: the ruins of a Roman town. Ahead of us a narrow bridge spanned a dark, fast-running river, and beyond it fortress walls showed the broken mouth of a gateway, black as the gates of Annwn itself. "Well," I said, "the gods send we find a dry lodging for the night over there! Where would you be thinking we are?"

"Na, I am not sure," said Neirin, counting on his fingers.

> "*Corstopitum* a-top her Wall,
> *Vindomora* in the moorlands;
> *Longovicium*—long its welcome,
> *Vinovia*—bend of river…

"but after that I am not remembering. Something, something *by its bridge*, something *loud with falling water*…"

"This one is loud enough," I said as we came to the bridge. "Let us hope that the arch is sound—I am not for *falling* into this *water* tonight!"

"True that is," said Neirin. "Wait—let me be crossing it first." Obediently I stopped my pony and waited; behind me the pack ponies halted and fell to grazing greedily on the weeds and grasses that covered the stony hummocks beside the road. Neirin's gray paced slowly across the bridge, hooves ringing hollowly on the stones above the shouting of the river. On the far side he reined the pony in. "Do you come," he called, and I set the string in motion again, very conscious of the tumbling water below me, and of the dark gateway beyond.

Slowly we rode into the town—the ruins of the town. Dark and cold it was, empty and derelict like all its sisters we had seen south of the Wall—houses crumbling to weed-covered mounds like the hollow hills of the Old Ones, grass and bracken rooting in the stone-paved streets, and young elms growing tall in the dirt-clogged ditches along their sides. We were cold and wet and weary, our bellies growling with hunger, and the ponies were not in much better case. What we needed first in this man-made desert was shelter, and then a fire.

We found the shelter a little way into the town, in the shape of a low stone building on the west side of the road. It was still partially roofed, and black inside as a moonless night could make it. Again I held the ponies while Neirin ventured in a little way—just far enough to be out of the rain—and set to work with flint and steel to make a spark. The rush-light he lit from his tinder flared bravely in the dark, and showed us that end of the long single room unexpectedly tidy and hospitable, with firewood stacked against the north wall, and piles of old bracken like bedding around the blackened stones of a hearth. "This place," said Neirin, putting my thoughts into words, "is still in use—by someone."

"Well," I said practically, "I do not care who uses it, as long as he will share it with us tonight. Do you help me with the ponies, and we will start a fire to welcome him home—supposing that he comes!"

"I am with you on that, brother," said Neirin, grinning, and we set to work.

With five ponies, ourselves, and a campfire in it, the room was rather full; but it was mostly dry except in the far corners, and that was what counted. The ponies did as much as the fire to heat the place, and by the time we had them all tethered at one end of the room with their nose-bags on, and our gear unloaded and stacked in the driest spot we could find, we were warmer for the work, and almost too tired to care about our empty bellies. Neirin dug some dried deer-meat out of the bottom of our food-bag, and we sat around the flames chewing on the leathery strips. Then we built up the fire to last for a while, and rolled ourselves up in our blankets on the dusty-smelling piles of last year's bracken; and sleep came down on us like a dark wave, and carried us away.

I do not know at what point in the night I became aware that we were no longer alone. There was a sort of silvery light in the room, not bright, but filling all its corners, and in it the figure of a man stood silhouetted against the dark doorway behind him. At first he seemed translucent as a ghost, but as I watched he became more and more solid: a thin man with a tangle of grizzled hair and beard and a no-color robe of undyed woolen stuff that came below his knees. He was looking around the room, and frowning as he looked, like a house-holder who comes back from a long journey to find unwelcome changes in his home. The ponies seemed aware of him; I heard them shifting uneasily in their improvised picket-line, but the ropes we had rigged in the doorway to give us early warning of an in-comer were still in place.

This night of all nights Neirin and I had chosen to sleep somewhat apart, feeling a false security from the stone-built walls around us and wanting each of us a side towards the fire. I would have liked to reach him now, to waken him with a touch; but when I looked sideways I saw him already sitting up in his blankets, awake and alert. As I watched he spoke to the man in the doorway; but the words were strange to me, of no language I had ever heard. They echoed like music; they had a pitch and a timbre I could not match. But the stranger heard, and answered: and his words rang like bronze, speaking not to my ears but to my mind, to my heart. Beyond the years I remember them, and this is what he said.

"Who are you," he asked, "that stable your beasts in the place of the God? Do you come to make the offering?"

"Na, Old One," said Neirin. "We did not know this was a holy place. If we have offended you, we ask pardon. Of what offering do you speak?"

"The sacrifice to the God," said the stranger. "The Dark-Offering, the Blood-Offering, to the One born in winter. Long it is now since any has made it; the stones beneath you cry out for blood. Do you not hear them?"

"Na, but I do not," said Neirin. "And I have never been deaf before! What god do you serve, Old One, and how do you come to be here in this place?"

"I ask: I do not answer," said the stranger. "I come when the time is right. Do you not know the rhythm of the seasons, the pattern of the days? Who are you?"

"I know them well, or so I think," said Neirin. "As to who I am—

"I am the seeker on the path,
I am the hawk upon the wind,
I am the word that shapes the breath,
I am the fire that wakes the mind,

I am a string strung in the harp,
I am a spear held in the hand,
I am the light of summer stars,
I am the life within the land,

I am the crown that makes a king,
I am the singing of his song,
I am the speaking of his word,
I am the light that brings the dawn,

I am the oldest living thing,
and I have never yet been born."

"Not hard," said the stranger, and laughed. "And your friend who does not speak? Who is he? Is he also a bard?"

"He is," said Neirin. "Gwernin? You can speak if you will. Do not be thinking first, that is all. Only do it."

"I—I am a storyteller, Old One," I said. The words felt very strange in my mouth; it was hard to speak them, and then it was easy. "I—I am not a poet, not yet, I only seek the *awen*. But what is this place we have come to? How is it called?"

"Hawk-on-the-wind?" said the stranger. "Do you know?"

"Na, I am not sure," said Neirin, "but I do not think it is the Roman town you are meaning. That is only the shell, the gateway. If you were a priest here, Old One, it was long ago; you are not one of theirs, for all you speak in their words. The gods change their names, but not their natures: is it not so?"

"*Sa*, it is so," said the stranger. "You are reminding me … of who I was before. True it is—true it is." He sighed. "You are not the sacrifice I seek, that is clear—unless you offer?"

"Na," said Neirin again. "My time is not yet, and my place is not here. And neither is Gwernin's. On the day appointed, the one appointed will come: is it not so?"

"It is so," said the stranger. He seemed to be fading, fading like the silvery light which had come with him. "And yet the gods will have their way here before long, and the stones will be red with their blood…" And with that he was gone, and there was only the faint red light from the dying fire, and the sound of the rain dripping from the roof outside.

"Neirin?" I said after a moment. "Was that—are we awake?" Almost it had seemed like a dream, and yet not quite.

Neirin chuckled. "As much as ever we were, brother." And standing up, he went to get more wood for the fire. As the dry sticks blazed up under his hand, the light seemed momentarily to paint his face like blood. Neirin paid it no heed, but poked the wood until it settled, then went to the doorway and looked out. "Still black as Annwn out there, but I am thinking the rain is for letting up. Maybe we can ride on in the morning."

"I hope so," I said, lying down again and closing my eyes. "I do not much care for the company here." I heard Neirin laugh again, and then I was asleep.

The next morning, unfortunately, the rain was still pouring down, and there was no question of riding on that day, however full of ghosts our lodging might be. Venturing out, I found a nearby pit filled with water, and we took turns leading the ponies there to drink. When that was done Neirin measured out their morning feed, shaking his head at the limpness of the sack as he did so. "At this rate, we have enough for two or three more days at the most. There is no help for it, we will have to stop for a while as soon as we find good grazing."

"Maybe we will find a farm where we can barter," I said hopefully. "They will have the new harvest in now, and we have silver. And you speak the Saxon tongue, you could convince them we are friends."

Neirin grinned. "I doubt me I speak enough of it for that! Making friends, *sa*, that I can do, at least with girls… But I am thinking there would be nothing to stop your farmers from killing us both and taking our goods and gear—or maybe worse. Do you want to wear a Saxon thrall-ring, brother? I do not."

"Na, nor I," I said and sighed. "If we went west into the hills, might we not find a British farm?"

"*Sa*, we might," Neirin agreed. "I will think on it. Better it would be, though, if I knew where we are now, before I choose." And with that he knotted up the grain sack neatly, and added it to the stack of pony packs against the dry north wall.

The rest of the day we spent in cleaning our gear and grooming the ponies, a pastime they enjoyed. Neirin's dapple gray especially loved the attention, leaning into the brush so hard that he more than once pushed his master into the adjacent pack-pony—not a good thing, as the pack-pony had a tendency to kick. Fortunately no one was hurt this time. By the end of the day we were both tired, dirty, and ready for a good dinner, but of course we did not get one: our rations were even shorter than the ponies'. We had debated for a while the idea of setting snares among the ruins in hopes of catching something, but the heavy rain dissuaded us. After a scanty supper of barley stir-about and dried deer-meat, we fed the ponies again and rolled into our blankets beside the diminished fire, hoping for a quiet night. We did not get that, either.

I am not sure what woke me. It might have been the restlessness of the ponies, and it might have been my own empty belly. Whatever it was, the hour cannot have been late, for our banked fire had not burned down to embers, but was still showing little tongues of blue flame which lit the room clearly enough to my eyes. As I lay blinking sleepily and wondering if a drink of water—we had filled our leather bottle that day from a clear pool of rainwater—would stay my hunger enough to let me sleep again, one of the ponies suddenly raised his head and whinnied, as a horse will do when he smells another of his race. And like an echo, he got an answer from somewhere close outside.

At that, all desire for sleep left me. It was one thing to converse quietly with ghosts or spirits, but another horse meant another man nearby, one now aware of our presence as we were aware of his. And Neirin this time was asleep, breathing softly in his blankets on his side of the fire, and too far away for me to touch. I was unwilling to call out to him, afraid that other ears would catch my words. Instead I reached as quietly as I could for my belt where I had placed it beside me when I lay down, and drew my knife silently from its sheath. It was not as good as a sword, but it was a great deal better than nothing. Then I waited, listening to the sound of the rain and trying to steady my breathing.

Drip … drip … drip, and then the crunch of a stone under a heavy foot, brief in the relative silence. A pause. Then, on the edge of hearing, the foot-sounds came again: those of one man only. He had left his horse somewhere, and was searching for ours. I wished then that I could keep our ponies quiet; but even if Neirin had been awake to help, the thing was impossible with so many. Instead I lay and waited, until I saw within the doorway the loom of a body: a man of middle height and bulk, and familiar. Bleiddig had come back to us after all.

Whatever his intent, he was unlikely to be friendly. Even as his left hand found the rope we had strung there, and he moved to cut it with the knife he held in his right, I was up from my blankets and crying out, "Neirin! Wake up, wake up! We have company!" I had time for no more; Bleiddig rushed upon me like his namesake the wolf, his knife glinting red in the firelight. I sidestepped, striking out in my turn, but he blocked my stoke and followed me; then we were hand-locked, each grasping his enemy's wrist, neither able to strike.

It lasted only a moment—as before, my strength was no match for his. Savagely he threw his weight against me, hurling me back into the stone wall behind me. In the impact I lost my grip on his knife-wrist, and he struck. Twisting like an eel, I evaded the worst of it, but still the steel ripped through my tunic and burned along my ribs like fire. Faster than I can say it, he drew back his arm for another blow. Then Neirin's hand clamped down upon his knife-wrist from behind, and Neirin's choking arm around his neck jerked him backwards and away from me.

Locked together so, they staggered back and forth across the cluttered room, stumbling on my blankets and trampling through the fire so that the sparks flew wide. Then Bleiddig's scrambling left hand found a purchase on Neirin's right, and I heard Neirin cry out in pain. They fell apart, gasping, and I did not wait, but launched myself at Bleiddig in a body-tackle that caught him by surprise and brought him crashing down amidst the snorting ponies.

In falling, his knife-hand had been trapped between us; he struggled to free it, and I to keep it there. Hot fire ripped across my belly, but I ignored it and brought up my own knife. Bleiddig caught my wrist with his free hand; then with a convulsive heave he rolled us both sideways under Brith's belly. The startled pony neighed and kicked out, hitting our linked hands. I yelped and dropped my knife, and I heard Bleiddig grunt; then with another heave he rolled back, breaking my grip on him, and came to his knees ready to strike, just as Neirin descended on him from behind.

Again Bleiddig grunted and threw himself backwards, landing beside the fire with Neirin underneath him. The impact broke Neirin's grip, and Bleiddig rolled away. He came to his knees again, but before he could strike at Neirin, who lay gasping and half-stunned with his hair almost in the embers, I scrambled up and threw myself upon his back. He collapsed under me with a cry, and coming to my knees astride him I struck him on the head with my clubbed fists, so that his face hit the floor with a crash. Again and again I struck, until he went limp beneath me; until Neirin crawled across and stopped me, and took the knife from Bleiddig's unresisting hand. Then I leaned back and got off of him, still shaking with rage and pain.

"Are you hurt, brother?" asked Neirin thickly, trying to staunch the blood that was pouring from his nose. "I saw him try to stab you!"

"Na, I—ah! A gash along my ribs, I think—nothing worse. It will keep while we tie him up. How are you?"

"I am thinking he broke my thumb," said Neirin, hissing through his teeth as he felt of it. "Na, maybe—it is—only sprained. Gods! I feel sick! Get the thongs, can you? They are in the pack over there. My head—is going round…"

"Lie down for a moment, then, while I tie him." I bound Bleiddig's hands behind him with leather thongs from the ponies' hobbles and rolled him on his side. His face was bloody, and he was breathing heavily, but clearly he was still alive—not that I would have minded at that moment having killed him. My own left side was sodden-wet with blood, and as my fighting-madness ebbed I was becoming aware of pain.

While I worked Neirin had brought wood one-handed to build up the fire, and now he helped me out of my tunic to assess the damage. It proved to be a deep gash along my ribs at the level of my heart, and a shallower cut across my belly from Bleiddig's knife point. Neirin had a broken bruise on the left side of his face which was fast closing his left eye, as well as the gushing nose-bleed from Bleiddig's having jerked back his head in his attempts to get free. We were both battered and shaken, and surprised to find ourselves alive. And we still had to deal with Bleiddig.

Neither of us had used a knife on him: Neirin because he had not had time to find his on awakening, and I from lack of ability and maybe lack of will. Neither of us was ready to cut his throat in cold blood, though that was doubtless what he had planned for us. "And still I do not know," I said as Neirin was salving my wounds, "why he should so want to kill us. He was well away—ow!—and had paid himself handsomely for his trouble, if our guess is correct. What are you doing to me there? You are binding it very tight!"

"Na, I must stop the bleeding, and I am—somewhat less deft—than usual, just now," said Neirin through his teeth. "So—so. There! Now you may have your revenge." And he held out his bloody and swollen right hand. "I am thinking my thumb is not broken, after all, but it is certainly sprained. Do you bind it up for me—ah!—and the wrist as well."

"You will not be playing the harp with this for many days," I said as I followed his instructions.

"Na, true that is." Neirin was still swiping ineffectually at his nose with his other hand as I worked. "Gods! And what we will do with him now I cannot think! I cannot stop this blood."

"Do you lie down on your back and pinch it closed," I said, getting cautiously to my feet. "I will bring you a wet rag—there is plenty of water outside! Then I am going to look for his pony—but first I want to tie his ankles as well. We both need rest, and I do not fancy getting kicked to death in my sleep!"

"Na, nor do I. But—I am thinking we have more company," said Neirin, looking toward the doorway. That was when I turned and saw the stranger.

This one was no ghost. Six feet tall, he must have been, and broad and solid in proportion. His pale hair and beard, wet though they were, looked red-gold in the firelight, and the cut of his clothes and the long knife in his belt shouted *Saxon* to me. He held a horse's lead-rope in either hand, and he was smiling, but I cannot say I was reassured. "*God æfen*," he said. "*Ic grete eow*. Good it is I bring more wood, yes? We will need it soon. Ælfred I am called— be welcome in this place."

"*Hai mai!*" said Neirin ruefully to me under his breath. "I am thinking the owner of this house has just come home!"

He was right in that. If the room had seemed full before, two more men and three horses made it packed to overflowing, but we soon found reason to be glad of Ælfred's coming nonetheless. Not only had he brought wood, but food as well; and not only food, but fresh cow-meat! While he unloaded his packhorse, I built up the fire, and soon we were toasting strips of it on sticks over the coals.

The scent of it brought the warm water into my mouth, and set my belly growling like a hungry wolf. I ate my share greedily, though it was charred on the outside and bloody-red within. Seldom have I enjoyed a meal more.

Our host cooked his own portion more carefully, smiling at us as he did so, but ate with equal appetite if not with equal haste. We learned he was a small trader, traveling around the Saxon farms on the western fringes of Deira, and using this place as a stop-over on his way north and south. "British people in hills to the west do not mind trading, too," he said in his thick accent. "I speak British tongue good, I come in peace. Happy they are to see me."

"Happy are we, as well," said Neirin, licking his fingers. "Maybe you can tell us, Ælfred—what is the name of this place? Or how far to the west is the nearest British town? For as you have seen, we have a problem."

"*Sa*, you do," said Ælfred, looking over at Bleiddig, who was stirring in his bonds. "As for the name, I do not know it; but little way south of here, a road runs to the west, and one or two days' ride brings you to *wealisc* people. I will show you in morning—I go south now to winter in Eforwic-town. Do you feed your problem?"

"Na, not tonight," I said. "Morning will be soon enough for that. He is not weak from hunger."

Ælfred looked from one of our battered faces to the other and grinned. "Na, that I see," he said.

The next morning he helped us feed Bleiddig, still dumb-sullen in his bonds. We tied him on his led horse, his hands still bound behind him, and set off into a moist cool morning which promised sun before long. Two miles to the south we came to the track Ælfred had spoken of, and bade farewell to him there. As we turned west I saw beside the road a small gray standing stone—a Roman milestone—and pointed it out to Neirin. *CAT*, the letters on it read—the British word for *battle*. "I wonder what that meant," I said.

"I think," said Neirin, "it was for *Cataractonium*. Catraeth, we would call it now. That was the last name in the verse, the one I could not remember." And we rode on into the west, little knowing how that name would echo down the years of our lives.

But that, O my children, is a story for another day.

The Might-Have-Been

The *llys* of Virosidum, home to Dunod mab Pabo Post Prydein, lay in the Spine of Britain between Rheged and Deira, not far north of the northern border of Elmet. Surrounded as it was by the high tops of the fells, those great round-headed hills which rise almost sheer from the flat valley floor below, it had an air of sheltered serenity made stronger by its gray Roman walls. There we were made welcome at the end of a long day's ride, and handed our captive to Dunod's astonished *teulu*. It was not usual for bards to come bearing British prisoners.

Dunod himself was a tall, heavily-built man of middle years, his curly hair and beard still dark as a Pict's, but his eyes an astonishing light gray. A gracious host, he allowed us time to wash and change our clothes and drink a cup of wine in his sumptuous guest-house before inviting us to join him in his hall. Had it not been for hunger, I think we both would rather have lain down and slept, but we knew a command when we heard one, and we came.

During that day's ride the gash on my ribs had opened and bled, and I was holding myself somewhat stiffly as a result. The left side of Neirin's face was purple as a thunder-cloud with bruising, his eye a mere amber slit in its puffy folds. It clashed wonderfully with his red hair and beard, and with the multi-colored tunic he had got in the Pictish lands. Dunod's pale eyes opened wide at the sight of us, but he greeted us politely all the same. "Welcome, strangers," he said. "I hear that you are bards, and have a tale to tell."

"*Sa*, we do indeed," said Neirin. "An ugly tale it is, but it is true. What is the penalty for theft in your kingdom, Lord?"

Dunod frowned. "Much as it is in any British place. For secret theft admitted, death. For lesser offences, something less. Do you have a case to bring before me?"

"I do," said Neirin, "and against the one we brought here bound. Will you hear it now, Lord, or may it wait until tomorrow?"

"I think," said Dunod, glancing shrewdly from one of us to the other, "that tomorrow will be soon enough. For tonight, eat and drink and rest yourselves; you look in need of it. But may I know what names to call you?"

"Gladly, Lord," said Neirin. "I am Neirin son of Dwywei, sister's son to Gwallawg Elmet, and this is my friend Gwernin Storyteller from the court of Prince Cyndrwyn of Powys. We ride under the command of Taliesin Ben Beirdd."

Dunod's eyes widened. "These are names I know—names I know well! Be welcome, son of Dwywei, and use my court as your own. I see that you are injured—shall I send my doctor to you after the feast?"

"As to that, Lord," said Neirin, "my injuries are only what you see, but my friend was wounded by the man whom we brought with us. The help of one skilled in bandaging would be good."

"You shall have it," said Dunod. "Now join the feast, my friends. Soon enough you shall tell me what befell you; for now, be at peace, eat and rest."

He was as good as his word, and troubled us with no questions, though he seated us at his high table in all honor. For my part I did my best to make up for many days on short rations, eating my way through a heaping platter of pig-meat. As the edge of my hunger was blunted, I had time to notice the pretty young woman who was pouring my mead, and I saw Neirin eyeing her, too. By then it was a moon and more since we had left Dun Eidyn, and for most of that time there had been no girls around. After we had eaten, the promised doctor came to our lodging, and with a full belly, clean bandages, and a soft bed, I slept sound that night. How Neirin slept I am not sure, but we neither of us rose early the next day.

Dunod came up to us as we sat making a good breakfast in his hall. "Good day to you, Lord," said Neirin—I had my mouth full. "What is your will for us this day?"

"I would ask some questions of you, son of Dwywei," said Dunod, seating himself informally across the table from us. "I have been speaking to the one you brought with you, and find his story strange in the extreme. I would hear your version now, before we come to open court."

"That is easily done, Lord," said Neirin, and outlined briefly our reasons for hiring Bleiddig, and the events that followed. "When we had overpowered him," he concluded, "we knew not what to do with him, and so we brought him here to face your judgment. All men have a right to justice, even such as he."

"Yes, I see," said Dunod, frowning. "And yet there are still points which make no sense. I think I will have you all in open court together this afternoon, and sort the matter so."

"Gladly will we come, Lord," said Neirin. "But may I make one request?"

"Speak it," said Dunod.

"We did not search the saddlebags on Bleiddig's horse when we took him prisoner, and they are not now in our lodging. If your *penteulu* has them, let him bring them to the court and show the contents there. I think something of interest may be revealed."

"You shall have it," said Dunod, and with that he stood up and left us.

At the time appointed we came into the hall, both dressed in our best, to find the order of things there somewhat changed. Where the high table had been there was now only the King's chair, with another lesser chair on either side of it. The trestle tables were cleared away and stacked against the walls, and only the benches were left. These were disposed at the high end of the hall, facing the chairs, and assorted persons were standing about among them, waiting. I saw one or two faces familiar to me from the night before, including the doctor, a thin gray man with clever hands and a kind face, who greeted me and asked the condition of his bandages.

While I was assuring him that my wounds were much improved, there came a tramping of feet behind us, and I turned to see Bleiddig being brought into the hall, escorted by several of the *teulu*. He wore shackles on his wrists, but his legs were free, and his head was held high. He did not look like a man expecting death. Beside him came the *penteulu*, bearing the saddlebags we had requested. They came to a halt on the left side of the hall, as we were on the right, and stood awaiting the King.

In a little while Dunod entered the hall accompanied by two men and took his seat, while they sat down at his sides. One of them, from his cross and his tonsure, was clearly a Christian priest; the other, Neirin whispered to me, would be the chief judge. The *penteulu* and one of his men went and stood behind the King, ready to deal with any disruption that might arise. Then the silencer called out for silence, and the audience sat down, and the case began.

"Let the accused and the accuser stand forth," said Dunod, "and let the accuser state his name and his birth and his rank."

"I am the accuser, Lord," said Neirin, speaking loud and clearly in his trained Bard's voice. "I am Neirin son of Dwywei, daughter of Lleenawg Elmet. My father was Cynfelyn Eidyn, Mynyddog Mwynfawr of Dun Eidyn. My lord is Taliesin Ben Beirdd."

"And the accused?" asked Dunod.

"I am the accused, Lord," said Bleiddig, and deep though it was his voice sounded thin beside Neirin's. "I am Bleiddig son of Eulad Hir, who is the son of Cynrain, son of Cadlew, son of Dyfynwal Hên. My father is third cousin to Elidyr Mwynfawr himself, and *uchelwr* under him at Buiston crannog in Aeron. Three years I was in Elidyr's *teulu*, and three with Clydno Eidyn, and now I ride south to seek another lord."

"Let the accuser state his case," said Dunod.

"I accuse this man of theft," said Neirin. "Theft unmitigated, theft in secret, and theft from me who was his lord. Let your *penteulu* open the saddlebags that were on his horse, and show what is found therein."

At Dunod's order the *penteulu* stepped out from behind his chair, and knelt to unstrap the saddlebags he carried and empty their contents on the floor. Most of it was personal possessions such as any man might carry on a journey—spare tunics and trews, an extra brooch for his cloak, a bone comb, a whetstone, a leather purse containing a few silver bracelets and rings, a horn cup, a woolen hood. Two things there were, however, that did not belong. One was a leather bag, small but heavy, which clinked as it struck the floor. The other, bent and broken and wrapped in a piece of cloth, was the remains of Neirin's silver circlet.

He had looked for it earlier that day while we were dressing and had not found it, but thought he had merely misplaced it somewhere in our gear. Seeing it now, stripped of all its beauty and turned to mere hack-silver, he stood for a moment open-mouthed in shock. Then his mouth set hard, and the unbruised side of his face darkened with anger. Dunod's pale eyes took note of these changes, and he frowned. "What do you see here that you recognize, son of Dwywei?" he asked.

"Let your *penteulu* pour out what is in the bag, Lord," said Neirin, and his voice was steady. Dunod nodded silently, and the *penteulu* opened the bag. A stream of gold rings and coins, enough to fill a man's cupped hands and more, spilled out onto the wooden floor of the hall. Necks craned to see the sight, and there was a thoughtful silence all around: this was a princely treasure, more than most men would ever own in a lifetime. There was no way a simple soldier like Bleiddig could have come by it honestly. Almost unnecessarily Neirin said, "I recognize the gold, Lord, and the bent silver. They were part of my reward for winning the Contention of the Bards at Dun Eidyn this summer."

At this all eyes turned to Bleiddig and settled there. There was sweat on his forehead, but he kept his bold face and held his head well up. "I deny the taking of these things, Lord," he said. "These men beat me and held me captive for a night and a day; they could have put the gold and silver in my gear easily enough to condemn me. It is only their word against mine; and I am a free man and independent, while they are still their master's pupils."

"What do say to that, son of Dwywei?" asked Dunod.

"I say and swear, Lord," said Neirin, "firstly, that it was Bleiddig who attacked us as we slept with a will to murder; we fought only to defend ourselves. Secondly, I say and swear that he took the gold and silver before we turned him off at Corstopitum for disobedience, and had it with him when he followed after us to kill us, for reasons that he himself knows best. Lastly, I say and swear that I am as free and independent as he is, for that broken silver which lies on the floor"—and his hand as he pointed at it was not quite steady—"is the Bard's Crown I won at Dun Eidyn: by that winning I am now *pencerdd*, a Master Bard myself, and pupil no longer. Is it likely, I ask you, that I would break the Crown that I won, and dishonor my oath, only to bring death on a follower, when I could if I wished have cut his throat and left him for the ravens along the great north road, and no man the wiser?"

"Bleiddig?" said Dunod. "Your word has been met by your accuser's: is there anything else you have to say?"

"No, Lord," said Bleiddig, and paused. Fear seemed to have crept on him unaware; it showed in his eyes and in the twitching of his mouth, but still he kept his countenance. "I will swear by holy Church that what I say is truth; will he do the same?"

"That is well said, my son," said the priest, speaking out of turn. "Lord, you should ask them both for holy oath."

"Neirin?" asked Dunod. "Will you swear the same?"

"I will, Lord," said Neirin reluctantly, "if you require it. My mother took me to the priest for my naming, or so she told me, though I am not now a follower of the Christ. I would rather swear by the *awen* I serve and honor: but it shall be as you choose."

"Lord," said the priest urgently, "I hope you will give more weight to a Christian oath than to a heathen one."

"I will think on it, Father," said Dunod. "Is there anyone else here who would add his voice to this case, before I reach my judgment?"

"I would, Lord," I said, coming to my feet beside Neirin. "I also have a word that I should say."

Dunod looked at me with interest, and most of the rest with surprise. "Speak your word, then, Storyteller," he said. "But state first your name and station."

"I am Gwernin Storyteller," I said, "son of Gwenfrewy, daughter of Cadell Coch, of Pengwern in Powys Cynan. I do not know my blood father, Lord; my father in name was Ynyr son of Huwel. I am freeborn man, and my master is Talhaearn Tad Awen, though I travel this summer on Taliesin's orders, and subject to my friend Neirin."

"He does admit, Lord," said Bleiddig, breaking in, "that he is pupil still and not independent. You should not take his oath."

"I know the law in my own court, soldier," said Dunod shortly. "Gwernin, speak on."

"What my friend Neirin does not say," I said, "is that while we all traveled together, Bleiddig made a murderous attack on me, which almost cost me my life. He later denied it, and it puzzled me for long why he should do so: only now in this court have I found, as I think, the answer. Bleiddig, as he told you, comes from Buiston in Aeron: Buiston *crannog*. Ask him, if you will, why he left home."

"Bleiddig?" said Dunod, frowning in puzzlement. "What does this mean? Do you know?"

"Na, Lord," said Bleiddig, but fear was written plain on his face. "He is the storyteller; let him tell the tale. Why should I hate him? I never knew him before we met in Dun Eidyn."

"Because," I said, speaking directly to him now, "you thought I knew your story when I spoke of a tale I learned in Aeron. I did not then remember it, but now I do. Your mother told it to us when we stayed on a crannog in a lake, at a place whose name I never heard. Where is your sword, Bleiddig? Where is your brother's grave?"

"No!" cried Bleiddig, and his face was ugly to see. "No, it is not true, I did not kill him! He died in battle, in battle—it was not me!" And he made a lunge for me, and was pulled up by his startled escort, who wrestled him to his knees. Again he said, almost wailing, "It was not me!"

"I think," said Dunod, "that this concludes the proceedings before this court. Take him away, *penteulu*, and hold him safe while we consider the sentence. And restore the gold and silver to Neirin son of Dwywei, who has proved his case." And he turned away to hold a low-voiced conversation with the judge, while beside him the priest looked sour.

The soldiers took Bleiddig out; the *penteulu* gathered up the evidence and brought it to Neirin. He took the gold absently, but looked long at the battered silver where it lay in his bandaged right hand; and his face was sad, and his eyes bright with unshed tears. "Why did he do it?" he asked of no one in particular. "Was not the gold enough? He might have had that, and welcome, but this—!"

"He was a destroyer, and a mad dog," I said. "He did it to hurt you, because he feared you."

"But why?" asked Neirin, still puzzled. "Why?"

"Because we are bards, and might tell his story," I said. "*The guilty flee where no man pursues*: is that not a saying of the Christians?"

"I think he will not have much longer to flee," said Neirin.

Even as he spoke, there came a shouting from outside the hall. It climaxed in the sound of a furiously ridden horse departing into the distance. After a moment the *penteulu* ran back into the room and stopped before the King. "Lord," he said, "shamed I am to tell you, but the prisoner has escaped! A man was riding into the *llys*, and he broke from us and pulled the man from his horse, and rode off on it. We are saddling our horses to pursue him; he cannot get far!"

"Do so," said Dunod grimly. "I will not have my justice made a mockery. Catch him if you can, kill him if you must: he is self-confessed by his actions, and his life is forfeit."

"At once, Lord," said the *penteulu*, and ran headlong from the hall. Neirin and I looked at each other, and reluctantly we grinned. "*Hai mai!*" said Neirin. "Somehow I do not think they will get him—but at least he will be too busy to follow us on our way home!"

We stayed for three more days at Virosidum to see the outcome, but as usual Neirin was right. We spent the time resting, eating, and enjoying Dunod's hospitality; entertaining him at night, too, although it was I who did the harping along with Dunod's own bard, a dark young man called Cywryd who reminded me of someone I could not place. It was when we were taking our leave that Dunod paused and looked long into Neirin's still-bruised face. "Did you know, son of Dwywei," he said at last, "that it was I your mother should have married? If things had been different, you might have been my son."

"Na," said Neirin, grinning, "I am thinking in that case I would have been different, too. But I thank you for your hospitality, son of Pabo and might-have-been father—and for your justice." And with that he mounted his gray pony, and we rode off on the long straight Roman road that would take us to Pengwern.

But that, O my children, is a story for another day.

The Wind in His Wings

The sky was a sword-blade gray that promised rain before night, and a cold east wind was stripping the last of the autumn leaves from the willows along the Severn when Neirin and I rode up to the gates of Pengwern *llys*. The bright leaves floated on the water like golden minnows, like the summer days gone by through which they had grown and aged. Now their time was done, and the river carried them away: so it was with our days of journeying; so it is with the lives of men.

We had come from the east, by way of Viroconium—the ruins of Viroconium—and had stopped there on the riverbank to make ourselves fine, stripping to bathe in the cold water and emerge, shivering and dripping in the sharp wind, to dry our chilled bodies and dress in our best. Now we rode like princes—or at least, like successful Bards. Even Neirin's bruises had mostly faded, though it would be a while yet before he could play his harp.

Pengwern sits on a knob of rock in a broad plain, encircled on three sides by a loop of the Severn, and has been a strong place time out of mind. To me, coming back to it after so long, it seemed at once familiar and strange. There were details here and there which had changed—some strengthening of the gates, new thatch on this or that hut—but nothing great. It was I that had changed. Pengwern now seemed like any other Prince's court to me, although one that I knew exceedingly well. It was not where my heart lay; it was no longer my home.

I said as much to Neirin as we clattered up the hill to the Prince's compound, and he nodded. "*Sa*, so it was with me at Dun Eidyn: a stranger where I had been familiar, however welcome. Will you stay long here?"

"Na, no longer than I must," I said. "I am wanting to see Talhaearn again, and Rhiannedd. Much can happen in half a year."

"Indeed, and it can," said Neirin, and with that we reached the courtyard, and gave our horses to the stable boys who came running to take them. "But where is Taliesin?" And he set out through the maze of buildings that filled the place.

"He cannot have known we would arrive today," I said, trying to keep pace with him. Neirin said nothing, but only walked the faster. People turned to stare at us as we passed—two well-dressed young men hurtling through the court like boys late for supper. At last we came to a spacious hut—almost a house—built against the wall of the compound close by the Prince's own quarters. Very fine it was, stave-built of new timber, with a red-painted door and two real glazed windows—a rare and precious luxury. But the red door was closed, and I knew, even before Neirin set his hand to the latch and opened it, that Taliesin was not inside.

Clearly he had not left. In the main room his harp sat on a table, out of its case, and a scroll lay half-unrolled beside it. The air was cold, but only with the chill of autumn, not of emptiness, and the brazier in the corner was fresh-laid for the evening's fire. When Neirin pushed aside the hanging curtain at one end of the room, the bed-place beyond showed neat and unoccupied. But where was he?

"Perhaps he is in the hall," I said. "It is likely, on such a day."

"*Sa*, you are right," said Neirin, but he was frowning. "Yet somehow I thought he would be here."

"Ah, but I am," said a voice from behind us. We jumped like startled thieves, and turned as one. Just for an instant the figure in the doorway seemed larger than a man, and unhuman. Then it dwindled, and stepped into the room, and was Taliesin again.

"Master—!" said Neirin, and paused. There were silver threads in Taliesin's dark beard which I did not remember from the spring, and his face looked somehow older. He seemed shorter, too, or else Neirin and I had grown again. But the sense of power in him was as strong and focused as ever, and his blue eyes were just as keen. They were smiling now as he looked at us, though his face was stern.

"Well, Little Hawk?" he said after a moment. "What is it to be? Word has come to me from the North of the Contention. Are you ready for your freedom?"

Neirin opened his mouth to speak, and paused. "Na," he said after a moment. "I am not, but I will take it from you if you bid me."

Taliesin's smile reached his mouth. "In the spring, then," he said, and opened his arms, and Neirin went into them like the hawk returning to the glove. After a moment, though, he remembered me, and whispered something in Taliesin's ear. And Taliesin grinned, and held out his right arm to me as well. That was when I truly came home.

My meeting with my blood family was different. My aunt and uncle also seemed smaller and older, much older, and my cousins had all grown up in my absence. My uncle grumbled that he had missed my labor on the farm this past summer, and he hoped I had got this bardic nonsense out of my system and was going to settle down, but my aunt only smiled. Taliesin had told them, of course, where I was, so they had not been thinking me dead for the last year, but if he had told them more they had not understood it. They were surprised that I would not stay, and a little offended that I chose to sleep in Taliesin's house rather than their own. But I had been gone a long time, and they had got used to it, even if they would not admit it, so we parted friends.

It was much harder saying goodbye to Neirin. In the end there were no words, and we simply embraced. Taliesin had promised we would meet in the spring—"before," he said, "the Hawk takes wing again." More than that he would not say, and we had to be content with his assurance.

I was thinking back to that conversation as I jogged along on Du, leading my little red pack-mare behind me. Taliesin had given me the black pony—"For," he had said, "Cynan would gladly give me a dozen more if I would let him, and you two have got used to each other. I would not send you back to Talhaearn on foot, and besides, you will need him next summer." And he had smiled.

Unlike Pengwern, Llys-tyn-wynnan looked just the same, and when I rode into the courtyard, Talhaearn and Rhiannedd were standing on the steps of the hall as if waiting for me. It was he who had the most to say—particularly the next day, when he found I had not kept up with my verse practice!—but she who had the final word. The two of us were standing in a corner of the courtyard before dinner, and I was kissing her—making sure that she fitted in my arms as she had before!—when she leaned back a little, the better to look at my face. "Gwernin," she said, "did you know you are growing a mustache at last?" And she traced it with a finger and smiled, and I kissed her again.

This was on Samhain Eve, the night of my homecoming, when bards rest from their travels and storytellers settle down beside the fire to start their winter-tales. So I did in my turn; but in the spring, though I did not know it, I would be off again, on some new adventure at Taliesin's pleasure. For as all rivers flow to the sea, nowhere in life can we ever truly stand still.

But that, O my children, is a story for another day—or another Samhain night!

Author's Postscript

The 6th century in Britain is in some ways the darkest part of the European Dark Ages (or the Early Medieval Period, as it is often called nowadays). As direct evidence of people and events in this period, we have a handful of poems, Gildas' *De Excidio Britonum*, a few historical references in accounts written a hundred or more years later, and a set of genealogies of doubtful value. In addition, there is a growing body of archeological material, some of which contradicts (or at least fails to support) the above sources. In attempting to write a series of somewhat historical stories based in this period, the prospective author must leap from rock to rock, occasionally walking on water in between. Inevitably there will be some splashes.

For those who care about such details, then, the following summary is provided. Actual physical locations (i.e., towns, forts, roads, etc.) are based on archeological reports where available, but details (buildings, general appearance) of these places at the time of the story are speculative or wholly invented. Territorial units such as kingdoms fall into this category as well; there are no maps of Wales or of the lands of the Men of the North from the 6th century. Most of the kings or princes are at best names in a poem, history, or genealogy, and their characters (to say nothing of their appearances) are largely inferred from their reported actions. Five of the more important bards are listed (as names only) in *Historia Britannica*; from two of them—Taliesin and Neirin (later called Aneirin)—we have poetry as well, although the degree to which these poems may have mutated during oral transmission is debatable. This poetry, incidentally, provides a large amount of the detail for material and social culture in the courts of the time.

Finally, a word on the magical or supernatural element in some of these stories. One of the "supernatural" characters encountered by Gwernin—Gwydion mab Dôn—derives from the story *Math mab Mathonwy* in the collection of Welsh medieval tales called the *Mabinogion*. Others are invented to fit the history of the place where he meets them; the King in the Ground, for example, is based on Lindow Man. In a time and place where there was no clearly perceived distinction between spirit world and "real" world—one need only read the biographies of the early saints to support this!— I submit that these characters would have seemed, to a person in touch with their stories, to have as much "reality" as many of the "historical" ones. Indeed, so I have found it myself on some of my own journeys through Britain, over 1400 years later.

Appendices

A Note on Welsh Pronunciation

The spelling used for Welsh words and names in these stories is mostly that of Modern Welsh. The most important differences between the English and Welsh alphabets are these:

Welsh	English pronunciation
c	k
dd	th (as in "breathe")
f	v
g	always hard g (as in "game")
th	th (as in "breath")

The Welsh "ll" has no English equivalent; an approximation can be reached by putting the tip of the tongue against the roof of the mouth behind the teeth and hissing—good luck!

Names of Some People and Places

key: **historical**   invented   *legendary/mythical*

(**accent** usually falls on the next-to-last syllable)

Alt Clut (ălt klēt)—Dunbarton Rock west of Glasgow

Bannawg (băn-năoog)—hill country south and east of Sterling in Scotland

Bleiddig (**blāēth**-ĭg)—warrior from Aeron

Broichan the Druid (brōĭch-ăn)—mentioned in Adomnan's life of Saint Columba

Cadell (kă-dĕll)—son of Urien, listed in the genealogies

Caer Iddeu (kăĕr ĭth-ū)—Sterling in Scotland

Ce (kā)—name of one of the sub-kingdoms of the Northern Picts, here used as a name for all of them

Cenau (kĕn-ăw)—son of Llywarch Hên

Claddedig (klă-**thĕ**-dĭg)—"the buried one", the King in the Ground: Lindow Man

Clydno Eidyn (**klēd**-nō ī-dĭn)—king of Gododdin

Cromar (**krō**-măr)—Pictish settlement

Cynan Garwyn (kĭn-an **găr**-win)—prince of eastern Powys whose court was at Pengwern

Cyndeyrn (kĭn-**dāē**-rĭn)—(invented) prince of northern Powys whose court was at Deva (=Chester)

Cyndrwyn (kin-**drū**-in)—prince of western Powys whose court was at Llys-tyn-wynnan

Denw (**dĕ**-noo)—daughter of Prince Cyndeyrn

Dere Street (dē-rĕ)—Roman road from Edinburgh to York, passing through the Saxon kingdom of Deira.

Deva (dē-wă—Chester

Dun Eidyn (dŭn ī-dĭn)—Edinburgh

Dun Moreu (dŭn **mō**-rĕw)—hilltop fortress south of Perth, Scotland (Moncreiffe Hill)

Dun Nottar (dŭn **nōt**-tăr)—Dunottar castle, Aberdeenshire, Scotland

Dundurn (dŭn-**dŭrn**)—Pictish fort located near Lake Earn

Dunod mab Pabo Post Prydein (dŭn-ōd)—King of an area between Rheged and Deira

Dwywei (**dooē**-wāē)—Neirin's mother

Dyffryn Mawr (**dĭf**-rĭn **mă**-oor)—Strathmore (Welsh equivalent)

Elidyr Mwynfawr (ĕ-**lī**-dĭr mooĭn-**vă** oor)—king of Aeron

Finaet Du (**fī**-năĕt doo)—sub-king of the northern Picts

Goddeu (**gō**-thăē)—Gwenddolau's kingdom, north of Rheged

Gododdin (gō-**dō**-thĭ)—kingdom centered around Edinburgh

Gwallawg (**gwăll**-ăoog)—King of Elmet

Gwenddolau (gwĕ-**thō** lăē)—King of Goddeu, area north of Carlyle

Gwernin Kyuarwyd (**gwĕr**-nin ke-**văr**-wid)—Gwernin the Storyteller, the narrator of the story

Gwion (**gwē**-on)—Taliesin's boyhood personal name

Gwydion mab Dôn (**gwĭd**-yon mab dōn)—Gwydion son of Dôn, the magician (Mabinogion)

Gwynedd (**gwĭn**-ĕth)—kingdom in northwest Wales

Ida—king of Bernicia

Inoide (ī-**nōĭ**-dĕ)—sister to King Mailchon

Llys-tyn-wynnan (llēs tēn **wĭn**-nan)—Cyndrwyn's court, near Caereinion in mid-Wales

Maelgwn Hir (**măĕl**-gūn hēr)—"Maelgwn the Tall", King of Gwynedd (deceased)

Mailchon son of Bridei (**māĭl**-khŭn son of **brē**-dāē)—King of the Northern Picts

Mamucium—Manchester

Metcaud (**mĕt**-kăood)—Lindesfarne Island

Modron ferch Afallach (**mōd**-ron verch a-**vă**-llach)—wife of Urien Rheged; possibly legendary.

Mynyddog Eidyn (mĭ-nĭ-thŏg ĭ-dĭn)—title of the king of Gododdin (my conjecture)

Nechtan son of Drustan (**nĕch**-tăn)—King of the Southern Picts

Neirin (**nāĕr**-in)—Taliesin's bardic apprentice; the poet Aneirin

Pengwern (pen-**gwĕrn**)—Court of Cynan Garwyn, possibly located on the site of modern Shrewsbury

Powys (**pō**-wes)—kingdom in east-central Wales, including part of today's Shropshire

Rheged (**hrĕ**-ged)—kingdom in the north of Britain

Rhiannedd (**hrēăn**-neth)—Gwernin's girl at Llys-tyn-wynnan

Rhun mab Maelgwn Gwynedd (hrēn măb **măĕl**-gun **gwĭ**-neth)—Rhun the son of Maelgwn Gwynedd

Rhydderch Hael (**hrĭ**-thĕrch hāēl)—king of Strathclyde

Talhaearn Tad Awen (**tăl**-**hāĕărn** tad ă-wen)—Talhaearn "Father of the Muse", Gwernin's bardic teacher

Taliesin Ben Beirdd (**tă**-lē-ā-sin ben bāĕrth)—Taliesin "Chief of Bards", most famous bard in 6th century Britain

Talorc son of Uoret (**tă**-lōrk son of **fō**-rĕt)—southern Pictish nobleman

Tristfardd (**trēst**-varth)—sometime bard to Urien Rheged, and killed by him; the name means "Sad Bard"; probably legendary.

Ugnach mab Mydno (**ēg**-nach mab **mēd**-no)—bard of Caer Sëon who competed against Taliesin at Caer Seint; possibly legendary.

Urien Rheged (**ēr**-eun **hrĕg**-ed)—King of Rheged in the North of Britain

Viroconium—Wroxeter, Shropshire

Other Welsh words

afon (**ă**-von)—river

bardd (**bărth**) pl. beirdd (**bēĭrth**)—bard

caer (**kăĕr**)—fortress, castle

cerdd tafod (**kĕrth tă**-vod)—poetry; literally, "craft (of) tongue"

coch (**kōch**)—red

du (dē)—black

dyffryn (dĭ-frĭn)—valley

ferch (vĕrch)—daughter (of)

galanas (gă-lă-năs)—blood price; compensation paid for a death

glas (glăs)—blue, gray, green

gwas (gwăs)—lad

ie (ēā)—yes

llwyd (llŏēd)—gray

llys (llēs)—court, fortified complex

mab (măb)—son (of)

pencerdd (**pĕn**-kerth)—chief bard, master bard, bard of the court

penteulu (**pĕn-tăē**-lē)—chief of retinue, leader of the body-guard

rhyd (hrĭd)—ford

sarhaed (**săr**-hĕd)—insult price; compensation paid for injury or insult

teulu (**tăē**-lē)—retinue, war-band (modern meaning: family)

tŷ-deyerin (tē **dĕē**-rĭn)—earth house, souterrain: underground storage place.

uchelwr (**ēch**-ul-ur), pl. uchelwyr (**ēch**-ul-ēr)—nobleman, literally "high man"

Old English Dialogue

Hwæt is ðin nama? Hwa aert ðu? Saga hwaet ðu hattst!—What is your name? Who are you? Say what you are called!

Ic hatte Wulfstan—I am called Wulfstan.

Englisc—English

læce—leech, healer

Eala, ic bidde þe, alies mec!—Please, I beg you, release me!

Na, ne geat—No, not yet

Wes stille, bida, deor! Froend ic beo—Be still, wait, dear! I am a friend.

Hwaet ðu hattst?—What are you called?

Ic hatte Ælfgifu—I am called Ælfgifu.

þes is forðæm ðe—this is for you

God æfen, Ic grete eow—Good evening, I greet you.

wealisc—Welsh, British

Suggestions for Further Reading

A full listing of the sources I consulted for this book would run to many pages. For those wanting to read on, however, some places to start:

Clancy, Thomas Owen, 1999, The Triumph Tree: Scotland's Earliest Poetry AD 550-1350: Canongate Books, ISBN 978-0862417871.

Evans, Stephen S., 1997, Lords of Battle: Image and Reality of the *Comitatus* in Dark-Age Britain: The Boyell Press; ISBN 0-85115-662-2.

Ford, Patrick K., 1977, The Mabinogi and Other Medieval Welsh Tales: University of California Press, Berkley, California; ISBN 0-520-03414-7.

Smyth, Alfred P., 1989, Warlords and Holy Men: Scotland AD 80-1000: Edinburgh University Press, ISBN 0748601007.

For further information about the *Storyteller* series, see

http://tregwernin.blogspot.com
or
http://aldertreebooks.com